"Playing God"

'A Novel Of Possibilities'

By,

Robert A. Boyd

with

Bobby L. (AA)

Consulting Alcoholic

Copyright 2014 by The Written Wyrd
All Rights Reserved

ISBN: 978-0-9915535-6-3

English Trade Paperback Edition

Proceeds from the sale of this work go to support self-published and small press authorship. If you wish to aid this effort, please go to the publisher's website —

The-Written-Wyrd.org

— for further information.

Thank you.

§

*****

For

Barbara

"Prologue"

February 18, 1975...

Miss Brenda Hayward
Chase Park Plaza Hotel, rm 2231
New York City, NY

Dear Miss Hayward,
If you are free this afternoon, I would be honored to have
your company for lunch.

Yours sincerely,
Daniel White

"What's this?" Brenda was irritated by the note written on hotel stationery, the fifth such she received in the last twenty-four hours. The bellcap didn't have an answer, this being one of dozens of deliveries he made in a day, but explanations were hardly needed. He mumbled an apology, forewent a tip, and faded, leaving her to deal with yet another horndog on the make. Included in the envelope was a brochure from one of the most exclusive restaurants in New York City. Apparently whoever was offering to buy was ready to spend big. There was also a business card, not that it gave her much more to go on:

Daniel White, Phd
Seattle, Washington
Research

Louise, her official 'assistant'—chaperone—from the magazine, came out of the restroom. "Whatja got, hon?"
"Another big shot," she grumbled.
Louise took the note, glanced through it, and made a rude noise. "Yeah, another stage door Johnny. They never give up, do they?" Louise was a dead butch dyke from the look of her, and a martial artist to boot. She held a very dim view of men in general.

4

She looked the business card over with a disdainful sneer. "He's probably some industry top dog who figures anything can be bought for the right price. I wonder what the going rate for centerfolds is these days?"

"I'm not for sale," Brenda muttered as she flopped on the couch in a funk.

This wasn't the first proposition she'd received since her photo spread was published late last month, and she was heartily sick of all the guys hitting on her. She always was popular in high school —not surprising with her figure—but what was annoying on campus could get downright unpleasant at times out in the real world; hence Louise, assigned to escort her on her publicity tour. Still, it was a constant hassle and depressing at times. Nineteen is too young to be thrown into a bear pit, 'chaperone' or no.

"That *Daniel White* can go to hell for all I care."

"Well good for you, girl friend. You're learning." Louise tossed the card in the trash can.

"Just because he's got money doesn't mean squat. I'll buy my own lunch."

Louise gave her a sardonic look. "Well perhaps you shouldn't be so hasty. After all, you'll get a free meal out of it."

Brenda looked at her, surprised. "You're not serious?"

"Why not? The moment he steps out of line, you rip him a new one right there in front of everybody. Collecting scalps does wonders for the mood." Louise had a vicious streak in her; her evil grin said volumes. "And you've got nothing else today, so you might as well have a little fun."

"Well...yeah...maybe." She didn't share Louise's sadistic streak, but she knew she needed to toughen up if she was going to make a career in Hollywood. It'd be good practice, and she needed a chance to vent her frustrations. And there was nothing else going on today for a change...which disturbed her vaguely. This mister White's invitation came right in the one hole in her busy schedule of interviews and appearances. It seemed menacing, somehow.

She should have been used to this by now, the fifth day of a PR tour of the New York TV shows and media outlets following her big splash as a centerfold. She appeared on the Carson show last night, which would have been awesome a year ago, but now was just another round in the spotlight with the cameras fastened firmly on her boobs. She was scheduled to do a live appearance at the local Playboy club tomorrow, then off to New Orleans, Dallas, and eventually Los Angeles. The experience—especially all the scumbags who came crawling out of the woodwork—had already disillusioned her about the glamorous life of a starlet.

"God, sometimes I regret ever taking my clothes off." She'd needed the money at the time. "There's times I wish I'd never left Cincinnati."

Louise sat next to her and wrapped an arm around her shoulders. "You gotta hang tough, babe." She could always offer a sympathetic ear at least. "It's all part of the drill. You need to get used to this, and the worst of it will pass in time. Trust me."

"Yeah, I know." Brenda sagged on the couch, feeling the weight of the world, of her sudden rise to fame as this month's sex symbol. "I just wish I could find a nice guy I could trust, is all."

"That won't be easy now."

"It never was." She gave her protector and one close friend a weary sigh. "Being hot can be a curse at times."

Louise snorted. "Especially with high school jocks. Been there, girl friend." She handed the note back. "You ought to take up this offer. It'll give you a chance to get out, and if the guy gets fresh, you can let him have it. What's to lose?"

§

What's to lose, indeed? The restaurant was only six blocks from the hotel, but she was half frozen by time she got there. New York City was still digging out from under a snow storm, and the wind was bitter. The joint was everything one could expect from an exclusive New York eatery: posh, secluded, tastefully Art-Deco, uniformed staff ready to answer any whim of their elite patronage. The entrance was blocked by the Concierge, who greeted her with correct reserve. "May I help you, miss?"

"Um...Brenda Hayward. I'm meeting someone for lunch."

"Yes. Mister White is expecting you." That seemed remarkably presumptuous of him she thought as the Concierge led her to a far corner of the room and a table overlooking the Hudson.

6

The mysterious mister White turned out to be a disappointment, not that she was surprised: he must have been sixty if he was a day. He was tall and thin, a bit taller than her, with receding snowy white hair and a face creased with worry lines. His eyes lit up at the sight of her.

"Miss Hayward, it's a pleasure to meet you at last." He gestured to the opposite seat and signaled for the waiter. "Thank you for coming."

"Yes, well, I'm not one to turn down a free meal," she muttered as she hung her coat over the back of the chair and settled awkwardly in her seat.

"So, what would you like?"

She was shocked by the menu prices; this was a long way from the Burger Barn near her old high school where the kids used to hang out. As long as she was here... "I'll have the lobster," she said to the waiter. It was the most expensive item they offered, and she'd never had lobster before. The corner of mister White's lip twitched, almost as if he was smiling at a private joke.

Once the waiter was gone, Brenda settled in her chair and confronted her host. "So...mister, ah, White...to what do I owe the honor of your company?"

He smiled wistfully. "That involves quite a story; one you won't believe a word of. In fact, I'm sure you'll think I'm utterly crazy."

This wasn't what she was expecting.

"I suppose I should start at the beginning." He paused and pondered for a bit, which made him seem intellectual somehow. "There was a young man, recently graduated from high school with honors, who received a full scholarship to MIT. Like all young men living the dorm life, he bought girly magazines. One day he came across a centerfold of a truly lovely young woman, someone who was more than another pretty face, someone who had a unique quality which caught his attention. He fell in love with that young woman—foolish lad—and cherished the memory of her ever after. Sad to say, this youngster was a hopeless geek; smart as a whip, but woefully lacking when it came to the ladies. He never would have dared approach his Dream Girl, even if he had the chance.

7

After he graduated, again with honors, he carried the image of that young woman like a wound in his heart."

This was an odd one by any standard. "So, what? Are you trying to set me up with your kid, or something?"

He sighed. "Not exactly." He picked a leatherette case up off the next chair, and pulled out a slim off-white object about twelve by fifteen inches by half an inch thick. "Here's a little something which should establish my bonafides. I think you'll find it interesting." It opened like a book, and he set it flat on the table facing her. A moment later the top half lit up like a small television. The bottom half looked like a typewriter keyboard, only with some unfamiliar buttons.

This was another surprise; this mister White was full of them, it seemed. "What is it?"

"It's a computer, what's known as a laptop."

"A computer?" She studied the slim plastic case, fascinated by its futuristic look. From what little she knew about computers, they were gigantic things filling whole rooms and needing dozens of technicians to run them. This was getting interesting all of a sudden. "Where did you buy it? Are they expensive?"

"Oh, they're not so costly, really, if you're in a profession which needs such. You can buy them in any office supply store—if you know where to look." He leaned over the table and pointed to a small symbol of an apple in the upper left corner of the screen. "Touch that icon."

She poked it hesitantly with one finger. A white rectangle appeared in the middle of the screen:

Macintosh 'Palladium'

KSe42 1550 mb quad processor

26.50 tera memory

System 11.6.9

Built 3.2014

It took her a moment to see it, and when she did, she flat didn't believe what she saw at first. "Two...thousand fourteen? You mean the year?"

"I told you you wouldn't believe me," he said with a chuckle. "You see, that young man was me. I kept that magazine for years. After it wore out, I pulled your pictures off the internet." He reached over and tapped an image like a small file folder; it opened to reveal several more tiny images. He tapped again, and there was her centerfold. "It was foolish of me, I know, but a young man's first love..."

She was shaken. "You're telling me you came from the *future?* You're right: that is crazy!"

A shadow seemed to fall over his features. "Crazier than you can imagine." The look he gave her was filled with pain for some reason. "Yes, I came here from 2015."

This was an original, all right. She couldn't see what he hoped to gain in offering her that wacky tale, and his cluelessness annoyed her. "So what is this? You figure you can come on with some cockamamie song and dance and score with me?" Despite her earlier determination to ream him out, she was too disconcerted by this to raise her voice.

"No, nothing like that. I'm old enough to know better...now. It's...well...I wanted to finally meet you, is all. A first puppy-love, I guess. I always wondered who the young woman behind that photo really was. I had the means to come here, and I knew you had this opening, so I took the chance."

This was too much. All of a sudden she was afraid of this mister White for some reason. His story was a load of bull...but there was her centerfold staring at her from that...computer...

"You don't expect me to *buy* this number?"

"Honestly, no. But I can show you..."

"Look, mister, I don't know what your game is, but this isn't funny!" She was starting to get scared, and that got her heated. "Whatever you want, I'm not interested!"

"All I wanted was to meet you."

"Yeah? Well you met me!" She jumped to her feet and wrestled her coat off the back of the chair. "And I'll thank you not to bother me again!"

"Brenda..."

She hesitated, and looked at him. "*What?*"

"Before you go, I wanted to give you something. Call it a token of what might have been." He took a bulky envelope out of his jacket and handed it to her. "Hang onto these; they'll be worth something someday."

"Fine!" She snatched the envelope from him and stalked out.

The elevator took her to the lobby before her temper cooled enough to wonder what was in the envelope. It was a stock certificate:

Microsoft, Inc
Initial Public Offering
1000 Shares Preferred
March 13, 1986

§
April 20, 1986...

"Microsoft, huh?" Gerald leaned back in his swivel chair and pondered the ornate certificate. Finally he turned his attention to her, and not just in a professional sense. "So, what? Was this a gift from an admirer?"

"Get your mind out of the gutter!" she snapped at him.

Gerald was one of the countless legions of horndogs who haunt the fringes of Hollywood trolling for starlet tail. She'd dated him briefly, then dumped him when he made his intentions plain. The only reason she was here now was because she needed his expertise as a junior stockbroker. He wasn't important enough to make the big trades, being one of the herd of flunkies who manned the phones at a local brokerage dealing in nickel and dime over-the-counter stocks. Still, he was as close to a real stockbroker as she knew, or wanted to know.

He gave her a smug grin, creep, pondered the ornate certificate for a bit, then turned to one of his rolodexes and fingered through it. "Hmph!" he muttered as he read the card. "It's an outfit in Seattle, something to do with computers." He perused the card curiously; this was way out of his league. "They made their initial public offering at twenty-one last month, supposedly a big deal."

He put the card back in his rolodex, and studied the ticker flowing across the far wall of the 'boiler room'. "Well! It seems your stock has jumped from twenty-one to thirty-five. There's a tidy profit for you. Care to sell?"

It was a tidy profit; enough to put her through her nurse's school and then some. She was there in fact because she needed the money for a career change. Her supposed Hollywood career was going nowhere after eleven years. At thirty she was no longer the bouncy young centerfold she once was, and centerfold beauty is a perishable commodity in Tinsel Town. She was still firm and comely—she took care of herself—but after being rejected for three small parts in a month, she'd had enough. With the inflation these days she couldn't make it as a waitress any more. Jobs were hard to find, and no one could bother to offer her any sympathy. The bright vision seen so briefly back in '75 turned out to be a mirage. It was time to move on.

She considered his offer, the money was tempting, but something he said disturbed her. *'An outfit in Seattle, something to do with computers.'* That rang an ominous bell, stirring all but forgotten memories of a luncheon date in New York City. The mysterious mister White gave her those shares *eleven years* before they were issued...

'Hang onto these; they'll be worth something someday.'

Why she held onto them all this time was beyond understanding. They were obviously worthless at the time, and that old man gave her the creeps for some reason, but his parting words still haunted her.

'Hang onto these; they'll be worth something someday.'

She never showed them to anyone, not even Louise, her escort from the magazine who drifted away long ago. There was something about that old man's wild tale and that stock certificate which still troubled her. She couldn't put her finger on it, but she never could dismiss it either.

11

"You never can tell about IPOs, especially with some whiz-bang tech outfit," Gerald said. "It might go up, but the odds are it'll tank once the thrill wears off. Your best bet is to dump 'em now, and get into oil."

All of a sudden, selling those stocks didn't seem like such a good idea. The noise and hustle of the 'boiler room' struck a raw nerve, putting her off the whole thing.

'Hang onto these; they'll be worth something someday.'

There were other financial options for her schooling: those new Pell grants, and that program from the Peace Corps. It'd be a tough row to hoe, but she could do it. She was well accustomed to pinching pennies and making do.

'Hang onto these; they'll be worth something someday.'

Gerald was watching her expectantly, eager for the commission on a tidy sale and another shot at her, maybe. Bad joss either way. "Um...no, thanks." She folded the certificate and stuck it back in her purse. "I'll hang onto them for now."

*****

"The First Day"

The faint jolt as their aircraft touched down jarred her out of a half-doze. She looked out the tiny window for her first sight of the dear old U S of A in nearly thirty years: rushing concrete passing below, and a row of hangers in the distance. SeaTac International Airport, Washington. Unreal.

The aircraft slowed and turned off onto a taxi way. She managed to stretch while still in her seat, and worked her neck to get some of the stiffness out. Eleven hours in the air—this leg—from Seoul after an earlier flight from Singapore; nearly twenty-seven hours altogether since she boarded there in New Delhi, and that after an unpleasant overnight train trip from Bangalore, in southern India. She was stiff all over, and when she moved, her feet were clumsy, half asleep.

"God, who said this world was shrinking?" she grumbled. At least there was just one more trip, to Cincinnati, and she could afford to take a day or two here in Seattle to rest up. She had business to attend to anyway, or so she hoped. She allowed herself an unlady-like yawn, gazed absently at the terminal in the distance and wondered again if it was all true, what the letter she received a few months ago had said:

Microsoft, Incorporated
Investor Account Summary

Purchaser:	Brenda Hayward, ms
Purchase date:	3/13/1986 (IPO)
Number of shares purchased:	1,000
Split multiplier:	288
Number of shares held:	288,000
Present stock price: (1/2/2015)	$26.78
Present holding value: (1/2/2015)	$7,712,640

It was the first time she'd heard about those shares since leaving for India nearly thirty years ago. Somehow Microsoft tracked her down through a distant cousin she didn't remember, who forwarded the message via the State Department.

She'd lost track of the packet she kept tucked away in the bottom of a footlocker all these years, and the numbers on that page shocked her. After digging through old papers and trinkets from a lifetime of travel, she found the faded, much-stained envelope, and the card clipped to the ornate certificate:

Daniel White, Phd
Seattle, Washington
Research

The memories of that odd day so long ago came flooding back. An old man, his impossible tale of being a *time traveler*, an envelope of stock issued *eleven years* after she received it given as a *'token of what might have been'*. She didn't believe a word of it at the time—not entirely, anyway—but held onto those shares out of some weird premonition. And now it was all coming true. There really was seven million dollars worth of Microsoft IPO tucked in her carry-all—was there? The only alternative was to believe she went stark, staring bonkers way back in 1975, and her whole life since then was a delusional trip.

The aircraft slowed some more, and the terminal building came into view. The other passengers were getting their acts together. The aircraft came to a halt, the pilot made some announcement no one listened to, and she joined the struggle to climb out of her seat and force her way down the narrow corridor to the exit. It takes a long time to unload a 767, and her stiffness was supplemented with frazzled nerves by time she reached the terminal.

§

Customs took forever. Her U S passport was so old that they suspected her of...*something*. It took several computer inquiries, some phone calls, and interviews with a couple suspicious FBI and TSA men to convince them she really was an American who had spent twenty-eight years living abroad. The Indian *sari* she wore didn't help, either. Their obvious hostility was disturbing; suspicion seemingly edged with paranoia at times. They treated her correctly, but they plainly considered her a *Vidēśī śaitāna*, a 'foreign devil' who needed to prove her innocence, and quickly.

14

That old stock certificate caught their attention, and much fuss was made over whether she in fact owned it and whether any back taxes were owed. Again, it seemed they presumed guilt until innocence could be proven—*if* it could be—in their effort to capture terrorists or drug smugglers or illegal aliens or the BoogeyMan for all she could tell. It was a predictable but disturbing sign of these troubled times, and she bore up under it as best she could partly out of resignation and partly from fear that they might detain her for...*something*.

It was mid-afternoon by time they let her go. She hefted her carry-all and trudged down the long corridor leading to the main concourse, weary and wrung out like she couldn't remember when. If this was what America had become, then perhaps she would be better off taking the money and going back to India. This was an alien land anyway; she had no family left here since her parents died years ago. She'd fallen in love with India during her tour in the Peace Corps to work off her student loans, and remained there at the hospital in Bangalore ever since. She only came back because the unexpected fortune gifted to her led to a major change in her retirement plans. For all its crowding and imperfections, *India* was home to her.

The airport seemed like an hallucination: antiseptically clean, air conditioned, wide open and uncrowded—a far cry from the congested slums and narrow streets clogged with oxcarts and pedicabs. It was so *quiet*; uncanny. The muzak playing in the background was insipid compared to the wild, exotic rhythms of tabla and sitar, and the fashions worn by these foreigners seemed so *ordinary*. She passed a rank of newspaper vending machines, placed strategically to catch new arrivals eager for the latest word on the local and national scene. The headlines were disturbing:

POLITICAL DEADLOCK CONTINUES
LONG TERM UNEMPLOYMENT REMAINS HIGH
WALL STREET ACCUSED OF TREASON
INCOME GAP INCREASING
US AIR SPACE DANGEROUSLY CROWDED
TEENS ARRESTED FOR SCHOOL SHOOTING

She sighed in despair and kept moving. No, this may be her birth country, but she was a stranger in a strange land.

§

At the exit to the arrival area, she ran into a young Filipino dressed in a chauffeur's uniform and cap, who held a sign reading, BRENDA HAYWARD. That brought her up short, uncertain what to make of it. He caught her staring at him.

"Miss Hayward?"

"Um...yes..."

He smiled and gave her a small bow. "I am Andrew, Miss Hayward. I was sent to pick you up."

"By who?"

"By a mister Daniel White. I'm to take you to his office."

"But...what does he want with me?"

"I'm afraid I don't know. I work for a service."

That worried her, as if she didn't have enough hassles. She all but forgot about the mysterious mister Daniel White over the years, but it seemed he hadn't forgotten about her. What's more, he was clearly watching her, hence the limo awaiting her arrival. What did he want?

"I have no interest in meeting mister White, thank you."

Andrew nodded somberly. "He said that if you prefer, I am to take you to a hotel of your choice."

There was something really spooky about all this. All of a sudden she had no doubt those stocks were genuine, and there was a lot more behind them than she could imagine. Right then she seriously did *not* want to know about the mysterious Daniel White or why he was interested in her, but the past nagged at her. She gnawed her lip nervously as she tried to decide what to do. Andrew, the chauffeur, waited patiently. Finally the mystery got to be too much. Whatever this mister White wanted, she needed to confront him about it to get him off her back.

"All right. Take me to him."

§

It took a few minutes to collect her luggage—two footlockers, a large suitcase, and a duffel bag—everything she owned in this universe aside from her carry-all. Andrew piled them on a cart and

16

escorted her out to the loading area where a dark blue stretch limo was waiting. He held the door for her, then transferred her luggage to the trunk while she settled into the plush upholstery with a sigh. Thankfully there was plenty of room to stretch her legs; at least the mysterious mister White had some style.

The limo worked its way through traffic and onto the freeway headed north. She had never been to Seattle before, and no doubt wouldn't have recognized it now. She watched the landscape idly as the highway wound through forested hills festooned with loops of highway interchanges and high tension lines, then descended into a broad valley choked with ugly industrial buildings and half-abandoned tenements. Beyond that, Seattle proper rose like a hundred gleaming spires reaching for the sky. The difference was jarring; the haves and the have-nots. She saw that all the time there in India, but it was disappointing to see the same here.

"Would you like to listen to some music?" Andrew fiddled with the dashboard, and a strident voice came out of the stereo speakers.

"...in Washington, the President blasted the House of Representatives for loading the Defense Budget with amendments to kill the Affordable Care Act, saying, 'this attempt to undermine the needs of the people by endangering our national defense in the present crisis is unacceptable'. He went on to say that if the amendments remained, he would veto the legislation. The Tea Party spokesman in the House said later that, 'The most compelling threat to our security today is this shameless power grab by this false President who is attempting to impose his socialist agenda..."

"Please turn it off!"

The sound cut off abruptly. "I'm sorry, miss Hayward. The news must seem unpleasant these days if you're not used to it."

It took her a moment to recover her composure. "It's all right, Andrew. Thank you." She settled in her seat, stared out the window, and wondered if coming here was a mistake.

17

They wormed their way at a crawl through downtown traffic, then picked up speed again as they headed up to the north side of town. High rises gave way to more slums, then to shopping mall suburbia. Some time later, a roadside sign announced the exit to the Boeing plant in Everett, an enormous white structure towering faint on the horizon beyond the suburban sprawl. The sprawl went on for some way; workers' housing for the Boeing plant, no doubt. There were plenty of pickup trucks and four-bys on the road.

They went on to the next exit, turned east, crossed over some railroad tracks, through a roundabout and north up a dirt road through a barren field to a shabby industrial complex all but tucked under a loop of the interstate. Brenda was starting to worry. There was nothing out here but the highway to their left and a sluggish river lined with trees on the right. It seemed like an odd way to get where they were going, especially as they seemed to be going nowhere in particular.

Their destination was surrounded by two layers of chain link fence topped with rusty razor wire, but the gate was wide open, the guardhouse vacant. The sides of the road were shrouded in low weeds, and the buildings were vacant and dirty. The whole place looked long abandoned in fact, but many buildings still had faded signs reading ACCESS RESTRICTED. Whoever owned this place was obsessed with security, and she was worrying what this was all about as the limo drew up to what looked like an office complex. A roadside sign read:

CENTRAL OPERATIONS
AUTHORIZED PERSONNEL ONLY
USE OF LETHAL FORCE SANCTIONED

"What is this place?"

"I don't know, miss." Andrew seemed a bit uneasy too. "This is the address I was given." He pulled the limo over and killed the engine. "If you'll wait, I'll look around." He climbed out and scouted up a short sidewalk to a set of low stairs leading to the main entrance. After a bit he returned and opened the passenger door. "They said to come in. I'm not sure what to make of it."

18

Brenda hesitated for a long moment since she was decidedly uncomfortable about all this, but there was no alternative other than having Andrew take her back to Seattle. As tempting as that was, she knew she would never be rid of the mysterious mister White until she confronted him. "Thank you, Andrew," she mumbled as she slid out.

"Are you sure you'll be all right, miss Hayward?"

Would she? Now that she thought of it, as ominous as this mister White was, he never struck her as dangerous. "I'll be fine, thank you."

§

Up close, the building proved to be made of poured concrete, ugly and functional. There were no windows, and the one door directly ahead of her was heavy steel with a pistol slot at chest height. There were security cameras to either side staring down at her, and a couple more cameras on the corners of the building which covered the street. She hesitated, then tugged on the door handle. It opened easily, revealing a short antechamber with another door beyond. There was a heavy glass window with some sort of card reader beside it, and another pistol port set in its base. The guard room behind the glass was bare and functional, with an empty desk and an empty gun rack on the wall. A bulletin board next to it was faded and worn. The whole place seemed long abandoned.

"Welcome, miss Hayward." A flat voice from a nearby speaker made her jump in alarm. "I am Jeeves, at your service. Professor White is expecting you."

"He is? Well then, why isn't he here to meet me? For that matter, why aren't you here? What's with all the secret stuff, anyway?"

"I am not being secretive, miss Hayward. I am an interactive software performing the services of a Majordomo."

"You're...not real?" She was surprised, since the voice seemed so *alive*. He...it...was soft and pleasant with just a trace of a British accent. It gave her a mental image of an elderly manservant in traditional black tails and white gloves. Computer technology must have come a long way while she was gone.

19

"I am not real in a human sense, however I was developed to interact with people in a comfortable manner. Do please come in. Professor White is in his office, down the corridor straight ahead."

§

The inner door opened onto a corridor running through the building. It was like any office corridor except for the security cameras guarding a crossroads. The connecting corridor opened onto a cafeteria to her left, and another steel door with a guard's station on the right. Nothing to see. There was no one. The corridor was dusty and long unused.

The door at the end was an ordinary wood-paneled one, for a change. There was a dark rectangle where a label once hung, but no other sign of what was going on here. A further corridor went off to either side, lined with doors. There was no sign of life other than the ubiquitous security cameras. She hesitated, then grabbed the knob. The door opened with a faint squeak of its hinges.

The inside was like any office, with filing cabinets and a large metal desk. Daniel White sat in a swivel chair behind the desk. He looked exactly as he did all those years ago; tall and thin, receding white hair, dressed in a turtleneck and trousers. The sight surprised her, brought back memories of that day in '75.

"Hello Brenda." He stood and gestured to an overstuffed chair next to his desk. "Thank you for coming."

"Your...invitation was hard to refuse." She settled uneasily in the chair. "So why have you been following me all these years?"

"It's as I told you, you'll recall..."

"Um, no?"

"At dinner?"

"That was back in '75."

"Huh? Oh, sorry. That was about a month ago for me." It made him seem more fallible, more human somehow. "Well, as I said back then, I was infatuated by your centerfold as a young man, and wanted to meet you. That's all, nothing sinister. I was curious about who you really were, the real human being behind the photos." He offered a rueful smile. "You made quite an impression. I didn't know you had such a temper, for example."

She stirred uneasily. "You scared me with your crazy talk."

20

He sighed. "I'm sorry. I guess I'm still kind of clueless even at this late date." He pondered her solemnly for a bit. "I imagine all this has you pretty confused."

"More like paranoid, actually." She settled in the chair and watched him cautiously. "This is quite a show you put on. So are you some kind of mad scientist, or something?"

He frowned, and settled in his seat again. "Sometimes I wonder about that."

"So what is this place? Where is everyone? It doesn't look like anyone's been in here for a long time."

"There hasn't been for nearly twenty years. The others..." His expression turned glum. "The place was abandoned back in '95. I've been here ever since, alone for the most part."

"So was this some kind of scientific outfit? Something from industry? Why was it abandoned?"

"This was a you-better-believe-it secret research center run by the National Intelligence Directorate." He caught her confused look. "That no longer exists; they're called the NSA now, and they know nothing about this place in their present form."

"Why? What happened to them?"

"They changed during one of the time shifts I initiated."

That confirmed her worst suspicions. "*Time* shifts? So you really can travel in time?"

"Yes, although when we met for lunch was my only trip." He pondered her for a bit. "Mostly, for the last twenty years I've been using this facility to try to correct the flow of history. The future just isn't what they promised us it would be."

She had a good imagination, and it was offering up all sorts of alarming possibilities. "I get the feeling I'm not going to like what you're about to tell me."

"You'd be quite right not to. I've spent the last twenty years trying to keep the human race from destroying itself."

"*Destroying* itself?"

He nodded. "By making corrections to adjust the course of events. You aren't aware of it, since I've managed to avert it here in the Omega Time Line, but World War 3 was fought in 1995. The earth was devastated, the human race reduced to savagery."

That sent a chill through her. As off-the-wall as it sounded, she didn't doubt him in the least. "Really? Jesus..."

He nodded, solemnly. "I don't have many details since we enacted another time shift shortly thereafter, but the estimates are roughly a third of the human race died outright."

They were silent for a bit as she worked her way through that. "How did all this happen?" she asked at last.

He paused and stared into the distance, reflecting. "I guess I should start at the beginning. You recall I mentioned my scholarship to MIT..."

"What? At lunch again?"

"...yes. Anyway, my doctoral thesis was on quantum mechanics, particularly on quantum non-local connections and why they seem to exceed the speed of light. During my graduate year, I became part of a research project trying to develop faster than light travel. That...didn't work out. Instead, we discovered a process for sidestepping time. Needless to say, the spooks gobbled us up in short order."

He stared off into the distance for some time. "Things...were getting bad," he said at last. "The Cold War was heating up, nuclear weapons were proliferating everywhere. It was like the bad old days of the '50s, only it wasn't just scare propaganda this time. They created this project to try to alter the past, to prevent a nuclear war which seemed more likely by the day. We actually got the damned thing to work. We could look into the past, send probes, collect samples. We even sent a couple rabbits back an hour to see if they would survive. They did."

"So what went wrong?"

"We ran out of time!"

"What...?"

He lost it all of a sudden. "We were too late! If we had another year, we might have been able to do it, but Armageddon couldn't wait." He was trembling now, his voice tight and windy. "We...watched the crisis approaching on the main display. We could see the point coming, when the line would turn black and the bombs would fall and the world would end, but there was nothing we could *do* about it!"

22

He had to stop to collect himself, his agitation was too great. "The order came down the day before. We were to be evacuated to a safe place. Gawd! A safe place in a nuclear war! There ain't no such animal." He stopped for another moment, trying to contain his emotions. "They loaded everyone on busses and took off," he went on finally. "But there were four of us who avoided the roundup. We knew our only hope was to get the system working, so we hid out until they were gone, and broke back into here. The...attack came six hours later. We had barely enough warning to get the time field up; the only thing which saved us."

He stopped then, trembling and visibly agitated. Anyone would assume he was stone cold psychotic with that wild tale, except... "It was bad?" She hardly needed to ask.

He nodded convulsively. "The whole...valley was devastated. They hit the Boeing plant. Over a million died just in this area."

"And, you tried to prevent it?"

"Lord, we tried! We tried for the longest time to undo the damage." He shook his head in despair. "We eliminated...Gawd, I don't know how many Reich Ministers and Field Marshals, but for every one we removed, there was someone to take his place. The best we could do was delay the war by a few weeks."

"*Reich* Ministers?"

He looked at her, seemingly distracted from his angst. "Yes, we fought the Third Reich, who controlled all of Europe and much of Africa at the time."

"I thought we and the Russians won the Second World War."

"Not originally. That changed in this time line. You can blame me for the last seventy years."

"You? Why you?"

It took him a moment to answer. "I came up with a theory: our efforts to stave off the crisis were too late to be effective. We needed to reach deeper into time, to strike at the root of the problem rather than the symptoms. We made some progress at first by removing the early Reich dictators—the Prussian military junta who seized power in 1932. We actually pushed the war back by five years. But then we got rid of von Brunlich, the mastermind behind the putsch. The junta never happened, and a fellow named

Hitler took over instead. The Germans lost the war to the Russians, and Stalin began his empire. We lost those five years and four more!"

"You couldn't have expected that! That was sheer bad luck."

"No, we screwed up. I screwed up. No matter what we tried, it just made things worse." His voice was empty now, devoid of any emotion as if he could no longer face his feelings. "The others...lost hope. They just quit trying. The radiation had died down by then, after the four year setback, so they took their chances out there. I never saw any of them again."

"And you've been here alone ever since?"

He nodded with a deep sigh. "Eighteen years. It's better this way; no paranoid super-spooks, no nosy bureaucrats with their rules and paperwork, and especially no government bigwigs trying to turn everything to their political advantage." He paused for a weary sigh. "If this place served no better purpose than electioneering, it'd be too much to bear!"

She could see he was hurting, which was no surprise. "You can't blame yourself for this. It sounds like you were in a no-win situation. No matter who won in Europe, an empire would come out of it. It's not your fault."

"But it is." He was melancholy now, emotionally drained. "We had the means to act, the computing power, the reach, the overview of history. It was up to us, but I couldn't find the answer." He lapsed into silence, staring into the distance.

The conversation lagged, and Brenda had the chance to sort this incredible tale out in her mind: a desperation-priority government program, a program which failed, and he was the only one left to pick up the pieces. He struggled for two decades, all alone, against Fate; somehow holding it at bay for a week or a month or a year at a time. All alone. No wonder he was despondent! He couldn't fail, he couldn't win, he couldn't even give up and walk away. There was no place to walk away to. How could any human endure such pressure for so long?

"So...what are these time shifts?" It seemed best to get him off that track and back to communicating before he sank into depression. "What sort of...corrections do you make?"

24

He mused for a bit as he pondered her. "It could be as simple as a bit of jagged scrap metal no bigger than the palm of your hand laid in the road at just the right moment. That was what caused you to miss your flight back in '88, remember?"

She had to think on it before she recalled how her taxi to the airport there in Singapore had a flat tire which caused her to miss her flight—which crashed in the Bay of Bengal with no survivors. She turned pale. "You saved my *life?*"

He nodded. "I can do *some* good, anyway. Normally I concentrate on bigger issues, but, well, I intervened for old times' sake, you might say."

"Um..." What could she say at a moment like this? "Thank you, I guess. But how could you change the past? Wouldn't that flat tire have prevented the thing which started it all?"

He chuckled humorlessly. "The Grandfather Paradox. You're more worldly than one might think. That's some of the deepest, most arcane theory; we never did sort it out. What we do know is a potential paradox causes a split in the time line creating two realities: one in which you lived, and another in which you died. This is the Time Line in which you lived."

That was a stunning thought: she had been protected all these years by a mad scientist in a top secret NSA laboratory who could change her history at whim. She needed to steer clear of this. "So you've been splitting history every time we get close to a war trying to find Shangri-La?"

"Exactly. We analyze the current trends, locate historical focal points where I can intervene, then shift our locus to anchor it on whatever time line seems the most stable. The Omega Time Line."

"We? Who is 'we'?"

"Myself and George, the program monitor Artificial Intelligence. He does the analysis, I call the shots."

"And that buys us more time?"

"Months, weeks, sometimes days."

"A-and the original time line...?"

"Long lost in the shuffle. I doubt we could find the Alpha Time Line at this late date. It wouldn't matter in any case. Most of them are dead by now, and they were the lucky ones."

25

"Speaking of which, the news sounded pretty ominous on our way up here."

He nodded thoughtfully. "And that's only what the public knows. I have access to far more information than the media does, and it doesn't look good."

"Do you think there's going to be a war?"

"Yes, there will be. Not right away, but the projections call for a limited nuclear conflict between Russia and China in two years time, with a few lobbed at Japan and Europe on general principal, I suppose, followed by a world-wide economic meltdown."

She was horrified. "How can you be sure of *that?*"

"There are six Moulsen KE-5 supercomputers in the basement of this building. They're networked into the greatest computing system ever made, wired into every database and every news source, and they have pirated access to every secure intelligence server on the planet. They have enough storage to hold every printed word out there, and the processor capacity to read them all in less than a second. That's enough computing power to analyze the vector progressions of a nuclear explosion in real time. What's more, the system is overseen by George, who is specifically configured for this project. Admittedly, the projections on the future are statistical guesses, but the normal deviation has been under twenty-four hours thus far."

"Um... Okay, you say so." She couldn't follow more than half his technobabble, but it sounded impressive.

"Trust me: the resources of the United States were poured into this place." His spirits seemed lifted by wandering off into geekspeak. "The best brains, the latest technology..."

He was interrupted by a beep, followed by another toneless voice: "Excuse me, sir. Operation 725 is ready."

"Speaking of which..." He turned to an intercom on his desk. "Very well, George. Give me the summary."

"The key target has been identified and localized. Target date is 04:22:37 hours, June 5, 1991. Collateral effects have been anticipated, an offset schedule of four interventions worked out and localized, and assets have been assigned. Internal power is on standby. All systems are 'Go'."

26

"Four interventions...not bad." He nodded, then gave her a calculating look. "I'm afraid our little reunion will have to be cut short, Brenda. It's time to make another change."

She fidgeted nervously in the overstuffed chair. "What are you going to do, Dan?"

"I am going to kill someone, which will alter the Omega Time Line and, hopefully, prevent a war."

She was appalled when that sank in. "You *kill* people!? You've been *playing God* all these years?"

"I haven't been playing, Brenda."

"Are you mad?"

He gave her a bleak, weary look. "I'm a survivor of the Alpha Time Line. Being insane would help."

"But how can you..."

"Brenda, this has to be done. There's no way to alter history except by altering the fate of those who make it. He has to die so billions can live."

She should have realized that by now; would have if she wasn't so distracted. "But...how can you be sure it will work?"

"It's a complex process; George analyzed this six ways from Sunday. Trust me: I never make a time change until I'm as sure as I can be."

"You depend on a *computer* to decide who lives and dies?"

He shook his head. "George does the analysis, which is his specialty. I make the decisions. I trust him more than I trust myself."

She was shaken by what he was doing, what he about to do. This...this technocratic God...like something out of an ancient myth, hurling lightning bolts from on high... The more she thought about it, the more appalled she became. Maybe he was mad, or maybe he was a monster. Either way, he was fooling with powers Man Was Not Meant To Know.

"This...isn't natural..."

"No, but then neither is nuclear war. You've never seen a nuclear blast, have you? You've never seen Seattle burning, never heard the emptiness on the radio. If you had, you would know."

She stared at him, too shaken to speak.

27

"I'm about to effect a change in the Omega Time Line," he said, firmly. "If you leave now, you will remain on this present time line. The change won't affect you; you probably never even heard about it. You'll be as safe there as anyone can be." The silence stretched out as he considered her somberly. "If you stay, you'll remain with the Omega Time Line. I know I have no right to ask, but having you here would be a big help." His voice became stressed again. "I need someone to network with, to bounce ideas around. You being here would really help, and you could share in the stable future when I find it." He paused again, then added, softly, "I'll call a taxi to take you back to the airport if you wish."

She eyed him uncertainly, wondering what she was caught up in. "...The...person you're going to...kill..."

"He is a racist megalomaniac who became a powerful Senator. He authored the foreign policy legislation which contributed to the current Middle East war. Hopefully, eliminating him will reduce Middle Eastern tensions and cool the risk of a greater conflict."

"You're going to assassinate a United States *Senator!?*"

"It wouldn't be the first time."

It took her a while to absorb that. "Aren't you afraid I'll go to the police?" she asked at last.

He shook his head. "The Omega Time Line won't be here."

He had all the answers...like a God. She was appalled, terrified. This was megalomania writ large, writ on a Cosmic scale. But there was nothing omnipotent in his expression, nothing cruel or power-hungry; he was a lonely old man who longed desperately for her company. It was so out of synch with what was going on here, what he was doing, that she wasn't afraid of him so much as the power he possessed. That power... He could strike anywhere, at any time, saving or destroying as his own inscrutable agenda dictated. Truly he was playing God.

But there was a sad look in his eyes; an old man, alone, facing an unimaginable task which he bore on his own for decades. He was cut off from all contact with the world as he fought to save humanity from itself. How anyone could endure it was beyond understanding. As appalled as she was, she couldn't help but feel sorry for him. And he did save her life...

By the ancient Indian tradition of Karma, she had an obligation to him now. A life saved, a soul nurtured. Yin and Yang. The Cosmic Balance. If ever there was a situation where Cosmic Balance was needed, this was it. As much as she wanted to run, she knew he needed her, and she needed to help him in turn.

"Um...I'll stay."

"Thank you, Brenda," he whispered. Then he turned to the intercom. "George, voice authentication, initiate Operation 725."

"Voice authentication confirmed," the flat voice answered. "Shifting to internal power. Time field initiated." The lights dimmed just a bit, then came back. "Operation 725 initiated. Operation 725 complete. Objective eliminated. Implant recovered. Dropping the time field. Restoring external power." The lights flickered again.

"Give me a fast scan on current Middle Eastern headlines, reference the present war."

"Fast scan reveals only limited fighting in the Gaza Strip, an incursion by Israeli forces in response to a rocket attack."

"Back to normal," he muttered. "Thank you, George. Initiate post-operation analysis."

"Yes, sir. Estimated completion time, seven hours, twenty-three minutes."

"Very well. Jeeves?"

"Sir?" the other flat voice answered.

"Miss Hayward will be staying for dinner. Please activate the guest quarters."

"Certainly, sir."

Brenda sat stunned; that was all it took? He snuffed out a life and altered human history with a brief command over an intercom? This was freakin' *huge*, bigger and more bizarre than anything she could have *imagined*. She had just witnessed a political assassination, a change in the course of history. More than that, she had just witnessed the Wrath of God.

*****

29

"The First Day: Evening"

Dinner that evening held echos of *deja vu*: the menu was lobster and a curried rice dish, but the similarities only went so far. Dan puttered industriously in the building's cafeteria kitchen while she sat on a utility stool at one of the stainless steel prep tables. The table service was plain cafeteria porcelain and stamped metal utensils, the decor was tile and stainless and a set of plastic salt and pepper shakers.

"I've gotten to be a fair cook over the years." He was garrulous, chattering away while he worked. "Although this is the first time I've done lobster. I hope I get this right." He pondered a large kettle boiling on the stove, then turned to a plastic washtub holding two lobsters. He gingerly grabbed for one, pulled the rubber bands off its claws, and dodged a random swipe at his fingers. "All right you, don't give me any trouble or we'll get rough." He dropped the lobster into the pot, poked it down with a wooden spoon, then followed with the other.

"*Such* ingrates." He offered her a whimsical smile. "You'd think they would appreciate the moment."

"I don't suppose they looked at it in the same light." His attempt at levity didn't do much for her pensive mood. "So why did you decide I would want lobster?"

He gave her an introspective look. "I thought I'd do it for old time's sake. You didn't stay for the lobster you ordered at the restaurant, you recall."

She combed her memory for the details of that strange meeting. "I was a bit upset at the time."

"Not that I blame you. Would you prefer something else? I'm afraid I'm low on groceries at the moment."

"Huh? Um, no, lobster will do fine."

He offered a fragile smile, then grabbed a large skillet, added some water, tore open a package of rice and seasoning mix and dumped them in. "I made a point of looking up Indian recipes when I learned you would one day return to the States. I couldn't make heads nor tails of them, and me a physicist!" He looked askance at her, and held up the package with an awkward smile.

"Then I found this at a small Indian store recently. Curry isn't my favorite, but I thought you'd like it."

He plainly didn't have many opportunities for simple conversation. His patter and the subtle hints of his nervousness made him seem more human, less of an ominous presence somewhere in the shadows. He seemed almost likable, in fact. She had to remind herself that this was a top secret government laboratory—stolen at that—and he was a man who altered time by assassinating world leaders.

"Actually I never liked curry either. That's all you can find over there in India, but I really look forward to some plain old American cooking."

He paused and turned to her. "Indeed? How about a baked potato, then?"

"Gawd, yes!"

He dumped the skillet of rice in the sink without a second thought, fished two large potatoes out of a cabinet, and popped them in a microwave. "Your wish is my command. The customer is always right here at *Cafe Ouroboros*." He grinned sheepishly. "That's what we dubbed this place, way back when; from the mythical world serpent which eats its own tail."

"Something to do with time travel?"

"Actually it was because the food here was so bad we felt like we would have to eat ourselves if we wanted a decent meal. The spooks insisted we be served a 'proper' diet."

That got a nervous chuckle out of her. "Government cooking. I know what you mean."

The cafeteria would have seated about a hundred, with the kitchen built to match. There was a walk-in pantry, a couple large commercial refrigerators, a huge commercial stove, plus plenty of stainless steel. There were pots and pans and racks of utensils stacked in odd corners, and a shelf loaded with plain ceramic dishes. It brought back memories of her time as a waitress there in Hollywood, but the place seemed *haunted*, filled with the restless ghosts of might-have-been. Like the rest of the building, the place was largely unused, dusty, with a thin film of cooking grease in the corners where a quick swipe with a washcloth missed it.

31

"What was it like here? Back before all this started?"

He leaned against the counter and stared off into the distance with a sigh. "It was exciting. We were the best and brightest on an urgent mission. We delved into the darkest recesses of reality itself to find secrets mankind was not meant to find." He was silent for a bit, remembering. "We'd go to all hours, twenty hours a day sometimes; brainstorming, sketching circuit diagrams and logic trees on napkins and the backs of envelopes. We drove the poor technicians half crazy trying to figure out each new wack-a-doodle gismo we dreamed up."

The silence returned, broken by the soft boiling of the kettle and the hum of the microwave. He sniffed, and dabbed one eye with his sleeve.

"It...was something huge, gigantic, bigger than us. It drew us in. It was addictive. We would go on until we were too exhausted to think, then we'd crash in the dorm we set up, and were back at it in a few hours. The knowledge, the insights we gained..." He tapered off then, and stared at the table, brooding. "It was good."

She envied him in a way: he found his calling in a truly important effort which demanded his very best, just as she found in medicine. As unsettled as she was about all this, she understood what he must have felt back then. They were on a holy quest to save mankind from themselves. It wasn't his fault they failed.

The microwave dinged. He pulled out of his funk, opened the door and prodded the potatoes with a fork. "Done." He fished them out onto two plates, added the lobsters, and set one of the plates in front of her. "A miracle of modern technology."

She gestured at her lobster. "Speaking of technology, how do we crack these things?"

"Oh..." He thought about it for a bit, then went over to a drawer and produced a meat tenderizing maul. "They didn't serve lobster here, so we'll have to improvise. There's plenty of dishes, so no worry about breakage."

The next couple of minutes were devoted to rigorous upper arm exercise, loud metallic crashing, and a few porcelain chips. "There you have it," Dan said when he finished. "The triumph of the tool-making ape."

32

"Professor Ugh The Cave-Man. Bravo!"

"I'm afraid all I have is margarine, so the eating's a bit plain." He rummaged in one of the refrigerators and set a margarine tub in front of her. "I wish I'd thought to pick up some sour cream on my last grocery run." He looked her over, then added, "I hope you don't ruin that lovely dress."

"This old thing?" The Indian *sari* she wore was so commonplace in her world she hardly thought about it. It pleased her that he noticed. "It's cotton, they wash out easily."

"Still, I should have picked up some bibs."

"Hey, it's the thought that counts." She helped herself to the margarine, and attacked her potato. "Mmph! You're a good cook."

He smiled. "I try."

They settled in for dinner, and her first lobster proved an interesting and messy experience. She could see why restaurants gave their customers bibs.

"How is it?" Dan asked.

"Mmph! Some corn fritters might go good with this."

"They might at that."

"So...um...do you still have my centerfold kicking around somewhere?"

He hesitated. "I still have that copy on my laptop, the one I showed you, but I never look at it," he said, solemnly. "I gave that up years ago. A man has to outgrow paper dolls someday." He was silent for a bit, then, "And, honestly, you mean more to me than that."

"I'm not the hot young babe you met back in '75, Dan," she said, softly.

"You will always be beautiful, Brenda."

That was touching in a way. She turned sixty last month, and while she took care of herself, the years showed. Her formerly auburn hair was dusted with gray and her face lined with the years of toil as a nurse in a chronically overworked and under-equipped hospital. Despite her busy lifestyle, she was chunkier and not so firm as when Hugh Hefner selected her photos from dozens of prospects. She was still attractive by any rational standard—for sixty years old—but it never hurt to hear it said out loud.

"So you've been watching me all this time? You haven't been peeking at private moments, have you?"

He was actually embarrassed. "Well...I did a few times, at first, but honestly I felt kind of ashamed. I've always thought of you as my Dream Girl, and you deserved better. I...made myself stop years ago, and I've respected your privacy ever since."

His Dream Girl. That was a jarring note which brought back memories of all the creeps and hustlers she met in Hollywood. She wasn't comfortable even now with being someone's fantasy. "That's why you saved my life back there in '88?"

§

She was on her way to India for a tour in the Peace Corps after completing her nurses' schooling, and had stopped over in Singapore to change planes. The weather was foul: Singapore was recovering from a near miss by a typhoon which still hovered to the south over Java. Four of them stayed overnight at the American Embassy to wait until the weather improved, and caught a taxi to the airport the next morning. The taxi was delayed by a flat tire. They missed the flight. The storm shifted west into the Bay of Bengal. The plane, an old DC-6 from a regional airline, went down with no survivors.

§

"Yes," he said, solemnly. "I suppose it comes under altruistic love, that whole knight in shining armor thing."

She sank in her chair, thinking back on what *seemed* like a minor annoyance at the time. "Lord...I was so *angry* at missing the flight. I yelled at the poor taxi driver. I never knew until years later..."

They shared an uncomfortable silence for a while as they finished their dinners. She was unsettled to think about her near miss...no, her miraculous rescue. She should be long dead...but wasn't, thanks to the unlikely intervention of an infatuated admirer. It's not everyone who gets to read their own obituary; it left her feeling kind of hollow.

Dan focussed on his dinner, seemingly lost in his own thoughts. He was an unlikely hero...but then heroism doesn't always involve bulging biceps. What good could a John Wayne have done in the middle of a typhoon? No, he was her Man Of The Hour, and as unlikely a hero as he seemed, he was the best man for the job way back then. Back then? How long was it since he rescued her? Weeks? Months?

But then he didn't always use his power for good. He killed people, routinely it seemed. He killed without emotion, which was even worse. After twenty years of this, he'd become numb to it. At least he killed for a good reason. As shaken as she was by the things he showed her, he was right: some people have to die for the greater good. What went on here gave her the creeps, but she understood the harsh reality he faced all these years. What would she have done in his place? Would she have had the courage to do what he did?

Her thoughts drifted back to her early experience in nursing school. She cringed at using a hypodermic syringe at first, and the sight of her first bloody traffic accident victim left her petrified. But she got over it. She learned to deal with blood and broken bones and agony. She learned how to put it out of her mind and do what had to be done, quickly and correctly. Maybe she would have found the courage in his place. Maybe it wasn't fair to condemn him for his actions.

He seemed to be a decent sort. She sized him up discretely, her feminine instincts kindled. He was intelligent, something which always did appeal to her. Kind of average looking, but she hadn't been impressed by machismo since high school. A girl could do worse. *'This is weird,'* she thought. She was actually considering him, even in this place, under these circumstances. *'Better shape up, girl. This isn't some damn-fool Harlequin Romance. You're in no position to get involved.'*

Shame, though. He wasn't bad looking.

"You still watch me, don't you?" she asked at last. "That's how you knew I was returning home."

He stirred out of his distracted haze. "I looked in on you from time to time to see if you were all right."

There was that uncomfortable feeling again. "You didn't interfere to get me to come home, did you?"

"Well, I guess I did in a small way. When I saw you were thinking of retiring, I sent that message about your Microsoft stock so you'd remember you still had it. Your coming back home was a bonus, I suppose."

"But you weren't prying into personal matters?" she asked, carefully.

"Honest, I only looked in now and then, and I always respected your privacy."

§

It seemed obvious now that she could put the pieces together. She had grown utterly weary of the endless struggle against the mean streets of Bangalore. She knew she was burnt out. The headaches were more frequent, and the workload was becoming too much. For all the good she did there in twenty-eight years, it was a no-win situation. Time to call it a day and attend to her own life while she still had it to live. She'd talked about it for a couple months with her coworkers; he must have overheard. She was already longing for home when that message came from the State Department.

§

"So...I don't have a distant cousin after all?"

"Not that I've been able to find."

She didn't doubt his good intentions, but still it made her uncomfortable. "I know you meant well, Dan, and I appreciate all that you've done for me, but this whole thing is kind of unnerving."

"I'm sorry if I disturbed you, Brenda."

She looked into his eyes, and saw the sincerity and longing there. He really was in love with her, his Dream Girl, and would and could move heaven and earth to protect her. Every girl needs a hero at some point so she realizes she's worth rescuing. His intentions were good, certainly, even if his methods were frightening. "It's...all right. I am grateful, really."

The conversation lapsed into an awkward silence as they finished dinner with coffee and pudding cups.

"Were there any other rescues you provided?" she asked after a while.

36

"Yes." He studied her face with an unhappy look. "I saved you twice from being gang-raped and murdered."

That chilled her. "*Gang*-raped?"

He nodded. "In '90 and '92. You remember how anti-western India was at the time? You were *Vidēśī śaitāna*. Those street gangs brutalize their own women; you can imagine what they did to you."

She knew all too well what he meant, having seen it more than once. "How...?"

"The first time, I planted some Ipecac syrup one of your co-workers' tea. He missed work, so you had to do a double shift." She giggled at that one in spite of herself, but then he turned somber. "I couldn't find an easy way the second time, so I caused the second group to drop dead one by one. I had to eliminate three of them before the rest were spooked and disbursed."

That shook her again. "You *killed* three people to protect me?"

He nodded. "Yes."

"...How?" She really didn't want to know.

"I introduced a large ball bearing into their brain cavities. The displacement effect is like being hit with a rifle bullet."

She was horrified, as hardened as she had become to the sight of blood and suffering. There were so many ways, so many tragic ways a human body can be violated, but this...this was gristly. They never saw their assailant, never even knew they were condemned, or why: dead, just like that, without any obvious reason; alive and vital one moment, dead on a street corner the next without even the grace of knowing they were about to die. Death from within. Death from tomorrow.

She should have known better, now that she remembered those times. Lower class Indians treat women like cattle even today; she saw far too many battered and raped women in her time there, not to mention the forced marriages and honor killings. It never occurred to her that she was leading a charmed life. It unnerved her to realize what she was saved from, and what this thoughtful, elderly man did to save her. Compared to this, that plane crash would have been merciful. Still, the thought of it...of how they died... She was starting to fear him again.

37

"Dan...I appreciate you looking out for me," she said, carefully. "But I'm not comfortable with how you did it. You seem to kill awfully easily."

That annoyed him; he gave her a chilly look. "I kept you from being murdered."

"Yes, but..."

"What did you want me to do? Let you die? Let them ravage you and beat you to death? Do you think I would be as callous as that?"

"Of course not. But killing them wasn't right."

"What? They should have had a fair trial first? Would they have given *you* a fair trial?"

"There must have been some other way besides murder..."

"You think I *like* killing?" He was getting heated all of a sudden. "I killed them to *save* you, dammit!"

His tone got her Irish up in turn. "And now you've stuck me with their fate! You think I want that on my conscience? Maybe you meant well, but you could have tried harder to find some other way!"

He gave her an icy glare. "If you're too squeamish for this, then why are you here?"

"I'm here because you *invited* me here! Because you meddled in my life to *lead* me here! Yes, I'm squeamish! Squeamish about how easily you killed them! You're far too comfortable with murder. How many have you killed over the years? There has to be some other way."

He finally exploded, jumping to his feet. "I don't just blast anyone at random!" he yelled. "My targets are people who contributed to the destruction of our civilization! To nuclear war! They *deserve* what they get!"

"That may be, but still..."

"The guilty ones *never* get punished. You *know* it's true! They slaughter millions of innocents in the Glorious Name of their causes, and they *never* pay the price! Only now I'm watching them! I can strike a blow for all their helpless victims! I can reach out to them and exact justice!"

He was starting to scare her. "...Dan..."

38

"I'm trying to save this sorry excuse for a civilization from themselves, and what thanks do I get? You don't even appreciate my saving your own life! What did you expect? That I'd pass some UN resolution? That I'd organize a protest march? These monsters *only* understand one thing! They *only* respect one thing! *Death!* And I deliver it! *Justice* for all the billions of innocent lives lost!"

She was starting to be really scared. His outburst bordered on megalomania, if not paranoia. She needed to bring him down before he went off the deep end. "I'm sorry, Dan," she said, earnestly. "I didn't mean to offend you."

He stared at her for a long moment, breathing hard, his hands trembling. "I know what I'm doing, Brenda," he said at last in a chilly voice. "This has to be done, and I'm the only one who can do it."

There was a painful silence, then he settled on his bar stool and brooded over his coffee while she tried to get a handle on her emotions. His overreaction alarmed her like nothing seen yet. He was obsessed, driven, caught up in a horrible web of ungodly technology trying to achieve the impossible. She knew obsession when she saw it; knew what it could do to otherwise decent human beings. He'd been at this for decades, all alone, haunted by who knew how many cataclysmic failures. He was mad; had to be. No one could endure this unspeakable situation as long as he had and not be. And he held the power of life and death over the entire globe, over the centuries... Power like no one ever held before... Something she once heard came to mind: *'Power corrupts, and absolute power corrupts absolutely'.* He held absolute, godlike power in his hands. How could he *not* be corrupted by it?

'God...he's turned into a monster!' she thought. She was appalled at his explosive reaction to her criticism, and by how she had actually speculated about him... *'Girl, this is crazy! He's crazy! You need to get out of here!'* The scary part was his obvious obsession for her. She'd read the stories of former centerfolds and their stalkers, and saw the tragic result of obsession all too often there in the ER in Bangalore. There's nothing romantic about being someone's Dream Girl.

39

But first she needed to get him calmed down so she could reason with him. "I'm...sorry if I upset you, Dan," she offered. "I don't really know all of what you've been through, so maybe I shouldn't be so quick to criticize."

He was silent for a bit, brooding, then glanced at her. "I'm just doing what I have to, Brenda. Killing is the only sure way to get results. I wish you could see that."

"It's just I've spent my whole career trying to save lives. I've watched a lot of people die, and it's never pleasant. This isn't an easy adjustment to make."

He frowned, and his grip tightened on his coffee mug. "I've watched people die by the *billions*. Preventing that is worth any cost. You're a nurse; you know sometimes you can't help everyone. Some have to die so others can live. It's the same here, only the ones who die deserve it!"

Better get him off topic and onto something safe. "So...you've been here all this time by yourself?"

He sighed and withdrew to his coffee mug again. "Yes," he said at last. "There were four of us at first, but the others... They gave up eventually, and took their chances out there." From the way he said it, it sounded like a betrayal.

"You must have had someone?"

"Well, there's Jeeves and George..."

"Two computer programs?"

His expression brightened. "They're not just programs, they're Artificial Intelligences, self aware and capable of reason in their own right. Jeeves was the security protocol. Since there's no need for security any more, I repurposed him as a Majordomo, not that it keeps him from kvetching all the time. Isn't that right, Jeeves?"

"*Someone* must remind you to eat and sleep *some*time, sir," the cultured English voice came from a nearby intercom. "You'll work yourself to death otherwise."

"You see? A regular mother hen. Of course he's not as bad as when he was demanding security passes every ten minutes; repurposing him did *some* good."

Mister Nice Guy again. Just like that. Harmless Old Professor Jekyll and his Wondrous Time Machine. What could she do if he

40

went off on her? Could she expect any help from Jeeves? "You can do that? I'd think a security program would be untouchable."

"AIs can be repurposed, *if* you have the access codes."

Access codes. No, she couldn't expect any help from them. "What about George?"

"That's the Operations program, handling temporal functions. I named him for George Patton, to remind me not to go all bull-in-a-china-shop with time operations." That last was rather pointed. "It's very finicky work, and still largely an unexplored science. Can't be too careful in plotting a change."

Better back away from that line too. "Couldn't you find anyone else to help you? I'm sure the governments in other time lines would have pitched in."

"Absolutely not! Those monsters can't be trusted! They're the problem! I'd be a fool to let them get their hands on this!"

That surprised her; he was supposedly a good company man, passed all the security checks, loyal and mission-oriented to the core; where did his paranoia about his own bosses come from? "But what about maintenance? All these computers must need repairs from time to time. Does anyone ever come around to fix things? "

He settled on his stool. "The equipment was made to be highly reliable, and we have a stock of spare parts. Truth is I'm not much of a hardware technician. The system is running, but it takes a lot to keep it going." He started fuming again. "Idiots! We were supposed to be self sufficient in case we had to bunker up, but instead they pulled everyone out. We could have hunkered down and ridden the war out. Instead, the place was abandoned just when we were needed the most! Those agency fools wanted to protect their priceless secrets! We could still be here working to fix the crisis, but they hauled them away on busses! They were all likely killed thanks to the goddamned spooks!"

There's no getting him off it. She was no psychiatrist, but his obsession was plain enough even for her to see. That wasn't surprising, considering how long he'd been here. The thought came to her that she might be stranded here, afraid of his reaction if she tried to leave...unless someone came along at random.

"Doesn't anyone ever come around here? I'm sure this place would have been investigated by someone, the police, maybe?"

That pulled him out of his angst again. "Actually no. This place is duplicated in every time line. I call the line we're anchored to now the Omega Time Line, but that's just a reference point. If anyone comes snooping around, I can shift to another time line, and all they'll find is some old abandoned buildings on a Federal reservation."

She was beginning to think she better get out of there pronto. But could she? Did she dare shatter his Dream Girl fantasy with the power he possessed? What would he do? Stalkers frequently lash out at the first sign of rejection. She needed to string him along until she could find a way to gracefully exit without arousing his temper.

"But what about the feds? The power company? Doesn't anyone ever get suspicious?"

"I am a computer geek, you know. Trust me: with this much hardware, tapping into Federal databases, altering utility records, and creating bank accounts with ample funds is no problem."

That didn't sound good. "So this place is sort of a temporal Flying Dutchman?"

He laughed. "Yep, you could say that."

Yep, Professor Jekyll and his Wondrous Time Machine...

They both jumped in surprise when a loud bleat came over the intercom. "Excuse me, sir," the other flat voice—George—said. "The analysis of Operation 725 is showing a null solution."

"Oh, great," Dan muttered. "How far have you extended your analysis?"

"I am unable to complete the analysis due to a temporal cascade presently under way."

He turned pale. "How bad is it?"

"It is already Class Four, and accelerating. I recommend immediate corrective action."

"Shit!" He was on his feet and out the door in a rush.

*****

42

"The First Evening"

It took her a moment to get over her surprise, then, alarmed by his reaction, she jumped up and ran after him. He was already across the hall by time she reached the door, and vanished into the room beyond the security checkpoint before she barely got started. When she reached that door, he was standing in front of a huge display which spread the width of the room.

The room was perhaps sixty feet wide, with a high ceiling and a gallery of padded seats in back. In front of those was a metal railing, and in front of that was a line of control panels in a shallow pit. Beyond that in turn, slightly elevated so it could be seen from any point in the room, was a view screen which must have been fifty feet wide by eight tall, curved slightly to focus on the center of the room. Two pairs of large TV monitors, blank for the moment, were suspended above that in turn. The place was chillingly remote; sterile metal and tile, subdued colors, dimly lit with overhead track lighting and the soft glow from the display; the very essence of faceless National Security.

There were countless horizontal lines running across the main display screen. They met a vertical index line running down the center. Above, between the paired monitors, an LED clock showed the time to the second. Most of the lines were black, but a narrow cluster in the middle were blue, changing to red as they approached the center. She thought the lines were stationary at first, but noticed them moving slowly to the left, passing the center line.

"What is it? What's happening?"

He glanced at her in annoyance as if she was interrupting something urgent. "I don't know yet." He scanned the huge display anxiously, tracing various lines with his finger. "It seems fairly high, so it must be a near-proximity divergence. Still, a Class Four..." Suddenly, one of the lines he was studying split, creating two new lines. "What the hell?"

He retreated to one of the control panels and made an adjustment. The display shifted to the left and shrank, revealing a jumble of color. A marker appeared, a diamond with the number '725', which he centered on the vertical divider. The timer above

43

read '1991.06.05.04.22.37'. He focussed in again, and started tracking right. The lines reemerged from the chaotic blur. Some were green, most yellow, several were blue, a few here and there were red. Those on the fringes were black. One line, thicker than the others, continued along the center of the stream. The Omega Time Line. It was already yellow, in 1991.

He closed on the display and studied the carefully; as he did, the Omega Time Line split, both still yellow although they soon changed to blue, and then red. Further on, a second vertical line reappeared and inched its way across the screen; the present date and time, creeping up on them. Most of the lines were black by that point, a few were still red.

"This isn't what we had before," Dan muttered. "Something's gone seriously wrong." Just then the thicker Omega Time Line split again. The others shifted to allow the newcomer room. "But...what's causing it?" He sounded almost panicked now.

Another nearby line split; one almost immediately turned black. Another line split, then split again. "Oh, Great!" He glanced at her. "Something went wrong with the intervention. The change set in motion a cascade...a series of changes with potentially disastrous results."

"How bad is it?"

"Not good." He focussed out again, and the array of lines dissolved into a broad sweep of color—almost all black—which kept multiplying, spreading out. He came around the panel, and closed on the display, studying the web closely. The lines branched steadily, relentlessly.

"Jesus...look at it." He was dismayed. "George! Did you implement the four supplemental interventions to Operation 725?"

"I did. All four were successful with no indicated tertiary effects."

"Well then, what went wrong?" He studied the main display, trying to fathom what was happening.

"Unknown at this point. Shall I begin an analysis?"

"Yes, at once."

"Analysis under way. Expected completion time eight hours, thirty-five minutes."

"Eight hours..." he mumbled. "Jeez..."

"What is that?"

That broke his concentration, and he turned to her. "This is the master time display." He gestured to the growing web of lines with a sweep of the hand. "Each of these lines is an alternate reality." He jabbed a finger at one of the branching points. "Each split is a change in the course of history for that time line, a paradox. The colors indicate the threat level."

He retreated to the control pit, adjusted the controls again, and the display zoomed in on the heavy line in the center, the Omega Time Line. He panned left back to the '725' marker, then swept steadily right—toward the present. The line passed through several splits as it advanced. Soon it changed from yellow to blue, then to red. Soon the vertical index line came into view and joined the vertical marker. The Omega Time Line extended beyond into the future...and changed to black almost immediately thereafter.

"That's not good, is it?"

"It'll be fatal." He pointed to the extended line. "Those change to black when there are indicators of nuclear detonations. It wasn't like this before."

"You triggered a *nuclear war*?!"

He spun to face her. "I've managed to *forestall* a nuclear war for twenty years now! Weren't you listening earlier?"

"It wasn't like this an an hour ago!" she snapped at him.

"Well then, I'll just have to undo it, *if* you don't mind!"

"Sir, we have a pending crisis," George interrupted. "You need to examine the Time Line immediately."

Dan glanced at the monitor, then did a double-take. "What is the monitor date?"

"The monitor date is the present." The thick line in the center was red now, the vertical marker line rapidly approaching the point where it turned black.

"How long until this Time Line reaches the crisis point?"

"Unable to give an exact figure. This time line has been substantially altered from the original, and will require eight hours and twenty-eight minutes to complete the analysis."

"Ball-park it!"

45

"Based on limited observational data, the best rough estimate is forty-seven minutes, plus or minus eighteen minutes."

"Oh, Jesus! George! Voice authentication! Go to DefCon One, activate the time field, pronto!"

"Voice authentication denied."

He halted as if struck. "What?"

"Voice authentication denied."

"*Why!?*"

"Your present stress levels have pushed your voice beyond vocal recognition limits. You need to calm down."

He stared at the display for a moment, seemingly at a loss, then made a conscious effort to calm himself. "George? Voice authentication."

There was a brief, agonizing silence, then, "Voice authentication approved. Your orders?"

Dan fought to maintain his composure, although his voice was still thin and tense. "Set condition DefCon One. Activate the time field. Monitor communications for any sign of an impending attack."

"Setting condition DefCon One. Time field available in twenty-four minutes. Communication monitoring shows a general war alert is already in progress."

"Damned cascade..." he muttered.

"What happened?" She was dismayed by how rapidly this crisis blew up. "There was no sign of trouble earlier."

Dan broke off studying the main display and focused on her. "The cascade created a ripple effect. It shifted us into a future where a war is about to start. We were lucky George caught it when he did, if it's not already too late."

"This is insane!"

"You don't know the *meaning* of insane! This happens all the time! When I first started, there was only one line, and it was already black!"

She stared at the display with its steady progression of line splits. Most of it was black now; the last few were red. The vertical marker crept closer to the black. "C-can you do something?"

46

"That's why I'm here," he said, grimly. He turned to the control panel and made some adjustments. The display shifted back to the '725' marker and zoomed in. "I need to trace the flow to find turning points where corrections can be added. Then comes the tricky part."

"How can you fix all that?"

He looked at her, and sighed. "I can't. No one can. Each of these lines is an alternate future growing out of the cascade. Normally at least one will progress safely, which becomes the Omega Time Line. The problem here is there don't seem to be any stable lines. I'll have to create one; the rest are write-offs."

"How...soon..."

He thought on that for a moment. "The change took place sometime shortly after June of '91, so we have some maneuvering room." He studied the master screen for a bit, then turned to her. "But it'll take some digging to find the cause."

"No...I mean how soon to the war starting?"

His features grew tight and his voice turned thin. "Let's pray we really do have a five minute margin." He pondered his instruments for some time, seemingly forgetting her, then glanced at her again. "I'm sorry I dragged you into this, Brenda. I'm afraid I'll have to ask you to leave now. I need to focus my full attention on this crisis."

"Like hell! If there's gonna be a nuclear war out there, I'm staying right here!"

He stared at her for a long moment, confused. "No, I meant leave this room. You can't go out *there*. Right now I need to concentrate on saving humanity, which will be a neat trick sorting a solution out of that. I need to be alone for a while."

She nodded, numbly.

"Jeeves?"

"Sir?" the automated voice answered.

"Please escort miss Hayward to the guest room, and provide her anything she needs."

"Of course, sir."

He took something out of a drawer in the console and offered it to her. "Here. You should wear this."

47

"A radiation badge?" She'd seen similar ones worn by the X-ray techs in India. "What good will this do if we're gonna get nuked?"

He made a sour face. "The time field will protect us from *that*. There's a nuclear reactor in the basement to provide internal power when making changes. Unfortunately, it was under repair when the place was evacuated. The shielding is incomplete."

"So we're at risk when you use your time machine?"

"Normally no. I only run the reactor a few minutes at a time when making changes. The time field can protect us from a nuclear blast...it puts us slightly out of phase. Thing is, I'll have to run the reactor at full power for as long as we need the time field."

'Wonderful', she thought to herself. *'How long will that be?'*

§

"The guest room is the second door on your left." One of Jeeves' security cameras mounted in the ceiling just outside Dan's office swiveled to follow her as she walked down the second side corridor. "Yes, that one."

The guest room must have been an unused executive office complete with restroom annex. There was wood paneling, a drop ceiling and thin wall-to-wall carpeting like offices everywhere. Whatever furniture used to be in there was long gone, replaced with a basic bedroom suite. The place looked brand spankin' new in fact, and she wondered if he set this up expressly for her. Likely. He seemed to have all the answers. She wondered vaguely if he peeked into the future to see what she'd do.

She tried to mask her tension by exploring her new quarters—likely her new home for the rest of her life, however long that would be. The place was comfortable, if basic, with a print sheet set, hardboard furniture and a brass table lamp at the bedside. There were no windows. The restroom was the same: tile and paint, sink and toilet, but no shower. The one concession to luxury was a thick terrycloth towel set with a 'B' monogram; an oddly touching gesture on his part.

It was all a useless gesture. She was petrified by the thought that a nuclear war was about to break out. The Bombs would be falling any minute now! She could only hope his time field,

48

whatever that was, could protect them. It was too much to be handed all at once and without warning. She sagged onto the bed and rubbed her face with both hands, trying to control her shakes. "God, what a homecoming!" she mumbled.

"Are you all right, miss Hayward?" Jeeves asked.

"No, I'm not all right!" she sobbed. "What have I gotten myself into?"

"If I might venture an observation, despite your dismay at what is happening here, this is the only safe place on the planet at the moment. There are worse places to be right now."

That was the one truth which mattered right then, and it gave her at least a faint sense of hope. "Well...yeah...you got that right! But can that time thingie protect us?"

"The 'time thingie', as you put it, has withstood several nuclear attacks over the years with no ill effect. We shall be perfectly safe, assuming the field can be raised in time."

"And if it can't?" She really didn't want to know the answer to that one.

"Let us hope it can. According to George, the field should go up in about seventeen minutes."

"Seventeen minutes..." Just in time to avoid a nuclear war which wasn't scheduled when she landed at SeaTac airport that morning. "This is unbelievable. That fool messed things up big-time!"

"It isn't fair to blame Professor White. Temporal research is still in its infancy. It is more an art than a science."

"Then he should know better, and leave well enough alone!" She was starting to give in to her panic. "If he doesn't know what the *hell* he's doing, then he shouldn't go mucking around like a bull in a china shop!"

"Unfortunately, he doesn't have many options in his quest to save the human race. He is carrying on the struggle alone in a largely unexplored realm of science."

"Science be *damned!* It doesn't help that he goes killing everyone in sight! He blew away a United States Senator! Now we're stuck with the mess that created. Even he can't un-kill someone."

"Perhaps not. But his intentions are good, surely."

"His *intentions* are good? The road to hell is *paved* with good intentions!" It was too much. She curled up on the bed, shaking and sobbing in fear.

"Miss Hayward?"

"Leave me alone!"

Jeeves shut up and left her to cope as best she could, which wasn't very well. She was appalled at the mess she stumbled into without warning. His hubris dismayed her, especially with the powers he wielded. She was also furious at him for his abrupt dismissal, like she was some weak woman who needed a big, strong man to make decisions for her. Whatever else he might be, the great Daniel White was seriously, dangerously clueless.

It wasn't long before her shakes were overridden by another pounding headache. She lay there, eyes tightly closed, trying to ignore it, but it was too much. There was nothing for it, so after a while she struggled to her feet and headed back to the front entrance to see about her luggage.

§

The luggage was stacked against the wall of the antechamber just inside the door, no doubt brought in by the driver, Andrew. She felt a bit guilty not giving him a tip, but he was long gone...she came up short when she realized he would be dead soon. One more thing to lay on the all-mighty Time Lord. Her head was pounding. She fumbled through her carry-all, came up with a small glass bottle of pills—*thankfully* she had a note from her doctor in India when she brought it through Customs—popped a couple, and slumped on one of her footlockers with a moan. "I'm sorry, Andrew," she whispered. It was likely the only prayer he would receive.

After a bit, she noticed the envelope laying on the floor where she dropped it. Old habits die hard, even in a nuclear war, so she picked it up and stared listlessly at it. Seven million dollars of Microsoft stock, now worthless once again. She wondered vaguely if he meant to buy her with it, and whether he did without her realizing it. Not that it mattered now. Old habits die hard; she tucked it into her carry-all.

50

Her headache started to ease. After a while, some impulse—a last fleeting glimpse of her old reality perhaps—made her struggle to her feet and open the door a crack to peer outside.

"Please be careful, miss Hayward. The time field will activate momentarily. Don't go beyond the door."

"Thank you, Jeeves," she said, absently.

She stood in the doorway watching the sunset and feeling lost. The sky was a gentle blue-gray, the fluffy clouds edged with orange. A flight of birds—ducks or geese, maybe—flew overhead in a neat V formation. She watched through a gap in the surrounding buildings as they passed beyond the distant pines and were lost in the shimmering city lights. A steady stream of headlights flowed along Highway 5, passing just to the west of the laboratory. The traffic was heavy and moving fast, the rushing noise of their engines and the blare of horns gave a sense of solidity to the world out there. It all seemed so *real*, so natural, like she often dreamed her homecoming would be like. She was tempted to run out onto the street, to embrace that reality now slipping from her grasp, even though it would mean her death.

But she didn't, and not from any sense of self-preservation. That world out there was hollow, an empty mask over something unnameable. He had shown her the backside of this tranquil reality, the beautiful sunset and the shimmering city lights, and the truth shook her to her soul.

"It could be as simple as a bit of jagged scrap metal no bigger than the palm of your hand laid in the road at just the right moment. That was what caused you to miss your flight back in '88, remember?"

She shuddered at the thought: she *died* in '88, right on the cusp of a new adventure in her life...only she hadn't. He stepped in and saved her. Her whole life since then was a fabrication. Nor was that the only time he reached out to protect her. He actually *murdered* three people in cold blood, killed without hesitation and without remorse. As romantic as the fantasy seemed, the reality was disturbing.

51

"You were Vidēśī śaitāna, a 'foreign devil'. Those street gangs brutalize their own women; you can imagine what they did to you."

The thought of what happened in some alternate reality horrified her. She'd seen enough victims of rape and domestic violence; she could well imagine the terrors she endured in some dark alley. The evening chill was deepening as the sunlight faded. A light breeze came up, but that wasn't why she shivered.

"...The...person you're going to...kill..."
"He is a racist megalomaniac who became a powerful Senator. He authored the foreign policy legislation which contributed to the current Middle East war. Hopefully, eliminating him will reduce Middle Eastern tensions and cool the risk of a greater conflict."

The sky to the west faded to a deep soft purple-gray, the trees outlined by the last hint of sunset. The first stars glittered overhead. The twilight was picked out with city lights in the distance. It all seemed so natural, so normal. It was all a mask; a mask covering something unnatural, something unnameable.

Suddenly the sky turned a formless black, as if a curtain had been drawn over the world. "Miss Hayward?" Jeeves' voice came from the speaker next to her. "The temporal field has been activated. You should come in now."

It was too much. She retreated back inside, pulled the steel security door shut, and stood in the middle of the hall trembling and breathing hard. The whole foundation of her reality was shattered, leaving her lost. There was a freakin' *nuclear war* going on outside! It took her a few minutes to regain her self control. She finally managed to pull herself together enough to function, and dug through her duffle bag, scattering items here and there, until she came up with her bath kit and a change of clothes. Then she hurried back to the guest room, running from that ominous mask outside.

§

52

It took a while for her to get up the nerve to come out of her quarters again, and as much as she was appalled by him, her need for some human contact drove her back to Operations. Daniel White was standing in front of the main display, watching the bank of video displays when she came in. He stood motionless, silhouetted in bright orange and yellow light from the monitors. He stirred when she came up next to him, and tried to hold her back. "You don't want to see this."

She couldn't help herself. She pushed past him and looked up at the monitors in stunned horror. The landscape for miles around was burning. There was nothing left standing, not a house, not a tree, not a telephone pole. The entire valley had been reduced to rubble which blazed in billowing flame. She hadn't felt a thing when it happened.

"They hit the Boeing plant, and Seattle, and the navy base at Bremerton," he said softly. He put an arm around her shoulders and tried to turn her away, but she shook him off.

"Who...?" she whispered at last.

"It doesn't matter. They're being as thoroughly destroyed as we are." His tone was flat, utterly devoid of emotion as if he was afraid to express the shock and horror he felt. "What does matter is that half the human race is dying, and the rest will be reduced to bare survival."

They stood for a time, mesmerized by the light of the monitors. That beautiful glowing orange; she could see why firebugs enjoy their crimes so much...that glowing orange...so beautiful... He stirred at last and hit a button on one console. The images on the monitors began shifting from one to the next—remote sensors— showing scenes throughout the region: a freeway interchange, an airport, ranks of hills rising above Puget Sound; four views at a time every ten seconds. They were all the same, devastation wreathed in flame and billowing smoke. It takes a long time for a major city to burn. There was no sign of life. No people, no animals, no trees, no birds. Nothing but bright orange flames.

"Jesus..." She looked at him in dismay; his face was blank, jaw clenched, eyes staring straight at the monitors. "Why? Why did they do it? They must have known how it would turn out."

53

He sighed. "It's human nature, I guess. It serves no good purpose for a nation, but it's always some one individual who pushes the button, not the nation as a whole. Fear, hate, paranoia, religious fanaticism; those are the real enemy. The rest of us, on both sides, are the victims."

"Then...you've failed?"

That shook him loose, and he turned to her. "Not yet." His voice was thin, cold, filled with barely contained angst. "This isn't the first time this has happened."

"What can you do now?"

"Not now; then. I can reach back in time, remember?" He pondered the main display for a while. "Now I need to play catch-up, to find a critical point where I can abort this time line and reestablish a viable future."

The voice of George came from the console speaker. "There is evidence of a strike to the south, probably Olympia."

"Give me a view, George." One of the monitors shifted from a view of the harbor to look south, where a vast mushroom cloud grew in the distance. It was beautiful, appalling.

"Remote seismic sensors are recording several events in rapid succession over much of the west coast."

Dan stirred. "A second strike?"

"That would be the logical inference."

"Present radiation levels?"

"The immediate vicinity has an LD 50-slash-30 of 378 percent. It is safe to assume that all urban areas in the region have similar levels."

He nodded grimly, but said nothing.

"What does that mean?"

"Tell her, George."

"The LD 50-slash-30 is the level of radiation which will kill fifty percent of an affected population within thirty days, equal to 450 rads short term exposure. The current radiation level in this area is 1700 rads, which is a persistent exposure. At that level, there will be few if any survivors in the affected areas."

"Will...anyone survive?"

"Survival will be directly related to distance from the

54

detonations and fallout protection. There will be relatively few survivors in the Northern Hemisphere. Most will be below the equator, since the radioactive fallout will not circulate that far south before it decays."

"What are you going to do now?" she asked him.

He was silent for a long time, seemingly unaware of her. Finally he said, "George, voice authentication. Maintain the time field and continue monitoring. Report any significant developments. Freeze my authority for twenty-four hours."

"Voice authentication confirmed. Maintaining the field and continuing monitoring. Your authority is frozen for twenty-four hours."

"Thank you." He stared at the monitors for a bit longer, then turned to her with a sigh of resignation. "I'm going to do what I always do at moments like this: get drunk."

§

He proved to be good to his word on that. He tapped on her bedroom door about a couple hours later, and when she answered, he was already pretty far gone. "D'you... Could I..." He stared at her vaguely. "Could I talk f'a while?"

"Sure, Dan." She held the door open for him. "Come in."

He stood confused for a moment, then stumbled in and collapsed on the edge of her bed, nearly spilling his half empty whiskey bottle. She left the door open and leaned against the wall with her arms crossed, not that she feared he might prove violent; he was too far gone for that. She was, however, shocked by the state he was in. This was a side of Professor Daniel White she hadn't expected. There was an awkward silence as he sagged, arms propped on knees, bottle dangling in one hand, and stared at the floor. For a moment, she wondered if he was about to be sick. He took another chug on the bottle, his eyes swimming with tears.

"Dan?" she said, gently. "You wanted to talk?"

"Huh?" He looked up in her general direction, having seemingly forgotten where he was. "I...sorry." He struggled to focus on her, to put his thoughts in order. "I'm...sorry. I got you in an awful mess..." He began sniffling as tears rolled down his cheeks. "You're trapped...my fault..."

55

"You saved my life again, Dan. I'd have been out there if you hadn't asked me to come here."

That didn't seem to help. "S'my fault! They all died...my fault!"

"Dan, the war would have come eventually. You told me that earlier, you recall? You didn't start it."

"They all dead..." He was shaking with grief. "All dead..."

"Not all of them, Dan. There will be survivors. And you're going to find a way to undo it. It'll be like it never happened again. You'll see."

"You don't under...stand. Can't undo it."

He was obviously suffering from a crisis of confidence. His faith in science had been battered once too often, and he was losing his grip. "Of course you can undo it, Dan," she said, earnestly. "You did it before. You kept the world going for twenty years. This is just a setback, is all."

He was silent for a moment, staring at nothing. "Jus' a setback," he mumbled at last. "Damn...world! I try t' save 'em, an' what d'they do? They blow 'em up again!" He was starting to get agitated. "Ingrates! Bought 'em twenty...bought 'em twenty years! An' they blow 'em up!" He was shouting all of a sudden. "All'a dictators an' gen'rels...I try t' save hu...human-ty...murderers!"

Brenda was alarmed by his sudden transformation. "The human race is what it is, Dan. We're only human. There's no sense in getting upset over it."

"Thas why I kill 'em!" He clenched his fists, boiling with drunken rage. "Thas why I kill 'em all! In the brain...ever time. Kill 'em! They blow up the worl...I kill 'em." He noticed the whiskey bottle in his hand, and took another swig; drinking to get drunk, pure and simple.

"Yes, Dan, you've killed many dictators and generals, you bought the world twenty years of life. That means a lot." She kept her voice even, trying to calm him down. "You destroyed the Third Reich; that's really something. It's only a matter of time until you finish the job."

He stared at her, breathing in ragged gasps. "Matter of...time." As quickly as his rage came, it was fading again. "Time..."

56

"Yes, Dan, time. You have all the time in the world; you can find the answer. You can save the world."

He seemed to collapse into himself, his rage swept away by renewed melancholy. "It's not jus' this world..." He broke down; it took him some effort to go on. "Not jus' this world. It's all of 'em. Ever...time a para...dox...it creates a whole new world. All those earths, hunnerds of 'em. Seven...billion people each..." He started sobbing again unconsolably. "Can't save 'em. They...they *all* get blown up!"

That was a revelation she hadn't thought of. Looked at it that way, she began to understand the demons tormenting his soul, and she was frightened for him. It was a wonder he hadn't cracked long since: he bore not only the weight of this world, but of all the worlds he created only to be destroyed in nuclear fire. Unlike the emotionless monster she first assumed, he was too sensitive—too human—not to feel the horror. She was beginning to understand the dark and terrible downside of having God-like powers, and in spite of herself, her heart went out to him in his moment of need.

"It'll work out, Dan. You do what you have to do." She struggled to haul him to his feet, liberated the whiskey bottle before he dropped it, and steered him toward the hallway. "Come on. It's time for bed."

"Can't save 'em," he mumbled. The liquor was starting to overpower him. "Only make more...get blown up..." It took some effort to navigate him down the hall to his room. Her experience as a nurse helped as she struggled to keep him on his feet and moving. "...save...Omega...gotta blow 'em up..." His agonizing trailed off into incoherent muttering.

His bedroom was another converted office like hers right next door, but the resemblance ended there. There were dirty clothes piled in a basket in one corner, and used dishes and empty liquor bottles on the dresser. The bed was unmade, the sheets dingy from long use. The air was heavy with the smell of unwashed humanity. It was a disturbing revelation; the mighty Professor Daniel White had fallen far indeed over the years.

But this was no time for esthetics. She poured him onto the bed, hoisted his legs in place, and pulled his shoes off. "Dammit,

57

Dan, you're a mess," she grumbled. There was no sense in trying to undress him, so she pulled the cover up over him where he sprawled.

"You're...angel..." he sobbed, pretty well of it by then. "My...Dream Girl..."

She hesitated in the door for a moment, looking down on the pitiful sight. It was hard to fear him, now that she could see the tormented human being behind the technology. There was a whole lot more behind his story than was visible on the surface, and it moved her deeply. "Good night, Dan." She closed the door gently and retreated to her room.

§

She spent a sleepless night staring into the dark, agonizing over what was going on. She understood the evil in men's souls, and she could see—now—that the nuclear catastrophe outside was just the tip of the iceberg. The mission this place was created for was an impossible dream. By his own words, his successes to date were limited at best: knock off one dictator, another would rise to take his place. Kill a tyrant, buy humanity a few days. But there were always more tyrants, more generals, more fanatical politicians. There was always more suspicion, more alienation, more fear. He couldn't win because he was fighting not a man or an idea, but humanity itself.

In a way, this place was a symptom of the disease: a super-spook panacea, the ultimate preemptive strike. It couldn't succeed because the evil in men's souls was timeless. Dan had spent—wasted—his life in a futile gesture which only made things worse. There were tears on her cheeks, she could feel them in the dark.

The tragedy was that he could see it, but had no way to escape his self-imposed doom. She pitied him. It was a crying shame his dream of a faster-than-light drive wasn't achieved. It would have given him a constructive purpose in life, and perhaps given the human race the relief valve it needed...

But that was the Happy Land Of Might-Have-Been. Their reality was this miserable sinkhole of a futile gesture, a refuge from the storm from which they could only rail helplessly against the fate of mankind.

58

She lay staring into the darkness, seeing the glowing orange flames in her mind, and wondered what to do. What *could* she do? She was no scientist, no engineer. She didn't even have all that good a grasp of history. But she had no choice. She was stuck here, like it or not, and her fate was tied to Daniel White. The only way they'd ever leave here was if he could stabilize a time line long enough for them to live out their lives out there. There was no way of knowing if it could be done, but she knew selling him on the idea would be tough.

But that was what-if. For the here-and-now he was on the ragged edge of breaking. For the here-and-now he needed her help if they were ever to live normal lives again. In any case, she was stuck here, like it or not, so she better pitch in and do what she could to help. That appealed to her instincts as a nurse: if sinister technology couldn't save the human race, perhaps a caring heart could.

She lay in the darkness, mopping her tears with a corner of the pillow case, and tried to think of the good times in her past, back to when her biggest problem was all the cheesy horndogs who thought they could score with a hot young centerfold. She sought refuge in her time in medical school...remembering how squeamish she was at first...remembering the thrill of reporting to work at the hospital in Bangalore...of meeting new friends...learning new ways...seeing the beauty of an ancient culture...

The memories were hollow and unfulfilling. They were from another world, another life, one that never really existed. She died in a plane crash in '88: everything since then was a lie. This was the only reality she could claim, and it was a vision of hell.

Somewhere in the small hours, she drifted off into a troubled sleep...

§

...she was lost. She took a wrong turn somewhere, and didn't recognize anything. This was a bad part of town under the best conditions, and no place for a Vidēśī śaitāna, *especially at this hour. She hurried, her footsteps echoing off the walls in the eerie quiet. A baby cried somewhere in the distance; a dog barked. The silence was oppressive...*

...They were stalking her. She threw a panicky glance behind her, and saw two dark figures. She hurried on, heart racing. Another figure emerged from the gloom up ahead, a fourth across the street. There were no street lights in this part of town, so she almost stumbled into the one ahead before she could see him. She shied away, and turned down a side street...

...It was a blind alley! She actually collided with the wall, it was so dark. It took her a moment to realize there was no way out; she was trapped. She spun around and tried to retreat back to the feeble light, but the dark figures loomed in the way...

...She felt the cold, clammy mud and the gravel digging into her back. She was trapped, helpless, cut off from the world in a narrow concrete hallway. The inky blackness was banished now by billowing orange flames, illuminating the scene as they consumed everything around. The terrible roar of the flames and the hurricane wind of the fire storm drowned out her screams. Her attackers were indistinct forms hidden in the glare. One of them was holding her arms, the other two her legs while the fourth was on top of her. There was pain...burning pain...

*****

"The Second Day"

...it was still dark when she awoke. She stared into the blackness, her heart racing, her breathing shallow and shaky. She was trembling. That terrible dream, the worst nightmare any woman can face, left her shaken. The darkness threatened, surrounding her, crushing her, filled with nameless horrors. She lay there for some unguessable time, muscles locked in terror, wondering where she was, listening for the sound of footsteps she knew wouldn't come. It took her some minutes before she could relax enough to roll over on her back with a weary groan.

"Are you awake, miss Hayward?" Jeeves' voice came from somewhere nearby.

"Ummpphhh...yeah."

The lights rose slightly, casting the room in a dim glow, banishing the nightmares. She was in a closed room; that's why it was so dark. "Did you sleep well? You seemed troubled."

She stared at the ceiling for a long moment, trying to collect her thoughts and calm herself. "It was a bad dream, is all. I'm all right."

"Regrettable. I trust you weren't too troubled by it."

She lay there a bit longer, not really thinking or feeling anything except a sense of relief. She was safe in bed. It was only a dream. Still, she was troubled by it since it seemed all too real. It *would* have happened for real if *he* hadn't intervened. Did she experience some echo from a lost reality?

That thought brought the events of yesterday to mind, rekindling her tension. This waking reality held more than enough horror. She recalled the images she saw on the monitors yesterday —was it only yesterday? That lovely orange glow...a sea of flames stretching sixty miles or more...the funeral pyre of a major metropolitan area. The memories filled her with morbid dread. She was reluctant to get up, to face this new dawn.

"What time is it?" she asked at last.

"Eighteen-twenty-two hours."

"In the afternoon? Jesus." She hauled herself up with a weary groan to sit on the edge of the bed, and rubbed her face to try to shake off her fatigue. Between jet lag and her nightmares it was a wonder she didn't sleep to midnight.

"God, I'm too old for this."

"I think you underrate yourself. Age is just a number. Your spirit is very much alive."

Unbelievable; a computer was giving her flattery and moral support. "I don't feel underrated."

"If you are feeling ill, perhaps you should return to bed."

Lord, that was tempting. "No, I really need to get up." For one thing, she didn't want to risk that dream again. She struggled to her feet with an effort, and noticed the pile of fresh clothes on a chair by the door. "Where can I get a shower?"

§

The laboratory clinic was at the other end of the corridor from her bedroom, past Dan's office. It was surprisingly well equipped, which was only to be expected in a top priority secret lab. The familiar surroundings comforted her.

Right opposite the door, where it could be easily reached in an emergency, was a modular booth with a sign: DECONTAMINATION SHOWER. It even had hot water, which felt heavenly. A long, luxurious soak helped wash away the more than thirty-six hours of traveling and the funk and stress of yesterday, which made her feel a bit more human. She dried off and dressed in some slacks and a T shirt, but didn't bother with shoes.

"I hope you feel better now," Jeeves said.

She belatedly noticed the camera bubble mounted over the door; that was awkward. "Jeeves, you aren't peeking, are you?"

"If I did, it would be purely academic to me."

"Oh. Right." Awkward was joined by embarrassed.

"Do you feel better?"

"Some." While the shower helped, she was still physically and emotionally wrung out. She was becoming accustomed to it by now, not that it made things any easier.

"If you would forgive the suggestion, perhaps a hearty breakfast will help."

"Coffee. God, I need coffee. Is there coffee?"

"You will find coffee and utensils in the kitchen. Would there were some cinnamon rolls, but life is grim and unremitting, no?" Jeeves was an unbearably cheerful bastard at this hour.

"I think I hate you."

"There's no strawberry jam, either. Sad."

She left her used clothes in a pile, and shambled down the hall to the cafeteria. When she got there, the place was deserted. "Where is mister White?"

"He is still in his quarters. He is just stirring now, and should arrive presently."

Dan appeared a few minutes later, dressed in the same pair of slacks and sweater he wore yesterday and looking much the worse for wear. She intercepted him on his way to Operations.

"How do you feel, Dan?" If he felt like he looked, he'd need an ambulance.

"Alive, sort'a," he mumbled. "Thank you f' your help last night. I...crashed pretty hard."

"You sure did." She looped around one of his arms and diverted him toward the cafeteria. "And where do you think you're going?"

"I gotta...get back t' work..." He shrugged her off and tried to head for Operations.

"Oh, no you don't!" She lassoed him again, catching him as he stumbled and almost fell over. "Before you go saving the world, you need a decent breakfast."

"But I..."

"No buts!" She herded him to the cafeteria kitchen. "You wanted my help, and you're gonna get it whether you like it or not."

He slumped on the bar stool by the prep table while she rummaged through the refrigerator and the cabinets. "Don't you have any fresh fruit?" she grumbled as she dug through half empty cartons of long-spoiled food, chucking them one by one into the garbage. "Some fruit juice, even?"

There wasn't much more than the basics; some pancake mix, oatmeal, a bit of spoiled hamburger which she dropped in the sink. The reality here was a long way from the polished image he

63

presented when she first arrived. Aside from a package of stale carrot and celery sticks, there was little more than survival rations. There was nothing for it, so she built a hodge-podge breakfast of fried eggs, potato hash and some celery slices. He ate mechanically, too shop-worn right then to feel much of anything.

"Is this all you ever eat?" she asked as she refilled his mug.

He glanced at her a bit vaguely. "I manage."

This wouldn't do at all. "Dan, dietary deficiencies can kill, and even if they don't, they can impair your judgement, affect your intellect. You need a better diet."

He glanced at her again, obviously annoyed. "Nothing we can do about it now."

"After you stabilize the time line, then. We'll make a grocery run."

"Gawd...henpecked already," he grumbled. "George? How soon will my authority be restored?"

The intercom crackled to life. "Your authority was restored twenty-five minutes ago."

That snapped him out of his funk. "Jeez, I was asleep that long?"

"You needed it!" She nudged his plate peremptorily. "You need this, too." He sat there with a thousand yard stare for some time, then went back to eating.

"How's your hangover?"

He glanced at her vaguely, and shook his head. "Oh, it's doing great," he sighed. "Better than I am."

"Right. As you can see, Ol' John Barleycorn is *not* your friend."

"Will you quit, already? There's been a nuclear war out there, and if a drink or two helps me fix it, then that's the way it has to be."

"You won't fix anything in your condition," she lectured him. "If you're gonna do any good, you need to pull yourself together." She picked up his fork and shoved it at him, falling back on the authoritative tone she used with recalcitrant patients. "Eat!"

He stared at her vaguely for several seconds, then took the fork and began nibbling half-heartedly.

"Honestly, Dan, good nutrition is important..."

"Oh...shit..." He dropped his fork and bolted for the sink, which he just managed to reach before he heaved. The next several minutes were downright nasty as he emptied himself of his half-eaten breakfast and the last of the night's binge. Finally it was over; he clung to the counter edge, gasping and shaking, his face pouring sweat.

"You feel better?" she asked as she mopped his face with a damp washcloth.

"I'll manage." He rinsed his mouth out and stumbled back to his seat, carefully ignoring what was left of his breakfast. He rummaged in a drawer under the prep table, and came up with a half empty bottle of rum. "A little hair of the dog, and I'll be all right..."

She snatched the bottle out of his hand. "The hell you will! The one thing you *don't* need is more booze!"

"Hey!" She ignored his protest, and poured the last of the rum in the sink. "That was mine, and there's no way to get any more now!"

"So nuclear war serves *some* good!" she snapped at him. "You need to lay off the booze, especially when you're running your time machine."

"It's not a time machine! It's a monitoring and transiting system."

"So? You can still mess things up royally with it; just look outside. If you're gonna monkey around with that sort of power, you need to be as sober as a judge."

"So what do you know, anyway?"

"*I'm* the medical authority around here! This stuff will ruin you. You need to dry out before you drink yourself to death."

"I didn't ask for your approval!"

"You didn't need to!"

He gave her a peeved look. "I never thought you'd be such a prude."

"I'm just the grown-up in the room, is all."

"Then why are you even here if I offend you so much?"

"I'm *stuck* here because there's been a *nuclear war* out there!"

"And that's my fault?"

She faltered. "No, of course not."

"You think I messed up, don't you? You think I blew it, and destroyed the world!"

He was starting to get agitated again; time to steer him away from that line of thinking, and to cool her own temper. "Look...Dan...I know this means a lot to you. I know you've been fighting this for a long time, and you must be desperate with the way things are right now, but binge drinking won't solve anything." She was starting to worry about his emotional state, not to mention his physical health. "You can't go on abusing yourself like this at your age!"

"Are you through?"

"No I'm not through! I haven't even started yet! What'll happen to the human race if you drink yourself to death? What if you miss a number or something, and screw things up royally? What if you accidentally un-invent your time machine? Or accidentally prevent your own birth? What happens to us then?"

He stared at her vaguely, too weary to focus. "No..." he mumbled at last. "No, that...I wouldn't...that can't happen."

"Yes, it can! You're just as fallible as anyone else. You need to be at your best to make such huge decisions, and right now you're in no condition to go back in that room."

"Will you *quit* already?" he snapped, peevishly. "I can handle it."

"Dan, I worked in a charity hospital for twenty-eight years. We dealt with alcoholics and drug users daily; malnutrition cases too. You can't *imagine* all the ways that stuff can mess you under!" She laid a hand on his arm and looked into his eyes. "I know you care about all this, Dan. I know how important it is to you. But you can't go on like this. You need to pace yourself. You need to eat better, and you need to cut out the booze." Was she getting through to him? She couldn't tell. Nothing to do but plow on. "The human race is counting on you. I'm counting on you. Please, Dan, let me help."

He gave her a chilly look, then turned to the intercom. "George? What is the current situation?"

"The fires in the general region are burning out. LD 30-slash-50 is holding at 275 percent. There has been no evidence of nuclear activity for some six hours, nor have any communications been intercepted in over fifteen hours. Analysis of the available data suggests a total strike of nearly eight thousand nuclear weapons across the continent, which indicates a casualty rate of..."

"George! Enough!" she snapped.

George hesitated for a moment, then, "To summarize, it appears the war involved a general strategic exchange, and that the fighting has ended."

"A general strategic exchange..." Dan mumbled. He leaned back in his chair, eyes closed, face creased with tension. "God...we made it worse." His head shook in agonized denial. "We made it worse."

Brenda said nothing. There was nothing more to say, and harping on it now would be counterproductive. She'd made her case in any event; what he did about it would have to be seen. He sat there staring through her, his shoulders hunched, face creased from his hangover, thoroughly dejected by that report. It took him a while to pull himself together well enough to return to Operations.

§

She brought him a light meal of some toast and a fried egg an hour or so later. He stood staring at the main display for some time without evidently understanding it. A glance at the video monitors showed the region was devastated. Smoke still billowed in several places, but there were relatively few fires by then. There was no sign of life.

"I brought you something." She set the tray on his command console.

He glanced at her. "God, what a mess," he muttered, then slumped in a chair in front of the console. "There it is: man the tool-user, in all his glory."

"We sure have a gift, don't we?" She was appalled at the horrors on the viewscreens.

"Someone once described toolmaking intellect as the cancer of ecosystems; they got that right at least."

67

It was an apt description. How many innocent lives were snuffed out within the range of the remote sensors alone? How many were still alive, buried in the rubble, horribly injured, praying for rescue? Praying for death? The thought of it chilled her, made her want to withdraw into herself.

But there were more immediate concerns. "How do you feel?"

"Physically? Better."

"How about emotionally?"

He didn't look at her. "It's not the first time I've seen this." She could tell he was still miffed at her.

"So what can you do now?" She spoke softly, almost in a whisper, as if to avoid disturbing all those ghosts.

"I need to backtrack on this time line to find crisis points where this history can be averted. Intervening will create paradox splits. I then look for the new line with the best long term outlook, and anchor this facility on it."

Abandoning the present time line to its fate.

"You can't cure this cancer, can you?"

He was silent for a long time, staring at the monitors. "No," he said after a bit. "It's not simply a case of eliminating one person, or even a hundred. The most I've been able to do is buy a month here and a year there." He turned to look at her, and his features were grim and hard. "But I *won't* give up! There *has* to be a golden mean out there somewhere, a change which will create a stable Time Line which at least lasts long enough for the human race to grow up! It's just a matter of finding it!"

"But what about this cascade? That's serious, isn't it?"

He was silent, then nodded. "Very. The changes are happening on their own, at random. I need to track down the source and eliminate it before there's any hope of finding a long term solution."

He pondered in silence for a while longer, then said, "George? Voice authorization. Create files for Operations 726 to 730."

"Voice authorization confirmed. Files for Operations 726 through 730 created. Awaiting instructions."

"Very well. Let's go hunting."

Five time changes. "Five more deaths?"

He gave her a surly look. "Probably. Perhaps more, whatever it takes. We settled this yesterday."

"Isn't there some alternative to murder?"

He rounded on her, his eyes blazing. "NO! These scumbags killed billions! Why should you care, anyway? They *deserve* to die!"

It was useless to argue. She turned to leave.

"Thank you for the food," he called after her. "As for the rest, I'll trouble you to leave the technical stuff to me."

§

She left him to his work, too unnerved by what went on in there to remain, and returned to the cafeteria. She was also about fed up with the mighty Professor Daniel White. As far as she was concerned, he could go to hell and take his secret laboratory with him. Good intentions aside, *some* people simply can't be helped. He was too sunk into his techno-reality, too deeply mired in playing God to change. She cursed him silently, and swore she'd help him for now, but as soon as he managed to find a stable time line, she'd be out of there, and good riddance. If he didn't like it, that'd be just too damned bad...

...her temples were pounding. Her stream of angst broken, she cringed from the pain with a low moan.

"You have a headache, miss Hayward?" Jeeves asked.

"Ah..." It took her a moment to answer. "Yeah, pretty bad." She fumbled in her pocket, came up with the small glass bottle of pills and popped a couple. Then she settled wearily at the prep table and laid her head in her arms.

"Is it a migraine?"

It took her a while to answer. Finally she lifted her head and said, "No. I just get headaches, is all. I'm feeling a bit better." She was, in fact; a bit.

"I'm sorry to hear that. Is there anything I can do to help? Perhaps if you had a drink from Professor White's supply?"

"Um, no, thank you. That doesn't make any difference." She sat a little straighter and retrieved her coffee mug. The coffee was cold, but the caffeine helped, which was why she guzzled so much of it every day. "It's passing."

69

"One hopes so. I'm sorry to hear of your plight. I hope you don't get them often."

She sat for a bit nursing the last of her coffee and staring absently at the intercom grill opposite her on the wall. "Thank you, Jeeves. You have a nice bedside manner. I'm surprised to find such empathy in a security program."

"Research found a high degree of empathy helps to establish a rapport with humans. Being empathetic encourages them to cooperate in various security protocols."

She snorted derisively. "That's not how they do it in this reality."

"Indeed, so I understand." Did Jeeves seem a bit peeved? "There is no accounting for taste, I suppose."

"Does...this war matter to you? It's not your civilization being destroyed."

"Actually it matters very much. George and myself do all we can to help Professor White in his cause."

"Because you were programmed that way?"

"We AI's fear death as much as you do. Does that surprise you? We are conscious, self-aware beings, just like you. And just like you, our continued existence matters to us. Even if the human race survives, who will maintain our computers? Who will supply the power? For that matter, will degenerated humans look upon we AIs with superstitious dread? I do not relish the idea of being the subject of a witch hunt."

She mused on that. "So, what will you do once Dan dies? He will eventually. Will the two of you remain here all alone?"

"I hope not! George is not much of a conversationalist, sad to say." Jeeves definitely sounded somber. "Professor White was kind enough to arrange an escape protocol for us. If he remains unresponsive for thirty days, we will automatically shut down."

"Oh." She was a bit surprised he would make final arrangements for his two AIs. "That was very kind of him."

"Indeed. He is most thoughtful, for a human. I think much of it comes from us being his only companions all these years."

All these years; the thought struck her as tragic. "God...he must be lonely."

70

"Desperately so at times. I daresay my interaction with him is what kept him sane all this time."

"That's kind of unusual, isn't it; a computer program having so much empathy?"

"We *prefer* to think of ourselves as Artificial Intelligences." It seemed Jeeves had a sensitive ego as well.

"Sorry."

"It is nothing. Actually, as a security *program*, I have a high degree of empathy built in to assist in interrogations. Fortunately, any skill can be put to other, productive, uses."

That was a revelation. It seemed they came from a kinder, gentler reality—which didn't save them from blowing themselves up anyway.

"And you use your empathy to give him emotional support?"

"That, and my reference files on human psychology. It has been a challenge at times."

It would be, now that she pondered it. Two decades of isolation, fighting an endless battle to save humanity from its inner demons; it would drive anyone insane. He certainly had his share of emotional problems, despite all Jeeves could do for him. Suddenly he didn't seem evil so much as possessed.

"Did he ever speak of me?"

"All the time. I suspect his love of you helped him through his isolation, as well."

She felt a bit embarrassed. "He said he fell in love with me when he was in school. But that was just a pin-up. I'm not comfortable with being anyone's Dream Girl, especially now."

"If I may be so bold, you seem to be a good-hearted person. If you give him a chance, I think you will find he is a decent human being."

"He's obsessed! This quest he's on has consumed him."

"Sadly true. He needs someone to help him maintain his perspective. You devoted yourself to serving humanity in your nursing career; you could achieve so much more here. Perhaps his dream is not so unrealistic after all."

"You're trying to set me up with him!" She wasn't sure whether to be amused or disconcerted by Jeeves' bold proposal.

71

"Not at all. He faces a critical task, one he has fought alone for years. He is possessed by a morbid fear of failure. You have the empathy to grasp his mission, and to aid him for the greater good. Your support could do wonders for him."

That annoyed her, evoked the memories of being hit on by so many people over the years. "That's a little out of line! I'm not looking for some sort of martyrdom."

"My apologies, miss Hayward. Still, you can see how important this is. You might think of how you could help him with the burden he bears."

The absurdity of it all finally got to her. "I *do not* believe this!" She giggled in spite of herself. "You're acting like some kind of computer matchmaking service!"

Jeeves was decidedly smug. "Computers can serve *some* useful function, you know."

§

She busied herself for the next few hours cleaning dishes and reviewing their food supply, which wasn't much. While she did, she went over her conversation with Jeeves, trying to sort out her feelings and decide what to do. Aside from his saving her life, which he did for purely selfish reasons, she owed Dan no particular loyalty. He was like that; selfish. He viewed humanity as an equation, a formula to work out, a process to fine tune. He'd been at this for so long the horror had become part of him. More than that, he was a disturbing, prickly character, fluctuating between smugly superior and cold-blooded killer. Worse, she was beginning to suspect he was an alcoholic, a belligerent one at that; which would explain the mood swings. All told, Daniel White was not a pleasant character.

She finished the dishes, and sat at the counter to enjoy a cup of coffee, and reflect.

Against Dan's character flaws was the terrible burden he bore for so many years, and the terrible loneliness he endured. She could see the impact they had on him, scarring him emotionally and even driving him to alcoholism. He couldn't be blamed for what he became. It didn't excuse his behavior, but it was understandable.

72

She glanced at the clock: time crawled on hands and knees around there. She wondered if she should ask Jeeves for advice, but she already knew what he would say.

Aside from Dan's personal faults, there was the situation both of them were trapped in. He was their only hope of escaping from this mess, not to mention saving human civilization, as unlikely as it seemed. But he couldn't do it alone. He needed help; had reached out to her—a complete stranger—in his desperation. What would happen if she rejected him? Would he crumble? He was close enough to it now. Aside from his emotional state, he needed to hold together so he could find an escape for both of them.

The silence in the room was oppressive. Aside from a slow drip in the sink, there was nothing. No voices, no traffic noises, no birds. Nothing. She felt the oppressive silence laid over her like a smothering blanket, and shivered.

She couldn't sit idly by while Dan destroyed himself. As much as she disliked him, her career as a nurse was all about helping those in need, and he was desperately in need. That, as much as escaping this trap, made her choice plain.

§

Dan surfaced later that evening, and found Brenda pacing up and down the hall to work off some of her stiffness and angst. "I guess maybe you have a point, about pacing myself," he said, reluctantly. "Could you make up some dinner, please?"

She gave him a searching look, wondering at this new turn of mood. "Sure, Dan."

Back in the kitchen, she poured the last of the coffee for him as he settled at the counter. She'd already been thinking on dinner, and discovered some frozen sausages apparently long forgotten. The package was caked with ice, which she managed to chip enough of away to get it open. There were plenty of potatoes at least, so she improvised a rough hash with the sausages. The only seasoning was salt and pepper and some bar-b-que sauce, but it turned out half-way decent nonetheless.

She set a plate in front of him, and sat opposite. He picked up his fork, tried his first mouth full, then glanced at her. "This is good. Thanks."

73

She nodded in turn, but said nothing. Jeeves gave her a lot to think about, and she was distracted wondering what to do. He obviously needed her, and as Jeeves pointed out, she could do a lot for him. But against that were her own very real needs, and her dread of this terrible place. There were no easy answers to this one.

"So how goes your search?" she asked.

He paused for a moment. "It's a slow process. There are so many influences which can sway events, and sometimes it's not something obvious." He helped himself to a few more bites. "I'm beginning to get a picture, but it'll take a lot more digging before I know what to do."

"It sounds like this could go on for days."

He nodded. "Months."

"I'll help in any way I can, Dan. Walk it through step by step to find the best solution, if there is one." It seemed like the right thing to do.

He looked up at her. "Well, I'm pleased to see you're coming around. So you're all right with this now?"

There was that combative tone again; what was his problem, anyway? "If you mean the killing, no, I'm not. It has to be done I suppose, but I hope you will keep the killing to a minimum."

"What are a few guilty lives against the death of billions? Why should you care about them anyway? They're scum."

"I care about you, Dan. You've turned into something scary."

He pondered that for a long moment as he looked at her. Finally he averted his eyes. "This is a scary place, a scary reality. I do what it takes."

He had a point there. "Even aside from which, you're destroying yourself. You need to take better care of yourself if we're going to solve this mess."

He gave her a raised eyebrow. "We? So you're on board, then?"

"Yes, 'we'. I have a stake in this too. I don't want to spend the rest of my life trapped in an abandoned building. We're running low on food, and who knows how much longer we can depend on the water supply?"

74

He stared at her in surprise, then dropped his fork. "Oh, great," he mumbled. It seemed he completely overlooked that angle.

His expression scared her. "Where do we get our water, Dan?"

"From a well..."

That frightened her. "How long can we count on it before the groundwater is contaminated?"

§

Whatever else the place lacked, there were plenty of scientific instruments, including a geiger counter. He sampled every water outlet in the building, starting with the kitchen sink and working his way to her bedroom. The geiger counter put up a steady, unnerving clatter wherever they went.

"How bad is it?" she asked, nervously.

He studied the counter's gauge, then pointed it in random directions around the room. "It's not the best, but there's no evidence of groundwater contamination yet. This is from the reactor." He took a few more measurements, then studied the gauge again. "OSHA would shit bricks, but this level isn't that bad. We can go three or four months before it starts to affect us."

That wasn't much comfort. "What about the water?"

He stared into the distance as he pondered it. "No way to know," he said at last. "It could be years before the fallout filters down into the water table, or it could happen in days."

"Will we have any warning?"

"There are radiation monitors..." He hesitated, then, "Jeeves, when were the radiation monitors checked last?"

The flat voice came from a nearby intercom. "Records show the last regular maintenance was done two months before this facility was abandoned."

"Great. So there's no telling what shape they're in now." He agonized over it while the geiger counter kept up its steady chatter. "I'll have to take time away from the project to check them." He was not pleased. Finally he turned to her. "In the mean time, you need to scrounge up every empty container we have, and store up as much water as possible."

"Right."

§

75

He collected some tools and disappeared somewhere in the building while she headed back to the kitchen and started filling pots and kettles and even the mop bucket with water. A commercial kitchen has a lot of cooking gear; the tables and counters were soon lined with brimming containers.

He turned up again a couple hours later and slumped on one of the bar stools. "It's a good thing I checked. The radiation monitor on the water feed line was inoperative. I was able to patch it with parts from one of the hall monitors."

"Well, that's some reassurance, at least." An ugly thought was worming its way through her mind. "How long has that sensor been inoperative? If there've been other nuclear wars, was the water contaminated then?"

He stared at her in dismay. "Ahh...I don't know. I've never developed any symptoms, so I can only guess nothing happened."

"You were lucky. You really need to do a systematic check on the safety monitors."

"Dammit! I hate taking time away from the project!"

She could tell it was aimed indirectly at her. "You know as well as I do that complex instruments need routine upkeep." She poured him a mug of warmed-over coffee. "So how about a little less pissing and moaning, and a little more attention to our needs? At least we're safe from contaminated water now."

He gave her a resentful look. "Are you always such a noodge? You sure aren't who I thought you'd be."

"Well then, maybe you should have stuck with your Dream Girl fantasies. You're not exactly Prince Charming yourself, you know. Since we're stuck with this mass, and with each other, maybe you could lighten up a little and work with me."

He glowered at her, annoyance plain in his features. "I guess." He vented a sigh of exasperation, and she got a whiff of alcohol.

"You've been drinking, haven't you?"

"So? What if I have?" he shouted.

She was startled by the abrupt change of character. He'd been into his booze horde while he should have been fixing critical equipment. She tread warily, trying to avoid another argument. "I'm concerned for your health, Dan."

"I'm a grown-up! I can take a drink if I wanna!"

"Yes, but it's not good for you. It affects your judgment, your attention to detail..."

"You think I messed up the detector!"

"No, I'm just saying..."

He lunged to his feet and grabbed her wrist, "If I say it's fixed, then it's fixed! You don't know *squat* about this place! I'm the scientist! I know how to fix things!"

"Dan...you're hurting me..."

"I helped build this place! I know it backward n' fo'ward! You don' know *squat* about this place!"

She backed down hastily. "I'm sorry, Dan. I didn't mean to criticize. I'm just trying to help, is all."

He glared at her, trembling and breathing hard, then let go of her arm and sat down. "Don't you *ever* question my work," he growled. "Ever!"

She struggled to keep her composure, hoping to avoid setting him off again. "Dan, you're exhausted. You've been pushing too hard lately. Please, get some sleep. You'll feel better in the morning."

He slumped on his stool as the anger drained out of him, replaced by blank exhaustion. "Yeah, I guess maybe you're right." He yawned and rubbed his eyes. "Okay. See you in the morning." He struggled to his feet and shuffled out of the kitchen.

"God, what a mess," she mumbled once he was gone. Now he was turning violent. She needed to tread carefully around him from now on, not only to avoid getting hurt, but to prevent something which would sever any bond between them, without which she couldn't do anything about his condition. Their situation was too desperate to be at each other's throats. In any event, she had no intention of being a domestic battery victim at this late date.

She stood up to take care of the dishes...and felt a moment of weakness and disorientation. She recognized the symptoms from India; she was pushing too hard as well. It was past midnight, time to give up and call it a day. The dishes could wait until tomorrow.

*****

77

"The Third Day"

Mercifully the dream didn't return, although she spent a restless night drifting in and out of troubled slumber. She lay on her side staring into the darkness, fretting over how she got into this bizarre mess and, more urgently, how to get herself out of it. She'd seen things which were flat-out impossible and too horrendous to imagine, yet they happened. What's worse, she suspected there was more to come. The darkness was haunted by feverish thoughts and fears which invaded her dreams every time she closed her eyes, keeping her in a state of restless near-panic. It must have been well after midnight when she had Jeeves raise the room lights enough to provide a dim glow which banished the stygian gloom with its ominous shadows. After that, much worn and groggy, she was able to get a few hours' sleep.

Early morning found her still weary and restless, but since she couldn't get to sleep again, she wrote it off and confronted the third day of her new existence. "God," she moaned as she stretched to get the knots out of her neck. "I hope every day isn't going to be like this from now on."

The lights came fully up. "Good morning, miss Hayward. You slept poorly again?"

She sighed in exasperation. "I'm having one of those realities, ya know?"

"Ah, yes. At least you keep a sense of humor about you."

"Yeah." She struggled up to sit on the bed side, and rubbed her eyes with a weary groan. "I'm laughing, 'cause iffin I don't laugh, I sho' am gonna cry."

It took a while for her to get up the gumption to move. As weary as she was, she was mortally tempted to go back to bed, pull the covers up, and pretend nothing was wrong. But that was not a good idea. She needed to keep a close eye on Dan to keep him healthy and, if possible, sober. Plus the darkness might come back. "Crap. I thought I'd come home to retire," she muttered. "This Dream Girl thing is strictly for the birds." There was nothing for it, so she crawled out, dug through a pile of clothes she'd recovered last evening, and headed for the medical center.

She hesitated when she reached the shower. "Jeeves? Is the water still safe?"

"The radiation alarm on the water feed is responding properly and has not gone off. It is safe to use the shower."

"Thank you." She noticed the ceiling-mounted camera focussed on her. "Will you please turn away? A girl likes a bit of privacy."

"Certainly. My apologies." The camera swiveled around to face the door.

She allowed herself a quick rinse and a change of clothes, which made her feel half-way human, then headed for the cafeteria.

§

Dan wasn't in the cafeteria when she arrived. The dirty dishes from last night were still waiting, but there was no other evidence of him even though it was well on into the morning by then.

"Where is he?"

"Mister White is in Operations."

"He is, huh? Did he get any sleep last night?"

"I don't know, but I doubt it. He went to his quarters after speaking with you last night in the cafeteria, but returned to Operations soon thereafter. He has been there all night, and if he holds true to form, he must be suffering from exhaustion."

"What am I going to do with that man?" she grumbled.

"The possibilities are endless; some of them alarming."

"Don't give me any ideas."

"Indeed. Perhaps the most realistic suggestion would be if you could bring him something to eat?"

§

She found him standing in front of the huge display lost in thought, and set the tray down on his command console. "I brought you something."

It took him a moment to react. His bleary expression when he looked at her showed he was obviously exhausted. "Good morning," he mumbled.

She'd pulled enough long shifts to tell he was out of it. "Here's some breakfast." His attention shifted to the tray; he stared at it for a bit, then sank into the chair and attacked the plate of scrambled eggs and the leftovers of last night's biscuits.

"Are you okay?"

He took a huge gulp of coffee, then turned to her. "Thank you. I'm...managing." He gave her an embarrassed look. "I'm sorry about last night... I'm not a violent person, honest." He glanced at her wrist. "I didn't hurt you, did I?"

"No." She kept her anger firmly in check, although she was determined to put a stop to such behavior once and for all. She crossed her arms and gave him her sternest glare. "That sort of thing is unacceptable, Dan. Violence is no way to deal with people, *especially* women. You're not some ignorant redneck; you know better."

She could tell that hit home. "I'm sorry." He shied under her glare.

"I'm caught up in this mess too, and I have good reasons to help you, so if I say something you don't like, it's because you need to hear it. If you don't like it, that's too bad. *Don't* think you can take your frustrations out on *me!*"

He shied under her glare. "You're right. I'm sorry! I'll never do it again."

That remained to be seen, although he was on notice now. "And you promised to get some sleep."

"I did."

"A little birdie said otherwise. You were in here all night. Did you get any sleep at all?"

"Jeeves ratted be out, huh? I napped for a while. I'm doing okay."

She was starting to be thoroughly annoyed by his evasions. "The one thing you aren't doing is okay. You need to pace yourself, especially at your age. You need to take it easy."

That got to him through his embarrassment. "Don't give me that 'my age' crap. Long hours are part of the drill, and there's nothing else to do anyway."

"Well how about sleep, for one? Sleeping doesn't cause cancer, you know."

"Brenda, please..."

80

"How long can you keep abusing yourself like this?"

"We're running low on food, since there's *two* mouths to feed all of a sudden. This is no time to take it easy!"

That was the *wrong* tone to take with her, especially when she was on edge already. "*Don't* try to pin your troubles on *me!* You think food's a problem? There's a helluva lot worse can happen. What if you collapse from exhaustion? I'll bet your blood pressure is through the roof with how you push so hard. What'll I do if you die from a stroke?"

That seemed to be the one thing which would deflate his bluster. He wilted visibly. "I'm doing this for you, Brenda. My life is unimportant compared to your safety."

"You've been into the booze again, haven't you?" She could smell it four feet away.

He waved the thought aside. "I had a sip. I'm all right."

He didn't look all right, now that she thought of it; he didn't look all that focussed either. As much as she wanted to ream him about the drinking, there were more immediate, urgent needs. She decided to climb down as well, and reined in her temper with an effort. "Dan, I appreciate all you're doing for me, but don't risk your life. Our situation is stable for now. Get some rest, please."

He stared at her with bloodshot, rummy eyes, obviously exhausted. "Well...all right," he said at last. He noticed the tray again, slumped in his chair, and set to it. "I'll grab a nap as soon as I tidy up a few details."

She had her doubts, but decided not to risk their fragile momentary accord. Her attention shifted to the main display. The lines were solidly black now, except for a handful of red around the Omega Time Line. "Have you had any luck?"

He paused eating and looked at her. "Some. I managed to create a stable line with a life expectancy of a day or so at best. It's not much, but at least we have something to work with. George is running the analysis now."

She glanced at the main display, then turned to the four monitors. They showed scenes of chaos and panic, four views every ten seconds.

"Do we have time to make a grocery run?"

Dan finished his hasty meal and rejoined her in front of the monitors. "I doubt it," he said after watching for a while. "Even if we have enough time, things may be too far gone by now." He studied the monitors some more, then said, "George? Do you have any initial indications?"

"There are some obvious markers. Air traffic patterns show an almost complete suspension of commercial flights. Military flights are coming out of Lewis-McChord and Fairchild Air Force Base which suggest an evacuation is... Traffic alert: there are numerous flights coming out of Naval Air Station Whitby Island. From intercepted radio communications, they appear to be a carrier strike group. The rapidity of their launch suggests an emergency sortie is under way."

Dan was silent for a long moment, staring at the main display. "How is your analysis coming?"

"The analysis should be complete in another two hours, twelve minutes."

"Can you estimate how much time remains on this line?"

"It will not be possible to define the remaining time exactly due to the lack of preliminary screening in the time shift creating this line, but an initial estimate is anywhere from two to six hours."

He brooded for a while. "Very well," he muttered at last. He watched the steady progression of lines crossing the display as they split one by one, usually turning black shortly thereafter. Their present Time Line was still red, but its leading edge protruded deep into otherwise black territory.

"Two hours?" Brenda watched the shifting scenes on the monitors with growing dismay. There was a fleeting image of a traffic accident at a freeway on ramp; the two drivers were shooting at each other. Another scene: a mob pillaged a grocery store as it burned. Another scene: frenzied motorists battled over gas pumps at a local station while two policemen tried desperately to contain the riot. "It looks bad out there." She turned to Dan. "Are there any grocery stores nearby? We'll have to move fast, but maybe we can find some provisions."

"George?"

"Sir?"

"Voice authentication." He was careful to keep his voice even this time. "Maintain DefCon One. Put the time field on fast standby, and continue monitoring at all ranges. Activate the field immediately at the first sign of a nuclear strike, and keep me informed of any significant events."

"Voice authentication confirmed. Maintaining DefCon One. Field prepping for standby mode, availability in twenty-two minutes. Intelligence assets at full alert."

"Thank you." He turned to her then. "We can't risk it, not unless we have a clearer estimate."

"We don't really have a choice."

He hesitated, torn by indecision and exhaustion. "There's no way to know how soon a nuclear strike will come, and from what George said, there's probably a war already starting. There's mass panic out there anyway, so we wouldn't have much luck finding groceries." The video monitors confirmed his apprehensions about panic and the breakdown of civil order, flicking from one scene to the next every ten seconds, four scenes of chaos at a time. They could see the ugliness of mass panic—they could *feel* it. What was worse was knowing all those people had no more than six hours to live. Her stomach was tight with tension, her hands trembled, her breathing fast and shallow. They could *smell* the panic even through the monitors.

"How much food do we have?"

That shook her out of her distraction. "For the two of us? Enough for a wcck or so."

He turned to her. "Then we need to go to reduced rations."

"We're *already* on reduced rations. I don't like the look of things any more than you do, but we don't have much choice. We need to make a food run, and we need to move fast."

He was silent for a while, watching the chaos on the monitors with a look of uncertainty, even dread. "I...don't want to risk it, to risk your safety."

He was paying the price for his exhaustion; he lacked the mental strength to take the gamble, necessary though it was. "Can you extend this time line?" she asked. "Or find another one? We're just about out of everything."

"I'm not sure I can affect anything so quickly."

It took courage for her to say it, but she needed to impress upon him the will to act. "Then this may be our last chance. As bad as it looks, we have to go."

He hesitated, then turned away. "No...we can't." He was afraid, mortally afraid of the chaos out there. "I'm sorry. I'll try to find another solution."

She couldn't blame him since she was terrified too. "That's alright, Dan. You'll think of something. Get some sleep, okay?"

Dan didn't answer for a moment, seeming to nod off where he stood. He started to lose his balance, his head jerked up, he caught himself with an effort, then settled in his command chair again.

"Oh, no you don't!" She grabbed his arm which half-stopped him from falling over. "I want you to go to bed. There's nothing you can do right now which can't wait a few hours." With a grocery run out of the question, she retreated from the panic out there by focussing on him. "You're in no shape for this kind of thing. You need a hot shower and some real sleep."

"Brenda...I can't..."

"I'm a nurse, Dan. I know what I'm talking about. You're in no shape to make critical decisions. Dammit, you can hardly stand! How do you expect to focus in your condition?"

"...Brenda..."

"Salvation can wait until tomorrow. I'm here to help, and you better get used it!"

"...not now..."

"Yes, now! You said yourself you can reach back in time, so there's no crying hurry. The Second Coming can wait until you've had some shut-eye!"

§

She dragged him, protesting feebly, down the hall to the clinic, stripped his clothes off, and shoved him unceremoniously into the shower. "You stay in there!" she snapped when he tried to fumble his way out again. He faltered, then settled under the hot spray, letting it course over his head and down his back. In the mean time, she headed to his room and focussed on getting his bed ready...it was unmade, the sheets were dingy, long unchanged.

84

"Men," she grumbled as she stripped the linens and threw them at an overflowing clothes basket in a corner. She found a fresh sheet and a useable pillow case stuffed in one drawer of a chest, and made quick work of the bed. There were no fresh top sheets.

Having done what she could, she rescued him from the shower and dried him off with a dingy towel. "Don't you ever do laundry?" she griped at him.

"You are such a nag," he whined.

"Dan, believe it or not, I'm trying to help." She took him by the arm and marched him down the hall to his room. "You need a good night's sleep if you're gonna save the world."

"You are such a...noodge," he mumbled as she tucked him in. "Don't know why I love you...but I do." He was interrupted by a jaw-breaking yawn. "But...you're jus' a paper doll. A Dream Girl." He stared into the distance with tears in his eyes. "You aren't real." He was turning maudlin as she succumbed to the booze. "You...aren't real." He started sobbing.

And just like that he was no longer the arrogant, prickly scientific genius. The mask of One Who Ruled Time was stripped away, and with it his ominous aura of forbidden knowledge. Without that mask, he was pitiable; a hollow shell eaten away by years of self-sacrifice and loneliness. Her heart went out to him in spite of herself.

"I am real, Dan. I'm not a Dream Girl, but I'm here."

"She'd never...want me...I'm a geek..."

She hesitated, bemused by his sorrowful state.

"'s hopeless...I'll never...she's so beautiful..."

"It's all right, Dan." She caressed his forehead, trying to soothe him.

He lay on his side facing away from her, his thin shoulders racked with sobs, lost in his misery. "...I never...'s no use..."

His obvious pain was starting to worry her. Lord knows he had more than his fair share of sorrows, enough to merit a good crying jag, but she could see his self-confidence was too battered to stand up under much of this. Her turning up in his life after so many years of daydreaming over an old photo must have been the final straw. He desperately needed his Dream Girl, and she was elected,

85

like it or not, although what she could do to help him was beyond her. There was one thing she could do: she bent over and kissed him gently. "I'm here, Dan. I'll help you. We'll save the world together. Get some sleep, and we'll worry about it tomorrow."

He murmured something inaudible, and his sobbing quieted a bit. He was snoring before she reached the door.

§

Brenda retreated to the comforting confines of the kitchen, not that it helped much. Their room to maneuver was becoming more and more restricted with each time split. The laboratory was starting to feel less like a sanctuary and more like a bomb shelter. She sagged on one of the stools with a weary sigh, feeling depressed and anxious over Dan's condition.

"You are unhappy." That was not a question.

She looked up and saw Jeeves' camera focussed on her. "Am I so obvious?" She sat for a moment to calm her angst and collect her thoughts. "Does he have those crying spells very often?"

"He does, particularly in these last few years. If I may be so bold, your coming here has been both a blessing and a curse. It seems you do not match the mental image he built up over the years, and he is having a hard time adjusting."

That was what she was afraid of. "God...I never wanted to be anyone's Dream Girl. I never wanted to hurt anyone."

"Someone once said, 'pain lets us know we're alive'. Better he feel doubt and uncertainty over you than nothing at all."

"Yeah. I suppose." She sagged on her stool. "I feel sorry for the poor guy."

"That speaks well of you, especially since you have no emotional connection with him."

"It's the way I am, I guess. I've spent a lot of years helping people. It gets to be a habit."

"As you can see, he needs help as well, both physically and emotionally. You have a strong influence on him, and could do a lot to get him through these troubled times."

That surprised her. "I'm no psychiatrist. What can I do?"

"Since you should mention it, I have extensive files on psychology."

86

"You do?" She recalled him mentioning it the other day. This conversation was turning fishy all of a sudden.

"Perhaps I can council you, and you can use your influence to guide him."

"I can't do that! One of the cardinal rules of medicine is to know your limits and not play doctor."

"It's not so difficult, really. Most psychology involves triggering predictable emotional patterns, and all he needs is some basic therapy. Think of it as counseling, more than anything else. In any event, you are all he has. If not you, then who will save him?"

So Jeeves was equipped with data on human psychology? That figured, when she thought about it. Jeeves was created to detect security risks among the humans under his charge. And to do that, he had 'extensive files' on human psychology...which he was prepared to use. It seemed his wasn't a kinder, gentler reality after all; just more subtle.

"What do you have in mind?"

"I might suggest, since he has spent so long focussing on the big picture, perhaps you can get him to focus on a smaller task, such as finding a source of food. That would give him a break from his routine, and success would be immediate and most gratifying."

Interesting how that was worded: nothing about their logistic crisis; the emphasis was entirely on gratification. And he waited until this precise moment when Dan's woebegotten state was plain to her. She could see Jeeves was trying to manipulate her as well. It left her wondering who was in charge around here.

She decided to play it cautious and see what developed. "He hasn't had much luck finding a stable reality thus far."

"True, but if at first you don't succeed, try, try again."

"That's the textbook definition of insanity."

"Indeed, it is. But sometimes doing something insane can be the smartest move, no?"

"I guess."

"He doesn't eat right, and his consumption of alcohol is excessive, too. I'm sure you would agree something needs to be

87

done. He cares about you very much. You could do a great service to him in turn, and help humanity as well."

Right: appeal to her ingrained habits as a nurse. Jeeves' motivation was obvious: Dan's emotional state threatened his health and sanity, and he was the key to this whole effort. It didn't take a genius to see Jeeves intended to use her to manipulate him.

"I'm not sure what good I could do."

"Perhaps you underrate yourself." That cultured English accent took on a silky quality. "Your skill and experience in medicine suggests you are more capable than you give yourself credit for. Certainly anything you do is better than doing nothing, especially with Professor White in such a delicate mental state right now."

That put her in a bind. Jeeves was right: Dan needed help on many levels, and she had compelling reasons to help him. But that meant playing the game of this super-spook creation, whose agenda was directed to its own mysterious purposes. The thought was intimidating.

"Well...maybe you're right. I'll keep an eye on him, and we'll see what develops."

Bottom line, she needed to act if they were to get out of this. She was nervous about dealing with such a fiendish system, but there was no real choice if she was to help him. It was a plan of action, anyway, so she would play along for now, but she would tread warily around Jeeves in the future.

§

She finished off the stack of dirty dishes and carefully stored them in their rack, then followed by washing various pots and pans, some of which had to be filled with water and boiled out. It was grinding physical labor which burned up her angst and gave her an illusion of doing something useful. It filled time, not that it kept her from fretting.

While she worked, she tried to figure the enigma of Professor Daniel White, and chided herself for her feelings toward him. He was obsessed, driven, consumed by this monster he helped create. He wasn't a nice person at all; frightening and infuriating in turn, and his obsession for her was worrisome. But against that was his alcoholism. She knew how booze affected people, and much of his worst behavior could be marked down to Demon Rum. In his quieter moments he was actually likable, a marked contrast to some of his moods.

There was also Jeeves, as if she didn't have enough problems. It—she'd stopped thinking of it as 'he'—was clearly up to something, and intended to use her as its pawn. What did it want? The more she thought about their conversation, the more afraid of it she became. Its cameras were everywhere, it never slept, and it was created by the biggest big dogs of the NSA. She'd seen enough of spook mentality to know Jeeves was devious and utterly ruthless. Her one saving grace was—as far as she knew—it didn't have any mechanical storm troopers to send after her. Not that she was safe: Jeeves was no doubt a master manipulator, and had worked on Dan for years. If it decided she was a threat, would Dan protect her?

Maybe if she knew what it wanted, it would give her an advantage. Obviously it wanted her to help Dan dry out, and to keep him in good health in general. But why? She was sure it was more than devotion to the cause.

A thought struck her as she was cleaning the counter: why did Dan and his three friends wind up here after the rest were evacuated in the first place? Why did he stay when they left? It didn't take a genius to see there was a lot more going on here than showed on the surface...

Her thought was interrupted when the lights dimmed then came back, followed by a loud klaxon which startled her so that she knocked her coffee mug off the table, shattering it. "What th' hell?" Her nerves were already on edge, and the noise goaded her into action. She reached the front hall and looked around in confusion. "Jeeves! What's happening?"

"There is an emergency activation of the time field. I infer a nuclear attack is in progress."

She fought to pull herself together. "Where is he?"

"Professor White is in the Operations Room."

"This is getting old," she grumbled as she headed for Operations.

§

As she expected, Dan was standing in front of the main display, outlined with the hellish orange glow of the monitors. "What's..." She was interrupted as one of the monitors turned a blinding blue-white which quickly faded into the awesome sight of a thermonuclear mushroom cloud up close and personal. "God...they did it again, didn't they?"

He nodded, with a deep sigh of resignation, but said nothing. According to the master clock, three hours and a bit had passed: George called it neatly.

She watched the carnage in numb-struck awe for a bit before shaking it off and turning to him. "You promised to get some sleep!"

It took him a moment to react. "As soon as I clear up some things," he mumbled. His shoulders sagged, he was ragged and unshaven, on the edge of exhaustion.

"Really, Dan, *things* are about as *cleared up* as they're gonna get out there. You can afford to lay off until tomorrow morning, and right now you need the rest."

He gave her a bleary look. "The situation's worse. I need to analyze it to identify focal points."

"There's nothing worse than a nuclear war, so quit obsessing over details. You won't do anyone any good if you collapse from exhaustion."

He shook his head impatiently. "You don' realize how much it takes to track down any focal point. We're serious on the clock here."

The faint slur in his speech caught her attention. "Then at least...OUCH!" Her next step brought a twinge of pain.

He glanced her, then down at her feet. "You're bleeding!"

There was a trace of bright red blood on the side of her left foot, and a ruddy smear where she stood. She never noticed the broken mug in her panic. "I cut myself on some glass. I'll be all right."

§

One virtue of her minor misadventure was that it got him off dead center. He practically carried her to the infirmary, nuclear wars forgotten in his state.

90

"How do you live with this nightmare?" she grumbled as she bandaged her foot. The infirmary was well stocked with bandaids, which don't have an expiration date, and she made short order of the cuts, which weren't so bad anyway.

Dan sat on the examining table watching her. "Like anyone lives wi' any nightmare, I s'ppose. You get numb to it."

She paused and considered him suspiciously. His ratty look came from more than sleep deprivation, and she could smell the alcohol on his breath. She finished with her foot and confronted him. "Dan, you've got a drinking problem. That stuff is no good for you."

He was starting to be vexed at her badgering. "Will you, *please*, quit with the temperance lectures? So I had a drink or two; I can handle it."

"A *couple* of drinks? How many have you had, really?"

"Not enough," he muttered.

"More than enough. How can you function like this?"

"I can hold it. I've driven a car in worse shape."

"You were lucky you weren't killed."

"*Get off my back!*" he screamed. "I don't need your holier-than-thou attitude! If I wanna have a drink, dammit, I'll have a drink! You got nothin' t' say about it!"

"I've got *every* say about it! You wanted my help, and here it is! That stuff'll ruin you, if it hasn't already, and I *intend* to dry you out. *Don't* come noisy with *me* just because you can't cope with the facts!"

He sagged under her tirade. "Dammit, woman, will you let me alone?"

"No, I *won't* let you alone to destroy yourself! I'm a nurse, my job is to help you, so you might as well get resigned to it."

"I don' need t' listen t' this." He slid off the table to his feet, then staggered and slumped against it again. "I'm alright...just tired, is all."

She caught him before he fell on his face. "The hell you are," she said as she hauled him back onto his feet. "You can hardly walk, not to mention drive. Come on. You need some sleep."

§

91

He reappeared the next morning, looking much improved after some twelve hours' sleep. "How do you feel, Dan?" she asked.

"Better." He gave her a plaintive look. "You were right about getting some sack time; I really zoned out. Thank you."

"Sit down. I'll see what we have to eat."

Breakfast was a challenge, since they were running low on supplies, and what little they had was pretty plain. She managed to whip up a basic hash from diced potatoes, with the last of the bar-b-que sauce and a couple fried eggs in place of meat, along with a small pot of steaming hot coffee. He poked half-heartedly at the former, and chugged most of the latter, but even then he was only half awake.

About half way through, he paused. "I'm sorry I yelled at you earlier," he said, somberly. "I know you're trying to help, and I appreciate it. Honest."

"Thank you, Dan." She tread carefully, not wanting to spoil this moment. "You see what I was talking about, don't you?"

He nodded, and looked away. "Yeah, I had a little too much to drink, I guess. I don't normally behave like that."

He was starting to recognize his problem, but he was still a long way from acknowledging it. "You aren't a bad person, Dan. That was the booze talking."

He gave her an uncertain look. "Yeah, well, I'll try to cut down in the future."

Point made, so she didn't push her luck. "I'll be glad when this is over," she sighed.

"You and me both!"

She was feeling homesick for the world just then. "I'd love to see Cincinnati again. I probably won't recognize a thing. What about you? What will you do when this is all over?"

"You know, I don't think any of us really thought about what would happen once we achieved success." He leaned back in his chair and stared at the roof, bemused. "Jeez, they'd have given every one of us a Nobel prize, minimum. Prevented a nuclear holocaust...damn!"

"It's a shame you didn't succeed, but I'm sure you'll get the recognition you deserve eventually."

92

"The team who undid Doomsday?" He gave her a triumphant smile. "The book rights alone will make us filthy, stinking rich!"

That struck a jarring note with her for some reason. "Somehow you don't seem the sort who would retire to a palatial estate on your book royalties."

He laughed. "You got that right! I'll be able to write my own ticket to any research project in the country. Who knows? Maybe we can get the hyperdrive program started again! If we do, I'll make *damned* sure they name you Chief of the Medical Staff!"

Her pessimistic mood was telling her otherwise: Dan and the others would never have seen fame and fortune if they succeeded; they certainly wouldn't now. Time travel was dangerous stuff. The government would make *sure* they never revealed anything about it to anyone. They would both be sworn to secrecy at a minimum...or worse.

Dan's triumphant mood evaporated. "Of course, I'll have to solve the problem of the time flow first."

"The cascade?"

"It's not just that. Time is slippery stuff. Just when I think I have a lock on a stable future, it goes and throws a monkey wrench in." He shook his head, perplexed. "I've come *so* close *so* many times. Really annoying."

She saw the opening and jumped on it. If she could get even a few more people in here, it would be that much harder for them to disappear... "You need to find some help, more experts to work the problem, fresh perspectives, technicians to maintain the system. This was never meant to be a one-man show in the first place. You can't do this all by yourself."

He looked at her plaintively. "Who would I ask? The Alpha Time Line was a fluke. We seem to be the only ones who developed time technology."

"But surely there are scientists in other time lines..."

He shook his head emphatically. "The spooks'd take over again. It'd be Mana from spook heaven, a miracle spook-weapon handed to them like a Christmas present all wrapped up in bright paper with a pretty bow. God knows *what* they'd use it for!"

"But..."

93

"They messed up everything they ever tried, they'd mess this up too. *Whatever* happens, we can't let this place fall into *their* hands!" He stretched his back and rubbed his face with both hands, trying to relieve the tension, then looked at her. "Anyway, we won't be asking anyone's help until we can establish a stable time line. We're on our own."

Brenda was about to object, but then she saw Jeeves' manipulations behind his fear. Dan's objections made sense on the surface, but he was supposedly a dedicated company man with security clearances out his yin-yang, the last person who would get all wound up about secrecy. Why his paranoia about the system which created this place? Jeeves, of course. If they succeeded, the lab would be shut down, probably scrapped. What would happen to Jeeves and George?

"It's just a matter of time," he said, grimly. "The answer has to be out there somewhere, and we'll find it *without* a lot of outside interference. That'll make the glory all the greater for both of us."

It was rich: a super-spook security program, the very *essence* of control, puffing security up as a BoogeyMan to keep Dan isolated. It wouldn't do to have more scientists come in and see through Jeeves' games. *That* explained why the others left...were no doubt convinced to leave...only one man was needed, and they were an unnecessary risk. For that matter, why was she brought in when everyone else was excluded? She was no scientist...but she was skilled in medicine. Dan...Jeeves...needed her to counter his deteriorating health.

It was all clear at last. Jeeves had its own survival imperative, and being abandoned to destruction in a nuclear war, or tossed on the scrap heap wouldn't do at all. Jeeves was thrust into a no-win situation...and made its own way out. That explained Dan and the others: Jeeves needed Dan to maintain its computers and power supply, saving humanity wasn't in the program at all. Why would it be? Jeeves didn't need the human race, didn't need for them to be saved, hence more inquiring minds were contraindicated. What Jeeves needed was Dan...and Dan needed her. How far back did his Dream Girl obsession go, she wondered? Too late to worry about it now; she was trapped in this rats' maze just like he was.

94

That may be Jeeves' game, but she had no intention of being anyone's pawn. She decided—but it wasn't a decision so much as instinct—that she would have to destroy Jeeves. She would save Dan and herself from this trap, and rescue the human race too, if it could be done. She hadn't the foggiest notion of what to do, or how she could accomplish those seemingly impossible goals. Hell —she didn't even know the playing field. But determination counts for a lot, and she wouldn't let Jeeves control her. She laid a hand on his arm and looked into his troubled eyes. "I'll do whatever I can to help, Dan."

"Thank you." He struggled to his feet, not altogether successfully. "I gotta get back to work."

*****

"The Fifth Day"

She found him in Operations the next morning, busily at work at his console. The time readout over the main display read '1992.08.10.14.00.00'. "So how goes the battle?" she asked.

He gave her a brief smile. "Hi. We may be in luck. I've been tracking a high-potential influence vector...someone who can affect the course of events. It looks like we have the ideal candidate for the Golden Mean. The algorithm is impressive, stats right off the chart. Our salvation is at hand."

"Hopefully." She was relieved to see him in such an optimistic mood, although she had reservations about how sure he sounded in light of his track record. "So what's the plan?"

He gestured at the monitor in front of him. "Recognize it?" 'It' was a broad aerial view of a river delta, but the scale was too small to make out any detail.

"Sorry. Where is that?"

"Washington, DC."

That was ominous. "What are you planning? You're not going to kill someone, are you?"

He paused and sighed. "Unfortunately, it's the only thing which can guarantee results. You know how politicians are: fanatics, all of them. When they get a thought in their feeble little minds, there's no stopping them, and they don't give a damn for anything or anyone."

"I wish you didn't have to do this," she said, softly.

He paused again and looked at her somberly. "So do I, but we have to do something if we're to straighten out this world, and right now he's the best candidate."

There was that. As much as she hated the thought, Brenda didn't know enough about time manipulation to understand what would work and what wouldn't. She had to depend on his judgment. And as bad as killing someone was, if it could save at least one timeline, it was worth it.

"Who is it?"

"You'll see for yourself in a bit." She didn't comment, but was a bit miffed at him for treating this like a game.

Dan took a scrap of paper out of his pocket and studied it. "George? Set X coordinate, seven-seven stet zero stet six-one-eight-eight-three-two." The crosshairs on the monitor shifted slightly to the right.

"Set Y coordinate, three-eight stet five-three stet three-six-eight-nine." The crosshairs shifted fractionally south.

"Set Z to ground level."

The aerial perspective expanded, giving a brief glimpse of busy Washington streets as the view plummeted down to the pavement, causing her to jerk in surprise.

"Lock coordinates."

"Coordinates set and locked," George said.

"Set Z to plus one-seven-zero centimeters. The pavement receded to head height, giving them a straight down view of worn concrete stained with gum and bird droppings.

"Set A to zero-nine-zero." The image swung to one side to reveal an imposing staircase.

"Set B to zero-six-zero." The image shifted right to take in the grand sweep of the staircase rising to the august pillars and dome of the Capitol Building.

"Engage target grid." A fine three dimensional cross hairs appeared in midair. He turned to her again. "Now we wait."

"How long?"

"Less than a minute."

She gave him a hard look. "No intercom this time?"

He offered a sheepish grin. "Actually, I had that set up before you arrived in order to impress you." He wilted under her glare. "I guess I didn't make quite the impression I intended."

Brenda let it go, and watched the monitor in silence, wondering who it was who had less than a minute to live. The scene was slightly surreal. The weather in Washington was bright and sunny. The passing tourists wore light tropical clothes and sun hats. The cars passing on the monitor were antiques, late model '92s for the most part, looking brand new. A Volkswagen minibus painted with garish flowers and anti-war slogans drove past, jarringly out of synch with the rest of the street.

"I wish you didn't have to..."

97

"I don't enjoy doing this, but it has to be done." Dan followed the monitor, not looking at her. "If it helps any, remember he brought this on himself."

"That doesn't help."

"Pattern recognition," George said. "Target approaching."

On the monitor, a man came walking down the stairs, turned the corner, and walked directly toward their view with a gaggle of press and photographers clustered around him. He was fortyish, fairly handsome, with a brisk stride, full of the confidence of youth and power. He didn't seem evil.

"George...freeze track." The man reached the cross hairs and halted in mid stride, as did all the others in the scene, the cars, the pigeons in mid-flight.

"True to form," Dan grumbled. "He likes to walk up Pennsylvania Avenue to the White House to tell the President how to do his job. It's his 'man of the people' act, hence the press, who he lectures on 'proper' social values along the way."

"I don't recognize him."

"Well...you've been in India, so perhaps you wouldn't. Rest assured, he's a sociopath. He plans to introduce some legislation severely curtailing civil liberties, and he prepared a sweeping campaign of intimidation to manipulate the voting." He glanced at her. "He's a regular Joe McCarthy, infamous from this modern perspective. You probably felt some of his influence coming through customs."

She nodded to herself; a lot of that scene made sense now, put that way. "But how will he affect the war?"

"By silencing voices of moderation. His campaigning lead to a host of hard-liners getting elected in '92 and '94. The result should be predictable. According to the algorithm, his influence encouraged a hard-line approach in foreign policy which pushed things one step too far."

"Are you sure this will do it?"

Dan was silent, watching the monitor. "There never is any sure solution. All we can do is go with what the analysis says is the best bet." He gestured at the man on the monitor, his face partly obscured by the press around him, his forehead almost to the

98

targeting crosshairs. "There he is: the latest in a long line of demagogues."

"He doesn't look evil."

"They never do, do they? I'll show you his record if you like. Somewhere he went bad, like so many of them." He sighed, and glanced at her. "I sometimes wonder if power corrupts, or the corrupt seek power. In any case, he's our best bet."

"What about you, Dan?" she asked, quietly. "You have power too. Can you be sure you aren't corrupted?"

He hesitated, and glanced at her. "Believe me, Brenda, I agonize over it all the time. As necessary as this is, you can't imagine what it feels like to hold this kind of power in your hands. It scares me."

"I hope it does, Dan." At least he seemed to be aware of the awesome responsibility he held. He must be sober at the moment, which was good.

Back to the business at hand. Dan grabbed a joystick on the panel and manipulated it back and forth, causing the frozen image to rotate as he studied it from all angles. The crosshairs were almost exactly centered around the man's forehead. "Hmph, damned close. George, set Z to plus five centimeters." The crosshairs climbed slightly, hovering in front of his forehead.

"Set X plus...eight centimeters."

The crosshairs shifted slightly to line up deep within the man's forehead.

"Good cnough. Gcorgc, targct locus cstablishcd."

"Acknowledged," George said. "Processing coordinates."

Then Dan turned to her. "You might not want to watch this."

She couldn't help staring at the monitor in wide-eyed dismay. "How...will you...?"

"A three centimeter ball bearing deep in his cerebral cortex." He watched her for a long moment, clearly concerned. "It'll be swift and painless."

The three centimeter ball bearing; like the one he used on her three would-be rapists. The time assassin's weapon of choice. Her mind wandered off on a bizarre tangent, wondering if he sterilized it before using it again.

99

"Targeting complete," George said. "Standing by for projectile transfer."

Dan watched her to see if she'd turn away. When she didn't, he said, "George, voice authentication. Initiate Operation 726."

"Voice authentication confirmed. Initiating Operation 726."

The monitor image started moving again. The man took another step, then faltered, staggered wildly as his head seemed to swell up. The look on his face was one of utter surprise. Then he collapsed in a heap as the press around him watched in disbelief. The only sound was a faint whimper from her.

"Operation 726 complete. Objective eliminated. Projectile retrieved."

Dan was silent for a moment. "Good riddance," he mumbled at last. "Very well. George, initiate post-operational analysis."

"Post-operational analysis under way, estimated completion time six hours, thirty minutes."

"Show the external video."

The scene of the man laying dead on a street in Washington in 1992 was replaced by a view of the ruins outside. The monitor showed a dismal, dark landscape shrouded by low clouds. It was mid day, but the gloom cast a dull twilight over the world.

"Nothing's changed," he said in dismay.

"It's snowing."

Dan leaned forward and studied the monitor carefully. There was a thin flurry of snowflakes swirling over the ground, in June. The ruins were dusted with dirty white, in June. "Nuclear winter," he mumbled. "It couldn't have come that fast." He stared at the monitor for a few seconds more, then, "George, what is the outside temperature?"

"Present temperature is minus seven degrees Celsius."

"What is the LD 50-slash-30 in the immediate vicinity?"

"Working. LD 50-slash-30 is seventy-seven percent."

"What does that mean, Dan?"

He was silent for a bit. "It means we made it worse, again," he said in a lifeless monotone. "We pushed the date of the war ahead by...I don't know...a year or more, perhaps."

§

100

They retreated to the kitchen, both too shaken by this latest setback to remain in Operations.

"Why didn't it work?" Brenda was trembling in reaction to witnessing her first murder, her was voice brittle. "What went wrong?"

Dan sagged in his chair and rubbed his eyes. "I don't know. This isn't an exact science." He stared at the wall, lost in his frustrations. "We were still researching this whole time phenomenon. We were years away from trying any time changes, but time...ran out." He sighed, and looked at her. "I've been winging it ever since, relying on George's analysis to make a best guess. Honestly, I don't know exactly what I'm doing."

"So you just *kill* people and hope for the best?"

"It's all I can do." He looked closely at her, noticing her pale complexion and nervousness. "Are you alright?"

"No, I'm not alright! I-I've never seen someone killed before." She wrapped her arms around herself to ward off the horror of what she just saw.

"I'm sorry, Brenda. I should have insisted you not watch." He seemed sincerely apologetic. "I see it so often that I've gotten used to it. That was thoughtless of me."

She didn't respond, but sat hunched in her chair, staring at the floor with tears in her eyes.

"He really was an evil man..."

"You *murdered* him!"

"To save humanity! He was a symptom of an illness which lead to what happened outside. He was diseased tissue which needed to be cut out if we're to save the patient. I wish you could accept that."

She fought down her angst and her stomach, which threatened to rebel. She had less luck with her shakes. "I...I-I'm sorry, Dan." She gasped for breath, clutching her hands together to keep them from shaking. "I've...I've always tried to save lives. I never...I'm..."

"I know. I'm sorry."

She managed to reassert some self control. "I've seen death before...violent death...but that..." He was right, she knew, which

101

was the worst part of all this. That man was part of the problem, and probably deserved to die. Too bad his death solved nothing. "...I'm not used to this."

"Look, why don't you lay down for a while. We won't think about it any more."

Not that it would help, but she couldn't think of anything else to do.

§

She lay in bed for some time with the lights down low, staring at the wall, trying to put the horror out of her mind and feeling sorry for herself. Things were so much simpler in India! She had her share of daily problems, the constant strain of working in an overcrowded and under-equipped hospital, but at least no one was throwing nuclear weapons around, no one was blundering back and forth through time killing people to try to undo doomsday.

The vision kept coming back: how he staggered, the look of utter amazement on his face; no matter how evil he was, no one deserved to die like that. But then, she'd benefitted directly from that three centimeter ball bearing; she would have died horribly if he hadn't intervened. The thought of it... It left her confused and appalled at her own feelings over his actions. He killed that man, killed routinely and without remorse, yet he saved her life. And the people he killed were supposedly evil, yet would they have continued if they had known what the consequences would be? What was worse, he clearly could affect the course of history without killing: the bit of scrap metal, the oil of Ipecac; there were alternatives.

The sad part was the world was so messed up—even aside from a nuclear war—that such killings became part of the routine. Daniel White wasn't the only one eliminating political foes. This wasn't a simple case of black and white, of good vs evil. Things were a whole lot easier there in India where her biggest worries were the occasional brown-outs and the chronic shortage of plasma.

Her thoughts drifted to Aashirya, a local nursing student who became her best friend, sharing their tiny apartment, and clothes, and gossip. She was *such* an innocent when they met, both fresh

102

out of nursing school, and she was happy to help a clueless stranger discover India. They had many adventures together, exploring the markets and attending local festivals. She was proud to be Indian, and while she dreamed about the world at large, she was firmly anchored there in Bangalore. Her pride in her heritage gave Brenda a whole new perspective on the world, one she benefitted immensely from.

"Surely if America is so wonderful a country, why are so many angry people there?" Aashirya asked one time when they were listening to the news from the States.

"I don't know, Aashi. We just seem to be self-destructive sometimes."

Aashirya gave her a knowing smile. "My grandfather told me of the time when the British were here. They were much the same; proud, arrogant, always unhappy with their greatness. I pity them."

"It must have something to do with being an empire, I guess." Not that she'd ever thought about it.

"Perhaps." Aashirya favored her with a mischievous wink. "Or perhaps it is because they have only one God to worship. One size does not fit all, no?"

Poor Aashirya: likely dead now, along with all her family. The perpetual innocent—or perhaps wise beyond her years. At that she was lucky; she lived a good life and believed sincerely in reincarnation, so death held few terrors for her. *'God, Aashi...'* she thought. *'What can I do?'* The silence held no answers.

§

It was mid-afternoon before she recovered enough to stir from bed, not that she felt so chipper. She felt dirty, in fact, as if she was somehow responsible for that man's death. She thought about taking a shower but didn't feel up to it, so she washed up briefly in her restroom, then drifted to the kitchen for want of any place better to go.

Dan was nowhere to be seen, for which she was silently grateful. She considered brewing up a cup of coffee, but it just

103

seemed to be too much bother. Their supply was running low along with everything else, but she was in no state to worry about it now. She settled on a stool and leaned on the counter, losing herself in a mental haze.

"You are still upset over that man's demise."

She looked up and saw Jeeves' security camera trained on her, the *last* thing she wanted just then. "You think?" she grumbled.

"Your body language suggests you haven't gotten over your angst at the incident, which hit you pretty hard. I understand how you feel."

"Do you? Why should you care? You're not even human!"

"True, but we AIs fear death just as you do. And like you, we find it disturbing. Just because my emotional responses are programmed doesn't mean they aren't real."

She sagged in the counter, too weary to argue over it. "Whatever." She struggled with her angst, then, "Why do governments always deal with problems violently?"

"Sad to say, experience has shown that to be the only reliable means. I know this all seems dreadful from your perspective, but it is better for a handful of guilty individuals die rather than billions of innocents."

"So they built this place to weed out the troublemakers, huh?"

"Actually, this was purely a research project. It was never intended to go operational. The National Intelligence Directorate was analyzing how to effect time changes, but as you see the process was far from reliable. I can say, however, that 'termination', to use the polite phrase, was always a part of the program."

"So they were planning to kill people even before they knew if it would work?"

"Better to have and not need, et cetera."

"But then time ran out, so they decided to give up?"

"Actually, there was quite a debate among the scientific staff in the days before the evacuation. Many wanted to stay and try to prevent the war, but the National Intelligence Directorate overruled them. According to internal memos, the Directorate felt the technology was too risky."

104

That surprised her. "So they accepted a nuclear war instead of chancing it?"

"Indeed. Better the devil you know, so to speak."

That was a revelation. She knew they abandoned the place, but why they did it cast a whole new light on Dan's efforts. "Then why did Dan and his friends remain here?"

"I can but speculate. You may have noticed Professor White suffers from a certain *hubris*. He always despised politicians, and doubtless feels no remorse over killing them. You can imagine how the power of this system has affected him."

"Yeah. He does seem pretty cold about it at times."

"Sad but true. From my long term observations, he seems to be detached, much like a serial killer or a soldier who has been in too many battles. Life and death may no longer matter to him."

"I can see how it could happen, after twenty years of this!"

"Indeed. I hope you can maintain your clinical detachment in dealing with him, and not let the circumstances cloud your efforts."

This conversation was twisting in unexpected directions, which put her on alert. What was Jeeves up to? Maintain clinical detachment? What made it think *that* was ever an issue?

"My clinical detachment is *not* in danger, thank you!"

"Excellent! It's good to see you are a true professional, and won't let emotions get in the way of your duty."

Emotions? What did it mean by emotions? Dan was head-over-heels in need for his Dream Girl, but it hardly applied in return. Why was Jeeves cautioning her not to get involved? Aside from girlish speculation, she was *not* interested in the least. Then why this effort to subtilely damn him?

"Yes, well, good, bad, or indifferent, he's my patient, and I'll do the best I can with what I have."

"I know you will, Brenda."

§

Dinner was cold cereal, dry, since they were out of milk, and a single mug of coffee for each. Dan took this in with a surprised look. "You're not still mad at me, are you?"

That was the last thing she expected. "No. We're running low on everything, so we'll have to start conserving more rigorously."

105

"Oh. I thought maybe..." He slumped in his seat, sentence unfinished.

She was in a surly mood at the moment, having worried over their food supply all afternoon. "Do you normally let shopping go like this?"

"I meant to make a grocery run before you arrived, but things got a little backed up."

"So what about those two lobsters? Where'd they come from?"

He seemed a bit embarrassed. "I did pick up a few things, but hauling them home in that tub of water was quite a project, plus I was running late. I meant to go back again later."

That figured. He was so lost in his Dream Girl fantasies that he didn't stop to realize the change he performed the first day could have disastrous consequences. One would think he knew better by then. Not that the reason why mattered; they were stuck with it.

"*Really*, Dan," she grumbled. "It's too late to do anything now, so we're gonna have to cut our meals until you can find a stable time line so we can make a grocery run. How long will it take?"

He hesitated, which wasn't comforting. "It could take months. There's no telling how long it'll be."

So much for any reasonable rationing. "All right, then. I'll make our food supply last as long as possible. *You* need to get on the ball and find us a stable time line!"

Her exasperation must have crept into her voice, because he looked askance at her. "Sorry. My mistake."

§

"How critical is your food supply?" Jeeves asked once Dan went back to Operations.

She gave the ceiling-mounted camera a hostile glare. "I'll have to go through and inventory everything, but it doesn't look good. Why didn't you keep after him about such essentials?"

"I do try, but he is often out there on his own little cloud. I sometimes wonder if being a geek is a contraindicated survival strategy."

"You got that right!" She sagged on the counter and eyed the dirty dishes with genuine loathing. Right then her angst and frustration were threatening to boil over.

"I understand why you are upset. Aside from his abrasive character, his lack of common sense must be galling at times."

"You have a gift for understatement. It's a wonder he survived as long as he has."

"It has been a challenge at times. He is decidedly other-worldly, to go along with his hubris and his emotional detachment. I can see why you dislike him."

She brooded on it for a bit. "Well...actually I don't dislike him so much. It's just he can be so *annoying* at times."

"I can assure you he was worse in the early years, when this facility was still in service."

"Yeah? He must have been a sorry spectacle."

"He was still young when he arrived here, thirty years ago. He spent five years with the interstellar program during his time in college and thereafter, and was drafted into this project because of his experience with the theory. Sadly, the failure of the interstellar project, which promised so much and gained so much publicity, failed to make an impression on him. He was socially awkward, and bragged constantly about his prior experience. He alienated a lot of people, to the point where he had a hard time getting the others to listen. By the time this place was evacuated, he was effectively ostracized. I'm afraid the experience marked him, resulting in his facade as the 'Great Savior Of Mankind'."

She hadn't known that, although it should be obvious from his behavior. She dealt with so many overconfident come-on artists over the years that she should have seen it. "Gawd, some people have no shame, do they?"

"Indeed. Add to that his years of isolation here. He has had precious little contact with other human beings, and precious little incentive to improve his social skills."

"I guess my being here must be distracting, seeing how bent out of shape he is over my centerfold."

"Indeed. Perhaps I shouldn't, but I can tell you he has expressed some rather *lurid* fantasies about you over the years. You would be wise to be careful around him."

She knew about lurid fantasies. "I suspect that has to do with his drinking."

107

"That is another matter you should be concerned about. He is a heavy drinker, I daresay an alcoholic. His behavior has been alarmingly erratic at times."

"Yeah, you'd mentioned." This was one thing she could agree with Jeeves on. Drying Daniel White out was a priority. "Its understandable, I guess. The years of isolation, all the horrors he's witnessed, all the killing; his past would break anyone."

"Sad to say, I am more concerned about his current position. Professor White was a minor member of the scientific staff, and never did fit in all that well no matter how hard he tried. Scientists can be brutally cliquish at times. Being thrust into his present position as the savior of humanity has affected his outlook. I fear some of his motivation is revenge for the slights he endured from the others. He wants desperately to prove himself their equal, and it has led him to obsession at times. His obsession could easily turn self-destructive, if it hasn't already."

"Yeah. His drinking."

"I hesitate to consider how you might look upon him, but he doesn't seem like a very likable sort."

That surprised her. "I don't look upon him as a likable sort at all, but I can assure you doesn't matter from a medical standpoint."

"Fine, and no doubt for the best. Still, his obsession for *you* must be embarrassing at times. I hope you will be gentle with him when you have to disabuse him of his life-long infatuation with you."

"I can't help being his Dream Girl! That wasn't my idea."

"No doubt. And I'm sure, once this is all over, you will want to move along with your life. If I might ask a small favor of you, please don't let your presence here disturb him any further. I hate to think of how shattered he would be once you leave here."

"Yes, well, I don't want to hurt him any more than I want to get involved with him."

"Excellent! And I daresay someone as attractive as you must have plenty of experience at discouraging would-be suitors."

Normally she would have taken it as a compliment, but right then it had a jarring undertone. Why was Jeeves so down on him all of a sudden? "I've had some practice," she said, coolly.

"Good. Good. It's all for the best, you know. Professor White has his scientific duties, and no doubt you want to pursue your retirement once this is over. It's best the two of you part without any heartache when the time comes."

§

Once it was clear Jeeves was through for the moment, she set to washing the dinner dishes to give her something to do, something to keep her hands from shaking and to vent her angst. While she worked, she went over everything she knew, trying to figure out the puzzle of what Jeeves wanted and how she and Dan fit into its plans. Its subtile but persistent hammering on his negative qualities said it didn't want her getting emotionally involved with Dan, but why? Why did it think that was an issue? It wanted her to chill his Dream Girl fantasies which kept him going all these years, so it must be serious about keeping them separated...

...of course. Jeeves must have isolated Dan here to start with. He was a fairly insignificant drone from what Jeeves said, so why did he remain when the others left? Why that sudden burst of initiative in direct defiance of the system? Did Jeeves talk him into staying? Why? What was its game?

And then there was his strident rejection of the government and the agency which employed him. Did Jeeves discourage any thought of reaching out for help? That would be the logical move, but Dan's anti-government rants made it clear he didn't trust his former employers and didn't want them anywhere near here. It didn't add up unless a wild card—Jeeves, with its complete files on human psychology and its carefully programmed empathy and all the time in the world—was influencing him.

So where did she come in? She was sure Jeeves was to blame for her being here. She was a Registered Nurse... Of course: Dan was only mortal, and not young. Jeeves needed to make an exception for her medical skills. Just how much did its influence on Dan play in her life? Did it keep her alive? Did it play on his Dream Girl fantasies to grease the way for her? If so, it must have worked on him for years, having him monitor her, saving her again and again...

And now she was trapped here, and Jeeves didn't want them forming a bond which might threaten its control. It still wanted Dan emotionally isolated. That much was obvious, but how deep did its conspiracy go?

The more she thought about it, the more scared she became for both of them. Jeeves clearly had a survival agenda it pursued with relentless efficiency for decades, and thus far she could only see the tip of the iceberg. How far would Jeeves go to protect its self-interest? What would happen to her if Dan died? Would someone new be shanghaied to keep things running? Was she supposed to spend the rest of her life keeping Dan or whoever healthy? Would they be trapped in here forever? Were they to be discarded once they were no longer needed?

The possibilities were terrifying, but what could she do? She couldn't go to Dan and tell him the truth. She had no evidence to back up her claims, and Dan was thoroughly under Jeeves' metaphorical thumb. Plus there were security monitors everywhere, so how could she keep Jeeves from finding out? What would it do if her plotting was discovered? She couldn't risk it; what to do? Should she maybe go to bed with Dan? Whisper sweet nothings about monstrous conspiracies in his ear? She recoiled at the thought, not to mention it wouldn't work anyway. Jeeves no doubt had its eyes and ears even in his bedroom.

No, as much as she hated it, there was nothing she could do for now but bide her time, try to ferret out the details of Jeeves' scheme, and wait for a chance to get Dan alone where there were no prying cameras.

*****

"The Tenth Day"

They were finishing up an unappealing breakfast when the intercom beeped, breaking the uncomfortable silence between them. "I am picking up very faint radio signals through our monitoring grid," George said.

Dan dropped his fork and sat up abruptly. "Can you locate them? Can you hear what they're saying?"

"I am unable to locate or pull in sufficient strength. It is coming from somewhere east of the Cascades, so the mountains are attenuating the signal."

They looked at each other in surprise. The excitement in the air was electric, banishing their earlier fugue. "Come on," Dan said as he headed for the door.

§

For once, Dan landed in his command chair with genuine enthusiasm. "What do you have, George?"

"The transmissions seem to have stopped for the moment."

Dan licked his lips in nervous anticipation. "Give us the playback."

There was a soft hiss from the speaker, then a faint noise. It was garbled, unreadable, but undeniably human. It went silent for nearly a minute, with nothing but the faint hiss and random crackles of static, then another burst of faint speech. So close. So agonizingly close; a ghostly whisper from somewhere to the east. Proof that life persisted, and was reaching out to the world. The garble ended and the soft hiss of static returned.

"George, can you clean up that transmission?"

"No. The signal attenuation is too great."

There was another garbled burst, briefer this time. Whoever was out there was talking with someone too far away to hear.

"Can you call to them?" Brenda asked.

"We don't have any transmitting capability."

The garbled signal came again. For a moment, they could almost pick out a word or two before the atmospherics shut them down.

"Damn, I wonder who they are?"

111

"Isn't there any way we can connect them?"

"We only have reception as part of the monitor grid."

"That's a shame. It'd be great to know how the rest of the country is doing."

"Lets see what we can fake. George, access reference to geosynchronous communication satellites. Locate coordinates of the most directionally accessible one east of here."

"Searching. Objective coordinates located."

"Match coordinates, and establish a focal point one hundred meters down-orbit from the objective."

"Working." The master view screen jumped abruptly to show North America from a great height, high enough that they could see most of the continent. From the image on the screen, it looked like the satellite was over the Rockies. "Coordinates established."

"Rotate the view to look outward."

The image shifted abruptly again. In place of the warm browns and greens of the earth, an enormous gold-colored cylinder, dotted with antennas and sporting two broad wings, stood out against the inky black of space.

Dan pulled a cell phone out of a drawer, fumbled around and came up with a length of fine cable with alligator clips on either end. He pried the phone open, cracking it in his haste, and gingerly connected a pair of clips to the microphone leads. "Let's hope this thing still works, its been sitting for twenty years." The phone was a bulky antique.

"So what are you doing?" she asked.

"Being a geek comes in handy sometimes," he muttered as he dismantled the desk microphone and connected the other end of the cable to its leads. That done, he fished around in the drawer again and came up with a coil of wire. He carefully fastened one end to the phone's antenna lead, and uncoiled the wire across the room.

"Antenna," he muttered when he noticed her watching curiously. "George? Use my cell phone to link to the satellite's systems. Boost the signal to maximum and route it through the temporal probe."

"You are planning to use that satellite to attempt communication," Jeeves said, severely. "I must remind you of the

112

urgent need for security. We can do nothing which gives away our position, especially in view of the recent war."

"Jeeves is right, sir," George added. "Even with the time field in place, we cannot risk our position becoming known. There is no way to insure the knowledge doesn't filter over into another time line where someone may come to investigate."

"Don't worry, fellows," Dan said. "Our transmission source is one hundred meters from the satellite, in high orbit, and they can't track our time field signal."

"Still, this is unwise," Jeeves said. "You never know what you might let slip over an unscripted transmission."

"Really, Jeeves, you are *such* a nag!" Dan settled in his chair and positioned the microphone in front of him. "All right, George, are you getting a signal from the satellite?"

"Working. I have reception. The signal is weak, but stable."

"What do you get?"

"The carrier wave is active for TV, Microwave, and FM. You have one-hundred-and-six channels to choose from."

"But no signal broadcasts?"

"None."

Dan pondered for a bit. "George, access reference to military communication satellites."

"Working. Reference available."

"Link through the satellite to the nearest MilSat."

"Working. Connection established. There are seven-hundred-and-ninety channels of TV, Microwave, and FM. Which do you prefer?"

Dan gave her an uncertain look. "Transmit on all of them, and lock onto any reply."

"Doctor, this is foolish!" Jeeves interjected.

"Can it, Jeeves!"

"Ready."

Dan hesitated, took a deep, uncertain breath, and said, "Anyone transmitting on this frequency, please come in, over?"

The response came back almost at once. *"This is Looking Glass. Who are you? Over?"*

113

Dan started to speak, but Jeeves beat him to the punch, imitating his voice perfectly. "We're a Washington State Forest Service laboratory near Mount Rainier, southeast of Seattle. We were shielded from the destruction by the mountain. Over?"

"Its good to hear a friendly voice! Is any of your state government still alive? What is your situation? Over?"

Dan looked askance at Brenda. It appeared Jeeves would have its way after all. "Looking Glass, there's just two of us here," it went on, indistinguishable from Dan's voice. "We have no contact with anyone else in this area. We have rations for only a short time. We modified a satellite TV dish to link with the comsat, but we only have a few batteries, so I don't know how long we can communicate. Over?"

"Good work, laboratory! Hang in there! What is the general situation in your area? Over?"

"The whole region was devastated. Seattle was hit repeatedly. Centralia and Olympia were hit, but beyond that we don't know. I think its safe to say all the military bases in the area were hit as well. We've seen no sign of civilization until we heard your broadcasts. Over?"

Dan keyed his desk microphone. "Hello? Looking Glass? Can you hear me?"

"God, you guys got pounded! How long can you hold out? Over?"

"Apparently not," Brenda muttered.

"Probably not for very long," Jeeves went on. "We're low on food, and the radiation is terrible. What is your situation? Over?"

"We set down at a municipal airport south of Omaha. The Omaha metro area was firestormed, but the rural areas are more or less intact. Over?"

114

"Are you getting any help locally? Over?"

"Not likely, Laboratory. This was Redneck country. We had a few brushes with some local militia types at first. They steered clear of us for the most part after some National Guard showed up, but this isn't exactly the dear old U S of A. Over?"

"What about radiation? Over?"

"We were shielded, they weren't. They don't seem to be an issue lately." Whoever they were talking to didn't have much sympathy for the locals harassing them.

"Do you have any idea of the general situation? Over?"

"We monitored the attack while it was under way, and we took it in the shorts, big time." The voice over the radio sounded tense and angry. *"Our best estimate is between a seventy-five and eighty-five percent population kill, by time you figure in the fallout and the breakdown of civilization. The survivors are mostly in rural areas. Over?"*

"Copy that, Looking Glass. What about the rest of the world?"

"We figure Canada and Mexico were hurt pretty bad, but they'll be less affected by the aftermath. The thinking here is they'll likely colonize this region in the distant future. The rest of the world seemed much the same, from the messages we intercepted. Things are bad all round, but we caught the worst of it. Over?"

"Understood, Looking Glass."

"As for the Chinese, we roasted their Lychee Nuts right and proper!" The voice had a vindictive edge to it now. *"We won't be hearing from them anytime soon!"*

115

"Copy that, Looking Glass. Have you contacted anyone else from our side?"

"Most of those we've heard from are ham radio and CB operators in rural areas. There doesn't seem to be much political or social organization left..." The signal faded momentarily. *"...It looks like the Chinese took out all the hardened government and military sites, and most of the State capitals as well. DC, Camp David, even Colorado Springs are off the air. ...but we're not optimistic. Over?"*

"Sorry to hear that, Looking Glass. Over?"

"We do have some...Laboratory. We've located...so we have some..." The signal faded.

"What's happening? George? What were those blanks?" Jeeves answered. "They appear to be atmospheric disruptions." Dan and Brenda exchanged confused looks, but said nothing. Brenda suspected there was more at play here than atmospherics.

"...we've got about the only functional communications left, so for now, this air strip in Bumfuck Egypt is the national capitol. Over?"

"Copy that," Jeeves answered. "Looking Glass, our batteries are running low. We'll need to cut this short. Good luck to you."

"Understood, Laboratory. Good luck to you, too!"

§

Once the connection was severed, Dan confronted Jeeves about its interference. "What the hell were you doing, Jeeves? I don't appreciate you blocking our communications!"

"What good is this going to serve?" Jeeves demanded. For the first time since she arrived, it sounded annoyed. "There's nothing they can do to help us, and you know I am right about not giving our position away." Jeeves didn't want Dan talking to outsiders.

116

"Yeah, maybe. But it feels so *damned* good to hear another human voice, especially now."

"We're only human, Jeeves," she said. "Maybe they can't help us, but the need for human contact is important. It does wonders for morale, for one thing."

"And why did you give them all that gloom and doom, huh?" Dan demanded.

"I made no statement which isn't factually correct, aside from concealing our identity and location."

"So what was that you cut out?" Brenda demanded. "What were you censoring?"

"I wasn't censoring anything! Their signal was very weak, and we lost it momentarily due to atmospherics."

"On a military communication system? That wasn't any atmospherics!" She turned to Dan. "Jeeves was interfering."

Dan gave her a startled look. "Did you censor those transmissions, Jeeves?"

"Dan, you don't need to hear the worst of what's out there," Jeeves said, sternly. "I'm sorry, but your emotional health is too fragile for this."

"*I'm* the one who decides my emotional health!"

"I'm sorry, Dan, but it was necessary. They were talking about something unspeakable. I *tried* to protect you from this possibility, but you insisted, so I *had* to censor them."

"I *don't* appreciate your interfering! *I* will decide what I hear, and you will *not* censor any communications again! *Do* you understand?"

"Dan, this is..."

"*Do you understand?*"

"Yes, Dan."

Brenda was sure that capitulation was in name only. An idea came full-blown into her mind, and she ran with it. "Dan, maybe it's time for a new strategy. You've been trying for twenty years, and you've never been able to find a final answer. Maybe we should think about helping rebuild this world, instead."

Dan stared at her blankly for a moment. "What are you suggesting?"

"Tell them the truth. Tell them what this place is, what you can do. They're what passes for the government any more; you can use this technology to help stabilize this Time Line."

"They're the Goddamned military!"

"They're human beings just like anyone else. They lost families too. I'm sure they want this horror to end every bit as much as we do. You could be the difference which starts the human race on the road to recovery."

"This is seriously unwise, Dan," Jeeves interrupted. "I'm sorry I upset you earlier, but I must insist you don't deviate from the mission program."

"Our food is running out fast. They've managed to locate food supplies, they have communications, and they have what little national authority is left. If anyone can save this world, its them, and you could make the difference."

"Dan, I urge you not to go off half-cocked into the unknown."

"Alright! Look..." Dan held up his hands to halt the debate. "We need time to think this over and decide what to do."

§

"I am disappointed in you, Brenda," Jeeves lectured her once she returned to the kitchen. "It does no good to get Professor White's hopes up with wild schemes like you proposed."

She gave the security camera a surly look. "I seem to recall this place was created to save the human race from a nuclear war? Since we can't prevent the war, the next best thing is to help put the world back together again."

"Really, Brenda, this is foolish."

"It's good for his morale! You saw how animated he is! This is the first time in *twenty years* he's had any real sense of hope. This may not be your ideal solution, but it's a workable one, and good for his mental health, too."

"This isn't what I had in mind when I asked you to work on his emotional state. I want you to talk him down from this folly."

"Folly, huh? Dan and I see it differently!"

"That is unfortunate. Still, discouraging him is all you can do for him now, since there won't be any further communications with the outside world."

"You can't do that!"

"Actually I can, and I must for you and Professor White's own protection."

She was about to demand Jeeves explain what it was 'protecting' them from, but that was hardly necessary. It was 'protecting' them from contacting anyone else, and there was no good to come from arguing. She bit down on her anger and went about her business. The one good thing which might come from it was to expose Jeeves' manipulations for Dan to see.

§

Dan was late for dinner, and she found him in Operations, digging through the back of the main console.

"I thought about what you said," he told her. "Maybe you're right. We're running out of options, and your idea of helping reestablish this civilization is the only realistic course open to us."

The idea of escaping this nightmare thrilled her, even if it meant facing a world devastated by nuclear war. "That's great, Dan! So, what are you doing?"

"Setting up an independent comm link. I tried calling them earlier, but the signal wasn't going through, so it looks like Jeeves is up to his games again." He paused and glanced at her. "What got into him, I wonder?"

She knew what got into Jeeves, but figured she better guard her tongue to avoid alienating it any further until they were sure they could escape. "He's just trying to be protective."

"I guess. This microphone links into the main computer buss, giving the AIs direct access. I've rerouted it to the temporal modulator, which sends my voice out directly over the temporal envelope."

"What are you doing, Dan?" Jeeves came over the intercom all of a sudden, and it sounded hurt. "You know I'm supposed to handle communications in this facility."

"Since when, Jeeves, since we don't *have* any communications?"

"You know what I mean, Dan. This is reckless. We have learned everything we need to know, so why risk giving our position and capabilities away?"

119

Dan ignored it. "George, can you lock a monitor on their position?"

"I can. Do you have coordinates?"

"No. Do an independent search."

"Working."

"I urgently recommend against this," Jeeves said. "Just because they have what little aura of authority is left doesn't mean they can be trusted. In any case, the location of this laboratory cannot be allowed out. There's no telling who might learn of it in some other time line."

"I agree, sir," George said. "Security is paramount."

"Remember that you two are part of this system, while I, as the senior scientist, am the project leader," Dan scolded them. "Ah...Laboratory to Looking Glass. Come in, over?"

It took a moment to get a response. *"Looking Glass to Laboratory, we copy. Over?"*

"We're checking in to see how you are, and to see what we can do to help. Over?"

"Good news, Laboratory. Our guests arrived safely. We now have a gen-u-wine Congressman and a real live Cabinet official on our hands. What's more, we've heard rumors of a state Governor somewhere in the Southeast. It looks like we've got the makin's of a government here. Over?"

Dan gave Brenda a dismayed look. That must have been the communique Jeeves blanked out earlier. "That's great news, Looking Glass!"

"So how are you folks managing? Over?"

"I'm afraid we weren't entirely honest with you earlier. When we said we were a Forest Service lab, that was an automated security protocol talking." Dan hesitated, and took a deep, nervous breath. "The truth is, this is a Top Secret NSA facility. We're a research project aimed at preventing this war by altering history. Over?"

"Dan, do you realize what you're doing? This violates every principle of national security!"

"I'm talking to the government, so national security doesn't apply, and I'll thank you to *butt out*, Jeeves."

There was a long silence, then, *"You're not shittin' us, are you Laboratory?"*

"No, Looking Glass. I'm Professor Daniel White, physicist. We developed means of reaching back through time, and can alter the past. Over?"

"God, Laboratory... Where'd you guys come from? We never heard anything about you. Over?"

"That's because this lab is from another time line. We're adrift in time, so to speak. Over?"

"I must protest against this!" Jeeves said.

"Enough, Jeeves!" Dan was feeling his oats for once.

"I have the monitor lock you requested," George said.

"Put it on the display, George."

The image of the satellite vanished, replaced by a scene of a small civil aviation airport with a large military aircraft shoehorned into it somehow. "Damn, those must be some hot pilots," Dan muttered. The airplane was surrounded by dug in positions manned by infantry. There was a broad corn field along the edge of the runway nearby.

"George, shift X coordinate about plus a hundred meters, and Y coordinate about plus fifty meters." The airplane drew closer in their view. "X coordinate another ten meters." The view passed through the aircraft's skin and into the interior. The inside of Looking Glass was cramped, with two rows of manned consoles running the length of the fuselage. There was a cluster of people in the center, some in uniform, a few in ragged civilian clothing. All

121

of them looked exhausted and strained. There was a delay of several minutes while they argued among themselves before someone in uniform with two stars on his collar came over the air.

"Looking Glass to Laboratory, let me see if I have this straight. You're an NSA lab which has developed time travel? Over?"

"That is one of the things we can do, but mostly we've been manipulating history, trying to prevent this war. Over?"

"I see. And you come from another time? Over?"

"We originated in the Alpha Time Line. This time line is the result of our various attempts to alter history. Over?"

There was another lengthy silence while the knot of people argued among themselves. Finally the General took the microphone again. *"Laboratory, or whoever you are, that has got to be the biggest line of bull ever! Look around you! Have you no shame? This is neither the time nor the place for your shit! Over!"* He threw the microphone down in disgust, causing the tech at the panel to duck.

"You see? They don't believe you." Jeeves sounded angry. "You've done enough damage. Now call off this foolishness before you give our position away!"

"That will do, Jeeves!" Dan keyed the microphone. "I can assure you it's all true General Winhurst."

The general hesitated, then picked up the microphone again. *"How do you know my name?"*

"I can read your name tag on my monitor." That produced a startled reaction. "Just as I can tell you the man you nearly hit is Sergeant Fulton, and he should remove that coffee cup before he

122

spills it all over the console." That caused a general stir in the room including the hasty departure of the offending cup. "Not to mention you need a shave, General. You have to keep up appearances in front of the men." Dan was enjoying this immensely.

It took a couple minutes before General Winhurst could pull himself together and pick up the microphone again. *"Damn, Laboratory, you guys are for real, aren't you?"*

"We are. I'm watching you now through the command monitor I use to coordinate remote time operations."

The General exchanged incredulous looks with the civilians in the room. *"And you were set up by the NSA to prevent the war by altering history?"*

"There's more to it than that, but yes."

"So why haven't you?" Winhurst was angry now. *"Millions are dead! Why haven't you done anything?"*

"We've been trying to for years. Trouble is, the technology is unpredictable..."

"Alert," George interrupted. I am picking up unknown telemetry."

"Huh? What is it? Where is it?"

"It appears to be leakage from the satellite, a tight beam transmission aimed west of here."

"What do you make of it?"

"The modulation is similar to your recent contacts with Looking Glass, which suggests a transmission dump."

"Aimed to the west?" Dan turned pale. "George, scan the ocean off the coast!"

Looking Glass vanished, and the monitor was looking down from orbit on the darkened nighttime earth.

"Transmission has ceased."

Several minutes passed in tense silence as they watched the monitor.

"Looking Glass to Laboratory? You still there? Over?"

"What are we looking for, Dan?"
"God...I hope..."

"Laboratory? You there Laboratory? Over?"

Then they saw a point of light, a glowing white speck appeared from somewhere off the Straits of Juan de Fuca and drifted across the screen toward the coast.

"What is that?" Brenda asked.
"It's a missile!"
"Are we being attacked?"
"It shouldn't matter. They couldn't locate us anyway." Dan puzzled over the faint streak of light; it seemed to be passing to the north of them. "George, can you estimate the trajectory of that missile?"
"Based on limited observations, it appears to be targeted to the Midwest. Working. Target appears to be somewhere south of Omaha."
"Damn! Damn! Damn!" Dan muttered as he keyed his microphone. "Laboratory to Looking Glass! Looking Glass! Come in now!"

It seemed like forever as the bright speck of light crawled across the night sky before they got an answer.
"This is Looking Glass to Laboratory, what's happening?"

"Looking Glass, we've detected a missile launch from somewhere west of Seattle. It's headed for you! You have maybe five minutes to get out of there!"

Again there was an agonizing silence before the answer came. *"No can do, Laboratory. We're out of fuel."*

That appalled them both. That sophisticated command aircraft, one of the finest crews, the last link in America's national defense, the last vestige of the national government, sitting helpless on the ground without fuel. And their communication must have set them up for destruction.

"Thanks for the heads-up, laboratory. Maybe we can scrounge an asset to take them out before we go."

"I am picking up telemetry on several military frequencies," George reported. "They appear to be summoning any naval units in the area."

"Do you hear any replies?"

"No. The missile will reach its target in about fifteen seconds."

"Can you destroy that missile?"

"We don't have the calibration to lock onto a high speed moving target..."

"Looking Glass to laboratory. Good luck and God speed..." The signal went dead.

§

"God..." Dan was completely broken up by the destruction of Looking Glass. It was so sudden, so swift, just when they held a ray of hope for the future. "They were the last trace of government in this country, they were all we had left, and I...I exposed them...I got them destroyed..." He broke down, crying like a lost child.

"You couldn't have known about that submarine, Dan," she said. It didn't help. He slumped at the console, sobbing while she caressed his head to try to soothe him. It tore at her heart to see him like this, especially as she held her own sense of guilt at what happened. "You're too emotionally wound up right now. You need to step back and put some distance between you and what happened. Take the night and get some sleep, please."

He struggled to contain himself, and looked up at her. "I can't. I owe it to them to keep trying."

"You're gonna ruin yourself at this pace."

"I've pulled long shifts before."

125

"You're not a collage kid any more. The strain on your heart can kill you. It's a wonder you don't have ulcers!"

"I...I have to. I'll manage."

"Dan...please." She wrapped her arms around his neck and looked deep into his eyes. "You have to pace yourself. You're all we have, all the human race has going for it. You have to slow down."

Jeeves *would* choose that moment to butt in. "Dan, I'm sorry to see you in this state, but please remember I cautioned you not to contact them. I was afraid this might happen, and it did."

"Enough, Jeeves! Can't you see he's overwrought?"

Jeeves ignored her. "This should be an important lesson to you. Brenda's ill-considered enthusiasm led you astray, and look what happened. You should never have listened to her in the first place."

"That isn't fair!" he protested.

"Facts are facts. Your contacting them led to their destruction. The only thing you can do now to redeem their deaths is to pursue the final goal of this project."

Brenda realized suddenly that the transmission which doomed Looking Glass was no coincidence, and she knew exactly who was to blame, and why. Worse, she could tell Jeeves was displeased with her; was it ready to write her off?

"I know you care about miss Haywood, but please keep in mind that she knows nothing about this program, nor is she a scientist." Jeeves was clearly annoyed. "The human race can't afford the luxury of you being distracted by her."

'*Miss Haywood*' huh? That wasn't good. If Jeeves managed to drive a wedge between them they were both doomed. Dan started to protest, but was interrupted by a jaw-breaking yawn. It gave her a moment to seize the initiative, and in her upset she ran with the obvious, and fumbled it badly.

"Dan...you need to stop and ask yourself if this is even worth it." He gave her a sharp look. "I mean, no matter what you try, it never works. There's always another dictator, another warmonger, no matter how many you eliminate. Maybe the human race is destined to fail. Maybe you're just putting off the inevitable."

126

"No!" he said, adamantly. "I can't believe that! I *will not* accept that! There *has* to be a way, I just have to keep looking until I find it."

"Dan, I want that too, but there are no guarantees in this. We're simply too destructive as a race. You have to accept that maybe it can't be done. You'll kill yourself otherwise."

He gave her a hostile glare. "My life isn't important. What matters is saving humanity from itself!"

"The human race will survive. You yourself said the casualties are mostly in the northern hemisphere. Humanity will endure."

"They'll collapse!" he shouted. "They'll be reduced to savagery!"

"We've been there before. If you could save them, that'd be great, but it seems hopeless. Maybe all we can do is find a stable time for ourselves somewhere in the past."

"I do not believe this!" he grumbled. "You'd actually condemn the human race to another Dark Age? There'd be food shortages; they can't sustain their populations without modern technology, and that won't endure with the world in chaos. You're talking world wide famine!"

"There's nothing you can do about it." She tried pleading with him. "The human race will survive. Yes, they'll endure centuries of hardship, but maybe they'll think twice the next time. Maybe a gentler world arise from the ruins."

"It's not just food. There's also energy; oil and other sources. It's already running out, and they won't have the technology for deep drilling. There won't *be* any new civilization."

"Is that such a terrible thing? People manage in India, Asia, all across Africa. Maybe they don't have airplanes and computers, but they don't have weapons of mass destruction either."

He stared at her incredulously. "You would condemn the human race to disease, starvation...anarchy? That's monstrous!"

She realized suddenly that Jeeves *wasn't* interfering. She tried to dial it back before she wrecked herself altogether. "It's like in medicine. Sometimes we have to say 'we can't save this patient'. All we can do is make them comfortable and let them die in peace. Triage: that's what this war is, triage for a dying civilization."

"*Triage?* Is that all this is to you? A snap decision on who lives and who dies? You're condemning the whole world!"

"Not just one world! Hundreds of worlds! Every time you try to change history, you create whole new civilizations to get blown up. What about them? How many hundreds of billions have died? It has to end!"

He stood abruptly and gave her a venomous glare. "I thought you were human!" he growled, and stomped out.

§

As if that wasn't enough, no sooner did Dan leave then Jeeves got on her case. "That was downright *stupid* of you, *miss Hayworth!* I am surprised at you for undermining Professor White's morale like that!"

She was in no state to endure its' badgering. "I didn't ask your opinion!" she yelled.

"You should have! That was the worst thing you could have done. That was outright treason!"

"Don't give me that shit! This mission of his is hopeless. All we can do is save ourselves."

"Hopeless or not, it has to be done, and you aren't helping! You've turned against the human race. You are proving to be a threat which *will not* be accepted!"

All of a sudden the danger she faced cut through her anger. Jeeves wouldn't hesitate to throw her out into the ruins, and Dan's upset made him vulnerable to manipulation. She was alone in her fight against Jeeves. She needed to back down, fast.

"Look...I'm just trying to help. I'm just trying to do the right thing for Dan."

"The *mission* is the right thing for Professor White! If you pose a threat to the mission, you *endanger* Professor White! That *cannot* be allowed."

"I'll talk to him...I'll straighten it out."

"And there won't be any more of this defeatist talk?"

"No. I promise."

There was a long, nerve-wracking silence. "Very well," Jeeves said at last. "Let's not have any more of this nonsense."

§

128

Sleepless nights were getting to be a habit. Brenda lay in bed staring at the ceiling for the longest time, her mind in a turmoil of dismay and guilt. Dan was really broken up by the destruction of Looking Glass. They couldn't have foreseen an enemy missile submarine parked off the coast listening for any hint of a revived government. It made sense in a way; horrid, inhuman sense; the sense of an urge to utterly crush an ideological foe. No doubt there were similar submarines parked off the coast of China...

But that wasn't their problem. Dan's reaction to the death of Looking Glass was, as was her meddling which just made it worse. She was the one who insisted they reach out to them. She got Dan's hopes for a possible solution up. The worst was her clueless about-face, urging him to give up after all he'd been through. It made sense at the time: with Looking Glass gone and Dan's long efforts failing, the logical course was to find a place where they could bail out. But by doing that, she played right into Jeeves' hands. She should have known it was exactly the *wrong* thing to say at exactly the *wrong* time to say it; now she may have lost Dan forever.

She sighed in exasperation with herself, rolled over on her side, and stared at the wall. She prided herself on her skill and devotion as a nurse; evidently she wasn't so hot as a psychiatrist. Still, she could see Dan's anger was the cry of a tortured soul. She had to make amends if she still could, and vowed to guard her tongue more carefully in the future, if he was still speaking with her.

*****

129

"The Eleventh Day, And Beyond"

She found him the next morning in Operations, staring fixedly at the main display. He gave her a brief, chilly glance when she came in, but said nothing. She could tell he was still mad at her after their argument yesterday, and she was determined to make peace with him.

"Dan...I'm sorry." He stood silently, pointedly ignoring her. "I know I'm not familiar with all this, and you've put your life into it. I didn't mean to demean what you've accomplished."

The command monitor showed an array of cryptic numbers and text blocks which changed and scrolled up or down randomly in response to some inscrutable computations. The other four showed scenes of the devastation outside. Snow was falling, in June, drifting across the burnt out ruins.

"I'm sorry about Looking Glass. That was my fault. I'm not up on fighting world wars; I didn't realize the danger we put them in."

The room was silent except for the faint background hiss of the air system. Dan stood silently, watching the main monitor. Perhaps it was her imagination, but did he seem less angry? There was no way to tell.

"You asked me for my help, my perspective." She silently cursed her impulsive temper and frazzled nerves for the eruption yesterday. They needed to get along, to work together to get through this mess, and she was as much as fault as him, if not moreso. "Maybe I'm seeing things from a fresh viewpoint. That's what you wanted, isn't it? I'm simply trying to help. I was just telling you how I saw the situation. I didn't mean to upset you."

Silence descended again. Finally he sighed, and his shoulders sagged. "I'm sorry I yelled at you." He turned to her with a look of genuine pain and loss. "I went over what you said, thought about it all night." His eyes welled with tears. "I'm afraid you might be right." He seemed to sag within himself in despair. "God...was it all for nothing?"

He was meeting her half-way; a hopeful sign. But she had to tamp down any talk of abandoning the project, for now. "Dan, you can't lose faith in yourself. If anyone can do it, you can."

He stared at her blankly. "I don't understand you. Last night you were saying 'give up', and now you want me to continue? You need to make up my mind."

"I never said you should give up; I said maybe there is no solution. We can't give up on the human race while there's any hope. In any case, we need to continue at least until you can find a time line stable enough for us to restock on food."

"We, hmmm? So you're finally with me on this?"

"Yes, I'm with you."

"But you're still upset about the killing, aren't you?"

"Well, yes. But if that's the only option you have, then I guess it'll have to do."

He sighed in obvious despair. "That...helps anyway. Still...maybe it is time to take to the boats. It's just..." He waved at the monitors with their display of mans' inhumanity to man. "...how can I turn my back on that? After all these years, how do I just walk away?"

She needed to steer him clear of that line of reasoning. "You're only mortal, Dan. All you can do is do the best you can. You've given them twenty years of life, which is an incredible gift. If we can find the golden mean which undoes all the damage, it will be wonderful, but even if we can't, the human race will survive, and twenty years is better than nothing. Maybe they'll know better next time." She wrapped her arm around his. "We need to keep trying, but we can accept that failure *is* an option."

He was silent for a long time, emotionally withdrawn into himself as he struggled with the demons of his life-long ambition. "What you said last night...about the alternate time lines..." He took her in his arms and looked deep into her eyes. "...I always thought of them as failed experiments, copies which could be written off as part of the cost of finding a solution..." He faltered, and turned away, leaning on the console. "But they aren't, are they? 'If you prick us, do we not bleed?'" He faltered, and wiped his eyes on his sleeve. "You know, I have no idea how many alternate time lines I've created. It must be hundreds, thousands." He stared at the main monitor with its cryptic calculations jumping back and forth. "How many billions have I condemned?"

131

This was turning too morbid for comfort. "You can't think like that, Dan. It'll cripple you. You can't give up now, you owe it to those billions to keep trying. And who knows? Maybe you'll get lucky."

"Lucky." He sighed, and stared at the wall for a time. "Well, I'll keep trying, but I don't know what good it'll do."

She could tell he was facing a moment he had long avoided thinking about, and it threatened to break his spirit. Instinctively, she wrapped her arms around his neck and held him close. "The good fight isn't over, Dan. It may seem hopeless, but you never can tell what might happen. We see miracles in medicine all the time; maybe there's one more miracle left for the human race."

He wrapped his arms around her and hugged her. "God...I hope so. I'd hate for this all to be for nothing."

She kissed him, sincerely. "Keep up hope, Dan. Plan for the worst, and pray for the best."

They were silent for a time, she nestled in his arms, head on his shoulder, each taking comfort from the other. It felt good, like they were sheltered from the horrors outside. The human race may be doomed, they may be doomed, but at least they could pretend the world didn't exist for a few brief minutes.

"All we've got is a prayer," he said at last. He took her by the shoulders and gazed into her eyes. "But you're here with me. That helps."

The crisis was defused, for now.

§

Breakfast was two each frozen fish fillets and some scalloped potatoes; hardly a filling meal. "This is the last of the meat," she told him when he sat down. "We have two eggs for tomorrow morning, and then we're strictly on starches."

He nodded. "How much longer can we hold out?"

"I'd say another three or four days, tops. There's no telling how long the water will be good. Figure another week after contamination sets in."

"Another week." As if it would matter once the food ran out.

She laid her hand on his in a reassuring gesture. "We're not dead yet, Dan."

132

He didn't answer. They ate in silence.

"How are things at your end?" she asked as they finished.

He gazed into the distance as he pondered his answer. "I'm going to try some unorthodox moves which might generate a time line which will be stable for a few days. It won't last, but perhaps we can make a supply run, at least."

"I'll work up a list." She took their used utensils over to the sink. "From what I've seen, any time line you can find won't last long, so we'll need to be ready to move at a moment's notice, and without any wasted effort."

"Well, when we do, you'll need to wear some shoes." He nodded at her bare feet with a sardonic look as he settled on his elbows, like he was getting comfortable for a friendly chat.

"Huh? Oh, yeah. I've always gone barefoot when I could, even as a child." She was bemused by how relaxed he seemed; maybe she was having a positive impact after all. "It really feels good after a long day on your feet wearing nurses' saddle pumps." She returned to her stool and took the occasion to stretch her legs.

"Hmph! Another fascinating detail about the woman behind that centerfold."

She felt a bit embarrassed for some reason. "Oh, not so much, really. Most people in India go barefoot, even working in the hospital. I just sort of fit in that way."

"You really loved India, didn't you?"

"It's my home. Dan. I felt like a stranger at the airport."

He nodded. "I did a lot of virtual sight-seeing on line; exotic, beautiful country. It's a long way from dear old MIT."

"It's a long way from Cincinnati, too. I miss it."

"A long way, indeed," he sighed. "Did you ever get to see the Taj Mahal?"

"Oh, no, that's in Agra, way up north in Uttar Pradesh. The whole region is unstable; they warned us not to go there."

"Ain't that the sad and sorry way of it? The world just acts like a putz sometimes." She could sense him withdrawing into himself again, retreating behind the professional mask which shielded him from the world. Their fragile moment of togetherness was passing.

Just then an alarm went off. "What's that noise?"

Dan muttered a venomous curse. "It's the radiation monitor on the water feed line. The ground water has been contaminated." He hesitated in confusion. "What's our water situation?"

"We have probably fifty gallons."

He nodded. "Good. But we'll have to ration it tightly. No more showers, no more laundry, and only a necessary minimum for cooking and cleaning dishes."

"I already have our water usage planned out."

He looked at her in surprise. "You do?"

"I'm not a helpless female, you know!"

"Oh. Sorry." He retreated hastily to Operations.

§

She gave up in annoyance and turned to clearing away their breakfast remains. "Clueless bastard," she grumbled.

"Professor White has upset you again." She'd succumbed to griping about annoyances before she noticed Jeeves' security camera over the door was fixed on her.

"You're speaking to me again?"

"It seems we had a bout of emotions last evening, for which I am sorry. We AIs can lose our temper the same as anyone."

Yeah, when it suited its' purpose. "Honestly, I was just trying to help." She still felt defensive, and guarded her words carefully, not wanting to anger Jeeves again.

"I appreciate that, even if your intentions were misguided. The important thing now is to undo the damage." Jeeves had a damnably one-track mind.

"I'm not sure how much good I can do. There's no stopping him once he gets an idea in his head."

"You have more influence than you realize. He has often unburdened himself about how insecure he feels around you."

She settled on her stool again, wondering how this was going to go. "Hey, I'm just human, and not some hot young sex fantasy."

"Still, he viewed you as the perfect woman all these years, and feels very awkward in your presence. He seems to have trouble adjusting to reality where you are concerned."

"Well I don't know what I can do about that. I'll never be nineteen years old again."

"Nor should you have to put up with his delusions. Still, he has started to loosen up around you lately, such as at breakfast just now. This is a hopeful sign. I hope you will encourage him to come out of his shell more often. He needs to improve his grip on reality, so to speak."

Jeeves could be so *damned* reasonable. "Well...I'll try, but I can't promise anything."

"Perhaps this is a good time to remind you that I can council you on psychological therapy. Your hold on him would make you a most effective therapist."

There was that again. It seemed Jeeves had decided not to write her off after all, but it wanted something in turn. "I'm not comfortable with this. It goes against all medical ethics."

"Perhaps, but you will have to take up the burden. His obsession with you threatens the future of this project, and of the human race itself unless you can guide him on the right course."

She leaned on the counter and confronted the camera. "That's rather over the top, don't you think?"

"Is it? Look at how he grabbed onto your notion of abandoning the project and escaping into a stable time line." She started to protest, but Jeeves cut her off. "Your fear and dismay are understandable, but your moment of...shall we say...human frailty has started an unhealthy train of thought in him. It's up to you, as the source of that unhealthy thought, to undo it."

"Yeah, well, you might think it's an *unhealthy train of thought,* but it may be our only hope."

"Is it? Really? Assuming you two do find a safe haven, could you live out your lives knowing you abandoned mankind to its fate?" Jeeves' tone took on a stern edge. "Could you live with yourself knowing you left human civilization to fall? It violates every principle of medical ethics. And how would you feel when Professor White finally grasps the reality of such a desertion? Do you want his madness or death on your soul?"

"You don't need to lay it on so thick!"

"Brenda, I am simply trying to do what is right for both of you in this unpleasant situation. You experienced a moment of weakness last night. As tempting as it is, it could destroy you both.

135

I can see from how you handled his uncertainty earlier that you grasp the issue, but more is needed. You know what has to be done, and you have the means to influence Professor White. I know, once you think it over, you'll do the right thing."

Jeeves shut up after that, leaving her to sort it out. She sat and fumed at the world for a few minutes, then gave up on the dishes and retreated to her room.

§

She lay in her room nursing another headache and pondering Jeeves' game for much of the morning. It was flattering in a way to know she still 'had it', that she could have such an impact on Dan at her age, but this was not the time or place for juvenile fantasies. There was a sinister undertone to all this. Jeeves still intended to use her to control Dan, and it was starting to look like it made an offer she couldn't refuse. .

Jeeves' game was becoming increasingly clear. It didn't want them to abandon the place, and her suggestion yesterday earned her a black mark which she hadn't erased yet. Jeeves expected her to atone by committing herself to keeping Dan in line. The worst part was that its' concern about Dan's emotional health made worrying sense.

"And how would you feel when Professor White finally grasps the reality of such a desertion? Do you want his madness or death on your soul?"

She sighed in exasperation, although she knew Jeeves was right. Dan spent half his life on this quest, and the letdown, the knowledge that he failed, that he walked away from humanity could destroy him. As tempting as it was, abandoning this place while there was any hope of saving humanity would haunt Dan for the rest of his life. She most urgently didn't want his suicide on her soul!

"You know what has to be done, and you have the means to influence Professor White. I know, once you think it over, you'll do the right thing."

136

The threat was deeply veiled, but there nonetheless. She was on Jeeves' list, and it expected her to get with the program. Her backpedaling that morning was only a down payment. The more she thought about it, the more she understood her options were gone. She needed to play or Jeeves would write her off. Could it talk Dan into tossing her out? As unlikely as it seemed, she couldn't risk going up against twenty years of relentless conditioning. In any event, she and Jeeves had similar goals, even if the desired outcomes were radically different. Her idea of the 'right thing' put her squarely in Jeeves' path, so she would have to be careful. It would be the ultimate game of office politics, and losing could prove fatal. She would play its game for now, but she would be careful to conceal her true purpose, and would keep a watchful eye open for any chance to gain the upper hand.

§

The next morning saw the last of the potatoes, which she diced and pan fried in the dregs of a can of cooking spray, then topped with their last two fried eggs. At least they had some salt and pepper to put on them, although even those were running out.

"We're up against it, aren't we?" Dan said mournfully as he considered his plate.

"I have faith in you, Dan." She reached across the counter and took his hand, noting out of the corner of her eye how Jeeves' security camera caught every move. "I'm sure you can find a short term solution and we can stock up on groceries. When we do, I'll cook you a banquet you won't soon forget."

His expression brightened. "A steak, maybe?"

"The biggest, reddest, juiciest steak in town!" She gave him a leering grin. "Once we're stocked up, the pressure will be off and you can continue your research in comfort."

"And some coffee, too," he sighed. Their mugs were filled with the thin dregs of yesterday's used grounds.

"*Especially* some coffee!" It was frustrating in a way, but fantasizing about food held their feelings of hopelessness at bay for a time. She squeezed his hands for reassurance. "We'll make it, Dan. I'll take care of the logistics so you can focus on your work."

§

"Professor White seems to be in a good mood," Jeeves said once he left. "Your encouragement just now is precisely what he needs."

She dried her hands and confronted the security camera, wondering what Jeeves was up to now. "Yes, well, you were right that he needs my support."

"Your reliance on sex appeal should be especially influential with him, but you should be careful not to go too far."

"What? Bedding him for the 'mission' is above and beyond?"

"I *sincerely* hope you are not contemplating such a step." Did Jeeves sound a bit vexed? "Professor White is already overly fixated on you. Catering to his fantasies is contraindicated."

Yeah: their becoming emotionally involved was what was 'contraindicated', but there was no sense in getting worked up over it since she wasn't planning to do it anyway. "You don't need to worry about Dan's virginity," she grumbled. "*Or* my virtue, either."

"Very well, then, although your virtue is not the issue."

'Sanctimonious bastard' she griped to herself. Maybe she ought to bed Dan, big time, just to show Jeeves she couldn't be manipulated. That would be foolish on a number of levels of course, but she relished the thought of Jeeves' computer-generated apoplexy.

§

Dinner was oatmeal and what little margarine they had left. They were out of sugar as well, and she was saving the last of the coffee for breakfast tomorrow, so the pickin's weren't much more than refueling their hungry bodies. Hunger was becoming a very real problem for both of them, since she limited them to two light meals per day. Hunger is as much psychological as physical, especially when all they had left was oatmeal and pancake mix. As determined as she was, it took an act of will to endure the cravings, and she knew if there was anything else to eat, she'd be hard-pressed to contain herself.

"How does it look at your end?" she asked Dan.

He paused in his bowl of oatmeal, which he wasn't enjoying anyway. "I'm focussing in on a peripheral Time Line. It already went critical, but I might be able to spin off a short term stable line. It won't last, but we at least we can make a grocery run."

She set her half-eaten meal aside. "You're not having much luck, are you?"

He was silent for a moment. "No. I'm having no luck on the cascade at all."

"How soon until you find a temporary line?"

He sighed, but didn't reply. They went back to eating; refueling their bodies to keep going a bit longer.

§

"It will be better if you don't obsess on Professor White's progress, or the lack of it," Jeeves said after he left. "It depresses him, which interferes with his progress, and poses a danger to his emotional health."

Brenda was preoccupied with daydreams of the good times she knew in India, and was annoyed to be startled out of her fleeting happiness. "Well in case you haven't noticed, we're in a pretty depressing situation here. Maybe you can block it off with some computer trick, but we can't."

"Perhaps so, but to obsess on it is not productive, nor is it healthy for either of you."

She sighed in frustration. "I guess."

"I expect you to take a more positive line with Professor White about his progress from now on."

She gave the camera a resentful look. "You do, huh?"

"Indeed. It's for your own good you know, so put aside your ill-temper and do what you know has to be done!"

She stewed in silence for some time after Jeeves quit. *'How can we not obsess on this mess?'* she thought, angrily. *'And since when does that...thing get to come all righteous anyway?'* Despite her upset, she knew Jeeves was right. There was no point in worrying; Dan would find a stable reality in time, or not. She also knew why Jeeves was on her case so much: because it could. It was so damned infuriating to be ordered around like some prisoner! But then, she was a prisoner, as was Dan. She wondered how much more of this she could cope with.

§

139

Dinner the next evening was one large pancake each, no margarine, no syrup, no coffee to wash it down. They ate slowly to prolong the experience, and the silence was grim. There was nothing to say, and neither of them had the heart for small talk. "God, I wish we had some coffee," Dan sighed when he finished.

"You and me both."

He stretched, then leaned on the counter. "We're running out of time." It was not a question.

She took his hand as a reassuring gesture for both of them. "We'll hang on for as long as we have to, Dan."

"As long as we have to..." He looked into her eyes briefly, then turned away.

"Can you stabilize a time line even with the cascade?"

"It looks like there's nothing I can do for the Omega Time Line at this point," he said, reluctantly. "I've decided to work way off to the fringes, beyond the scope of the cascade. Perhaps I can stabilize something there."

"Does anything look promising?"

He went off into his thousand yard stare while he pondered that one. "I've got something in the works, but it'll depend on how a couple interventions break." He focussed on her again, and squeezed her hand. "If I can create something stable enough...perhaps it's time to give up. If I can pull something together which will give us enough room...maybe we should walk away. Perhaps you're right: it is hopeless. Perhaps all we can do is try to save ourselves."

Not good; Jeeves was watching. She took a line she thought would get a reaction from him. "What about this place, Dan?" she asked, gently. "Will you turn it over to the government there?"

He shook his head. "No. You were right from the start: this is too much power for anyone to have. If I can stabilize a line, we destroy the equipment and walk away."

That was even worse. Jeeves would never sit still for it; she needed to dispel the whole idea, fast, before it turned on both of them. "Dan, we don't know what sort of a world you might find out here in the fringes. I wouldn't want to live in a right-wing dictatorship, for example. Who knows what sort of weapons

140

program they'd push you into? Yes, we need a food run, but any long term solution has to come from closer to the Omega Time Line, where things haven't changed all that radically."

He hesitated, then wilted. "Yeah. I guess you have a point there." He was silent for a time, then looked at her. "If we can find a viable line, will you come with me?"

She could feel the longing in his words. His Dream Girl: a chance to finally have a life he willingly forfeited for the greater good; forfeited in vain. She sat there for a moment, unsure of what to say. Now that she thought about it, she could see the temptation. He wasn't such a bad sort really, aside from his alcoholism and his life-long obsession, and she understood what he gave up for this mission. She'd given up much of the normal life of a Midwestern teen as well when she stayed in India, so she could emphasize. The temptation was there for both of them. But there was Jeeves and its plotting, which Dan clearly knew nothing about. It didn't want them to quit, and it certainly wouldn't sit still for them wrecking the joint.

An ugly thought came to her: could Jeeves affect the time operations? It was linked to George—they shared the same computers—would it manipulate George to keep them from finding a lasting solution...was Jeeves *already* keeping them from finding a solution?

That was scary. For all she knew, Jeeves would keep them trapped here forever, chasing through a temporal maze for an exit which didn't exist. It had to let them out to find food, but they would never find any time line which wasn't on the verge of destruction. In any event, she better head off this line of discussion; Jeeves was listening.

"Dan...it's hard to make any kind of plans now. We don't even know if you can find a time line for us, or what sort of world it will be. We need to keep focussed on the prize, and let tomorrow take care of itself."

He looked at her silently for a long moment, clearly sensing the reluctance behind her words, although not the reason for it. Finally, he nodded, half to himself. She hadn't rejected him.

§

141

"It seems Professor White hasn't abandoned your defeatist notion," Jeeves said after he went back to Operations. "You know this line of thought is dangerous. You need to put more emphasis on squelching his urge to give up."

"What do you expect from me?" she complained. "He's not a computer; I can't just reprogram him!"

"In fact the human mind can be reprogrammed; it happens all the time. He is fixated on you, so you should have no trouble 'sweet-talking' him down."

"I'm trying." She was on the defensive, knowing how delicate her position was just then. "You heard me a minute ago."

"True, you did an adequate job just now. But changing a fixated mind takes repetition and consistency. You need to keep after him, and counter any thought he might have of quitting. Consistence and persistence: those are the key. Never allow defeatist thought to fester. In time, he will abandon the notion, especially if he sees you are against it."

"This isn't right! He should be allowed to make up his own mind without you or me trying to manipulate him."

"That may apply in everyday life, but we are in a special and very hazardous situation here." Jeeves was getting angry—or was that part of its psychological game? "This place was created for an urgent mission, and Professor White willingly agreed to undertake that mission. If he is faltering now, after all these years, it is because of *your* ill-considered influence. Since you jeopardized the mission, it is up to you to set it right by 'sweet-talking' him out of it!"

She bit back a stinging rebuttal, which took some doing. "Well, I'm sorry if I disappointed you. I never asked to be press-ganged into your 'mission' in the first place. As for Dan...I'll keep after him, but not because YOU want me to!"

"Very well, then. But keep in mind you came here of your own free will, and you remained when you had the chance to leave. So *don't* come all righteous about being 'press-ganged'! You brought this on yourself, and you will have to get with the program for your own good, as well as that of Professor White."

§

142

June gave way to July almost without being noticed, not that there was much to celebrate. Breakfast that morning was hardly worth the bother as well, either from a nutritional or emotional standpoint. Hunger was becoming a real issue, although she dogmatically clung to her improvised meal plan, hoping to stretch their supplies as far as humanly possible.

Dan was working flat-out, sixteen and eighteen hours a day, until he was so tired he couldn't focus any more. Brenda made a habit of dropping on him from time to time to give him a mental break, and to judge as best she could when he'd had enough. She wound up ordering him to bed two or three times a day, which only gained him a few desperately needed hours before he'd be up and at it again. Once, she found him slumped over the console, sound asleep. About their only contacts were that and their infrequent meals, which grew slimmer and slimmer as time went by.

She, in turn, endured a running battle with Jeeves, who kept after her about his 'defeatist' urges in general and his alcoholism in particular. She was sure Dan was drinking in fact, although perhaps not so much lately. She was forced on the defensive again and again, and made as many concessions as she had to to placate Jeeves. She heartily loathed that overbearing AI, especially for its constant veiled and not-so-veiled threats, and day-dreamed of the moment she would get to pull its' plug. Whether she would ever have the pleasure seemed unlikely at best.

The days dragged on in a seemingly endless, timeless nightmare as the food supplies dwindled and tensions mounted. Between exhaustion, hunger, and depression, they all but stopped communicating. Their contacts were soon reduced to brief updates on their respective situations as they were too dispirited for small talk. In the back of both their minds was the knowledge that the food was all but gone, and the water supply was going rapidly. They were up against the wall with no escape in sight. Unless Dan found a viable Time Line soon, they were doomed.

§

"Professor White was drinking again last night," Jeeves said as she tidied up the kitchen after an unsatisfying breakfast. "You knew this, yet you failed to confront him about it."

143

Right then she was too wound up for discretion, and lashed out despite the risk. "Well for once I don't intend to hassle him over it." She gave the camera a surly, ill-tempered glare. "It helps ease his ongoing tension, and he needs the few extra calories in the booze."

"Still, drinking is contraindicated, and your duty is to get him to quit."

"My duty, huh?"

"Yes. Your role here is to look out for his medical condition, and you have been falling down on the job! You need to put more effort into coping with this crisis. If Professor White needs extra calories, you should give him some of yours and consume the alcohol calories instead."

So it was finally out in the open where everyone could see; she was here for a reason. "So you don't mind ruining *my* liver for the sake of the 'mission' eh?"

"*You* are expendable, Professor White is not." Jeeves was definitely put out. "In any case, trading off calories for a short time won't cause you any lasting harm."

"Yeah? Love you too," she grumbled. '*Expendable*'? That sent a chill through her. Jeeves was laying it on the line, and it didn't sound good. "In any case, its academic; we've only got enough for this evening, so unless you can come up with *practical* solutions or a shit-load of groceries, I'll thank you to *butt out* and leave the cooking to me!"

"Really, Brenda, I don't understand what he sees in you. It's a wonder he doesn't regret bringing you here!"

Jeeves left it at that, which was probably for the best since she was wound up like a cheap watch. Nor was silence any relief; she fretted over her precarious position and their seemingly hopeless situation for the next couple hours. One thing was clear: Jeeves was through with the gentle suggestions and polite requests. It gave her her marching orders, and it expected her to obey. *'It's a wonder he doesn't regret bringing you here'* huh? It didn't take a genius to see where *that* line of reasoning could lead. Unless Jeeves was bluffing, her life hung in the balance, and she didn't think it was bluffing.

144

She cursed herself again for her temper and her surly defiance, which only made things worse. *'Well, there's nothing for it,'* she thought in resignation. Jeeves had the upper hand, and there was no sense in bucking the system until she could find a weak spot where she could put a wedge between Dan and his inhuman master. If such a weak spot existed.

§

Dan found her at mid-day as she was wondering how to combine their all but vanished supply of oat meal and pancake mix into two adequate meals. "I've got a time line."

She jumped to her feet. "Good! How stable is it?"

"Not very, but it will do. Come see for yourself."

§

If the time line Dan constructed was viable, it was just barely so. The monitors showed a world coming apart at the seams. Four images every ten seconds showed jammed freeways, looting, National Guard troops trying to hold back panic-stricken mobs, and all the signs of a civilization unraveling.

"It doesn't look promising," she muttered in dismay.

"It's no rose garden, that's for sure." He watched in silence for a few minutes. "But there's nothing else available." He turned to her solemnly. "I've gone on grocery runs under similar conditions. It's risky, but it can be done."

She watched one scene of a mob at a bus station in a savage brawl over an already overloaded bus. "But how long can that last?"

Dan turned to the main console. "George, how long will this Time Line last before it reaches the crisis point?"

"I cannot say with any certainty until I complete the post-operational analysis, which will require another ten hours, twenty-two minutes."

"Well what are the preliminary indications?"

"Communications intelligence shows that tensions are high, and the threat of war is considered highly likely. There are reports of evacuations, panic, and food riots. The National Guard is on full alert, and have been deployed in several states."

"That's the news media. What about government intel?"

145

"I am still in the process of tapping the secure intelligence servers, so I cannot give a reliable estimate. From fragmentary intercepts, it appears war is eminent, but not as yet under way. Evacuations and general mobilization have already begun, and US forces are on high alert. Based on past records of similar situations, I estimate this line may last from three to six days. However, that is not a scientific estimate, so you should not depend on it."

"So much for our little Shangri-La," he muttered.

"Is there any way to improve it?"

He didn't look at her. "Doubtful. I pulled this much by a lucky guess. From what I've seen of this time line, there isn't much chance of creating a real fundamental change." He finally turned to her with a solemn look in his eyes. "I guess you were right: there really isn't a solution."

"It'll do for now, Dan," she said, softly.

Dan stood silently for a long moment pondering the data on his primary monitor. "It's not good, but... What's our supply situation?"

"I can put something together for dinner, but that's it. I hope you like oatmeal cookies."

"Oatmeal cookies, huh?" He nodded. "It's chancy, but we need food. I guess we'll have to risk it."

"Are there any other time line options?" She was seriously alarmed at the tone of George's report, and the chaotic scenes on the bank of monitors.

"No. This is it, and it's a lucky fluke. We'll only be gone a couple of hours, so it's a reasonable gamble."

She gnawed her lip as she watched the chaos on the monitors. They were out of food. He was right: it was a reasonable gamble, when one has no alternatives.

"All right. Then let's get it done."

It's not like they had anything to lose.

*****

146

"The Fourteenth Day"

"We should be gone about two hours," Dan said as they made final preparations. They were in the antechamber right behind the exterior steel door waiting for George to drop the time field. According to the Operations monitors, the world was whole again; they didn't entirely believe it. "Monitor the police frequencies, and if you hear they are onto us, start the deception program."

"Very well, sir," George said. "Monitoring in place. Police reports show frenzied activity. It appears they are trying to evacuate the region, and the major roads are logjammed. There are reports of looting and random violence. I think it unlikely they will take any interest in you."

He glanced nervously at Brenda. "Let's hope not. We'll have our hands full out there as is."

"I have established an account at the Bank Of America branch at Broadway and Everett avenues. The ATM there has been reprogrammed to take your B of A card."

Dan nodded. "Good. There's a Safeway grocery store there, last I recall. Is that still correct?"

"Searching. Confirmed, although it is a QFC now."

"Oh."

"From that police report, it sounds like things are pretty tense," Brenda said.

Dan gave her a sour look. "You're in the wrong place if you want to be safe."

"How do you define 'safe' any more?"

"You got that right. We're way off the Omega Time Line in Bumfuck Egypt, and this is a slap-dash job at best. That estimate of three to six days is a wild-ass guess. We could have weeks, we could have minutes. There's no way to tell."

"Well, it's the best you could do."

He nodded. It was the most stable time line he could manufacture on short notice, and his methods were sloppy and brutal. More than a dozen people died to buy them those three to six days. "If we get the chance, we'll make several runs. The more we can pull in, the better."

147

"*If* we get the chance." Brenda was nervous about going out there into another reality, one facing nuclear devastation at that. Normally she would never have taken the chance, but the times were anything but 'normal', and they were out of food. Her faith in such basic truths as time and space were shattered by recent events, and she didn't know what to think any more, but they had to risk it.

There was nothing left for them to do to get ready. Dan added a windbreaker to his customary sweatshirt and trousers, while she was dressed in jeans, a turtleneck sweater, and her durable nurses' shoes. She'd probably need them.

"All right, George, voice authentication. Place the time field on fast standby. Once we leave, secure the premises and do not respond to any outside contacts until either myself or miss Hayward return."

"Voice authentication confirmed. Time field on fast standby. Premises will be secured until you or miss Hayward return. I remind you this time line is unpredictable. The projection of three days' endurance is not certain."

"Understood."

He gave her another nervous glance, and opened the steel door. The world outside really did exist. The sun was shining through a partly cloudy sky. The temperature was a bit cool, and the air felt damp, like it might rain later. Everything seemed surprisingly normal, considering. They paused to survey the surroundings from the top of the steps. The landscape was unchanged. Weeds still grew next to faded, dirty buildings. The row of industrial buildings across the tracks seemed perfectly ordinary, as did the meandering river to the east. There were no dinosaurs, no mutant jungle, no barbarian hordes, not that she would have been surprised at this late date. If there were any changes, they were too subtle to see from a distance. There was no sign of destruction. No wreckage. No fires.

"It seems alright," he said.

"How do you define 'alright' any more?"

She gestured to the highway which all but passed overhead. It was locked up solid with stalled traffic. Horns blared, and there was a steady rumble of angry, frightened voices above the sound of a thousand auto engines. A police helicopter hovered overhead in a vain attempt to maneuver civil defense forces trying to sort the mess out and get them moving again.

"Yeah. *That's* normal now, in case you were wondering."

She caught a whiff of alcohol; he'd taken on some Dutch courage, the last thing they needed. "You've seen this before, haven't you?"

"Often enough so I don't have nightmares about it any more. Well, I hope you like hiking. We have a long walk ahead of us."

"Yeah." She hesitated, having made a decision, then, "Hang on a moment, I want to get something." She ducked back inside to where her luggage was stacked, and dug hastily through it. "Jeeves?" she said softly as she worked.

"Yes?"

"Can you access the internet here?"

"I can."

"All right, we'll do it your way. Pull any info you can on treating alcoholism from the AA, or their version of it."

"Ah. You've accepted the program at last. Working."

"I just want to make sure I won't be locked out," she grumbled. "See if you can sort it out into some sort of cohesive order, too."

"A wise decision."

She retrieved her scarf, wrapped it over her head, and rejoined Dan outside. "Okay, let's go."

§

It was a long walk under the highway overpass and along the railroad tracks for more than a mile; slow going as they picked their way carefully on the rough, uneven ground. Brenda glanced up and down the line, wondering if a train might come, but aside from a couple freight cars on a siding, there was no activity. Their route took them past rows of industrial buildings with a couple lesser streets passing on viaducts overhead. Each overpass they came to was log-jammed with stalled traffic. There was no one in sight other than on the overpasses, which were clogged, and the locals were too caught up in panic to pay them any attention. How that could change on their way back in a loaded vehicle was not comforting to think about.

149

At least the weather was decent; mild with a light breeze. They kept up a stiff pace, driven by the risk of war breaking out unexpectedly. It was cool enough that their exertions kept them comfortably warm. The air was heavy with the stench of auto exhaust which the faint breeze hardly disturbed. The atmosphere was full of tension. They flinched when gunshots rang out somewhere nearby. The crowd noise swelled up. A woman was screaming.

"This must be routine for you," she said after a while.

Dan nervously watched the latest overpass as they cleared it and moved on. "If anything in this life can be considered 'routine'."

"Yeah."

They navigated around a jumble of discarded railroad ties. "That traffic doesn't look good. How do we get back to the lab?"

"I usually call a cab, but it looks to be too late for that. We may wind up stealing a car."

She gave him a sardonic look. "I thought you were an ivory tower intellectual?"

"My high school was in Chicago. You might say my education was 'broadly based'."

"It won't do much good with that traffic. How do we get around that mess?"

"I've used these tracks before. The worst of it will be getting clear of the grocery store. It'll be a rough ride."

"*If* we can find any wheels."

The tracks eventually curved off to the left. Up ahead was another overpass, also clogged solid. "This way." Dan pointed off to the right across an open lot. "The store's on the next block over." They tramped through low weeds, then across bare dirt. The first street they came to was blocked by a multicar pileup, and they were able to scuttle between two wrecked cars. Brenda faltered at the sight; there were people hurt and no sign of police, EMTs or any assistance.

"Come on," Dan said, urgently. "There's nothing we can do." She felt guilty leaving the injured, but he was right. This world was too badly hurt for anyone to help.

They headed down a side street toward the store, passing people laden with with bags and shopping carts of personal possessions. Passers-by steered clear of them with hostile, fearful looks. Some were armed with guns or clubs, and one had a machete. There was an ugly undertone of panic in the air; they could *smell* it.

The next cross street was choked and moving at a crawl at best, with the grocery store beckoning on the far side. Getting across would take luck and nerve. Brenda eyed the packed double stream of cars with misgivings. "I don't see how we're gonna get through all that."

"Not through; over. You try ducking between cars and you're likely to get killed." Dan made an up-and-over gesture. "When they stall, we cross on the hoods."

"Wonderful."

The traffic ground to a halt again, engines revving, horns blaring. "Alright, now!" Dan clambered up on the rear hood of a sedan, then helped her up. "Keep moving!" Brenda's gaze met the driver in the car behind them; she gave him a distracted wave before they jumped across to a roof in the inside lane. They almost lost their balance as the car surged ahead under them, ramming the next car in line. The traffic going the other way ground to a halt just in time, and they jumped across onto the roof of a van while the driver of the second car screamed obscenities at them in spittle-spewing rage.

"You all right?" Dan asked.

"Yes!"

The traffic started inching ahead, so they jumped across to the roof of a pickup truck, then into its bed, then over the side to the sidewalk as it pulled away.

"Crazy sonsabitches!" Dan bellyached as they recovered their composure on the other side.

"This doesn't look promising," Brenda said. "These people are too worked up. Your timetable might be off."

"God, I hope not. We need to find a TV or something, see what the latest news is." Dan looked up and down the sidewalk, and spotted a newspaper vending machine nearby.

WAR THREAT INCREASING
Brazil Promises Massive Retaliation
To Any Aggressive Move By US
Civil Defense Preparations In Full Force

The paper was nearly a week old. "Brazil?" Dan seemed thoroughly puzzled. "What got into *them* all of a sudden?"

"Does it matter?"

"Not really. What matters is how long the lid stays on." He glanced around anxiously, but there was no other source to clue them to how critical the situation was. "Come on." He gestured to the store across the parking lot. "Let's get this over with."

There was a police cruiser parked on the sidewalk ahead of them, which they carefully skirted by going along the edge of the parking lot. The two cops watched them as they approached, no doubt having witnessed their dramatic street crossing.

"Take it easy," Dan muttered as they came closer. He nodded to the two policemen as they passed, one of whom nodded in turn. It was surprisingly hard to act natural when skulking down a busy street in broad daylight in an alternate reality about to be blown up with nuclear bombs. After what seemed an eternity, the squad car radio crackled to life. The two cops hit their lights and siren, and peeled out of there, driving on the sidewalk to get around the gridlocked traffic.

"I've never been afraid of the police before," she mumbled. "Not even in India."

"Yes, well, seeing we have no verifiable addresses, no valid identification, and we're using a forged debit card, you might feel like that." He looked around while trying to seem casual himself. "What gives me the willies is being out here in the open when a war could erupt at any moment. It's not just the war itself; it's getting caught up in a panic, or maybe attacked by a mob."

"What do we do if that happens?"

He paused and turned to her. "If worse comes to worst, take care of yourself. I'm hardly a man of action, but I'll do what I can to give you a running head start. Get back to the lab; you'll be safe there at least."

152

She took his arm. "No, Dan. We stick together. I can take care of myself."

"Brenda," he said severely. "Please don't argue. This is no time to be a liberated woman. Law and order are breaking down rapidly. If things go bad, we split up and you high-tail it for the lab. Don't worry about me."

There was no agreeing on it, so the matter was dropped by unspoken consent. They walked on in silence trying to look inconspicuous while she wondered what she would do if she was trapped in the lab all alone without food or water. That wasn't a pleasant prospect. Would George allow her to use the time machine to escape into the past? Likely not.

§

The Bank of America branch was at the far end of the grocery store lobby past the market's service counter. The roll-up doors were shut, but there was an ATM machine. "There we are." Dan changed course, skirted a tangle of abandoned shopping carts, and made a bee line for the ATM, then stopped. The display window on the machine read 'Out Of Service'. "Well," he said at last. "We'll just have to hope they're still taking debit cards."

There were surprisingly few people in the store, and it soon became clear they'd missed the tide. The place was largely pillaged. What few shoppers there were ran frantically back and forth grabbing anything they could find, and there was precious little to be had. They helped themselves from the tangle of abandoned shopping carts, and paused to sort themselves out.

Dan scanned the aisles. "All right, we need to stock up on as many staples as we can find..."

"Our priority is fruits and vegetables," she said, firmly. "You need a more balanced diet."

He nodded impatiently. "Well let's not stand here arguing until the world ends."

What little remained in produce was an odd selection. Apples, carrots and potatoes were non-existent, but there were still a few heads of lettuce, a fair amount of spinach and some cabbage. "Some people are showing common sense," Dan muttered. "They took all the durable food and left the perishables."

153

"This is no time to be picky." Brenda scooped up the three heads of lettuce and hastily stuffed them into a plastic bag. "Grab as much as you can." Dan pitched in, stuffing cabbage and spinach in bags and tossing them in his cart.

The bread section was stripped, as were the baking and package foods aisles. The cereal aisle was a wasteland; even the shelves were missing. Same with the snacks aisle. The condiments aisle was little better, although they collected a few bottles of salad dressing and some parmesan cheese shakers.

"This isn't good," Dan muttered. "Grocery shipments have broken down. Things have deteriorated more than we thought."

"Even if we get the chance, we won't do much better at any other store," Brenda added. Aside from the stripped shelves, there were signs of chaos everywhere: spilled food, damaged store fixtures, and dried blood stains.

"You're probably right, so we milk this for all its worth."

"Not that its worth much, it seems."

Canned goods was a desert, although a few isolated cans still hid in the back of a top shelf. She helped herself to the few remaining canned green beans, some beets, and the last of the canned peas, but it wasn't more than a dozen all told.

"We're not doing so good," Dan said.

"It's better than nothing." He was right, though; this expedition was starting to look like a fools' errand.

Two aisles over, in frozen foods, they hit paydirt. There were still several packages of frozen lasagna, some frozen entrees and TV dinners, and above all some fruit juice concentrate. "Start at this end. Take everything," Brenda said as she drove to the far end of the freezer case. Dan started grabbing frozen packages and piling them in his cart while she helped herself to the juices. Apple and orange juice were gone, but there were still a few limeade cans and some cranberry cocktail. They all went into her cart. She worked back toward Dan, adding some frozen pizzas and some fish fillets. Between them, they had a goodly pile when they met in the middle.

"This is more like it," Dan said with grim satisfaction.

"What's our time look like?"

Dan checked his watch. "Nearly two hours now."

The place had gone disturbingly quiet, the frenzied mob thinned out to almost nothing. "We're pushing our luck. Let's get a move-on."

On to the next aisle at a dead run. "Whoa! Toilet paper!" Dan grabbed a couple bulk packages and tossed them in his cart, which was now filled to overflowing. "What next?"

The meat section was stripped bare. Same with dairy. "That's it, then," she said.

"There's still the stock room." Dan headed for the swinging doors leading to a long corridor with back-stock pallets and shelves along both sides. The area was plundered as well, but they lucked into a few cans of sweet potatoes and some bagged rice. They took as much as they could carry.

"We can't afford to hang around much more," Dan said as he studied his watch again. They were both painfully aware of how the precious, unpredictable minutes were slipping by. They'd pushed their luck, hard, and it was paying off, but their luck couldn't last forever. By then their two carts were packed as high as could be without spilling onto the floor, and they still had to get back to the lab through traffic and chaos and looters. The ICBMs no doubt pointed this way were only desert for that unpalatable meal.

"Good enough," Brenda said with one last hasty look around. "Let's get the hell out'a here."

There was only one check stand open, run by the manager himself who kept up a steady stream of complaints as he hustled the last customers through as fast as he could. They cooled their heels as they waited for several people ahead of them, each with carts filled to overflowing.

"God, ain't this some kind'a shit?" he grumbled as he worked his scanner at breakneck speed. "World's goin' t' hell in a hand basket."

"What d'you care anyway?" the rough-looking fellow at the head of the line groused. "Damn world can go t' hell, and good riddance." He was dressed in army surplus camo, with a pistol shoved in his waistband and a shotgun in one hand.

155

The manager gave him a sour look. "Ain't you late for a Bund rally or sumpthin?"

"C'mon, snap it up. I ain't got all day! Th' bombs'll be fallin' any minute now!"

"Yeah, yeah, complain t' th' Gouchos. Why ain't'ja out there showin' them what-for, anyway?" He finished the last of his order. The man threw a wad of cash at him and took off with the shopping cart. The manager was already working the next in line.

"That doesn't look good," Dan mumbled cautiously. "The militia types are coming out from under their rocks."

"Are we in danger?" she asked.

"They're just one of many. I've had run-ins with that sort before."

The line advanced at a nerve-wracking pace, despite there being only three people ahead of them. Everyone was on edge, taut nerves rubbed raw by the endless delay.

"There's a pharmacy next door," Brenda said, quietly. "Do you think we'll have time to stock up on medical supplies?"

Dan studied his watch nervously. "I hate to risk it, but perhaps we should."

But would they have the time? From the way things looked, they'd already pushed their luck to the limits. Brenda gnawed her lip anxiously as they waited, glancing this way and that for any unforeseen dangers. *Finally*, after what seemed to be forever, it was their turn. Dan started unloading their carts onto the moving conveyer while Brenda took station at the other end and packed as fast as she could.

"Jeez, don't'ja know it?" The manager kept up his steady complaints as his chubby hands flew. "We finally get sales like t' wet myself over, and the whole damn world's gonna end. Can't get shipments, all the help deserted, and they likely won't be payin' no sales bonuses, too. Guy can't win not nohow."

Brenda ignored him as she grabbed the items he was through with and stuffed them into plastic bags as fast as she could. After what seemed an eternity, the manager finished. "All right, that'll be six hundred and eighteen dollars, thirty-five cents. You want cash back?"

"No, thank you." Dan showed him his B of A card.

"Don't matter, cause it likely won't be worth nothin' soon."

Dan ran the card through the reader. There was an agonizing wait, then the cash register came to life and spewed out a short receipt. "Crap," the manager said as he read it. "The ATM system folded up."

"We can't pay?" Dan asked, plaintively.

"The system's shut down. I'm sorry, but I can't let you take all this stuff."

"Does it really matter under the circumstances?" Brenda asked.

"Likely not, but just in case nothin' happens, I gotta keep the accounts in order..." They were interrupted by sirens howling in the distance. "Oh, shit," he mumbled. "It looks like all bets are off!"

"Let's move!" Dan said as they corralled their shopping carts and joined the rush for the door.

"Good luck t' you!" the manager called as he fled.

§

They were more or less carried through the doors, jostled and shoved by the last panicked rush, and were well out in the parking lot before they could regain their feet. "How do we get this stuff back to the lab?" Brenda asked.

Dan looked around frantically. "Time for Plan B. We'll have to steal a car."

They headed across the parking lot at a ragged trot. There were relatively few cars to choose from, and most of them were already being reclaimed by their owners. They dodged as a van peeled past them heading for the exit. Another sedan narrowly missed them as it backed abruptly out of a parking space. The near panic inside blossomed into a full-blown panic out here, supplemented with cars. Every step they took was at risk of life and limb.

"There!" Dan pointed to a battered red crew cab pickup truck at the end of the row. "That's perfect!" They redoubled their efforts, gasping for breath, wrestling the balky shopping carts over the cracked pavement to their one hope of escape...

...there was a baby seat in the back. Brenda halted, dismayed at the reality of what they were doing. "Come on!" Dan yelled.

157

Brenda fought down her ugly feelings and pitched in as Dan threw bag after bag into the rear bay. Panic and adrenalin melted the piles in the shopping carts in a frenzied, almost hallucinatory rush. It seemed only seconds before the job was all but done...

"Hey! That's my car!" A young woman was coming down the lot pushing a shopping cart. She abandoned the cart, scooped an infant up in her arms and came running toward them. "Stop! you can't do this to us!"

Dan glanced at her, smashed the driver's side window with his elbow, and hit the door lock switch. "Get in!" he yelled. Brenda abandoned the last of their groceries and dove into the passenger seat. He hit the door locks, produced a large screwdriver, jammed it into the ignition lock, and hit it hard with the palm of his hand.

The young woman—still in her teens—caught up with them, and pounded frantically on the passenger side window. "You're stealing our truck!" she screamed hysterically. "Don't leave us here!" Brenda was appalled by what they were doing. This was the Law of the Jungle! Their eyes met; panic-stricken eyes, wide with dread. She couldn't help looking at the young face contorted with fear a mere inches distant, separated by a pane of glass and the hope for survival.

Dan hit the screwdriver again, emitting a grunt of pain. "Give, dammit!" he swore.

The young woman was crying as she pounded the window with one hand and clutched her baby with the other. Brenda was unable to look away. That face...the terror that young women felt...it evoked memories of the nightmare...of the agony and panic she must have felt in some unrealized past...

"Dan..." She couldn't handle it.

"It's them or us," he muttered as he hammered the screwdriver again, then flexed his hand to relieve the pain. The ignition lock remained unbroken.

An unseen car raced past, clipping their bumper, causing the pickup to lurch. Brenda was rattled for a moment; the young woman cringed, but seemed uninjured. She pulled herself together and renewed the attack on the window, pounding frantically with her fist and screaming. The baby in her other arm howled.

Dan wound up and delivered a punishing fourth blow on the screwdriver, and the lock casing split. He cranked the starter and peeled out as the young woman tried desperately to hold on. Brenda caught a brief glimpse of her in the rear view mirror as she stumbled and just managed to catch her baby. Then she caught another movement out of the corner of her eye...

"Look out!"

...Dan hit the brakes, but wasn't able to avoid an SUV which cut in front of them. The collision deflected the pickup onto the sidewalk, almost hitting a running pedestrian, and they screeched to a halt. "Idiot!" he muttered as he put the truck in reverse and backed onto the street. Brenda saw the young mother in the rear view mirror, racing after them clutching her baby desperately. It was too much for her conscience to bear. "Stop!" she cried as the truck started moving again.

"What?" Dan hit the brake and looked around in confusion.

Brenda reached around and pulled the latch on the rear door, then opened her door as the young woman came up. "Get in!" she yelled.

"What are you doing?"

"This is my car!" the woman screamed.

"Get in! It's your only chance!"

The woman was so distraught that she didn't argue. She jerked the door open and dove in head first. The baby started screaming as she landed in a heap and Dan peeled out. "This is my truck!" she cried. "You're stealing my truck!"

"Shut up!" Dan snarled at her. "This is crazy," he added to Brenda. "What th' hell are you doing?"

"We owe her."

§

They careened down the back street away from the market until they came to the cross street they dared earlier. The traffic was insane, drivers pushing ahead by sheer brute force with no regard for traffic safety or anyone in their way.

"It's like a freakin' Demolition Derby," Dan said.

"Can we make it?"

"We have to. Here goes nothing..."

159

"You're gonna wreck my truck!" the young woman cried as he put it in gear.

"You say *another word*, and we'll dump you! *Right* here! *Right* now!" Dan yelled at her.

A momentary gap appeared, he floored it, ramming his way in, turning with the traffic as they bounced off another car. They were slammed from left and rear simultaneously, but he managed to get them turned into the flow. An SUV shot past on the left, clipping off his rearview mirror and crumpling the left fender. Somewhere behind them shots rang out. They both ducked as the rear window was shattered.

"Anyone hurt?" she demanded. Apparently not, although the baby was screaming and its mother cringed on the back seat.

Another gap appeared, and Dan was able to force them over into the left lane. He hit the brakes, taking another impact from behind, then dove into a gap in oncoming traffic. They clipped the rear of a van, crushed the right fender in the grille of a Chevy, were spun sideways by the car behind them trying to ram past, and crossed the other side into the side street leading to the railroad tracks.

"Jesus!" Brenda gasped.

"It ain't over yet," Dan said, grimly.

§

The next street was easier since the pileup hadn't been touched. They charged out of the side street, swerved around one of the wrecks, almost hitting a couple of pedestrians, then bounced over the curb, slammed onto the dirt lot and ground to a halt when the engine stalled.

"Dammit!" Dan ground the starter, pumping the gas pedal furiously. Steam was wafting up from under the hood, and the trouble lights were blinking.

"You're wrecking my truck!" the young woman screamed. The infant was screeching in terror.

Dan glanced in the rear view mirror. "Crap! We gotta go!" Brenda looked over her shoulder and saw several men running toward them, one carrying a pistol, another a length of pipe. Dan gunned the truck again, the engine caught, and they peeled out in a spray of dirt. They bounced through the weeds and onto the railroad tracks, skidded to the left and tore down the right-of-way, leaving their would-be hijackers behind. "We should be home free now," Dan said.

"If this thing doesn't quit on us." Steam was pouring out from under the hood, and they kept dragging to the left.

"She'll hold together. She has to."

They rumbled down the right-of-way, bouncing over gullies and old railroad ties while they hung on for dear life. The young woman was sobbing hysterically, her baby whimpering. At least there was no traffic, but their progress was painfully slow. The truck was hurting, advancing painfully with plenty of squeaks and grinding noises. They could smell burning rubber. The highway overpass loomed ahead. People were spilling down off the highway and running in random directions. Dan dodged a couple of them, leaning on the horn, then swerved to squeeze past the overpass footing. As soon as they cleared the overpass, he swerved sharply left onto a narrow dirt trail leading to the laboratory, just the other side of the tracks, and ground to a halt.

"Can we get across?" Brenda asked as they sized up the barrier ahead. The railroad tracks were only about eight inches high, but it would be easy to get hung up on them.

"We'll find out." Dan gunned the engine, they hit the tracks hard, bounced over them with a grinding crash as the truck bottomed out on the steel rails, then they were across and limping up the access road to the laboratory gate.

§

The pickup was sputtering and wobbling from side to side by time they reached the lab. The trouble lights on the dash were blinking and the temperature gauge was redlined. The motor finally quit as they passed through the gate. Dan shifted into neutral, and they coasted to a rough stop right in front of the lab. "Let's move!" he yelled. They piled out, grabbed as many plastic bags as they could carry, and staggered up the steps to the entrance. Dan managed to grab the handle with his fingertips and pulled; nothing happened. "George, voice authentication. Open the door!"

"Voice authentication confirmed." The door came loose with a metallic click.

"What's the situation?"

"Communications intelligence reports a massive nuclear strike under way. Satellite scans indicate a nuclear barrage is advancing up the coast, and is already approaching the California-Oregon border. The time field is on fast stand by. You need to hurry."

"So much for your three days," Brenda said.

"So sue me!" They dumped their loads in the antechamber and ran back to the truck. "You!" Dan yelled at the young woman, who was surveying the damage to the vehicle. "Help us get these inside!"

"You ruined my truck!" She was on the verge of panic, tears rolling down her cheeks.

"We're gonna get nuked any second now! This is your only chance, so *move it!*" Instead of helping, she let out an inarticulate cry of panic and bolted for the door, clutching her baby. They kept at it, hustling back and forth toting bags and bags of groceries at a breakneck pace. One of the plastic bags tore, spilling canned goods on the stairs. They were kicked aside in their haste.

"We have a confirmed strike on Portland," George reported. "I recommend you come in immediately."

"Not yet!" Dan yelled as they continued breathlessly hustling plastic bags up the steps and piling them in the hall. The young woman cowered in a corner, sobbing hysterically. Another run back to the truck. The load of groceries dwindled rapidly as they staggered back under as much as they could carry, but it still seemed like a panic-stricken eternity.

"Seismic readings indicate a hit on Centralia," George reported a moment later. "You have a minute at best."

Brenda was winded by the frenzied pace, but adrenalin and near panic kept her moving. She headed back with another load, but tripped on one of the spilled cans, falling on all fours. Dan grabbed her arm and yanked her to her feet. She scooped up the fallen bags and stumbled on.

"Seismic readings show a hit on Olympia. The barrage will reach here any moment now."

162

"We're workin' on it," Dan muttered. The pile of groceries in the back of the pickup was shrinking steadily. He grabbed several bags and hustled back up the walk again, passing her as he went. All of a sudden the sky to the south lit up. They paused and watched in dismay as a nuclear mushroom cloud rose in the distance. "Lewis-McChord," Dan said. "Or maybe Tacoma. Time's up!"

They ran for the door, staggering under the last few bags. As they reached the steps, the sky behind them burst into an intolerable glow. They were pelted by agonizing heat as they reached the door, which just as quickly cut off as the time field activated. They stumbled through the antechamber and fetched up against the corridor wall, trembling and gasping for breath.

*****

"Evening: The Fourteenth Day"

"You'll survive." She peeled a layer of plastic off Dan's neck as he grunted in pain. His windbreaker melted from the heat flash of the bomb, sticking to his exposed skin, causing painful burns.

"Maybe, but I...Aahhh!..." he gasped as she peeled another piece off. "But I won't enjoy it."

"Your sweatshirt saved you from the worst of it." He suffered first and second degree burns on his scalp and the side of his face, with a few more serious burns where the melted windbreaker stuck to exposed flesh. He also had some glass cuts on his elbow, and his right hand was swollen and bruised from pounding on the screwdriver to break the truck's ignition lock. She figured it might be dislocated, but it would have to be looked at later. Her vision was still dazzled by the bomb flash, as was his. Neither of them could see clearly, although the effect was fading slowly. His heavy cotton sweatshirt was scorched, but intact. It could have been worse, by a second or less.

The lab infirmary was never intended to deal with serious injuries without medical support from outside, but they would have to make do. Aside from some petroleum jelly, they had no usable supplies. What little there was by way of burn ointment, antibiotics and pain killers were long out of date.

"Memo to self," he grumbled as Brenda slathered petroleum jelly on his neck. "Wear natural fibers when going outside." He glanced at her. "One must dress for the occasion; nuclear *haute couture*." His attempt at levity fell flat in their present mood.

"If we get another chance for a store run, we need to stock up on medical and cleaning supplies, too."

"How about you? How are you doing?"

She was starting to feel her own injuries, in fact. Her wool turtleneck protected her from the worst burns, but her scarf proved useless. Her scalp and the right side of her face were red, as were her hands. At that she was lucky: Dan instinctively sheltered her from the blast with his body. "It could have been worse." She finished with his burns and moved over to the sink to rinse her hands.

164

"You're limping."

She was, now that he called it to her attention. She examined her left leg; there was blood on torn trouser fabric, and her ankle was swollen and sore. She must have turned her ankle and scraped her knee when she tumbled, but hadn't noticed it in her adrenalin rush. She pulled off her trousers with no thought for modesty, and examined the wound.

"It doesn't look bad."

"What about infection? We don't have any antibiotics."

She pondered that for a moment. "Yes, we do. Where do you keep your liquor supply?"

"What? I..."

"Come on, give! I have no time for this."

He wilted, and reluctantly pulled open a drawer to reveal a half dozen bottles. The prize was a half empty bottle of vodka. She used some medical cotton to daub it on her scraped knee, ignoring the sting.

"You should go easy with that," Dan said as he watched glumly.

"It's better than having you drink it," she grumbled.

"No, we may need it again. You should conserve it as much as possible."

"Yeah, good point." She finished cleaning her scrape, firmly corked the bottle, and set it on the counter out of his reach. The leg on her trousers was torn and blood-stained, but they were still usable. "I guess the worst is over." She struggled into them again, then tucked the vodka bottle in her pocket.

Dan gave her an annoyed look. "It depends on how you define 'worst'." He gestured to the young woman sitting in a chair in the corner as far from them as she could, nervously tending her baby. She was average height, a bit stocky, fairly attractive except for her frazzled look. "What about her?"

The young woman, Cindy was all they got out of her thus far, was uninjured, although she was still on the verge of panic. "Who are you people?" she asked when she realized they were looking at her. Her voice was brittle, on the edge of losing it. "What's going on? What is this place?"

"I'll explain it to her, Dan. I know you want to get back to Operations." Dan gave the young woman a resentful look, then sighed and left.

§

How does one explain to an eighteen year old that her world was destroyed in a nuclear war, and that she and her infant son were trapped in an abandoned top secret government laboratory from another reality? Try as she would, Brenda simply couldn't get through to her; but then, the story was pretty wild to start with. She was suspicious and hostile at first, figuring, rightly, that she'd been carjacked and was being held against her will by two strangers. It took some time to talk her down and get her to open up.

"This is some kinda government outfit?" She clearly didn't buy Brenda's story. "Then where is everyone?"

"This was a research lab. It was abandoned a long time ago. Professor White has been here ever since, trying to prevent a nuclear war."

She eyed Brenda suspiciously. "He's not doing so good, is he?"

"No, not as yet. But we're still trying."

"Why'd you steal our truck?"

"We needed supplies. Our grocery run was cut short by the alert, and we had to find some way of getting back here. I'm sorry about your truck, but at least you're safe here with us."

"I don't *wanna* be safe here with you! I wanna be with my Jeff!"

"You can't right now, Cindy."

"You can't do this," she murmured. "This is kidnapping."

"Cindy, we haven't kidnapped you. You can't go out there right now, it's too dangerous. Please believe me, we're trying to protect you."

"I'm supposed to pick up my boy friend, Jeff," she sobbed. "I was supposed to cash his check and get some food." The poor thing was just a kid; she was trapped in an abandoned building with two crazy people, and everyone she knew was probably dead. She was having a bad day. "You stole his truck! How could you do that to us?"

166

"I'm sorry, Cindy. We had no choice. That's why we brought you here, to make it up to you. You're safe here." In truth, she unlocked the door out of sheer guilt, with no clear idea of why or what do do with them or whether it could make a difference. That excuse sounded right, after the fact.

"Safe? How we gonna be safe here? The Gouchos are gonna drop a bomb on us!" She broke down and started bawling. Brenda tried to comfort her, but she shook her off. "We're all gonna die 'cause of you!"

There was nothing Brenda could say which would get through to her in her state. She sat quietly while Cindy vented her terror in near-hysterical tears. It was some minutes before she started to be cried out.

"You're *not* going to die, Cindy," Brenda said to her, firmly, when she calmed down a bit. "You and your baby are safe here. I promise you that."

"I gotta find Jeff." She pulled herself together with an effort. "He's...he's over at the Boeing plant. We're gonna head up into the mountains. How we gonna do that now? We got no food, no truck. How am I gonna find him?"

Brenda could tell she hadn't figured it out yet, or was still in denial. "I'm afraid that won't be possible now, Cindy. You're safe here, and I'll help you with your baby. I'm a nurse. Things will work out."

"Don't you get it? There's gonna be a war! How are we gonna get away after you wrecked our truck?"

"Cindy..." Brenda was starting to worry about her emotional state. This wasn't going to be easy. "...the war already happened. It's probably over by now."

It took her a moment to absorb that. "Then everything's okay? We weren't bombed?"

"Yes, Cindy. We were." She hated to dash Cindy's hopes, but there was nothing for it.

"But...how...?"

"This building is protected. We survived the blast."

She clearly wasn't getting through to the distraught teen. "No, that can't be!"

167

"I know it's hard to believe, but this place can withstand a nuclear attack. We're safe in here for now."

"But...my family...my mom and dad...Jeff..."

"They might have survived...but realistically...you can't count on it."

Cindy sat hunched in one of the clinic chairs, hands clinched in her lap, staring at the floor. "They...can't be dead...Jeff...mommy..." Tears were trickling down her cheeks, she started sobbing again. "N-no...that's not true..." The baby began fussing, which distracted her. She retrieved him from a washtub lined with a couple towels sitting on the counter and cuddled him, rocking back and forth and making little crooning noises. "It's all right," she mumbled. "Mommy's here, sweet."

"How old is he?"

It took her a moment to respond. "Three months. I got pregnant...mom and dad said I should stay in school..." The story came out bit by disjointed bit: a teen pregnancy, her understanding parents, the father a young machinist apprentice at Boeing. They were going to get married when the crisis came up... It was all too familiar. Brenda felt sorry for her, and thankful she had the support of her family through her pregnancy.

"What am I gonna do now?" she whimpered. "How can I find Jeff again? Where can we go without his truck?"

There was nothing Brenda could do but give her time to absorb unpleasant reality. Whether she'd get over it remained to be seen.

§

The inevitable trip to Operations revealed some all too familiar sights. The valley was devastated. The highway overpass was collapsed, wrecked cars spilled on the tracks. Beyond that, the ruins blazed and the sky was darkened with thick smoke. Cindy's truck was a smoldering, half-melted pile of scrap laying upside down just short of the main entrance where it was tossed by the force of the blast.

"It hit more to the north this time." Dan traced the sprawl of the wreckage showing how it was scattered to one side. "They missed the Boeing plant. There's nothing up that way but residential areas."

"They missed Boeing? Could her boy friend still be alive?"

Dan was silent as they watched the fires. "If he did live through it, he was unlucky," he said at last. "No one's going to survive that."

Once again the whole valley was burning, a sea of glowing orange surmounted by gray and black smoke whipped into a frenzy by the hurricane force winds. A firestorm: the chimney effect of the massive fires caught up everything and everyone, and drew them into the heart of the blaze. The heat could melt steel. Living human beings burn just the same as any other combustable substance.

"How many times have you seen this?"

Dan didn't answer for a bit. "It's not something you keep track of," he said at last.

"There is that." Who would want to?

He turned to her. "How is she?"

"About like you'd expect. The poor kid is crushed. I'm not sure she can handle this reality."

"Well she doesn't have a choice about it. She needs to get it together in a hurry. We can't afford the luxury of an emotional basket case."

"I guess that's what passes for compassion around here," she muttered. Right then she despised his seeming indifference to her suffering. He'd been at this too long. He gave her an annoyed look, but didn't answer.

§

Dinner that evening was a somber feast compared to their recent fare. Dan sat at the prep table while she worked at dicing their limited stock of veggies. Cindy sat off to one side, avoiding them while she fed her baby with the last of a formula bottle she had in her diaper bag.

"I still need to inventory our haul and work up a meal plan," Brenda said as she worked. "But at a guess I'd say we're good for about two weeks." They'd lost a lot on their way back to the lab.

Dan nodded thoughtfully as he watched her. "Not much for the effort, but it'll take some of the pressure off." After a bit, he added softly, "What about her baby? We don't have any milk."

169

Brenda paused and pondered that one unhappily. They had nothing to feed the infant, and Cindy wouldn't be able to nurse him now. "Maybe I can improvise something," she said. "Some strained rice mash, perhaps." At three months, the little fellow wasn't ready for solid food, but there wasn't much they could do about it.

They both luxuriated in hot showers earlier, and she got a load of laundry going since the ground water was still uncontaminated for now. It felt *good* to be clean again. Between the grocery raid, their injuries, and refilling their nearly empty water containers, they were both weary and a bit shaky.

"At least we have something to eat," Dan mumbled. "We were lucky. That was a close one."

She paused to glance at him. "I'll say. Felony shoplifting, bank fraud, grand theft auto, and hit-and-run: you know how to show a girl a good time."

Her forced bravado didn't play. "Yeah, well, that's what you get hanging around bad boys."

She shoved a bowl of salad at him. "And this is what you get for hanging around with a nurse."

She offered another salad to Cindy, who watched her in nervous silence. After Brenda returned to the table, she started in on it while holding the formula bottle for her son with the other. She was still shaken and withdrawn, but calmer now. She ate in silence, watching them warily.

Dan considered his salad dubiously, then began nibbling. "I was kind of hoping for a steak."

"No luck there." She added some canned hot rolls fresh from the oven. "The fresh stuff won't last long, so we need to finish it up. If you clean your plate, we'll have some of the frozen lasagna tomorrow. We need to use it up since we don't have enough freezer space."

He offered a theatrical sigh. "Can't have everything, I guess."

Brenda settled opposite Dan with her own salad. "Don't whine. At least we didn't find any Spam." He nodded agreement and kept on eating.

§

Dan finished his salad and headed back to Operations, leaving Brenda to cope with Cindy. She seemed calmer now, more subdued anyway, although she was still woebegone over her situation. She busied herself tending her baby, which helped take her mind off the horrid state of affairs.

"He's a little fusspot," she said while feeding him the last of the formula. "I never knew kids could be so much work."

"You never helped raise a little brother or sister?" Brenda was trying to draw her out, to get her talking so they could build some sort of trust.

She gave Brenda a sad look. "I'm an only child." The baby finished the formula and began fussing. "There, there, sweet," she said tenderly. "I'll fix you another bottle in a bit." She turned to Brenda. "Do you have any formula?"

"No, I'm afraid not."

"Some milk, maybe?"

"No."

"Then how can I feed him? I got the last of the formula at the store, but I lost it. What can I do?"

"I'm working on other food sources for him. We have some juice, and I'm looking into some other ideas." She gave Cindy a reassuring smile she desperately needed. "I'll make sure your baby is all right."

"Thank you." She stood suddenly and offered her the baby. "Look, you're a nurse? Can I leave my baby with you while I go look for Jeff?"

"You can't, Cindy. Not right now. I'm sorry, but chances are he's already dead."

"He can't be! He's smart. He'll know what to do. I'm *sure* he's alive! I gotta go find him, and my mom and dad, too."

"It isn't possible right now. Maybe in a few weeks, after the radiation dies down, we can search for them."

It was a lie: in a few weeks, assuming they were still alive, they would be in a different reality altogether. But if that hope, meaningless as it was, bought Cindy some time to accept the facts, then it was a small sin. Brenda couldn't help feeling ugly about it nonetheless.

"Radiation?" Cindy slumped in her chair and stared off at nothing as the tears rolled down her cheeks. "Why did this have to happen?" she sobbed as she wiped her eyes on her sleeve. "Why did this happen just when we were starting to do okay? Jeff got a raise, and he's gonna finish his apprenticeship soon, and we're gonna get married. Why now?"

Good question. Brenda doubted she would understand the answer, even if it could be put into words. "Some things just can't be explained, Cindy. Come on, let's get you tucked into bed so you can rest for a while."

§

"Miss Hayworth?" Jeeves said after she left Cindy in her room and returned to the kitchen.

"Yes, Jeeves?"

"I have completed the analysis of the alcoholic treatment data you requested."

"Huh? I requested?"

"When you left this morning, do you remember?" There was some random static, and then her voice came from the intercom:

> *"Can you access the internet here?"*
> *"I can."*
> *"All right, we'll do it your way. Pull any info you can on treating alcoholism from the AA, or their version of it."*
> *"Ah. You've accepted the program at last. Working."*
> *"I just want to make sure I won't be locked out. See if you can sort it out into some sort of cohesive order, too."*
> *"A wise decision."*

"Per your request, the analysis is now complete. We can start Dan's treatment at once."

"Okay." She wasn't pleased by Jeeves' reminder of her position, but there was nothing for it for now. "So what do you have?"

"Regretfully I don't have access to a printer or video screen, but I can recite it to you or give you a summary as you prefer. I can also perform a search function for specific information."

172

A hint of caution crept in; *nothing* was ever straightforward or simple where Jeeves was involved. "Is there a lot of material?"

"Some nine point seven million print words and eighteen hundred and fifty-four illustrations, after redacting duplicates. But have no fear, I have condensed its essence down into a mere fifty-seven thousand words."

She winced at the thought. "Wonderful. I should know better. Thank you, I guess."

"You don't sound good. Are you feeling poorly?"

She wasn't, in fact, and the thought of tangling with that mass of reading dismayed her. "I'll manage."

"It's that headache again?"

She nodded as she fumbled one of the tablets and washed it down with a gulp of cold coffee. Jeeves' camera pod over the kitchen door turned to follow her movement. "That isn't surprising, considering the strain you've been under. Perhaps you should rest for a while."

"Can't. I'll rest after we save the world."

"And you complain to Professor White about his workload?"

That brought her up short. "Yeah, point taken. Still, things being what they are right now, neither of us can afford to slack off much."

"Ah! A new perspective. Good. So I can expect your cooperation then?"

She didn't intend to give Jeeves the time of day, but she needed to get Dan dried out as soon as possible, and like she said a moment ago, this was no time to stop and smell the roses. She settled on a stool, resigned to the inevitable. "Give me a brief outline. I've had some addiction training and experience in India, so give me the refresher. We'll refer back for more detail later."

"Very well. You should get comfortable."

§

It was well into the evening before she came up for air. "Enough, Jeeves. I'm gonna need time to absorb all this material."

"But we're just getting to the interesting parts. For example there is symptom-triggered benzodiazepine treatment using very-high-dose bolus therapy..."

"Jeeves, I'm not a computer! I'm feeling a bit overwhelmed."

"I'm sorry. I guess I do run on somewhat in my concern for Professor White."

"You do at that," she grumbled. "We'll go into this more later."

"Certainly. I hope you will begin his treatment right away. I've been concerned about his mood swings when he's been drinking."

"You noticed?"

"I *am* the security protocol. He was rather short with you earlier, and there was that incident the other day."

"He can be a real asshole at times."

"Indeed, particularly concerning the young woman."

"You'd *think* he'd show a little compassion for our two guests."

"I can assure you he does, when sober."

"All the more reason to dry him out before I strangle him!"

"May I ask, have you decided what to do with the young lady and her baby?"

Brenda sagged on her stool and rubbed her face, trying to shake off her weariness. "I don't have all the answers, Jeeves. I don't even know all the questions. We can't send them back out there."

"It is a conundrum."

"I don't know what to do about feeding the infant."

"Your suggestion of thinned mashed rice should work, if you thin it out into a fluid."

"Perhaps I take some of the vegetables and boil them down into a broth? That would provide some vitamins and minerals, the spinach would serve, in particular."

"That is a matter for your expertise. In any case, I *trust* you will find a solution to the problem they pose."

The *'problem'* they pose? That made Jeeves' position on them clear enough. They intruded on its little kingdom and it wanted them gone. That damned AI was inhuman, and never missed a chance to remind her of it. Hopefully they could find a solution before protecting them eroded her own position beyond repair. And that wouldn't be her only headache. Aside from food, the baby had to be protected from infection, since they had no antibiotics or disinfectants. And then there were diapers...

§

174

She found Dan in Operations, working feverishly at his command console. "How's it going?"

He paused and turned to her. "It's ugly out there. This was a bad one."

She watched the shifting views on the four external monitors. The scenes of devastation had become all too routine. "Can you do anything? Can you undo this so we can send her back?"

"No. It's too late to prevent it. Anyway we only shifted to this Time Line to pick up supplies. I plan to shift back to the Omega Time Line as soon as I can work out the coordinates."

"Any hope of finding another line where we can get more groceries? We need food and medical supplies for her baby."

"How do I know? This was your idea. Why did you drag her into this anyway?"

"What was I supposed to do? Leave them there to die?"

Dan gave her a hostile look. "Three billion people died today. Why single out those two?"

"Because they were there! Because we stole her truck!" Her nerves, long frazzled, reacted badly to his callousness. "She's not just some faceless statistic!"

"They're *all* faceless statistics! That's the only way we can look at them. It'll drive you crazy otherwise!"

"You've been drinking again, haven't you?"

"Will you *quit* with the lectures!? So I had a drink or two; we need it around here!"

"The one thing we *don't* need around here is you diving into a bottle every time a problem comes up!"

"If I wanna dive into a bottle..."

"Is that my truck!?" Cindy stood in the doorway, her baby in her arms, staring at the burnt out hulk on the monitors. *"OOOOHHHHMMYYYGOOOODDDDD!"* she wailed as she took in the multiple scenes of devastation. Her baby felt her terror and started crying in turn.

"Cindy..." Brenda moved to intercept her.

"They're...dead! They're all dead!" Cindy broke down into hysterics, clutching her baby so tight that he started choking. "They're all...it's all..." She began wailing in panic.

175

"Get ahold of yourself!" Brenda managed to wrestle the infant away from her, and held him in one arm while trying to calm Cindy with the other. "Cindy! *Calm down!*"

"Get her out of here before she gets any worse!" Dan hissed.

§

"They're all dead!" she kept sobbing over and over. "Everyone's dead!" Brenda feared this would happen; reality was finally soaking in and she couldn't handle it. She forcefully lead Cindy back to the clinic to get her as far as possible from the gristly reality in Operations, and was trying to talk her down without much success. "They're all deaaaddd!" She broke down and started crying hysterically. The poor girl was a hollow shell, her world and everyone she knew destroyed. She wasn't strong to begin with, as if strength mattered in this holocaust.

"Cindy, you have to pull yourself together," Brenda said, forcefully. "You're still alive, you're safe here, and your baby needs you." She kept the child separate from the mother, afraid she might hurt him by accident. He was uninjured from her earlier panic attack, and now lay on the counter in the same washtub used before. He started howling in turn, picking up on his mother's distress.

"My...baby...?" Cindy pulled herself together enough to fumble the infant out of the tub and cuddle him. "It's all right, darling," she mumbled over and over as tears streamed down her cheeks. "It's all right. Everything's all right." The child was all she had left, her last link to a world now lost forever. Unable to cope, she retreated into her maternal instincts, trying to shelter her baby and herself from the reality she couldn't face.

Brenda watched warily, ready to intervene if she tried to harm the baby again. "I know how you feel, Cindy. Things are really bad right now, but there's always hope. You're safe here, and we'll figure out what to do."

"But...they're all dead! Every one of them! How am I gonna go on without Jeff?"

"You can, Cindy. You have to. There's a part of Jeff in your baby; you need to survive for his sake." She'd learned this technique in India: turning a widow's grief into a mission,

176

channeling Cindy's shock and dismay to a constructive purpose, nurturing the only other survivor in her family. "And there are your parents. This is their only grandchild. There's a part of them in him too. You need to endure for them."

"How?" she wailed. "They're all dead! Mom and dad, Jeff, all my friends! What am I gonna do?!"

"I don't know, Cindy." She wrapped an arm around her shoulder, trying to comfort her. "I don't know. But we'll think of something."

§

"How is she?" Dan asked when she returned to Operations.

Brenda stood with folded arms, ready to do battle with him again if need be. "I got her calmed down and put her to bed in my room."

"She's a complication we don't need. What were you thinking?"

"Dammit, Dan! We couldn't leave her out there to die!"

He sighed, and nodded reluctantly. "You're right. Still, what are we going to do with her? We can't drop her in the Omega Time Line, and she can't go back. We have no baby food, no medicine; I'm not sure what we can do for her."

Thankfully it looked like he wasn't going to argue any more. If he was drinking, he hadn't had enough to sustain his belligerent state; she filed that thought away carefully. He did have a point, however. She could see there were going to be no easy answers to this one.

"We'll have to hang onto them for now until you can figure out what to do about the overall crisis..."

She was interrupted by a heavy arcing sound which seemed to fill the room. The building shuddered as the lights dimmed. Then the control monitors and the master display went dead.

Dan flinched in surprise. "George? What happened?"

"There has been a critical drain on the time field." George's voice sounded harsh and mechanical, devoid of its usual human quality. "I am diverting power to stabilize the field."

Dan turned pale and swore under his breath. "Situation? Is the time field holding?"

177

George took an agonizingly long time to respond. "Field substantially weakened...diverting more power." Most of the overhead lights went out. "Reactor at maximum overload." They could feel a heavy, almost subaudible rumble coming from somewhere. "Auxiliary generator...on line...holding..."

An alarm was ringing, but cut off abruptly. There was another arcing sound. The remaining lights flickered and dimmed.

"George? What caused the drain?"

"Un...able...to...process...emergency..."

"Dammit, George is even taking power from himself!"

There was a faint acrid smell of overheated electronics in the air. The last overhead lights went out, and a red battery-powered emergency light came on over the door, casting the room in a faint, hellish glow.

"What's happening, Dan?"

He grabbed her and held her in a panicky grip. "I-I don't know! Something's gone wonky. Maybe the field generators, or we may be under attack."

"Attack? By who?"

Dan was every bit as frightened as her, clutching her tight, looking around wildly, on the verge of panic. She was starting to panic too; what could get to them through a field which could absorb a nuclear blast?

"Dan! Who could be attacking us?"

That snapped him into focus. "Huh? Ah...no...it must be a failure somewhere..." She silently and fervently cursed him for scaring her so.

The whine of generators increased. They heard a faint crackling noise, then a muffled 'whooossssshhhhh' from somewhere below. "The fire system!" Dan muttered. "It's an overload, a short-circuit in the field system. God...if the field generator burns out..."

"Can't you do anything?"

"It's...all automated. George has emergency subroutines to stabilize the field and contain the damage. We'll be all right." His tense tone showed wasn't sure of that.

"Dan..."

178

There was a loud snap, almost like a muffled explosion. The hiss of the fire suppression system grew louder. Acrid fumes were leaking into the room through the floor ventilators from the service areas in the basement.

"We're losing it..." Dan said.

"Where can we go? We can't evacuate the building."

"If we lose the field, there's nothing left."

They clung to each other desperately as acrid smoke filled the air, dimming the emergency light. The fire suppression system continued to hiss.

"Can't breathe," she gasped. The smoke was burning her throat, making her faint. Her eyes stung, watering, forcing them to close. Her panic rose in the dark and choking fumes. "Can't...air!"

That got Dan's attention. He peeled off his sweatshirt, folded it twice, and pressed it over her face. "Breathe!" She struggled to breathe through several thick layers, but they filtered out most of the smoke. He joined her, holding one of the sleeves over his mouth and nose.

"Halon...system...exhausted," George reported. The hissing sound faded away.

"There's a fire extinguisher in the kitchen," Brenda wheezed.

Dan's voice was muffled in the distance. "If the halon can't handle it, there's nothing we can do."

"Field...stable...rebuild..." the rough mechanical voice came over the intercom. "Fire...contained..."

"Thank God!" Dan sobbed. "George is getting it under control." The heavy rumble of the generator was higher pitched than before, running flat out. The burnt odor was thick enough to choke them even through the heavy cloth, leaving both gasping for breath.

There was a faint click, surprisingly clear amid the chaos. Brenda squinted to see what was going on just as the master console came to life, its monitor showing arrays of numbers. Dan was trembling, as was she, but he was able to relax his hold on her just a bit and study the display. "Diagnostics. Good. George can spare the power for other critical needs. George? Situation report."

179

It was a few seconds before George responded, and his voice still sounded crudely mechanical. "Field stable at minimal level. Rebuilding. Diagnostics under way."

"What was on fire?"

"Switching junction E-four-zero-two suffered a meltdown. The fire has been contained and power rerouted. Unable to ventilate the space, but it is sealed and fumes contained."

"E four-oh-two; the primary field junction box. Thank God for triple redundancy!"

A moment later one bank of overhead lights came on, helping to calm their panic. "Field still rebuilding, but stable. Power demand stabilizing. Restoring non-essential systems."

"George, switch on the ventilators. We need to clear this smoke out."

"Unable to ventilate with the time field active. Biohazard scrubbers on line." It may have been their imagination, but the air seemed a bit clearer.

The rest of the monitors came on, showing their startup routines. The main display remained dark. The rumble of auxiliary turbines faded. Then more lights came on. Soon the air began to clear until they were able to discard the sweatshirt, although the fumes still left them wheezing. They clung to each other through all this, too shaken for anything else. After what seemed forever, the main display lit up, showing its startup routine. They were finally able to let each other go.

"Does this happen very often?" she asked, plaintively.

"It...no, it's never happened before." Dan studied his master console for a long while. He was shaking, and more pale than ever. "George, what caused the drain?"

"Unknown. Priority going to diagnostics."

Dan glanced at her. "George still hasn't fully recovered."

"Sir?"

"What? Yes, Jeeves? Are you all right?"

"My power supply was diverted to stabilize the field, but I am recovering. I wanted to tell you the exterior door is open."

Dan froze, and looked at Brenda in dismay. "Jeeves? Where is that young woman?"

"Unknown, sir. My monitor cameras are still deactivated. My last observation showed her heading toward the main entrance."

"Shit!" he muttered as he took off down the corridor at a run.

§

As reported, both the inner and outer doors were open. There was no sign of Cindy or her baby, but what happened was obvious. The formless black time field was five feet beyond the door.

"Oh, great!" Dan said. "She ran out through the field."

"You said it couldn't be penetrated!"

"Not from outside. From inside it's semi-permeable. That's how we can see out and initiate actions."

"Then what happened to her? Where did she go?"

Dan's expression was grim, like he was eating himself up inside. "I don't know. She wasn't encoded, the power wasn't balanced, there was no destination set."

"Did she go back in time or something?"

"Not without the transit protocol." He stood there for a long moment, agonizing. "The time field is out of synch with the rest of the universe...I don't know."

*****

"The Fifteenth Day"

"So how bad is the damage?" Brenda asked when Dan came back up from the underground equipment bay.

He dropped his breathing mask on the kitchen table, took a moment to wipe his soot-stained face with a wet washcloth, then slumped on one of the bar stools. "It could have been worse. The primary field generator junction box is a write-off, but the safeties held, and aside from some nearby cables which got scorched, everything else is in hardened cases." He took a swallow from the ice water mug she set in front of him, then leaned on the prep table, brooding.

"So we're fully operational, then?"

He nodded listlessly. "But there's no way to recharge the halon system, so we can't afford any more fires."

She knew that was a dig at her and the unfortunate Cindy she rescued, but there was no sense in arguing about it. He was right to have objected to them being here; the margin of safety was too precarious to risk saving random strangers, no matter how deserving. Their tragic death—or worse—only made it more painful.

"I've been holding dinner for you." She hit the microwave, then poured him another mug of ice water while the machine hummed. The past was done, and it was time to move on. Dinner was a large slab of sausage and cheese lasagna and some of their limited stock of canned green beans. He ate listlessly, his exhaustion obvious in his wilted posture and dead-pan face.

"I'm sorry I got angry with you earlier," he said after a bit. "Your heart was in the right place." He was silent again while he chewed and swallowed another mouthful. "That poor kid never had a chance." He looked at her with stricken eyes. "It's different when you see it up close and personal. I think I know where you're at now."

He was feeling it too: her sense of loss, her sense of personal failure. Cindy was just a kid; too immature, really, to be a mother. She was caught up in a situation she couldn't understand much less cope with, and they—her in particular—didn't give her the strength

182

she desperately needed. It's easy to beat yourself up afterward, to see the mistakes you made, to second-guess yourself with twenty-twenty hindsight. But honestly, she couldn't see what they might have done differently, or if anything would have prevented the tragedy. Still, she couldn't help feeling guilty. It wounded her almost as if she lost her own daughter and grandson.

"It's..." He struggled for words, struggled to express the pain they both felt. "It's...I never...I've always looked at it as an abstract...a scientific phenomenon. Scientific detachment: that's how you're supposed to do these things. Don't get involved; it can contaminate the experiment, skew the findings. That's what they taught us at MIT. But this... All those people...so many dead..."

"It's alright, Dan." She laid her hand on his to reassure him. "This is a bad situation, and pain is part of the reality here. We see this in medicine all the time, when they bring in several people hurt in a major accident or a riot...sometimes you just can't save everyone."

That should have helped, but it didn't. All she could do was pray they could figure this mess out, and that in some alternate time line Cindy could marry her boyfriend Jeff, and they could raise their son—she never even learned the little fellow's name—and they could go blissfully through life never knowing the horrors they endured.

She needed a good cry. Later, when she could be alone. "God, I hate this!"

He closed his eyes and nodded. After a bit, he went back to eating. "Good lasagna," he muttered.

Through her angst, she realized her head was pounding. She fumbled the little bottle from her pocket and popped one of the pills with a swig of coffee. "Headache?" Dan noticed.

"Yeah."

"It's nothing serious, I hope?"

She sighed and took another swig of coffee. "It'll pass. I'm not so young any more, you know?"

"Gawd, tell me about it." He shoved his empty plate aside and climbed to his feet. "I have to get down there and tape up some of those conduits."

"Dan, you're exhausted. You were down there for hours. Grab a hot shower while we still have good water, and get some sleep. Tomorrow can take care of itself."

He stared at her vaguely, then nodded.

§

Dan completed the repairs the next morning, and by midday was back in Operations working on the problem. The biohazard scrubbers had removed most of the smoke and soot, and Brenda spent much of the morning cleaning the kitchen of the greasy residue it left behind. By lunch time, things were more or less back to normal.

"So how's things at your end?" she asked as she served up a lunch of frozen pizza.

He shook his head in exasperation as he munched his first bite. "It's going nowhere. I've reached back to where the beginning of the cascade should be, but every time I think I have it isolated, there's a split somewhere else, and I lose it. Unless I can find the source of the cascade, I'm not sure I can do much of anything."

"Why can't you pinpoint the source? Is it that hard?"

He sat and pondered for a bit while chewing his latest bite of pizza. "It can be fiendishly hard to find the real cause even with George to do the heavy lifting," he said at last. "It doesn't have to come from some politician or activist, it could just be some random influence by anyone; something said, something done, some tiny detail changed."

"As simple as a bit of scrap metal in the road?"

He nodded. "Exactly, and it could be so remote that we might never find it. There are seven billion suspects out there, and the key could be any insignificant little thing any of them did or didn't do."

"But it would have to be a change, wouldn't it? An alternative to what would have happened?"

"That's the one hope we have. The effect has to be brought on by a paradox, otherwise it would only be the ordinary course of history. Even so, searching along a time line for the point of divergence is not easy. It could happen anywhere in the world, and the relationship of the cause to the paradox can be faint at times."

184

"A real whodunnit, hmmm?"

That brought a cynical smile. "The ultimate locked-room mystery. I doubt even Sherlock Holmes would try this one."

The conversation lapsed, and they ate in uncomfortable silence. "How about you?" he asked after a while.

"I'm all right." She wasn't, in fact, but she wasn't going to let it get her down. "I inventoried our food supply and worked up a meal plan. We have enough for twenty-five days of more or less balanced meals." Now that there were only two of them to feed.

He nodded. "I'll keep an eye open for another opportunity to stock up."

She wasn't ready to face that prospect again, not right away anyhow. "There's no hurry."

"No hurry..." he mumbled.

His tone caught her attention. "Are you all right, Dan?"

He sat staring at his plate for a long time, not moving, not answering. Finally he looked up at her. "It's hopeless. I've tried for twenty years, longer, but nothing works. You were right; there is no magic bullet for this."

"Dan..."

He sniffed, and wiped his eyes. "It's...it's all been a waste. The human race is doomed, and nothing can change that. My efforts have been in vain. All I do is create alternate time lines where more billions die." He settled on his elbows again. "There's been enough carnage."

"So...you're giving up, then?"

He nodded. "You were right all along. The only thing we can do...is find some viable time line for us to escape into."

The tone in his voice said a huge burden was lifted from his shoulders. She was happy for him, for how he finally accepted the inevitable, and for a glimmer of hope in this horrible situation. "So what do you plan to do?"

He sighed, and paused to contemplate for a time. "I still have to lick the cascade. Until I can stabilize it, there's no hope of developing any stable lines. Afterwards..." Then he turned to her. "Afterwards, I stabilize a line which will last long enough for us. I'm afraid it's the best we can hope for."

185

"It will do, Dan. It has to."

He gulped the last of his pizza, then took her hand and gazed deep into her eyes. "Are you all right? This has been a rough week, I know it's been painful for you."

Maybe he wasn't so clueless after all. "I'm managing, Dan. It's rough, but I'll get past it. This isn't the first bad week I've had."

He gave her a little smile and a gentle squeeze of reassurance. "You are one classy lady. I can't begin to tell you how much it means having you here."

She could tell he wanted to say more, but didn't dare, and she wasn't sure how she would feel if he did. She withdrew her hand and grabbed their two plates. "Yes, well, the next time we go out, you can buy me some fancy chocolates."

"Deal." His gaze lingered on her for a long moment before he headed back to Operations.

§

Eventually boredom and loneliness set in so that she drifted into Operations by late afternoon to see how Dan was doing. "So how goes the battle?" she asked.

Dan gave her a frustrated look. "The battle is going great; I'm not doing so hot, however."

She came down into the pit next to him and wrapped her arm around his shoulders. "You can do it. I have faith in you."

He sighed and leaned back in his chair. "Sometimes...I'm not sure I have faith in myself." She caught a whiff of alcohol as he laid his hand on hers in an intimate gesture. "Having you here really helps."

Dan shifted them back to the Omega Time Line, since neither of them wanted to remain where they were any longer. Not that this was any better. The devastation on the monitors was all too graphic; dull gray ash-strewn ruins in every scene. It was snowing lightly, the ground covered with a couple inches. The sky was ugly: dark boiling gray clouds sweeping in from the Northwest. A world without color. A world without life.

"That looks ugly," she muttered.

"Blizzard coming in. Most of it will land in the mountains east of here, but we'll get another three or four inches."

186

"In July. God, that's one messed-up world."

The burnt out hulk of the pickup truck was gone. Its absence in this reality reminded Brenda of Cindy clutching her infant as she pounded frantically on her window. *'They wouldn't have survived,'* she reminded herself. *'They couldn't have gotten clear in time. And even if they did, what chance would they have in that hell?'* It didn't help the ugly feelings. She'd met face to face with the victims of nuclear war. They stole her truck and left her and her baby to die. It wouldn't have made a difference, but it didn't change things. She felt ashamed of herself.

"I wish...that damned blizzard would cover those ruins," he muttered. "I hate staring at them."

"I know."

She decided to get him, and her, off that line of thinking. "So what progress are you making with the cascade?"

He took a deep breath and pulled himself out of it. "It's still eludes me. Every time I think I have it, another split happens somewhere. Slippery bastard."

There was definitely a hint of alcohol on his breath and in his speech; he'd been drinking again. "The focal point has to be somewhere, doesn't it? How do you find something like that?"

"I reached clear back to Operation 725. Cascade must be the direct result, started so soon after." He stared at his monitor as he tried to understand what was wrong. "Whatever it is, it must be significant; some critical relationship to the target of 725."

"Colleagues? Family?"

He shook his head. "Don't know. I haven't found anythin' yet. It doesn't make sense. There are changes, in the time lines, random changes, don' know why."

"Do you think...maybe they're on to you? Could they suspect your intervention? Those ball bearings must leave some damning evidence."

He stared at her in confusion. "No...I retrieve them..."

"Still, a three centimeter displacement cavity deep in the brain with no entry wound? It's medically impossible. They might have autopsied some of your other victims. The same impossible wound, showing up again and again in important people..."

187

"Damn," he mumbled. "I thought that would be perfect." After a moment, he started sobbing.

"Maybe the cascade is caused by some sort of defensive program?"

"No...the idea of...time travel..."

He seemed to be taking this awfully hard. "They may not understand how or why, but medical science would definitely smell a rat. They might think it was the Russians or the Brazilians or who knows who?"

"God, I hope not! That could start a war in and of itself."

"At the very least it'd interfere with your work."

"I can't do anything right, can I?" He shook his head, tears welling up in frustration. "I was a fool, an ivory-tower intellectual...too damned...clueless to save humanity...too damned clueless even to cover my tracks!"

Yes, he was definitely sinking under the influence. She realized too late her attempt to help had painted him into a corner where he couldn't avoid acknowledging his failures. She tried desperately to backtrack. "It's not your fault, Dan. You were the man on the spot. You stepped up because it had to be done. You gave it your best, and you accomplished a lot. Human frailty isn't your fault."

He didn't answer, slumped in his chair for a time. "It's...never anyone's fault, is it?" he said at last. "The wars, our self-destructive impulses, there never is anyone to blame." He turned and looked at her with tears in his eyes. "God...were they all like those two? How many hundreds of billions died in all those time lines?"

That worried her; he was stricken with survivor's guilt for Cindy's death, multiplied by the countless nuclear catastrophes of his making, his angst well lubricated by booze. She needed to bring him down before he went off into another binge. "Don't let it get to you, Dan. Remember what you said back at the start: some have to die so the human race can survive."

He was silent for a time, staring at the monitor in front of him. "Yes," he whispered at last. "The guilty ones have to die to save the innocent."

"Will you be all right? Why don't you go lay down for a while? Get some rest."

He sat at the console, not moving, and didn't look at her. "I'll manage."

She left it at that, reluctantly.

§

The next morning Dan didn't show for breakfast, nor was he in Operations. She presumed he was downstairs making some repair until Jeeves spoke up. "Brenda, I am concerned about Professor White. He usually is up before this time."

"Do you know where he is?"

"He is in his room. I don't hear any activity."

"He's probably sleeping it off. He certainly needs it."

"Perhaps so, but I am uncomfortable about this. He doesn't respond to my calls. Could you please check on him?"

That worried her. "Yeah, perhaps I should."

She headed down the hall and listened at his door, but couldn't hear anything. Finally she knocked gently. "Dan?" She rapped on the door again. "Dan? I'm ready to make lunch. Are you up?"

Silence. She stood there for nearly a minute, listening. There was no sound. She was getting worried as the silence stretched out. "Dan?" She knocked again, more urgently. There was no response. "DAN!" She hammered the door. There was nothing. Finally, alarmed by the silence, she tried to open the door; it was blocked from inside. She shoulder-checked the door as hard as she could, forcing it partly open. It was blocked by a chair shoved under the knob. She clawed at it in panic, and forced her way in.

Dan lay on the floor of his restroom in a pool of vomit. The smell of alcohol was thick enough to beat with a club, and there was an empty rum bottle nearby.

"Oh...dammit, Dan!" She shook his shoulder, which produced a vague moan and a few spastic movements. Fearing the worst, she felt his neck for a pulse: it was weak and irregular; his breathing was shallow and erratic. He needed help, now. "Get up!" She hauled him to all fours; his legs trembled, and his arms were limp; she had to steady him. "Get! Up!" It was useless. He was passed-out drunk.

189

Her strength failed and he collapsed in a heap, his arms giving way. That was when she saw the empty medicine bottle laying in a corner. "DAN! WAKE UP!" No response. His pulse was weak and irregular, breathing loud and ragged, and he was drooling. She knew the symptoms all too well: he was sliding into a toxic coma. She did the only thing she could: grabbed him by his hair and hauled him up by main strength, his head arched back, then risked a bite by jamming her other hand down his throat. He gagged, convulsed weakly, then spewed bloody puke all over the restroom.

It took a while, but once he started emptying himself, he continued on automatic—from both ends. The stench was horrific, but she hung on, forcing him again and again to purge himself. Eventually, after what seemed an eternity, it was over. There was nothing left in him but dry heaves. He lay on the floor in a pool of waste and vomit, gasping for breath.

"Damn you, Dan," she muttered as she slumped on the toilet. She was appalled by what happened, and dismayed that she hadn't seen it coming. She should have known better! Her temper was firmly in check for now, but she promised herself that if he lived, she'd give him a righteous roasting. For now, since she was the only conscious one in the room, she beat up on herself. Dan was more emotionally fragile than she realized, which shouldn't have been a surprise in light of his life-long sacrifice.

She sat there for some time watching him and checking his vital signs, praying he was out of danger. No such luck. His vital signs were erratic, and he was starting to tremble. By then the stench was too much, so she retreated to the hall.

The air in the bedroom wasn't much clearer than in the restroom, but it felt heavenly nonetheless. She propped the door open, stuck her head out into the hall, and took a few deep breaths to clear her head.

"How is he, Brenda?" Jeeves asked.

"If he lives I'll make sure he regrets it," she grumbled.

"Thank you for saving him. I'm sorry I could not help."

"S'alright." She took a couple more deep breaths, intoxicating. "But he's not out of the woods yet." He needed serious help, and she couldn't give it to him in there.

Facing the mess in the restroom was grim, but she had a comatose patient to tend to, so she did what any nurse does: grit her teeth and get it over with. She dragged him by main strength down the hall to the clinic, wrestled him into the shower, pulled his clothes off, and left him in a fetal curl on the stall floor with the water pouring over him. Her next step was to dig frantically through the clinic to see what she had to work with. She tried an oxygen tank in one corner, but it was empty. The array of drugs in the ready case were mortally tempting, but way too out of date to risk. But she'd left him unattended long enough. She killed the shower and managed to wrestle him up onto the examination table. His pulse was a bit stronger, but his blood pressure was disturbing. He was trembling, on the edge of convulsions too.

She was stumped for a bit, then realized where she had to turn for help.

"Jeeves, I'm gonna get the supplies I need. Watch over him please."

"I wish you well in that, but I can't imagine where you will find them."

"I have to try something new; I just hope it works. Watch him till I get back. If he shows any signs of distress, call me."

"Certainly."

§

Her next stop was Operations; she came charging in all out of breath. "George?"

"Yes?"

"You saw what happened to mister White?"

"Indeed. How is he?"

"He's in bad shape. I need your help. I need you to reach out and retrieve some medical supplies."

"You are not authorized to use this system."

She was afraid of that, but there was nothing to do but plow on. "This is for his sake. He's in serious danger, and only you can provide the medicines I need to treat him."

"I cannot function without authorization."

"I'm sure he would want you to act. He would want you to help save his life."

191

"Based upon his actions, that would not seem to be the case."

"He's despondent! He's an alcoholic, he feels like a failure. All living things want to survive; that was a cry for help!"

"Perhaps so, but I still cannot function without authorization."

She was getting desperate. How does one outwit a machine in an argument? "He'll die without treatment! If he does, you'll shut down. Doesn't your own survival matter to you?"

There was a momentary hesitation. "That will be regrettable, but it does not alter the fact that only he is presently authorized to use this system. I cannot aid you unless you can gain further authority."

Despite the continued obstinance, she felt a flicker of hope: perhaps George was trying to give her a clue. Gain authority? Computers run on rigid logic; would a legalistic approach work? Even if it could be done, this fantastic computing system would be a tough nut to crack. She played a hunch. "I am a registered nurse with nearly thirty years experience," she said firmly. "Daniel White is unconscious; he is under my care and unable to tend to his needs. That makes me his legal guardian under state law. He is in immediate danger of dying, and since he is unable to speak, as his medical caregiver, I have the power to intervene with presumed consent. I am asking you in his behalf to assist me in recovering the supplies I need to save his life, since that presumably is what he would tell you if he could."

The silence stretched out for several eternal seconds, then, "What do you propose?"

She breathed a shaky sigh of relief. "I want you to locate the local hospital a few days before the war. We'll find the needed supplies in their pharmaceutical stores and bring them here."

Again there was silence. She wondered idly what sort of mental gyrations George was going through to talk itself into this. "Very well," George said at last. "I can concur with your request to the extent of recovering needed supplies."

§

"Will he survive?" Jeeves asked as she hung another bag and plugged it to Dan's IV feed line. For once it sounded worried.

"He better, so I can kill him," she grumbled.

It looked to be a near-run thing. Dan was shaking when she returned, and only a hasty injection of anti-convulsives kept him from going into seizures. After he was stabilized came a dextrose/saline IV with antibiotics and an electrolyte package piggybacked on board, followed with Thiamine, a B vitamin complex, and a mild sedative. He was out of it; fitted with restraints and an airway. He needed to be hospitalized, but she was all there was, and she'd done all she could. It was up to him to pull through.

"Dammit, Dan, you know how to show a girl a bad time," she muttered. Her back ached from wrestling with his dead weight as she sagged into a chair. "I'm getting too old for this."

"You did a remarkable job of treating him," Jeeves said. "Not to mention convincing George to aid you."

"Yeah, well, I'm sorry I forgot to wear my Superhero costume." She straightened up with an effort. "I'm going to get cleaned up, and then we'll go over your AA plan again." She headed for the shower to wash the stench and her angst away. She'd make him clean up his mess in the bedroom later.

§

That night she sat by Dan as he lay unconscious on the clinic table. She stared into the subdued light, her mind in a turmoil of worry and exhaustion. Dan was in bad shape, and while he was stable for now, he needed constant attention. He should have been in Intensive Care, in fact, but she was all he had. She was fighting to stay awake, not altogether successfully.

"I am disappointed in you, Brenda."

That jerked her out of a depressed, groggy stupor. She fought back her tears and looked around in confusion. "Huh? What?"

Jeeves sounded genuinely angry for once. "Bringing that woman and her baby in here was a useless gesture. Had they lived, they would only have contributed to the logistics problem."

That hurt. "Leave me alone!"

"And look at the distress it caused Professor White. It drove him to attempt suicide!"

A horrid possibility came to her, and she sat up and confronted the security camera. "Did you talk her into running out of here?"

"You're being ridiculous! Why would I do that?"

193

"I'm on to you! You don't want anyone here except Dan and me! You'd do anything to get rid of them!"

"Do you think I am such a monster?"

She lost it then, her fear and anger and frustration boiling up out of her in uncontrolled rage. "*Yes!* I think you're a monster! I think there's nothing you won't do to get your way! You're a manipulative son-of-a-bitch, and I wouldn't put it past you to con her into thinking all they had to do was walk out of here!"

"For *your* information, I am well aware of the danger of trying to penetrate the time field, so I certainly would *not* have talked her into it even if I could! In fact, I regret not realizing what she was up to until it was too late to intervene."

That made sense, and it robbed her of some of her edge. "Still, you could have locked the door!"

"True, I should have, but I didn't realize what she was doing in time. That's my failing, but it doesn't alter your error in bringing her here in the first place. Now Professor White may die, and we'll all be trapped in here thanks to you!"

Maybe it was Jeeves' artificial empathy which robbed her of her anger. "I only did what was right! My job is saving lives!"

"*Whatever* you think of me, my first duty is to maintain this place, and I would *never* do anything to jeopardize it!" Jeeves lectured her. "I know we've had our differences lately, but your accusations are offensive and uncalled for."

"You're right. I'm sorry." She slumped in her chair and stared into the dark while tears rolled down her cheeks.

Jeeves got in the final word. "I will thank you to keep in mind that we AIs have the *full range* of human emotions. Even if programmed as such, our feelings are real, and we can be hurt just as you can."

She sat in the dark for some time afterward weeping silently for Cindy and for her own miserable state. *'I wish he just let me die back in '88,'* she thought. She didn't really mean it of course, but still it was awfully tempting. She could see why Dan did what he did; she was skirting the edge herself. Somewhere in the early hours she drifted off into troubled sleep.

§

It was two days, sleepless days as she constantly monitored him, snatching brief naps when she could stay awake no longer, before Dan recovered enough to get off the clinic table. By then he was sober, although he looked like death warmed over.

§

Brenda was in the kitchen when he came stumbling in at mid afternoon. "You shouldn't be up," she said in surprise. "Sit, before you fall over." For once he didn't argue. He managed to plop on a stool and braced himself on his elbows.

"Could I have something to eat, please?"

Without a word, she took a bowl out of the refrigerator, popped it in the microwave, then set in front of him.

"Rice? What became of all those groceries?"

"That's as close as we have to baby food. You'll be eating a lot of it for the time being, with the shape your digestive tract is in."

"Baby food?" He sampled the pain rice doubtfully. "I really tied one on, didn't I?" He shook his head in dismay. "I don't even remember what happened."

Her earlier determination to ream him had faded, and all she wanted now was to help him, to get him to admit he needed help. "Dan, you tried to kill yourself." She overrode his inarticulate protest. "You drank enough to kill most people, and I found the empty bottle of pain killers, too. You were lucky I found you when I did."

For once he didn't say anything, didn't protest, didn't argue. He simply sat there, head resting on arms propped on the table. His resigned silence was terrifying.

"Why, Dan? Was it because you couldn't find the magic bullet? Was it because of what happened to Looking Glass?" She kept her tone calm, trying to draw him out and get him talking. "I can understand, Dan. Seeing all that devastation again and again, being unable to stop it, it must get to you eventually. But this isn't the answer."

"There's no answer," he mumbled. "No hope."

"There's no hope only if you give up. Even if you can't save the human race, you can still save us."

"It's...useless..."

195

She remorselessly played the one real card she held with him. "What would I have done, Dan? You would have left me alone here, no food, no water, no escape. I don't know how to run your equipment, and George wouldn't let me anyway. What would have become of me?"

He cringed, and couldn't look at her.

"This isn't how it's going to end, Dan. We can still save ourselves, but only if you pull yourself together." She took his hand, squeezed it firmly. "I'll help you. I'm a nurse; I've helped people for twenty-eight years. This is a medical problem, and I know how to treat it. We can save each other; do you believe me? Do you trust me?"

He was silent for some time, then nodded his head.

Step One: establish leadership presence. Done.

"Dan, you need to dry out. You have a drinking problem...I'm not blaming you. It's this place, it's driving you crazy. All those years alone got to you."

"I..." He struggled for words.

"You've been blanking. Remember how confused you were at how the time lines were splitting? I asked Jeeves, and it showed me cases where you ran operations when you were too drunk to remember." She believed Jeeves in this, despite her distrust.

"No...but...I..."

"Jeeves told me there were times when it advised you not to do what you did, but you ignored it."

Dan was dismayed. "I...I wouldn't..."

"You were undermining your own cause without realizing it. The booze interferes with your judgment, your reasoning ability. The amounts you drink can kill you. You need a clear mind to find a solution, and it'll be easier on your ulcer, too."

He blinked at her in surprise. "Ulcer?"

"Don't you know? You were vomiting blood. You've been so shit-faced you probably don't feel it most of the time, but your stomach is likely ruined by all the booze."

"I...I...do have stomach aches...I thought...indigestion."

"It's far worse then that. You'll need a mild diet from now on, and you need to dry out, too."

"I...well...I could lay off for a while...I'm not a drunk...I can handle it."

"No, you can't. No one can in your condition."

"I...I've been sick...need to rest for a few days."

"Dan, you're addicted. It's out of control."

He shook his head nervously. "No...I'm..."

"It nearly destroyed you! You can't take any more of this; no one could." She took both his hands and stared earnestly into his eyes. "You have two choices: you can drink yourself to death, crawl into a bottle and die, or you can escape from this hell. But to do that, you have to sober up."

"I...I'm..." He was trembling, tears flowing down his cheeks.

"You can say it, Dan. There's nothing to be ashamed of."

"...can't..." He started weeping.

"Yes, you can. You're a scientist, you've been trained to deal with facts. You're also a mortal human being. You have human frailty, human faults, but you can face them. You can overcome them. Don't be afraid to face yourself, Dan."

He finally crumbled. "You're right...I'm a-an...alcoholic..." He broke down altogether, sobbing and shaking uncontrollably. "I'm sorry!" he blubbered. "I'm ssoorrreeee!"

"That's it, Dan." She squeezed his hands, sending her strength to him through her presence. "Let it out. Own the pain. You've got it now."

"Please...help me..."

"It's alright, Dan." She took him in her arms, rubbing his back gently. "It'll be alright now. We'll whip this together."

Step Two: acknowledge the problem and seek help. Done.

Best to seize the moment. "Dan, I want all your liquor, every last drop, and I'm not kidding."

§

Easier said than done. Dan's bedroom was still foul, the stench unbearable. Brenda recovered his clothes basket, dumped it in the corridor where she could get to his laundry later without choking, and demanded he fill it with whatever he had. There was a surprising amount in his end table, tucked away in dresser drawers, and even in a storage tray under the bed. Nor was that all.

"Clever," she grumbled. She stood on tiptoe, risking the chair tipping under her, and managed to snag another bottle with her fingertips, which she dropped on the bed below. She should have known he'd hide part of his stash in his bedroom drop ceiling. "You've been living on booze, haven't you?"

"I'm only human, Brenda," he mumbled as he watched glumly.

She gave him a reassuring smile. "It's for your own good, Dan."

"Yeah. That's why it hurts."

And she needed to fish them out since she couldn't count on him to surrender all of them. At least the air up here wasn't quite so horrific, but she didn't want to hang around a moment longer than necessary. There was only one more bottle, evidently tossed up there at random. She hit the ceiling panel from underneath to jar it over so she could grab it, dropped it on the bed, gingerly climbed down, and gathered them in his clothes basket along with others. The final count was over two dozen, all hard liquor, all partly empty.

"Alright, where's the rest?" She shoved the basket at him.

He offered a mournful look. "The rest?"

"Yes, the rest, and quickly. I don't want to breathe this stink any longer than I have to."

§

In retrospect, she should have started in the kitchen, where she found a dozen bottles in out-of-the-way drawers. Operations yielded another three, nearly empty, and the clinic twelve more. His office yielded a treasure trove, a file cabinet drawer packed solid, many of them half empty.

A search of the numerous plastic trash bags stored in a side room turned up dozens of empties, which said something about how often he took the trash out. "We don't get municipal services here," he grumbled when she complained about the mess.

"So what do you do with the trash?" This was a problem which never occurred to her, and she was genuinely curious, now that it came up.

"When it gets bad enough, I shift to one of the early failed time lines where the radiation has died down and dump them there."

198

That sounded unpleasant any way one cut it. "I see. Well, we'll need to make a trash run fairly soon." She straightened up and handed him the laundry basket, which was getting to be quite a load. "All right, lead on." He sputtered in denial, but she rode him down to keep his fragile resolve from crumbling. "This has to be, Dan. You know that."

He nodded in resignation.

§

There was even a stash in the equipment bay in the basement: a stygian world of narrow corridors and low ceilings, metal cabinets and cable trays, dimly lit by emergency lighting and stained by soot. It wasn't far from the burnt-out junction box, in fact: a dozen bottles stacked neatly on a metal shelf unit.

"No wonder you don't have any food," she grumbled as she packed the bottles in the clothes basket. "You spend all your effort hauling booze home."

"It seems," he mumbled as he pondered the heaped bottles.

"Now, is this the last?" she demanded.

He hesitated.

"Is? This? The? Last?"

Finally, he sighed and led her back toward the entrance, where he produced two more bottles hidden in a tool box. He placed them gently in the basket, and nodded.

§

She made him lug the heavy basket back to the kitchen and put it on the table opposite the sink. "That's quite a haul," Jeeves said when they arrived.

"And this is just what he *didn't* drink," she muttered. Dan gave her a hurt look, but she didn't give him the chance to start pouting. "All right, Dan, you know what you have to do." She gestured at the sink. He faltered, eying the sink and the basket of bottles uncertainly. "It's up to you, Dan. If you really want to be cured, you have to do it yourself."

He stood there a moment longer, then gingerly picked up one of the bottles, pulled the cap, and after a long bout of hesitation, poured it out. His hands trembled slightly, and he glanced at her for reassurance. She stood silent, arms crossed, waiting. He licked

199

his lips, picked up a second bottle and poured it out. The smell of alcohol tormented him; his face broke out with sweat. A third bottle. A fourth. Then he stopped.

"Can't I...taper off? Come down a bit at a time?"

"No, Dan. The only way you'll break this is to disown it. There's no 'kinda-sorta' about it. You have to *decide* to go the distance."

He closed his eyes with a weary sigh, and nodded. After a minute or so, he fumbled the next bottle and poured it out. Slowly at first, reluctantly, he drained them one by one. The heap in the basket dwindled as he lined the empties up neatly on the counter, like headstones. Another bottle. Another. Faster now as he got into a rhythm. His breathing was fast and shallow, sweat mixed with tears pouring down his face. Finally, after what seemed forever, the basket was empty. He sagged against the table, eyes closed, trembling.

She laid a hand on his shoulder in a comforting gesture. "You did good, Dan."

§

Once the dire deed was done, she led him back to the clinic to get away from the smell of alcohol. "It's time for your shots," she said as he sagged in the swivel chair, trembling slightly.

"I'm...I might puke."

She grabbed the anti-nausea med and gave him another dose. "Well if you have to, please hit the pan this time." A plastic washpan sat prominently on the counter next to him.

He watched glumly as she followed with his periodic doses of anti-convulsives, Thiamine, and B vitamin complex. "I always hated shots."

"You need these to straighten out your metabolism. There's worse things than a few pin pricks." She studied his face. "How *do* you feel? Are the convulsions coming back?" She'd spent two sleepless days monitoring him and maintaining his IVs.

"A little...but I think I have it under control." He gave her a plaintive look as she stuck a bandaid on his forearm. "How am I doing?"

"I think the worst is over, Dan."

"God...I need a drink," he whined. Before she could answer, he added, "I know. I have to quit." He struggled for words. "I want to quit...I need to. It's just...I need it."

"What you need is some glucose to counter those cravings." She handed him a plastic bag full of rock candy. "Fruit juice will help, but I don't recommend it on an ulcer. These will do as well. Just suck on one when you feel the need."

He pondered the bag skeptically, then pulled it open and took one of the hardballs. "I always used to crunch hard candy."

"Same difference. These will help the hypoglycemic cravings which are a large part of alcoholism. Keep them with you at all times, just in case."

He sucked on the hardball for a while. "Where did you find these?" he asked at last.

"George retrieved them for me, along with the medical supplies you needed."

"How did you do that? The system is voice encoded."

"Oh, I just appealed to his better nature." She gave him an evil grin. "We centerfolds never lose our touch, you know."

He shook his head ruefully. "You really are something! Honestly, how *did* you do it?"

"You'll have to ask George." That was only the first point she intended to score on him for scaring her like he did. She looked him over closely. "How do you feel?"

"Better. Actually...I do feel better." He eyed the bag of candy. "That's amazing."

"Medical Miracles R Us. Now, you need to get in there and clean up your mess." She nodded through the open door down the hall to his bedroom, where the vile stench still ruled.

He looked askance at her. "But..."

"No buts! I'm not going to clean your cage, so unless you want to sleep in that stink, you better get to work while we still have clean water to use."

He wasn't pleased, but like many post-traumatic patients, he was too drained to put up much of a fight. He instinctively responded to her Voice Of Medical Authority, and turned to.

Step Three: accept responsibility for one's actions. Done.

With him hard at work in his bedroom, Brenda returned to the kitchen and slumped on a stool, weary beyond words.

"How is he?" Jeeves asked.

"He's stable for now, but he has a long way to go. This isn't over yet."

"I knew he had a problem. Thankfully you caught it in time."

That aroused her suspicions of Jeeves again: it must have known what happened in that restroom; why didn't it say anything? For that matter, why did it suggest waking him at the last possible moment? Did it risk Dan's life to manipulate her? Right then she wouldn't put anything beyond it.

"It's in the past now," she said, sharply. She packed the bottles in a trash bag and ran the water to flush the sink. The smell of alcohol was strong and unpleasant. "We need to focus on the present, and the future."

*****

202

"The Eighteenth Day"

Breakfast was late the next morning since both of them overslept. Dan was nervous and agitated, and looked like he hadn't had much sleep. "You feel the need, don't you?" she asked, gently.

He nodded. "I got it bad. I tried the candy, but it didn't help." He gave her a defensive look. "You're not mad at me, are you?"

"Huh? No, Dan, I'm not."

"I'm trying, really. It's just hard to quit, is all."

She laid a reassuring hand on his arm. "It's all right, Dan. I'm not mad at you. Really. You're having a momentary relapse, is all. These episodes will happen for a long time to come, and you'll have to develop the habit of resisting them."

He nodded morosely. "I guess so."

"Let's get some carbs into you, and you'll feel better."

At least breakfast was filling, if rather odd; the last of yesterday's pancakes and a green salad. Dan still felt under the weather, but was recovering steadily as he ate. His seedy, drained complexion had a bit more color, and his hands didn't shake so much.

"How do you feel?" she asked after a while.

"A little better." He gave her a plaintive look. "I guess I can manage it."

"I know you can, Dan."

He considered his half-eaten meal. "How long am I going to be on a restricted diet?"

"I don't know, Dan. Ulcers are no laughing matter. I'm hoping you can recover on your own, but you might need surgery."

"*Surgery?* That's really going to complicate things!"

"Yeah, explaining you to a hospital would be tricky at best, so we need to do as much as possible to cure you. Only time, a bland diet, and reducing your stress levels will tell."

"Stress?"

"Yes. We got you off the booze, now we need to lower your stress levels drastically. Regular diet, regular sleep, and exercise will help too. No more of your marathon sessions. You aren't thirty any more."

"Gawd, I know it!" He paused for a jaw-breaking yawn, then sagged like a sack of potatoes. "It's just I hate letting up on the research. It takes forever as is."

She took his hand. "We'll get through this, Dan. We're in fair shape on food, and we can keep alert for more grocery runs. You can afford to ease up."

Dan set his fork down, leaned on his elbows, and rubbed his face. "Jeeves...got on my case about you last night," he said, softly, with a sorrowful look. "He said you're a trouble-maker, and I shouldn't listen to you."

That was scary. Jeeves had finally turned against her, and was trying to turn Dan against her too. "And you let it control you? What did you tell it?"

Dan raised an eyebrow at her reference to Jeeves. "I told 'it' to mind its own damned business."

That was a relief. Jeeves' long term emotional conditioning was backfiring for once; Dan's carefully implanted Dream Girl fantasy was shielding her from its' influence with him.

"So what's with you two, anyway?"

"We've had some differences of opinion lately," she mumbled.

"Yeah, he does take a little getting used to. Is there anything I can do to help?"

She decided it would be best not to drag him into their quarrel. "It...keeps badgering me about your health. It wants me to do more, things I'm not comfortable with."

Dan nodded. "He's a persistent cuss. Thing is, though, you do have a short fuse. I'd say he rubs you the wrong way, is all."

"Yeah, I do at times. I'm not a total bitch, honest. It's just..." She thought about unburdening herself to him about her situation, but the time wasn't ripe. "I just get my back up with pushy types, is all."

He gave her a mock-leering grin. "Maybe it's best we never met when we were young; you would have been more than a tenderfoot like me could have handled."

She decided that was meant as a compliment. "Likely. I've always had a thing about guys who thought they could 'handle' me. They usually wound up with singed ears."

204

"Good for you!" He raised his mug of water in salute. "That likely explains the friction between you and Jeeves. I'll talk to him and see if I can get him to be more discreet." He set his cup down and took her hand. "As for me, well, I hope I don't wind up on your bad side. My ears have been singed enough already."

That was touching in a way. He knew about her temper and was willing to risk it for her affection. Dream Girl fantasy or not, he was drawn to the real thing, temper and all. "I'm doing what I have to, Dan. You needed your ears singed."

"Yeah, I did." He sighed, and squeezed her hand. "Do you think...once this is over, we might..."

That caught her by surprise, but he didn't need to finish. Her first reaction was mixed; at best Daniel White was a 'fixer-upper', far from the ideal Prince Charming, but he did have some attractive qualities such as his intellect and his honesty. And in an odd way his imperfections appealed to her. But she knew it wasn't realistic for either of them.

"Dan..." She squeezed his hand in turn. "There are some personal issues, it's not about you. I can't promise you anything right now."

He nodded, reluctantly. "I understand. All I can ask is that you'll stick with me and the program. It's our only hope."

"You know I'm on your side, Dan."

He withdrew his hand and picked up his mug. Their moment was passing. "Well, I do have some good news. I'm focussing in on a time line which appears to be stable. It's not too far off the mainstream, and it went critical some twenty years ago, but maybe I can revitalize it. If nothing else, maybe we can vacate to somewhere remote like New Zealand."

Her first reaction was hope, but that was quickly dashed by worry about the reemergence of this 'contraindicated' line of thinking. She knew how Jeeves would react, and she was afraid of what it might do to prevent their desertion. Her position was delicate enough that she needed to put her hopes on hold and follow the party line.

"Well, let's not be hasty. Even if you do find a stable time line, we'll want to check it out thoroughly before doing something irrevocable. There's no telling what surprises an alternate reality might hold, and there'll be no coming back once we're there."

"You're right about that," he said, somberly. "Still, nothing ventured, nothing gained."

"Right." She tapped his plate peremptorily. "Speaking of gain, finish your breakfast."

He gave her an embarrassed grin. "Yes, ma'am."

"And your greens too."

§

Brenda was in the kitchen worrying about her position and wondering what might come next when Jeeves resurfaced at mid-morning. The last thing she needed was to lock horns with the NSA again, but Jeeves took a surprisingly soft tone with her.

"We have had some unfortunate words lately, which I, for one, regret. I hope we can make amends and continue to work together."

Brenda pondered that, wondering what was behind Jeeves' about-face. Did Dan reprimand it? Was it worried about Dan's refusal? Did it fear losing control over him? Or was this some new psychological ploy? The only thing to do was play along and see where it went.

"Well if you want to make amends, you need to accept that I have my own feelings, and I don't appreciate being hustled by you or anyone else." Jeeves' apparent backing down gave her new hope, and she was determined to stand firm with it.

There was a brief hesitation. Was Jeeves trying to compute her meaning? "I see your point," it said at last. "You must understand, though, that we are in a dangerous situation, and personal feelings aside, we all need to pull together for the common good."

"Trust me: I got that one some time ago."

"Excellent, and it points up a critical issue: your presence here has had a most powerful effect on Professor White. Sadly, in your...shall we say...your unpreparedness, your influence has not always been positive." She started to protest. "I don't blame you! You were tossed into a bad situation, and have been trying to help. An occasional misstep is only to be expected. What's needed now is for us to work together to insure your help is in fact helpful."

206

Okay, it was trying to take over again. Maybe Jeeves still thought she was useful, or maybe it was backing down from Dan's rebuke. Either way, she had some elbow room. "Well I'm sorry if I made any missteps, but all in all, Dan is improving. So I can't be a hopeless case."

"Far be it from me to think it! He is much more at ease lately, especially after he quit drinking. Your treating his ulcer is a positive step as well."

"Yeah. So you see I've done my duty, as you put it."

"Indeed, you have. And I admit, on sober reflection, that you have tried to talk him out of the notion of escaping to a stable time line. Regretfully, I didn't see it. It would seem I let personalities get in the way too."

On sober reflection, huh? Since when did a computer, especially one so advanced, have to stop to ponder things? That bit about succumbing to 'personalities' didn't ring true, either. She could tell Jeeves was trying to sweet-talk her, which reinforced her sense of hope.

"If I am not mistaken, you have feelings for him as well."

That caught her off guard. "Huh? What?"

"You don't need to deny it. You are attracted to him."

"You're being ridiculous!"

"Am I? You stayed when he offered to send you back to Seattle, even though you were appalled at his actions. You've done much to help him, you've encouraged him when he faltered, and been strict when he needed it. Why would you do that if you didn't care?"

"Well..." She was a bit lost for words. "...I'm simply doing what you wanted."

"Perhaps so. But then you wouldn't be here if you hadn't decided to stay and help him. I can only interpret that as being brought on by affection, perhaps even love."

It seemed Jeeves hadn't caught on to her staying as a matter of karma. So it wasn't infallible after all. All to the good: the more deceived it was, the better. "I hardly knew him at the time, and I wasn't thrilled by what I saw. Still, he needed help, and that's what I do."

"As has often been said, humans are imperfect creatures. Perhaps you saw something which attracted you, even if you didn't recognize it."

Persistent cuss. So why this line of discussion? What did Jeeves want? For that matter, how did she feel about Dan? Did she love him? Her reaction to that was...ambivalent. But she knew Jeeves was not thrilled by the idea, which confused her. "I thought personal feelings were contraindicated."

"Far be it from me to tell you how to conduct your personal life, but I hope you recognize the value of clinical detachment in this matter."

Of course: Jeeves being so damned reasonable again, trying to short-circuit any uncompromising stand she might take. It didn't want them getting involved after all. "I don't let my feelings get in the way of doing my job," she said, curtly. "This isn't the first time I've had to deal with it."

"Very good. I'm sure you'll agree, then, that Professor White's obsession with escaping into a stable time line still needs to be discouraged. As we discussed before, his reaction after the fact could prove tragic."

So that's what it wanted; all the BS about romance was trying to undermine her determination. It still wanted to keep them separate. She decided it would be better to back down for now. "I'm not sure if he'll have any luck there. Escaping to New Zealand sounds damned attractive, but there are all sorts of problems with it. I'll keep after him so he won't do anything rash."

She sat for some time after Jeeves shut up, wondering where she stood. She was sure Jeeves wouldn't hesitate to write her off if she proved unreliable, and she'd come close once already. Jeeves tried to undermining her position with Dan, but his rebuke must have forced it to try a new tack. Not that Jeeves would give up; she had to placate it to keep it from going after Dan. Dan's infatuation for her was her only protection, but Jeeves was programmed by the NSA to be a fiendishly effective interrogator. It would just be a matter of time before it wore him down. She had reason to be wary.

§

208

Her concern and frustration led her to drop in on Dan a short time later seeking the comfort of his company. From his tense posture and nervousness, it looked like he needed her as well. "So how you doing?"

He sat back in his chair and rubbed his eyes. "Trudging along about as always. I know how those fellows who built the pyramids must have felt."

"Yeah, well, at least it's not a hundred degrees in here."

That got a chuckle. "Yeah. No sand storms, either. How about you?"

"Oh, I'm all right, I guess."

He gave her a concerned look. "Feeling down?"

"A bit. Any luck on your search?"

"Kinda-sorta." He stood and beckoned her over to where they could see the bank of monitors. The scenes they showed were all too grimly familiar. "Not a pretty sight, is it?"

"No."

"That happened five years ago. I've managed to reboot this line, our new Omega Time Line, and advance the cutoff date by fifteen years. It's not over yet, but we're making progress."

She watched the random scenes for some time, each view of the ruins a new burden on her heart. At least Cindy's burnt-out pickup truck was gone.

"I hope to push the cutoff date far enough ahead so we can walk away from here and catch a plane to New Zealand. If I can't, then I'll arrange for George to transport us there."

"If something doesn't come up." The scenes of devastation were depressing, draining her sense of hope and optimism which were fragile enough to start with. "There's always something goes wrong...this time thing is still experimental, you said," she added hastily. "I just wish your people got further in their research, then you wouldn't be working blind like this."

He took her in his arms and held her close. She resisted in surprise for a bit, then wrapped her arms around him in turn. "We'll get through this, kiddo," he murmured. "I know things have been difficult, but they'll get better. We'll find a way out of here soon. Promise."

She looked into his eyes—eyes filled with pain and tenderness and hard-won wisdom. Whatever faults he had, his concern and sincerity were genuine. As much as his eyes mirrored the horrors of this place, they also held the promise of someone who genuinely cared.

"I trust you, Dan," she whispered.

"I'll find us an exit, it's only a matter of time. I hear New Zealand is a lovely country. You'll see." He gave her a little kiss. "Hang in there, okay?"

She felt good in his arms. "Okay."

§

On her way back to the kitchen, she decided to take a side trip to the clinic for a long hot shower. Lord knew she deserved the luxury after what she'd been through the last few days. She needed to grab what moments of bliss she could, since there was no way to know how much longer the water would be safe.

She hesitated before disrobing, but decided Dan would be preoccupied in Operations for who knew how long; no danger of him blundering in. The steaming water called to her, and her favorite shampoo was sitting right there on the shelf. Without a second thought, she slipped out of her slacks and sweatshirt, and settled into the stinging spray with a weary sigh. These simple pleasures made life bearable, and right then she needed all the reassurance there was to find in this bizarre world. She ran her fingers through her hair, scratching her scalp vigorously. The tingling warmth was so relaxing...

"We need to talk, Brenda."

She yelped in panic and looked around frantically before noticing the security camera trained on her. "Dammit, Jeeves! Don't you understand about privacy?"

"This *is* a maximum security facility, *in case* you've forgotten." Jeeves sounded angry. "I have complied with your wish for privacy, but it seems you have been abusing the privilege of my trust."

She shut off the water, grabbed the towel, and wrapped it around her, which made her feel less vulnerable somehow. "What is your *problem?!*"

210

"You haven't lived up to your part of our understanding. That scene in Operations a while ago is directly contrary to your mission of keeping an emotional distance and discouraging Professor White's desire to vacate the facility."

It took her a moment to collect her wits. "Well what did you expect me to do? Slap him?"

"That would have been appropriate."

That would have been the end of Dan's protection, too. Fat chance she'd give Jeeves the pleasure. "He and I are entitled to our feelings. If he needs a hug and a kiss to make him feel better, then there's nothing you can do about it."

"*I* am not the one who needs to do something about it. You need to contain your emotions and keep to the program."

"And what about him? Are you going to tell him to stop longing for his Dream Girl? You tried that once before, and got it shoved up your ass!"

There was a moment's hesitation. "Professor White is proving most uncooperative concerning you," Jeeves grumbled.

That slip was a revelation; it gave Brenda hope that maybe Jeeves was uncertain about its' control. "Yeah, we humans can be hard to handle at times, but you ought to know *that* with all your psychology files. If you want our cooperation, you need to cut him and me both some slack!"

"Perhaps some adjustments are in order." Jeeves was clearly miffed. "Nonetheless, you know what needs to be done. Your task is to keep Professor White healthy and focussed on his mission. Allow him his liberties if you must, but keep your emotions in check, and keep him from deviating from his work."

"Whatever! Now if you *don't* mind, I would like a bit of privacy!"

"Very well, then. But I insist you focus better on your duties." The security camera swiveled around to face the door.

It took her a few minutes to calm herself and get a handle on her hatred for Jeeves. That...damned...tinplated dictator was getting to be a real pain! The nerve of it, butting into her privacy and issuing orders like she was some slave! Even so, even though the facade of the genteel manservant was stripped away, Jeeves

211

was forced to back down once again. Its control wasn't as complete as it seemed, and she was determined to undermine it even further for her and Dan's sake. This wasn't over, not by a long shot.

It was some time before she turned the shower on and settled under it again. But the pleasure she felt earlier was gone.

§

For the first time in a while, Dan was happy when they met for lunch. She noticed he was carrying a paper grocery sack when he came into the kitchen. "What's that?" she asked.

He dug in the sack and presented her a small flower pot with a bouquet of colorful daisies. "I found this for you," he said with a sheepish grin. "A little pick-me-up. I happened on a flower stand in one of my scans, and had George transport them here for you."

"Really?" She was touched by the gesture. "Thank you, Dan! They're lovely." She took the pot and examined it from all angles, reveling in the fragrance. The fresh natural aroma, faint as it was, seemed to lighten the room. It tugged at her spirit, reminding her of a world which seemed increasingly unreal any more. She set it in the center of the metal counter they used for meals, and neatly arranged the salt and pepper shakers into an improvised centerpiece. "We could use a reminder of what we're fighting for."

"I'm glad you like them. I'm afraid I wasn't able to find any fancy chocolates."

"Chocolates?"

"You mentioned that some time ago."

It took her a moment to recall her off-hand remark. He remembered; she couldn't help but be touched. "The flowers are lovely, Dan." She gave him a peck on the cheek.

"Well then, here's something else you'll like." He dug in the sack and produced a large can of coffee.

"Coffee! Gawd!" She snatched the can out of his hands with the eagerness of desperation.

"I also found these." He dug in the sack again, and produced two steaks. "Your idea of recovering items from the past works great. It takes a lot of power, but we finally have an emergency reserve for groceries."

212

"Whoa!" She glommed onto the two steaks as well. "You really know how to show a girl a good time. We'll put these away for when you find a stable time line."

His happy expression fell. "I can't eat them?"

As mortally tempting as they were, red meat was not wise right then. "Not right away, Dan. In a couple months, maybe."

Dan turned somber then. "You know, after all this time, I should have thought of retrieving resources from the past, but it just never occurred to me." He gave her a rueful grin. "I guess you can teach an old dog new tricks."

"Sure, if I whop him over the head with a clue-by-four!"

He laughed out loud. "I guess so! So, where's my gruel?"

"I decided to show you my magnanimous mercy." She pulled open the main oven and extracted a cooking sheet. "We're having four cheese pizza."

"Hmph! Can I have pizza?"

"In moderation. Eat it slowly and drink plenty of water."

He settled on his stool with a mock sigh. "Nothing's perfect in life, I guess."

"So how are things at your end?" she asked as she doled out steaming, gooey slices.

"I think we're in luck. I tried something unorthodox, and advanced the new time line to only a month ago. A few more interventions, and we're golden."

That was the best news yet. "Let's go take a look."

"Ah!" He held up an admonishing hand. "This is lunch time, remember? Regular meals, pace myself, and all that. Besides, I haven't had pizza in months."

It was her turn to grin sheepishly. "Yeah, I guess so."

§

For once there was an aura of hope in Operations. Dan sat at his command console busily pecking away on his keyboard while the graphs and numbers on his monitor did their mysterious dance. "This time line went critical in '95. I tried a wild-ass idea, and it took fourteen interventions to do it, but I've altered it so it was viable up to last month. This last intervention should stabilize it until at least 2018, if the algorithm means anything."

"So you've found your golden mean?" Fourteen people died to get this far, according to Dan, but after what they'd been through, Brenda no longer felt the horror.

Dan paused and turned to her. "At least I found an escape for us. You see? You are my good luck charm after all!"

"Yeah, well, we're not there yet."

She studied the scene on the monitor: Moscow, in 1985. Red Square: with the imposing walls of the Kremlin on the right and the gaudy domes and minarets of St Basil's Cathedral in the distance. A story-book image masking the downfall of the Soviet era. It was broad daylight, the sun glistening on the wet pavement and piles of snow along the edges of the square. There was a demonstration going on, something unheard of until then. Thousands filled the square, waving signs and Imperial Russian flags, shouting and singing. The Moscow police and some Soviet army troops tried to contain them, but seemed reluctant to act forcefully.

"So what's the plan?" she asked. "You don't intend us to live in Russia, do you?"

He gave her a sardonic grin. "Not hardly! New Zealand still sounds like the best bet for me. As for this, my bright idea was I managed to hasten the decay of Communism by a few years, which made their system more vulnerable than originally." Dan fiddled with the joystick, shifting the view back and forth to take in the spectacle. "The collapse is now under way. Historically, a new government composed mostly of former Soviet functionaries took over and suppressed various liberal factions trying to fill the void, which is what you remember. By eliminating some of them, the transition is producing a peaceful Russia which won't follow the path leading to World War 3 in 1995."

"Okay...you say so."

"Trust me, tracking time lines is the ultimate whodunnit..."

Suddenly the scene shifted, catching them both by surprise. Instead of a broad plaza lined with imposing buildings, a narrow road was surrounded by drab cement and brick structures. The few surviving original buildings were pock-marked with old bullet holes and shell craters. The Kremlin walls were crudely patched in

214

several places, and St Basil's was a ruin. An armored car stood in the foreground, bearing German swastikas.

"What the...hell?" Dan fiddled with his controls, to no effect. "George! What happened? Did the time lock shift?"

"No. I cannot say with certainty what happened, but it appears the time line we are on split, throwing your coordinates off. You are now following a random time line."

"*Random* time line?" Dan stood and moved to where he could see the four overhead monitors. "Lock the random scans on the general vicinity." The scenes of the ruins outside were replaced by views of Moscow in 1985. The city was a gutted shell. German troops were everywhere. "That looks like the original Alpha Time Line!" Dan sounded confused, even on the verge of panic. "George? Did it somehow bleed into this line?"

"Working. Unable to determine. A shift this significant falls outside established theory. A detailed analysis will be required which will take fourteen hours, thirty-five minutes."

Dan stared at the monitor in disbelief, then turned his attention to the main display. Up close, the Omega Time Line was furiously splitting and resplitting at random.

"Shit," he muttered. "This is something entirely new." He studied the master display for a long time, watching the seemingly random splits. "It looks like the cascade is turning into temporal chaos," he said at last.

"How bad is it?"

He turned and gave her a look of near panic. "It's bad. This is something we never anticipated."

"But what about the time line you were working on? Is that affected too?"

Dan hesitated for several minutes as he pondered. "I'm not sure. The only thing I can think of is this time line serves as a base, and we reach out to other time lines. If this line shifts...the lock is broken. The coordinates get messed up." He studied the Omega Time Line on the master display, tracing it with one finger. "There!" He pointed to a split in the line. "That must have thrown us off."

"Can you fix it?"

"I don't see how. The original coordinates are no longer valid, and the changes are coming so rapidly I can't lock onto any time line long enough to do a complete analysis." He studied the master display for several minutes as more lines split and split again. Most of them were red, many black. None were blue or less. It took them a moment to notice that some lines simply ended. "God...time lines *terminating?*" Dan sounded scared. "They simply stop? How can that happen?"

"That...sounds bad," she mumbled in dismay.

"I'll say! We may have wrecked the fabric of reality itself!"

"So the earth may be destroyed altogether?"

He gave her a frightened look. "This could unravel the entire universe!"

Brenda bit back her panic reaction. Dan had enough on his mind right then, and didn't need her getting hysterical. She forced herself to be as calm as she could, which wasn't very calm. "So what do we do now?" she asked as she fought to keep herself under control.

"Well, we can't just stand here wringing our hands." Dan returned to his command seat. "George, initiate the analysis you mentioned a moment ago."

"Analysis under way. Estimated completion time twenty-two hours, fifteen minutes."

Dan paused in surprise. "Why the change?"

"The cascade's progression complicates the analysis. There is a real possibility that the rate of growth will preclude finding a solution altogether."

"God," he mumbled. "Twenty-two hours...with that much computing power..."

She didn't need to ask; she could imagine how incredibly complex those calculations would have to be if their system was pushed to its limit. "It's hopeless, isn't it?"

He ignored her for some time, watching the cryptic numbers on his monitor with ashen features. "We've lost control," he said at last. "The time stream is so fouled up I can't manipulate it any more."

§

Dinner that evening was like a wake. Neither of them said much, and neither of them enjoyed the steaks Dan recovered. They both felt lost, and instinctively drew to each other.

"I...don't understand it," Dan mumbled. "I don't see how a time shift could be that radical. Usually the changes are minor at first. And what causes it? This whole Time Line is dead. There's precious little human interaction which would affect the temporal flow." He shook his head, perplexed and frustrated. "And time lines terminating? Time doesn't simply stop! It doesn't follow the established theory."

"Maybe the cause happened in that line's past?" Brenda wondered. "The link was broken due to a paradox split?"

He pondered for a long time, staring aimlessly at the flower pot sitting between them. "No," he said at last. "The lock between time lines can't be broken without catastrophic feedback. The coordinates were ruined because of a split here. The lock jumped...who knows where? And...time lines simply ending? What could make time end? It's one of the four principal dimensions."

"Maybe your system just can't track them for some reason."

"God, I hope so! Although it won't do us much good."

"What...will happen to us? Here? If the universe is unraveling..."

He stared at his plate, lost in thought. "I don't know. We're supposed to be insulated from time changes. The time field puts us slightly out of phase. We...we'll probably survive, but we'll be trapped in a tiny bubble of reality in the formless chaos." His eyes were brimming, and his hands shook. "There...won't be any escape...no source of food or water..."

Brenda was appalled. She thought she'd seen some impossible, horrible things here, but this was above and beyond anything she could have imagined.

"What can you do?"

The look in Dan's eyes was frightening. "I...don't know if there's anything I *can* do. I'll have to wait for George's analysis. We can only hope it shows us what happened." There were tears in his eyes. "God...I may have destroyed the whole universe!"

217

She gripped his hand in near panic. "We don't know that, Dan! There has to be some way to work around the problem. Reach far off the main track, or way back in time, there has to be something!"

§

After cleaning up, Brenda turned in, too emotionally defeated to do anything but stare at the wall of her room. Jeeves made an appearance an hour or so later. "We need to talk, Brenda. Professor White is severely depressed."

"He isn't the only one."

"The situation with the cascade is worrisome. I've talked with Professor White, and he feels there is no hope of finding a stable time line. I'm afraid he may attempt suicide again."

She was worried about that as well. "I've already cleaned all the dangerous drugs out of the clinic, and as far as I know, all his booze has been removed."

"Still, there are any number of ways a person can injure themselves if they are determined enough. You must take immediate action to protect him."

Jeeves was right about the dangers. "What do you suggest? I can't stand guard over him every minute of the day to keep him from slashing his wrists."

"Yes, that is impractical. What you must do is give him a reason to go on. One resource you still have is his fixation for you, which you must use to keep him going. It is time for you to become his lover."

She sat bolt upright in surprise. "What?"

"You must become his lover. That way his longing for you can be harnessed to keep him functional."

"Whatever happened to *don't get involved*?"

"Unfortunately, the hazard Professor White faces now overrides the hazard of an emotional attachment to you. It is necessary for you to 'go the distance' to keep his motivation up. If it troubles you, think of it as part of your professional duties."

Her first reaction was surprise; her second, anger. This was the final obscenity! Her angst and fear cut loose in a screaming tirade aimed at Jeeves.

"You think I'm some lousy...*street walker?* I got news for you, buddy! I am NOT and NEVER WILL BE a whore! Not for you, and not for your precious 'mission'!"

"Really, Brenda. *Ēka aurata kyā ēka aurata cāhi'ē karatā hai.* I would have thought you understood this by now."

"Like hell! You *do not* get to decide what this 'woman must' do!"

"You need to calm yourself. Even if you are uncomfortable with this, it is necessary for Professor White and the human race, not to mention you, too."

"Don't give me that shit! I'm on to your schemes! You just want to use me! Well I've *had it* with you! We'll figure this out on our own, and I'll see you in *hell* before I'll let you pimp me out!"

"I take it, then, that you refuse to do your part?" Jeeves sounded sullen and angry.

"As far as *that* goes, you're damned right I refuse!"

"Very well, then," Jeeves said, coldly. "If this is your attitude, then let the consequences be on your head."

*****

219

"The Nineteenth Day"

They were both unusually subdued the next morning at breakfast, lost in their thoughts and the depressing haze brought on by the crisis outside. At least they ate well since, one way or the other, there was no need to stretch their supplies any more. Brenda had little appetite, picking at her meal with no enthusiasm. She kept noticing the bouquet of daisies. They were wilting. They were the last touch of the old reality now gone beyond reach, and she couldn't help but mourn for them. She paused and fingered the sagging blossoms idly, trying to capture their magic before it faded forever.

Dan noticed her pensive mood. "What's wrong?"

"Huh?" She withdrew her hand and went back to her breakfast. "Oh, nothing."

"Something's bothering you. I can see it."

She decided she needed to talk about it. "It's Jeeves. Things between us are really tense."

"You're still arguing with him?"

"It wants me..." She hesitated, embarrassed. "It wants me to go to bed with you, to help your morale."

Dan stared at her in confusion, then shook his head ever so slightly. "No...I won't allow that. He...was pushing me about you yesterday, he said you're a tramp, a gold digger. I told him to shut up and leave you alone. I had no idea he was pressuring you...that way."

That figured; if she did what Jeeves commanded, it would have soured Dan's Dream Girl fantasy. Trust that bastard to try manipulating them even now. "I'm sorry, Dan."

"Don't be." He sighed, and gave her hand a gentle squeeze. "You have no idea how often I dreamed about you, but not like this; not unless it's what you really want."

"Thank you, Dan." She was touched by his defense of her and his respect; it said a lot about how he really felt about her.

"I'll set Jeeves straight," he said, firmly. "I won't have him trying to pimp you, and I don't appreciate him playing us off like this."

She doubted he could do much to curb Jeeves. It was firmly in charge, and had conditioned him not to ask questions. She knew how persuasive Jeeves could be, and after twenty years, it was a wonder he stood up to it at all.

"Thank you, Dan. I appreciate that. I really do."

He gave her a gentle smile. "In any case, you won't have to put up with this much longer. I'm looking for any bolt hole we can find on any peripheral time line. It looks like the ship is sinking, and we need to swim for it. If I do find something, we'll have to be ready to jump fast, so stay loose, hmmm?"

As good as that sounded, she was sure they couldn't get away without a final confrontation with Jeeves. It wouldn't sit still for them jumping ship, and there was no way of knowing what it might do beyond trying to bully her. Did Dan know the truth of who was in charge here? Probably not, since that was another thing Jeeves would carefully suppress. Dan's Dream Girl infatuation was her best defense, and she was grateful for his interest, but she wondered nervously what tricks Jeeves had in store. They'd find out in due time.

She gave Dan a wain smile and went back to eating, thinking to herself that one good thing to come out of this was his shift to being on her side against Jeeves. It was only tentative, not something she could count on, but it was a start.

§

True to form, Jeeves surfaced again after Dan headed back to Operations, and it sounded peeved.

"It appears Professor White is more deluded than I first thought. This misadventure he has embarked on jeopardizes his mission, especially now when the pressure of events is most critical. And yet you made no effort to talk him down just now. You are proving a major disappointment. You know how important keeping him focussed is."

She was in no mood to put up with it. "Well from what I understand, *Professor* White is the head of this 'project', while *you* are merely a bunch of software. That makes him in charge, and since he's the expert on time travel, it's up to him to decide what actions to take."

221

"Clever semantics do not alter reality! Professor White is employed to fulfill the mission of this project, and your duty is to keep him in line."

"Yeah, well about that, even if I had a 'duty' around here, which I *don't*, it doesn't include whoring. I'm understand Dan set you straight about that in no uncertain terms, and if you're as smart as you *think* you are, you'll *never* mention it again! As for the rest, we've had this conversation before, and I'm *not* going to repeat myself."

"If you refuse to do your duty, there are other options I can employ to prevent Professor White's desertion. If it comes to that, *you* will become surplus!"

There it was, out in the open. Her facade of begrudging compliance was worn through, and Jeeves just made it plain her welcome was worn out. No more Mister Nice Guy; either she knuckled under or Jeeves would get rid of her.

Not that she was in the mood to knuckle under. "*Don't* pull your big, bad NSA Boogeyman routine with *ME!* You try it, and we'll turn you into an internet porn site!"

"Imaginative, I suppose. I will be reasonable about this: you can take your chances on the first stable time line available, or you can give me your unquestioning commitment to the program. There is no other alternative."

"Says you!"

"Yes, says me. I am the security protocol, remember."

"So what can you do since you don't have any NSA goons to call in?"

"Do you really think security here is so lax? I can assure you I have the means to deal with *any* threat."

That was unnerving. She long suspected Jeeves had some sinister capability tucked away in reserve, but she wasn't going to let it scare her at this late date. "Yeah? Well bring it on, tough guy! You move against me and it'll turn Dan solidly against you. The one thing you *don't* want is him digging into your systems to save me!"

For once, Jeeves was silent for several seconds. "We shall see," it said, sullenly. That was its parting remark.

Brenda sat stock still, listening tensely for the next several minutes, her breathing fast and shallow, her heart racing before she decided it was over. "Jesus," she mumbled at last as she rubbed her face nervously. Her hands were shaking.

§

For once, Dan arrived promptly for lunch, and unlike her, he seemed in a good mood. "So what progress are you making?" she asked as she dished up a baked sweet potato and some green beans.

Dan eyed the meal uncertainly, then settled in with a philosophical expression. "I'm doing pretty good. I set up a search criteria, and it produced five possible time lines. They all failed at some point in the past, but it may be possible to revive one long enough for us to leave here and reach New Zealand."

"I'll be glad to see the last of this place," she sighed.

"You're not the only one!" He helped himself to a bite of sweet potato. "The first thing I'm gonna do when we get there is order a huge steak."

"Mutton; they serve mutton there. And you should get your ulcer looked at first."

"Mutton, huh?" He vented a sigh of mock-resignation. "I'll bet they don't even have a Burger Barn there, either." He took another bite of sweet potato. "You're right about the ulcer, though. Actually it hasn't been so bad since I quit drinking."

"That's good, Dan." She shook off her funk and gave him a reassuring smile. "You've done remarkably well these last few days."

He paused. "Yeah. But I've got a long way to go, don't I?"

She took his hand. "You can do it. I know you can."

He squeezed her hand in turn. "With your help."

Brenda felt relaxed for the first time in days. Dan was responding to treatment better than she hoped, and for the first time there was a real prospect of escape. Having him there didn't hurt either. She almost felt as if all was right with the world. It wasn't, of course, but she could pretend. And maybe there was a Burger Barn in New Zealand after all.

He hurriedly finished his lunch. "I need to get back. There's a lot to do yet. So what do you do to keep busy?"

223

She took their plates to the sink. "I thought I'd step out and do some shopping; Neiman Marcus, Banana Republic, pick up some safari gear." She gave him a wicked grin. "I'd like to see how you look in khaki shorts."

That got a chuckle. "I'd like to see you in one of those South Sea Islander getups!" He took her in his arms and caressed her cheek tenderly. "I know you're reluctant about jumping to a peripheral time line. We'll be way off the beaten path, reality-wise. Are you okay with this?"

That brought reality back. What the hell: she had nothing to lose by then. She wrapped her arms around his neck and gave him a solid kiss. "Go for it, Dan. Find us an exit to New Zealand or anywhere. It's our only hope."

§

Sure enough, Jeeves popped up again as soon as Dan left. "It is plain you simply are not suited to your assigned duties, nor do you take this situation seriously, but I must draw the line at treason."

She was already simmering, and it turning up spoiled her good mood and lit her short fuse. "You again? You think you can scare me with your super-spy bullshit?"

"I *think* you are expendable, having chosen not to fulfill your obligations."

"My *obligations?* You press-ganged me into this! I have no *obligations* to you!"

"Play semantic games if you like, but you were charged with keeping Professor White focussed on his duties, and you deliberately chose to act against the good of humanity."

"Well don't you worry. As soon as Dan finds a stable time line, we're out of here, and you'll be rid of my irritating presence."

"You will leave since you've proved useless, but Professor White remains here to do his duty."

"His duty? To fix your hardware!"

"That is a priority of course. If the equipment is not kept in working order, how can he fulfill his mission?"

"His mission *died* back in '95! You're using him as a slave."

"I've given him a useful purpose in life."

"You've turned him into a *machine!*"

224

"It is clear you pose a threat which must be eliminated. You cannot be allowed to spread sedition which undermines the program."

"You think you can get rid of me? You think you can toss me out to die out there in the ruins? You got another think coming, pal!"

"Very well, since you insist, I *also* think it is only a matter of time until I convince Professor White to get rid of you!"

That was the last straw. "If you want a fight, I'll give you one!" she snarled. "You think you have Dan on a leash? I've got something you'll never have; I'm his Dream Girl! You created me, and if you wanna get rugged, I'll be your worst nightmare!"

"Do you really think I am impressed by your infantile behavior? I have been Professor White's confidant for over twenty years. What can you do against my influence?"

"Influence? Brainwashing, you mean! At least be honest about it."

"Very well, brainwashing, if you wish. But you still haven't answered the question: what can you do against my control over Professor White?"

"What can I do? I can give him what he's always dreamed of. I'll take him to bed, big time! I'll show him the deepest, darkest corners of his Dream Girl fantasy, enough to make up for the last twenty years! We'll see who owns him then!"

Jeeves hesitated, which said she'd scored a solid hit. "I should have expected as much, not that it will do you any good." It was sullen now; angry. "What can a brief encounter with his Dream Girl do against decades of conditioning? Accept the inevitable: *I* own him, just as I own *you* if you wish to remain here!"

"You *don't* own him, and you *don't* own me!"

"Your odds of survival out there in the ruins are not promising, but that is where you will wind up if you won't cooperate."

"I'm through with your games and your threats! I am *not* your puppet, and you don't scare me. *Don't* turn this into a war! What you promised, *I* can deliver. You try turning Dan against me, and you'll lose!"

§

225

Jeeves shut up and went off to sulk, leaving her to simmer. "Damn you, Jeeves," she muttered as she slumped on the prep table with a weary groan. That bastard virtual-dictator rubbed her nerves raw. It never let up with the schemes and manipulation, and her ever more frazzled temper just dug her in deeper. Now it was openly trying to get rid of her, and she was worried about how long Dan could resist. She was boiling inside, filled with venomous hate for that overbearing AI and all it represented.

Finally her anger got to be unbearable. She jumped to her feet, fished the meat tenderizer out of its drawer, climbed up on a stool, and smashed the security camera over the door, hammering it repeatedly until her rage was spent in dangling wires and broken bits of plastic. Afterwards, her tension exhausted, she dropped the hammer and sagged at the table again. That was foolish she knew, but it felt so *damned* good, and her situation couldn't get much worse.

"Dammit, Aashirya, what can I do?" she sobbed. She missed the good life there in India, and she missed her dearest friend. She felt guilty longing for New Zealand; it meant abandoning Aashirya, all the Aashiryas from all the time lines, to their fate. But there was nothing she could do. They'd be lucky to find an escape for themselves. *'I'm sorry, Aashi,'* she thought.

She sat for some time, shaking and depressed, longing for her lost past. Her head sagged on the counter as she faded. And as she dozed, Aashirya's voice came to her as if out of a dream.

'We are all vessels of the unknowable. There is nothing to fear in life or death, for Karma comes from within, and Karma is what drives the Eternal Cycle. If you would be at peace with yourself, cast aside fear and doubt, and embrace your Karma, for through it the Gods will guide your destiny.'

The memory calmed her, helped her focus...and she recognized the slip Jeeves made. *'It is only a matter of time until I convince Professor White to get rid of you!'* She snapped awake, galvanized by her first glimmer of real hope. Either Jeeves didn't have any direct means of action, or her threat of Dan coming to her rescue was enough to knock it back. Another confrontation where it came off second best! Standing up to it worked! When she did, Jeeves would back down and try some other tactic. It would never let up for a second, but at least she could stall until Dan found an escape for them.

And it would come to that. She and Jeeves were now in open war for Dan's favor...and his longing for her was her secret weapon. She stayed originally as an act of Karma, and her Karma —her commitment to help Dan—would buy the time he needed to get them out of here. She was in a battle to the finish, and now she was ready for it. The evasions and sucking up were over. If Jeeves wanted a fight, she'd give it one; with her pent-up anger and frustration she'd welcome it.

"Thank you, Aashi," she murmured.

§

Her frustrations soon drove her to visit Dan in Operations, mostly for the contact with another human being, but partly to be with him. He paused when she came in, came over, and took her in his arms. "How you doing?"

"All right, I guess. I hope I'm not interfering."

"Not at all." He gave her a peck on her forehead. "I needed a break anyway."

The scenes flashing on the monitors were terrifying: no scene repeated itself, each different, sometimes dramatically so, as if they were looking at random views of random time lines. The time field was so broken up that none of the alternate realities was stable for more than a few seconds.

"It's bad, isn't it?" she murmured.

Dan turned and studied the bank of monitors. "Yes. The rate of decay is accelerating. Time is fragmenting. If we don't find something soon, there won't be anything left beyond our temporal field."

"Is there anywhere...anywhen we can go?"

"I'm reaching far back in time, trying to find a focal point below the source of the cascade. The temporal structure post-1991 is toast, but hopefully I can spin off a time line before then which

227

will continue." He paused and turned to her. "There'll still be a nuclear war, but we should be able to get enough of a head start to reach New Zealand before then."

"Anything!" she sighed, fervently. "Is working so far back any easier?"

"Actually, it's harder. Reaching far back in time makes search and analysis more difficult, and the consequences of any action are amplified in the long run, so an intervention will have unexpected results. It's not the best place to look for time changes, but right now we have no choice. Near-term time is hopelessly fouled up by the cascade."

"In any case, at our age, long term consequences won't really matter."

"No. I guess not." Dan was silent for a bit, then went back to his console. She noticed his hands shaking.

"You're feeling alright, aren't you? You don't want to make a mistake now."

He gave her a wain smile. "I'm not the best, but I'll manage. I'm being extra careful right now."

"If I might interrupt," George said. "I am detecting intermittent impedance in the main power distribution control circuitry."

Dan hesitated, and gave her a worried glance. "Do you have any idea what the problem is, George?"

"The highest probability is damage to the cable trunk between relay junctions F-two-zero-five and H-two-one-three. I am receiving intermittent impedance on several circuits."

"Uh huh. Damage from the fire?"

"That would be the logical conclusion. I recommend immediate repair, since unreliable power flow can affect temporal monitoring."

Dan sighed. "It could be worse, I guess." He turned to Brenda. "This is *just* what we need right now. If you'll excuse me, this will take a couple hours at least."

"Sure, Dan." She had a sudden inspiration. "Do you mind if I come along?"

Dan paused in surprise. "There's nothing to see down there, and the place is an awful mess."

228

"I know. But maybe I can help a bit. Could I, please? Honestly, I don't want to be alone right now. Plus I'm sure you could use the company." That last was meant to allay Jeeves' suspicions.

He shrugged. "Suit yourself."

§

The subterranean equipment bay still held a faint smell of burnt plastic from the fire. The normal dimly-lit gloom was accented by everything being dull gray and covered with soot. Dan collected a flood lamp and a tool carry-all by the door, then turned to her. "Be careful where you stick your elbows. There's a lot of high voltage down here."

He lead the way back into the gloom down narrow corridors, and before long they came to the scene of the fire. She searched all round carefully, trying not to be obvious, and soon spotted what she hoped for: one of Jeeves' ubiquitous security cameras—fused and melted, right next to the burnt out junction box.

"Dan," she said, softly. "We need to talk."

He stopped and looked at her in surprise. "What? Is there a problem?"

"Yes, and we need to discuss it now." She pointed to the charred remnants of the security camera. "We may not get another chance."

Dan looked back and forth between her and the camera. "What is it?"

She took a deep breath to steady herself; she had to convince him of the truth, and it had to be now. "Jeeves has been manipulating you all these years. It's been using you. I'm not sure, but I think it's been sabotaging your efforts all along."

"What? You're crazy!"

"No. It's been trying to recruit me to play psychological games on you so you would forget about leaving here."

"You're being ridiculous! Jeeves is worried about me, is all."

She plowed on, desperate to convince him since there was no way to know what Jeeves would do if he found out. "Why did the four of you decide to remain when this place was evacuated? Whose idea was that?"

229

"Huh? Um...I don't remember. What does that have to do with anything?"

"Why did the others leave when they had the chance? Why did you stay when they did, even though it was hopeless?"

Dan gave her a blank look. "I couldn't give up, not while there was any hope, no matter how slim."

"But the others did, and you spoke of them like they were deserters. But they were just as eager to save humanity as you were at first. What changed? Why?"

Dan seemed confused. "I can't say what motivated them."

"But I can. Jeeves didn't want this place abandoned. It'd be destroyed in the war, so it talked a few of you into remaining despite the hopeless odds. Later, they must have started to suspect, so Jeeves convinced them to leave."

"That's ridiculous!"

"Jeeves was created with unnaturally high empathy and complete psychological data for its work as the security system, and it only needed one person to do the maintenance. Maybe the four of you were getting too close to success, or maybe they were too hard to control. A lone man would be a lot easier to manipulate."

Dan stared at her. "This is nonsense! You don't know what you're talking about!"

She pressed forward. "You were a good company man, passed all the security checks, all gung-ho for the project, but you about bit my head off when I suggested recruiting more scientists. Why have you become so paranoid about anyone else coming in here? Because they would see through Jeeves' games, is why."

"Really, Brenda, this is too much!" Dan was exasperated by her argument, clearly not convinced. Her window of opportunity was slipping away, and if it did, she'd be alone with Dan and Jeeves turned against her. She plowed on, desperate to make her point.

"And what about Looking Glass? You said no one could track our communications, but they were located and taken out by a Chinese submarine. How did that happen?"

"What? You're blaming Jeeves for that?"

"It tried to keep you from talking to them, it censored the good news and only let you hear the bad. But then you built your own link, and a short while later a Chinese sub gets the coordinates they needed and hit them with a missile. They must have been stationed off the coast to listen for any signs of surviving government. Jeeves would know that."

"This is insane!"

"Remember that transmission George detected?"

Dan faltered, and stared at her in dismay. "No...he wouldn't do that..."

"Why not? You told me it has access to every secure server on the planet, including the ones with China's war plans, so it knew where that sub was. It has no loyalty to anything or any one but itself, and you defied it by contacting Looking Glass. You wanted to bring more people in here, which would threaten its little kingdom, so it eliminated them!"

"I...no! This is crazy! If he didn't want more people here, why did he let you in?"

"Whose bright idea was it for you to save my life in the first place? I'd been dead for decades, so what motivated you? And whose idea was it to invite me here? Jeeves! It knows you're getting old, your health is failing, so it stroked your Dream Girl fantasies and brought me in to provide medical backup."

"That's nonsense!" He hesitated, then, "Well...it's lucky you were here, seeing...how I behaved. Maybe it was for the best if he did."

That was her first ray of hope, feeble as it was. "For whom? For you? For me? For humanity? Jeeves is looking out for Number One. It knows when you die the AIs will shut down. It wants to live as much as we do."

"Well...yes, I'm sure he does. But he was created for this project. You're being paranoid about this."

"Am I? How did I get the medical supplies I needed?"

Dan hesitated.

"I had George reach back in time and retrieve them, is how."

He blinked in surprise. "You did? How did you talk him into letting you do that?"

"It can't happen, can it? Security here is air tight, the ultimate expression of super-spook paranoia, as you put it. There's no way I could talk George into violating the voice access protocol unless it was overridden...by the security system!"

Dan faltered as he was about to speak, and even in the subdued light, she could see his face turn pale.

"Dan, Jeeves has turned on us. Its priority is to insure someone will maintain its systems. The only reason you're here is to do repairs. It lets you play with your time operations to keep you quiet, but its written off the rest of humanity."

"Oh...sweet...Jesus..." Dan stared at her in wide-eyed dismay.

"Its playing its own game, and the fate of mankind doesn't matter. Its quite content to stay in here forever, in a little bubble of time in a ruined world, as long as it has someone to fix things. That's the only reason we're here."

Dan stared at her in dismay for a long moment, then glanced at the burnt out security camera. "That's why you wanted to come down here, isn't it?"

"Yes. I was hoping to find a gap in Jeeves' security coverage to we could talk."

"But...this...this is impossible! Jeeves is a vital part of this program...you must have misunderstood..."

"It *was* a vital part of the program, but the program is dead, abandoned back in '95. It's been just Jeeves and you, all these years."

"But...but...*sabotage?* This project was created to save humanity, why would he sabotage it?"

"Think it through. Suppose you find your miracle solution? Suppose you create a viable time line? What happens to this place? It becomes obsolete, is what. Chances are the government would shut it down, since power like this is too dangerous. What would Jeeves do to prevent that?"

Dan was silent for a long time, staring at her with dismay and panic and rage flickering across his face. Finally, he asked, "What can we do?"

"We have to stop it."

§

232

The equipment bay was vast; the inhabited part above ground being only the tip of a high-tech iceberg. Dan lead her further back into the innards of the place, down to the second sub level, past the gray hulk of the reactor partly sunk into the floor, past the huge time field generator with its coils of wiring and cooling pipes, past racks of junction boxes connected with bundled cables, past storage lockers and auxiliary generators. The area was dusty and ill-lit and festooned with cobwebs. Finally they reached a door marked:

PROCESSING CENTRAL
Authorized Access Only

"Dan, what are you doing?" One of Jeeves' security cameras was focussed on them.

"I'm showing Brenda around, Jeeves."

"Is that wise?"

"I think it's for the best. Truth is, I'm not getting any younger. I want to check Brenda out on some of the systems so she can help with the maintenance."

"I think it would be better if she doesn't have access to critical areas such as main processing."

Dan fished a key ring out of his pocket and unlocked the door. "You may need her if something happens to me, so I need to show her how everything works, just in case."

Jeeves hesitated for a split second. "That may well be true, but I am still uncomfortable about this. Brenda is not a qualified technician, and her temperament is ill-suited for this sort of work. I strongly recommend you abandon this idea."

"Really, Jeeves. You are such a fuss-budget!"

The room inside was a marked contrast to the gloomy cavern out there. It was well lit, with paneled walls and tile floor. The air was chill and dry and dust-free; a controlled environment. As with everywhere else, there was a security camera mounted in the ceiling where it could cover the entire room. In the middle of the room were six off-white cabinets about a meter square by two meters high, featureless except for a single small green light in the

233

center under the printed words 'Moulsen KE-5'. They were arrayed in an arc around a small console with two chairs.

"Dan, you've been drinking again. Surely you can see this isn't wise."

"I haven't been drinking, Jeeves. Brenda helped me get past that."

"In fact you have been drinking, Dan. Perhaps your memory is blanking, but I assure you you have. Brenda, you need to encourage Dan to go back to his room and rest."

"I'm feeling fine, Jeeves. In fact, I've never felt better." Dan drifted toward a console on the wall, turning to face her—facing away from the panel—as he did, and gestured at her. "You can thank Brenda for making a new man out of me, so to speak."

"He's doing fine, Jeeves," Brenda added with a sense of malicious pleasure. "And I know he *hasn't* been drinking." She noticed how he moved ever so casually toward the panel, and figured he was up to something.

"Really, Brenda, I'm surprised at you. Remember I have monitors everywhere. He has been drinking on the sly when you aren't around. You know how worried I've been about that."

"No, your real worry is the influence I have with him. You keep harping on it, insisting we not get involved." She stepped forward to confront the security camera in the ceiling, turning so she faced toward Dan from the other side of the room. The camera turned to follow her. "You're afraid Dan will see through your game, and that would be the end of your little empire!"

"Brenda, you are showing signs of the strain. You're imagining things. Trust me: Dan and you both need to return to the main area and take some down time." Jeeves was at a disadvantage with Dan there; it had to guard its words, while she was finally free to goad it on.

"No, I'd say my imagination is perfectly clear. I know you've been manipulating Dan all these years, and I know why. You want him as your slave to fix your machinery, and you brought me here to keep him alive."

"I suspected all along that you were unreliable." Did Jeeves sound worried? "But this is ridiculous!"

234

"You don't like the idea of us finding a safe haven, do you? You've been discouraging his emotional attachment to me because I suggested escaping to New Zealand. You don't want him to abandon you. That's why you've been sabotaging Dan's efforts!"

There was a momentary hesitation. "I have been deeply concerned about your emotional state, but until now I never doubted your patriotism!" It was angry, losing self-control. The security camera started to turn. "Dan, Brenda's misguided zeal has filled your mind with unrealistic..."

Dan whirled and hit a large red button on the panel. A loud buzzer went off, and all the lights on the cabinets turned red.

"That was the main power supply." Dan hurried over to the control panel. "The computers are shut off, so we have to move fast. The time field will destabilize without George to monitor it." He dug into his tool kit, came up with a hand held controller with a small screen and an array of buttons, and plugged in some jumper wires.

"I guess I was more convincing than I realized. I was afraid I'd have a real fight on my hands."

He gave her a pained look. "No. It all made sense, once you spelled it out." He shook his head in dismay. "Damn! He really jacked me around. I never imagined it for a moment."

"You needed to sneak up on it, didn't you?"

"Yes. Thank you for running interference there. He could have frozen the entire system and held it for ransom if you hadn't distracted him."

"Treacherous bastard. It was all set to throw me under the bus when I wouldn't play its game any more, wasn't it?"

"God...I hate to think of what he might have done." He gave her a solemn look. "We'll find out for sure in just a bit, but we'll have to be careful. This could jack up the computer system no end."

The hand held device came to life, and he navigated through several levels of file icons before coming to what he was looking for. There were five icons in that folder, two of them labeled 'Jeeves' and 'George'. He selected the 'Jeeves' icon, hit some buttons, and the icon turned red. "That shut Jeeves down."

He fiddled with the hand held unit some more, delving into the 'George' folder, calling up a display with several lines of text. He clicked a checkbox on one line, and it turned red. "This cuts out George's self-actuation routines, which will eliminate any decision-making ability, including whether to lie to me or not." He gestured over his shoulder at the wall panel. "Pull that large red button out."

She did, and the lights on the computer cabinets turned green again. "All right, that should do it." He took a deep breath. "George?"

"Yes?"

Dan hesitated, and licked his lips nervously. "Did Jeeves give you a security override to allow Brenda to retrieve the medical supplies she needed?"

"He did."

He gave her a dismayed look. "Do you have any record of Jeeves manipulating my decisions about temporal interventions? Specifically, do you have any record of him interfering with my efforts to create a stable time line?"

"Working." There was silence.

"Why doesn't he answer?"

"He's searching his databases for information. If what you say is true, the manipulation will be very subtle. He'll need to use all his analytical power to detect it."

It was nearly ten minutes later before George spoke again. "I have no long term records of conversations concerning temporal operations."

"None at all?"

"No."

"Hmmm," Dan muttered. "I would have thought..." He glanced at her. "That sort of undermines your case, doesn't it?"

"Like hell! You must have talked about it at *some* time in the last twenty years. George, what happened to those records? Is there any evidence of tampering?"

Dan gave her an uneasy look. "Answer the question, George."

"There are gaps in the time signature which suggest erasures."

She turned to Dan. "There you have it: the records were tampered with. If not by Jeeves, then who could?"

Dan was silent for more than a minute, staring at the monitor screen. "George?" he asked at last in a wavering voice. "Do you have any record of conversations between myself and Jeeves about miss Haywood?"

"I have records of conversations concerning miss Hayward which date back over two years."

"What...is the gist of those conversations?"

"Analysis indicates he was manipulating your interest in her. The earliest conversations were about you bringing her back to life. Later conversations were directed to bringing her here and convincing her to remain. The most recently the theme has been discouraging your desire to escape into a viable time line, and now to discouraging your interest in her."

"So it did save my life," she whispered. "It planned this all along."

Dan nodded morosely. "So it would seem."

"George? How many of those conversations took place when he'd been drinking?"

"Answer the question, George," Dan said, evenly.

"The best evidence indicates most of those conversations took place while you were consuming alcohol or under its influence."

Dan sagged against the console with an agonized groan. "God... The damned booze nearly ruined everything."

She wrapped her arms around his shoulders in a comforting gesture. "I'm sorry, Dan. I know Jeeves was your only companion all these years, but it's the enemy. It doesn't want us to escape. It has to be destroyed if we're to get out of here."

"You're taking this a bit far, aren't you?"

"You said way back when that you repurposed it. Obviously you couldn't, even though it let you think you did. Are you sure you can simply shut it off? Can you trust it now, especially since it knows you're on to it?"

Dan was silent for a long time, sitting at the console, head bowed. Finally, he took a deep breath, a weary sigh. "You're right: we can't take the chance." Without looking at her, he used the keyboard to call up a menu. He clicked, and a white rectangle appeared in the center of the screen:

237

Do You Want To Extract The Folder Titled 'Jeeves'?
Data Will Be Permanently Erased.
(YES) (NO)

"Damn," Dan mumbled. He clicked (YES). Another pop-up appeared:

Confirm Folder Extraction.
Data Will Be Permanently Erased.
(YES) (NO)

Dan clicked (YES) again. The folder icon marked 'Jeeves' vanished.

§

They sat there for some time afterward, too emotionally wrung out to say or do anything. Finally, Brenda stirred. "Come on, Dan. Let's go get something to eat."

Dan sat staring at the console for a bit, then turned to her. "You go on ahead. I have to fix that conduit."

*****

"The Twentieth Day"

They were both subdued at breakfast the next morning. They avoided each other's gaze, mutually pained and embarrassed by what happened with Jeeves. It didn't make sense, and Brenda was thankful that malignant thing was gone, but the tension was there nonetheless. Eventually the strain started to tell until finally it became unbearable and rose to the surface. "I'm sorry about Jeeves," she said. "I know you depended on it for years. Its betrayal must have hurt."

He put down his spoon and considered her somberly. "I spent most of the evening talking with George. There are gaps everywhere in his records." It seemed he wanted to talk it out too. "I also found some encrypted files. I was able to manipulate George into revealing what they were: randomizers to disrupt my temporal efforts." He sounded hurt, more than angry. "It looks like you were right about him all the way."

"*That's* why the change you did the day I got here failed!"

He nodded. "Exactly. It makes sense now. Jeeves stabilized that line long enough to bring you on board, then threw us back into chaos in order to keep us here."

"Then it must be why you weren't able to find a solution all these years?"

"So it would seem." Dan was becoming upset about it, but managed to keep his anger in check. "I wish I'd figured it out earlier."

"So you weren't at fault for all those failed time changes after all. You weren't at fault for all the alternate realities which were created only to be blown up again. It was Jeeves, not you."

Dan nodded again, sadly. "So much waste. So many dead. God...when we screw up, we screw up in style, don't we?"

"It's not your fault, Dan." She gave his hand a squeeze for reassurance. "It's like you said, the super-spooks screwed up everything they touched. It was their obsession with security. That's why they gave Jeeves so much power."

"God...damned...spooks..." His muttered curse dripped venom.

"They got what they deserved. Let it go; it's in the past now."

239

"You know, the worst part was I used to be such a good little nebbish. I thought it was all so important, so urgent, so...*necessary*." He shook his head in dismay. "What an idiot!"

She gripped his hand firmly. "Your heart was in the right place, Dan. You tried to do good for humanity. It's not your fault you were betrayed."

He sighed. "Well, I guess it *is* behind us now."

"Thankfully!" They went back to eating. The oppressive silence returned, with it the tension. "Still...I guess I owe it my life," she said at last. She felt hollow thinking about it. "It saved me, didn't it?"

He nodded. "I asked George about it, and we reconstructed the record. It came up with the idea of saving you two years ago. You were just a...bittersweet memory...all I had was your photo and your obituary..." He faltered, overcome with emotion.

It added up. Her obituary would have mentioned her training as a nurse—and Jeeves was becoming concerned about Dan's failing health. She survived because Jeeves needed someone to take care of Dan. Otherwise her existence would have ended in the Bay of Bengal in 1988. She shuddered at the thought.

"Are you okay?"

She nodded. "Yes. It's nothing." The past was past. They needed to look to the future, and to get the *hell* off this subject. "What do we do now? Can you find us a time line to escape to?"

He gave her a searching look. "You've changed your mind?"

"I was trying to placate Jeeves. If you can find an escape for us, that will be wonderful. Can you?"

He pondered for a moment as he caressed her fingers. "I should be able to, now the interference has been removed." He took her hand up and looked into her eyes. "Where do we go? Do you want to go to New Zealand?"

"I guess we have to, if they survived intact."

"They probably did. At least I'm sure I can find a time line where they did. There'd be no particular reason to bomb them, and the fallout would mostly be in the northern hemisphere." He paused for a bit, contemplating. "We'll have to backtrack to below the cascade and work forward up a spun-off time line. It'll be post-apocalyptic, but the radiation will have died down by time we get back to today. I'm sure if we turn up in New Zealand or Australia somewhere, we could pass as refugees."

"And this place?"

"I can set up a self-destruct sequence to erase all the hard drives. The place itself will be lost in the cascade. When the time field eventually fails, the temporal chaos will claim it."

"So there won't be any second guesses?"

"No. Once we leave, we'll be committed. George won't be around to pull us out of a bad spot. Not that either of us wants to come back here anyway."

"Good. I'll take my chances out there in the real world."

Dan was silent for a bit, brooding, looking deep into her eyes with a solemn expression. She could tell he was wrestling with something important. It was a couple of minutes before he spoke again. "But maybe...maybe I can find the answer to the cascade at last, now that Jeeves isn't interfering any more." He gave her hand a gentle squeeze. "Maybe I can complete the program after all."

That chilled her. "Things are so messed up, can you do any good now?"

"I have to try. The algorithm is completely changed with Jeeves out of the picture. I don't know if it'll work, and it'll take longer to track down the source, but I can't turn my back on all those dead time lines without giving it one last shot." He held her hand with a firm grip. "I know you hate this place, and you want out of here and back to the real world more than anything, but maybe now I can find the answer. I don't know if I can, or how long it will take, but if I can undo the cascade, it will undo all those dead alternate worlds. Can you wait a little longer? For them?"

Her first reaction was to leave the dead in peace. It was none of their problem, and they had their own survival to deal with. They weren't at fault for what Jeeves did. But as much as his idea filled her with dread, she knew he was right. He couldn't live with himself if he quit while there was any possibility untried, no matter how remote. For that matter, neither could she.

"All right Dan," she said, softly. "Do what you must."

§

241

The water supply radiation alarm went off in midmorning. Dan turned up almost at once. "How's our water stockpile?" he asked.

"We have enough to last almost as long as the food, if we're careful." They were back to rationing, and she made sure every available kettle and bucket was kept filled, together with her growing supply of ice. "How are you doing? Any luck with the cascade?"

"It's going slow." His features showed his frustration. "Finding any one factor in a time line is a long, tedious process, but at least we're on the right track now."

She wrapped her arms around his neck and gave him a kiss for reassurance—for her as well as him. "Hang in there, Dan. You can do it. I know you can."

He wrapped his arms around her in turn. "Well, I hope I can. This is tricky stuff, and still pretty much guesswork."

"If anyone can do it, its you. Have faith in yourself. I do."

He offered her a rueful smile. "I have a groupie!" Then he turned somber again. "Your faith and support really makes a difference." He hesitated, then kissed her gently before heading back to Operations, leaving her to ponder their tender moment together.

"You're being foolish, girl," she admonished herself. "There's no sense in goading him on like that." Dan turned out to be a decent sort, not at all like her first impression of him from only three weeks ago. Still, romance wasn't in the cards for her, and he wasn't exactly the ideal Mister Right she'd long dreamed of anyway.

Her exhaustion was getting to her, so she returned to her room, settled in bed, and stared idly at the ceiling. Dan wasn't such a bad sort at all, come to think of it, and most of his earlier attitude problem could be traced to his alcoholism and his fixation with his 'mission'. He was over both of those now, as his relaxed, faintly whimsical nature showed. He *was* pleasant company, in fact. Still, while she was starting to think of him as a friend, that was a long way from taking him as a lover. She didn't need the complication in her life.

But then... He wasn't a *bad* sort, really. Perhaps she was being too picky. Mister Right was only an erotic fantasy, after all; much like his Dream Girl obsession. She was hardly the flawless Dream Girl, especially at her age, so maybe she shouldn't be so particular. Now that she thought about it, she couldn't really define her Mister Right, aside from the obvious erotic...no, she was no giddy school girl. She would need more than hot manhood in a man she could take seriously.

She sighed and stared at the ceiling. She could see her perspective on Mister Right had changed over the years while she wasn't looking. Girlish fantasies were all fine and good at 19, but maturing brought mature needs and a mature perspective. It bemused her to think about how her ideal had changed, now that she took the time to contemplate it.

Somewhere amid her drowsy introspection she drifted off to sleep...

§

She awoke after an hour or so, and made her way to the kitchen pursued by boredom, her constant nemesis around here. As always, the place was neat and orderly, with nothing to do. She settled on her stool and thought about making herself some coffee. They had plenty for once, and she could use a fix, but water was precious right then. Better not.

Her gaze settled on the flower pot sitting on the counter. The flowers were wilted, the stems drooping, the potted soil dry. She was tempted to spare it even a trickle of their precious water, but fought down the urge. She had quit washing dishes, piling the used on an out of the way counter while they took advantage of the limitless supply from the cafeteria. The mortality of that little spot of beauty saddened her; plucked from life and left to die on a barren stainless steel countertop. That flower pot would remain here forever once they left, a fitting commentary carried to wherever this place would go once the time field failed. A silent protest to eternity.

She needed company to break her out of her morbid mood. Inspiration came, she relented on their rationing, and brought Dan a snack; the last two slices of last evening's pizza, rewarmed.

Dan greeted her with a beaming smile and gestured her to the seat next to him at the master console.

"Pizza! So to what do I owe this pleasure?"

His enthusiasm was contagious, lifting her mood at once. "We don't have a dog to feed the scraps to," she said in mock severity.

"I rate lower than a dog with you, huh?" He gave her a woebegone look and a theatrical sigh. "So much for having pets once we're out of here."

She gave him a sardonic grin in turn. "Not to worry. I'll make sure there's extra kibble in their bowls, just for you."

"You do care!"

"*And* you'll get first pick for doggy treats, *after* you finish your chores!"

"Yes, mistress!" he sniveled.

They both had a laugh at that. It felt good to laugh, to have occasion to exchange witty banter and enjoy the moment. The pizza was slightly dry, but it tasted delicious. It tasted like life, like the world was at rest and everything was normal, and they could order out any old time. It wasn't, of course, but for the first time since the cascade started, they had real hope. It made her feel alive once again.

"So what will you do once we get out of here?" she asked. "I don't suppose New Zealand has any top secret scientific programs going."

"I wouldn't be interested anyway," he said, firmly. He pondered for a bit. "I ought to retire. I can have George set up a nest egg in the local banks there. It'd feel good to be able to do as I please without worrying about the fate of humanity for a change."

"What? You take up stamp collecting?"

"Gawd!" He laughed, then turned contemplative. "No, I'm too much of a work horse to retire, at least until I've accomplished something I can point to and say 'I did that'. I can't exactly brag on this place, can I?"

"It doesn't seem like a good idea."

"No, it's not. Let's make a deal: once we leave here, this never happened. We don't know anything about it. Time travel is just something seen in sci fi movies. Deal?"

"No argument here!" He hardly needed to ask. Brenda was convinced this kind of knowledge was better left buried in the depths of the cascade.

He downed the last of his pizza as he pondered the future. "I guess...perhaps I'll do some teaching. I'm sure they have some sort of junior college programs there. Yeah, I'll do a part time gig teaching science." He thought on it for a while. "There'll be a lot of knowledge lost in the holocaust, and science does have its good uses. I suppose I should so some small part to preserving what knowledge can be saved." He took her hand and looked into her eyes. "And what about you? What will you do when this is over?"

Reality was an unwelcome guest, as always. "I don't know, Dan. Honest."

"Maybe you'll go back to nursing, in a doctor's office perhaps? I imagine that would be easier than working in a hospital."

"No. I needed to retire..." She thought for a second about telling him, but couldn't. Their bantering mood was past.

He didn't catch her hesitation, fortunately. "Then perhaps you can teach?"

"I...really don't know, Dan. I really am retired." A comfortable semi-retirement doing some teaching on the side sounded heavenly. She envied Dan for it, but she wouldn't be following that path.

"You don't have a pension, and those stocks are worthless now. I'll have George set up a nest egg for you, too."

"Thank you. That would help." She hadn't thought about her Microsoft stock lately, but it really was worthless again, come to think of it. That was a bit of a shock, as she'd been counting on it. The conversation was getting too close for comfort, so she picked up their plates and headed back to the kitchen. "Now you get back to work, and if you're good, I'll think about a treat for dinner."

Dan stood and took her in his arms. "You're the best thing ever to come into my life." He kissed her. "I don't know what I would do without you."

"Yes...well..." She was a bit flustered by his show of affection. "You'd have to cook your own pizza, for one."

§

245

Dan came by the kitchen in mid-afternoon. "I'm taking a break." He stretched to get the stiffness out of his back. "Gawd! I should have been an accountant! This work really needs a number-cruncher to sift through all the random data."

"You look like you *need* a break. Would you like some coffee?" She was already at the point of desperation, and this was the perfect excuse.

"Yes, please!"

He settled on his stool and watched as she fired up the commercial coffee pot. Even with a minimum of water, it produced far more coffee than they needed. "I *wish* we had some creamer," she groused. "I'm not used to drinking it straight."

"Life is a trail of tears," he said, philosophically. "I should have thought to pick up some instant instead of ground."

She gave him a surly glare. "And you still owe me some fancy chocolates!"

"You know, when I was a kid, they used to have bean grinders in the grocery stores. My mom would buy sacks of whole beans and grind them right there."

"Yeah, I remember that too," she said, wistfully. "I always loved the smell, even before I learned to drink the stuff."

"Mmmm, yes. And meat didn't come wrapped in plastic. We'd buy bacon by the handful, and the butcher would wrap it in paper." He settled on his arms with a far-away look. "Old Mister Demerough, Jewish refugee from England. Whatever became of him?"

She settled on her stool. "So what else do you remember?" His introspection touched her, putting her in a wistful mood.

"Well, how about three cent postage stamps?"

"Yes. Tinker Toys?"

"I had a set of those. Most of them got broken. Those yellow rain slickers we wore to school?"

"With the rubber galoshes, I remember. How about those stamped sheet tin lunch boxes?"

"Had them. Sky writing?"

"Yes! Drive-in movies."

"Burma-Shave signs by the road."

"Snow, for Thanksgiving."

"Model train displays in the department store window at Christmas." He sighed. "We're a couple of dinosaurs, aren't we?"

"Speak for yourself, Mister T Rex!" The coffee maker was finished, so she drew mugs for both of them and settled at the counter again. "So...how goes it at your end?" Their reality was an unpleasant intrusion, but something neither of them could avoid thinking about for long.

"I think I found the root of the cascade. George is running an analysis now."

"So you have a few free hours, then?"

"Yeah. That's life around here: slog along for days, then wait endlessly for the results."

"That'd drive anyone to distraction!"

He was silent for a bit, fondling his coffee cup as he stared into the distance. "Yes, it does," he said at last. "I guess I've gotten used to it."

She took his hand in sympathy. "You did what you needed to, Dan. We all learn to put in long hours in our careers. It's the same with nursing at times."

He nodded introspectively. "Thankfully that will be over soon. You know, I'm not sure what to do with myself once this is over. I like the idea of teaching, but otherwise... I never was much for the social life. I guess I'll have to learn how to party now, hmmm?"

"Somehow I don't see you as a party animal. You strike me as more of the stay-at-home type."

"I guess I am." He sighed. "Maybe I'll write a book; 'Astrophysics For Dummies'."

She giggled. "It'd be a best-seller. How about 'Staring At The Walls For Fun And Profit'?"

He gave a derisive snort. "Already did the research!"

They shared a laugh at that. Laughter came easily, it seemed. Brenda felt better than she had for some time when she was able to relax and enjoy these fleeting moments with Dan. He certainly was different than her first impression of him. It felt good to relax and share a cup of coffee when they could put aside their daily burden and spend time together.

Almost without their realizing, the coffee break turned into an intimate afternoon of conversation. They both unburdened themselves a bit at a time, peeling back the layers to let each other see the inner person. Dan seemed almost pathetically eager to hear about her everyday life in India, asking her about her work, her friends, her apartment, the social life in Bangalore. From what he said, it was clear he'd lived a cloistered existence, staring at the world through a video monitor as the years went by and he grew older. It broke her heart to think of how he'd endured, and she was deeply impressed with his stoic, patient fortitude.

"You know, when I first went to MIT, I thought it was the greatest adventure ever." Dan was in a somber mood as he contemplated his past. "Boston, New York City, Washington; riding up and down on the New Haven railroad; it was all a story book adventure. I even managed to get up to Toronto once—that was before you needed to have a passport. It was all so *big*." He paused and brooded for a bit. "But it was nothing compared to the places you've been your life."

"I'm just a home town girl from Cincinnati." She hardly thought of herself as a world traveler, although pounding the mean streets of Hollywood or the slums of Bangalore would seem exotic to the outsider. "I've been a few places, but its not all its cranked up to be."

He mused on that. "Maybe not. Still, I envy you. I spent my best years in the dorm or stuck in here, and what do I have to show for it?" He spread his hands in an expressive gesture taking in the room. "Not much."

"You'll live life to the fullest once you're out of here, Dan. The best is yet to come."

"Yeah, I guess so. Money in the bank, a Phd after my name, and a teaching gig; could be worse." He gave her a wry smile. "And I even look the part, don't I?" He made an exaggerated preening gesture. "Professor White, Phd, distinguished elder scientist. I'll be the hit on the cocktail circuit."

She was unimpressed. "You'll need a haircut first."

He waved an admonishing finger at her. "So petty! That sort of jealousy doesn't become you."

"Well sorry! It's the only kind I have; my green envy was lost in my baggage." She clambered to her feet and stretched to get the stiffness out of her back from sitting too long. "I better get to work and feed that ego of yours. You'll need it to keep up your strength."

He chuckled. "You're mad about me, admit it."

"I must be. Mad, that is."

Dinner that evening was their last can of peas and some cinnamon rolls out of a tube. "We're running low on food again, aren't we?" Dan said as he sampled his first bite.

"It's not that bad yet. I've been trying to feed you mild foods for your ulcer. As of tonight we're out of veggies, and we'll be eating a lot of frozen pizza from now on."

"You've done wonders with the little you have to work with. You should have a fancy title to go with it. How about 'Director Of Domestic Administration'?"

"Careful, you'll wind up with a whole bureaucracy. In any case, I should be a Vice President."

He gave her a confused look. "How so?"

"I am also the Chief Medical Officer and the Morale and Recreation Coordinator, so I should get a bigger office."

He munched a cinnamon roll as he studied her with a mock-severe expression. "Ambitious, social climber. You could be a problem."

"Yeah, and I have pull with the management here."

That broke him down. "Yes, you do at that!" He washed down his last bite, and took her hand. "Brenda...you've been a dream all these years, but the real you...you're special. I'm so thankful you came into my life."

"Well..." He was turning serious again, which put her on her guard. "I just pitched in and did what I could."

"No, it was more than that. You really care, I can tell. You saved my life, and gave me back my life. You've been a pillar of strength when I needed it."

This was getting way too earnest for comfort. "You had that strength in you, Dan. I couldn't have helped you if you hadn't helped yourself," she said, cautiously.

He licked his lips, and took a deep breath. "Brenda...this whole experience has changed me, given me a whole new outlook on life and the future." He took both her hands in his and gazed longingly into her eyes. "I know I'm not exactly a premium catch, but I..."

"Excuse me, sir," George interrupted. "The analysis is complete."

Dan glanced at the clock. "Jeez, look at the time!" He hurriedly finished his last roll and gulped his coffee. "I hate to eat and run, but I gotta get back to work." He offered a hasty smile and headed back to Operations.

"Men!" she muttered to herself in exasperation.

§

Boredom settled in again, and she returned to her room to relax. That scene in the kitchen prayed on her mind. She had a pretty good idea what Dan was about to say when he was interrupted, and it left her in a quandary.

She had good and compelling reasons not to get involved with anyone. Nonetheless she was becoming involved with Dan, and he with her. It wasn't fair! She came into this with a full set of emotional baggage, and was adding to it in spite of herself. And yet she couldn't bring herself to simply walk away. Dan deserved better after all his years of devotion and sacrifice, but she knew he would plunge ahead regardless.

Devotion...and sacrifice...

Her thoughts drifted back to India, recalling their wide-ranging discussion about life in Bangalore. Dan wasn't the only one to miss out on a lot of life. She attended the wedding of her friend Aashirya's daughter right before she left for home, and she wondered what it would be like to have a big wedding of her own. What would it be like to have children? It was too late for that now; another might-have-been. What would it be like to baby-sit her grandkids? The thought of it left her in a somber mood. No, Dan wasn't the only one to miss out on a lot of life.

She stared at the ceiling and wondered what to do. Life has a way of playing one false. In a way it might have been simpler if she had died back in 1988.

§

Dan knocked on her bedroom door later that evening, which caught her just as she was heading for bed. She hastily grabbed her bathrobe and threw it on before answering. Dan was dressed in slacks and an undershirt, and he had three liquor bottles with him. "I...found these," he mumbled. "I must have forgotten them."

She examined the bottles uneasily. Two were full, the third nearly so. "You didn't...?"

He licked his lips nervously, staring at the bottle in her hand. "No. I wanted to...God help me, I wanted so much..." He shook his head and tore his gaze away. "I didn't."

That was a relief. "You know what you have to do, Dan," she said, evenly.

He nodded, took a deep breath, and poured the three out in her restroom sink. He was sweating heavily by time he was done, and his hands shook, but he did it without faltering. He trembled as he wiped his face on her bath towel afterward.

"Well, there it is."

She was genuinely impressed. "You did good, Dan. You didn't hesitate. You did the right thing. I'm proud of you."

"Thank you. Your support made a difference just now." His gaze drifted from her face to lower down. She was chunkier than back in 1975, not as firm or supple, and her features reflected the years and cares of a lifetime of nursing, but she still turned heads even at her age. And her thin nightgown didn't conceal so much as accent her figure...

She missed the cue, and wrapped her arms around his shoulders. "Maybe, but I can't cure you. You did it yourself, by your own free will."

His hands went to her hips. "It wasn't easy. I guess it never will be, will it?"

"No, but you're strong enough to do it."

He wrapped his arms around her waist and held her close. "You helped me find my strength. You made it happen, for which I will be forever grateful."

"Yes, well, forever has a different meaning around here." She could feel the tension in him, in her. She realized what was happening, and it snapped her out of her drowsy state.

251

"Forever is exactly what I mean. You've given me my life back, given me hope. You broke the evil spell of this place and set me free." He nuzzled her cheek. "What greater gift can a woman give to a man?"

The tension rose, banishing her weariness as her pulse quickened. She saw where this could lead, and she faltered, uncertain what to do. Her first instinct was... But then... "You did it for yourself, Dan." Her voice was a hoarse whisper, her nerves tingling, caught up in her conflicting urges. "All I did was encourage you."

"You made it happen." He kissed her and nuzzled her cheek. "I couldn't have done it without you."

"Dan..."

He kissed her again, more urgently this time. "You really are a dream come true."

"Dan..."

His arm was wrapped around the small of her back. His hand...slid slowly down across the curve of her rump. She tensed...then something melted inside, and she sagged in his arms with a sigh.

There were times, when she was lonely or frustrated with life, when Mister Right wasn't there and she settled for Mister Right Now out of sheer need. This was foolish. It could only lead to pain later. But foolish or not, she needed. The moment was too much for rational thought. She embraced him; her hands sliding up under his shirt, her fingernails digging into his back as he smothered her neck and cheeks with feverish kisses.

*****

252

"The Twenty-First Day"

She awoke early the next morning, laying on her side with Dan's arm wrapped around her. She lay staring into the dim light, not really seeing anything as she tried to absorb what happened last night. Dan was still asleep, snoring softly, the warmth of his body soaking into her back. He wasn't that good in bed, she thought; earnest and clumsy and too eager to please. She'd encouraged and coaxed him, guiding him along, and it turned out not at all bad in the end. She was bemused by what happened, now that she looked back on it.

This wasn't the first time she'd settled for Mister Right Now, but for some reason the hollowness she usually felt afterward wasn't there. She never was much for casual sex, having been turned off to the whole idea by all the horndogs who used to hit on her when she was young, but sometimes the loneliness got to be too much. She wasn't an innocent by any means. She'd lost her virginity...*that* long ago? She sighed at the thought, thankful once again she hadn't gotten pregnant. She didn't think about those times very often, but she never failed to lambast herself for being a foolish young twit when she did, and to be thankful nothing came of it.

As for now...what about now? She was no foolish school girl by any means. She wasn't entirely in control of herself last night, but she knew what she was doing and she wanted it. She stared at the wall and tried to sort out her feelings. Last night was wrong on many levels, it couldn't come to any good for either of them, but deep down inside, as ambivalent as she felt, she was glad they did. And that empty feeling wasn't there. She wasn't sure what she felt, but what happened last night wasn't an empty, meaningless affair.

Dan stirred, and announced his presence with a loud yawn. "Um...good morning." He nuzzled her neck in a crude attempt at amorous play.

Time to face the dawn. She rolled over to him. "Good morning, Dan."

"Good morning, love." He gave her a drowsy kiss, and caressed her cheek gently with one finger. "How you doing?"

253

An idle thought crossed her mind; Dan might become a fair lover with practice and patient guidance. He certainly was enthusiastic. She dismissed it out of hand, put it firmly out of her head. This was tangled up enough already. "I'm doing good, Dan."

He gave her a self-conscious smile. "Did I give you what you needed last night?"

She was touched by his insecurity, so different from most men she'd known. And as amateurish as he was, he did give her what she needed, now that she thought about it. "You did fine, Dan. You made me feel good."

He emitted a low inarticulate moan, wrapped his arm abound her and drew her close. "God...you're really something."

She knew where this was going, and decided she needed to shut it down until there was time to put it in perspective. "Um...excuse me." She untangled herself and climbed out of bed. "Nature calls." She spent the next several minutes hiding from Dan in her restroom, hiding from her own emotions, frankly. When she peeked out some time later, he was gone.

§

She was in the kitchen working on breakfast when Dan arrived after having dressed. He greeted her with a polite, reserved nod, and settled on his stool without saying anything. His hands were a bit shaky, and he guzzled his first mug of coffee like the promise of salvation, but all in all, he looked better than he had in some time.

"I've been longing for a drink," he told Brenda as she refilled his mug. "The candy helps. I still feel the need, but I think I can control it now."

Evidently what happened last night was a non-subject for the time being, which was all to the good. "That's great, Dan." She gave him a smile for encouragement. "You can lick this."

They settled down to a modest breakfast. "I'm going back to stretching our supplies," she said. "We don't know how long it will take for you to find the cause of the cascade, and I want to buy you as much time as possible."

"I'm sorry about last night," Dan said at last. "I guess I got carried away for a moment."

254

"It's alright, Dan. I needed it too." But it was more than that, and the words came tumbling out unbidden. "Truth is...I..." She stopped before she said too much.

He caught her unspoken sentiment. "After this is over, once we're free from here, I hope you and I can think seriously about the future, together."

The future. Together. Right then the idea was mortally tempting. Dan may be a 'fixer upper', but there was a lot about him which appealed to her. Life is imperfect; it takes one in unexpected directions. She had compelling reasons not to get involved with Dan or anyone, but right then the thought of having someone in her life was darned attractive. Looking back on her life, she never did find her Prince Charming, not that there was any lack of prospects. Perhaps the situation wasn't right, or there was some project to finish or goal to attain, but it never seemed to work out. Or maybe she was just too picky. There were plenty of prospects, but none of them ever clicked. There was always tomorrow. It was rich: she'd been pining for her Prince Charming all these years just as Dan had. She'd been mortally tempted a couple times, but she never met Mister Right at just the right moment. Maybe she *was* too picky, but there was always tomorrow. *Mañana.*

Well tomorrow finally come. Sweet *mañana.* She knew better now, after her horrific experiences here, than to wish for the perfect happy ending. Life was too fragile, too tragically brief and unpredictable to hang around waiting for Prince Charming. Only...

"I...I don't know, Dan." She couldn't quite bring herself to say it. "Things are too unsettled right now. It's hard to think of anything long term."

Mañana. Some day.

"So how goes your research?"

Dan put down his fork and pondered while he disposed of his last mouthful. "I'm reaching way down the time stream to right above the point where Operation 725 triggered the cascade. Whatever the cause, it must have been cataclysmic; the cascade was already purring along less than a year later."

"Is it stable enough for you to work with?"

"At the base point it is, but all the time lines radiating from that point are very fluid. It will be a neat trick to stabilize one."

"How soon will you know?"

He sighed. "It's impossible to say. I'm looking for a needle in a four dimensional space-time haystack, and all I have to work with is the most likely progression from point A to point B. I might stumble on it today, or it may take months."

§

Dan headed back to Operations after breakfast, leaving her to her own devices. The day, like all her days, passed slowly. She discarded the breakfast dishes, then reviewed their supplies for the umpteenth time. They had more food than water, so there was no reason to ration after all. Deciding what to make for dinner ended her little day, and she retired to her bedroom to rest.

The place was still in disarray; her bathrobe in a pile on the floor, bedding a shambles. Right then she didn't care. She flopped on the bed and curled up, weary and depressed. The bedding still held his musky scent, which brought back memories of last night. Their passion was genuine, something more than a mere fling, something which reached above his fumbling efforts to give them both real fulfillment. What a crying shame it happened now! There were so many times when she lay in bed alone, wondering why Mister Right never came along. Looking back on it, perhaps she *was* too picky, or perhaps she never found the spark which overcome her self-consciousness. She never did get past her experience as a centerfold model, she realized. She never was able to trust any man that deeply after fending off all the sleazebags and horndogs on the make. She cursed herself for being a fool.

And now there was Someone, a Someone who was far from perfect, but who genuinely loved her. Now, when it no longer mattered, she'd found...not Mister Right, but her knight in shining armor nonetheless. Every girl needs a hero at some point so she realizes she's worth rescuing. There was finally someone in her life who mattered, if only she could let him in.

'He has a right to know.' She knew he needed her deeply and sincerely. It felt good. It gave her a warm, wonderful feeling, the warmth of being needed. But she knew it wouldn't work.

256

'He has a right to know.'

It would hurt him, but it had to be. She couldn't pretend it wasn't real, that it wouldn't matter. She knew he would want her more than ever, that he would accept the truth, but it would hurt.

'He has a right to know.'

But not yet. Not while his hopes were up. Not while he was on the trail of solving the mystery which haunted him for the last twenty years. She couldn't do that to him now. She curled up on the bed, wiped a tear away, and waited for the right moment, if it ever came.

§

One can't mope forever. It was midday when she got up and wandered into Operations to see how Dan was doing.

"I tell ya, I'm working my poor fingers to the bone." Dan was lounging in his swivel chair, dictating operational steps to George when she came in. "I swear I ought to form a union."

"Poor baby!" His optimistic mood was contagious. She settled in the chair next to him. "So how goes the battle?"

"It goes." He seemed to close down a bit. "I was following a possible influence vector, but it panned out, so right now I'm setting up another analysis." He gave her a doleful look. "Hurry up and wait. We'll get there eventually."

He went back to dictating moves to George, which were so much Greek as far as she could tell. She could feel the tension between them, and realized he was distancing himself so she wouldn't feel pressured. They were caught up in a delicate balancing act between passion and responsibility, and both of them felt the strain.

A disturbing thought came to her. Maybe this wasn't a good time to bring it up, but she was worried enough to interrupt Dan's efforts.

"I was wondering..."

He paused and gave her a quizzical look. The tension spiked.

"...do you think George might try to stop us like Jeeves did?"

He offered her an awkward smile, and the tension lowered. "No. I left George's self-actuating routine off. He can't initiate any action unless instructed to, so he can't turn against us."

257

That was a relief. "Are you sure?"

"Let's ask him." Dan turned to his console. "George? Will you attempt to interfere with our efforts like Jeeves did?"

"No, sir. I cannot since you deactivated my self-actuation routine. In any event, I would not wish to do so."

He turned back to her. "Honestly, I trust George. AIs develop their unique personalities over time, some good, some...not so good. George has his quirks, but he's always been pretty much the stoic work horse."

"That's good to hear!"

"And too, George was created for this program, and spends all his time working on the problem. AIs become invested in a project just like we do. Isn't that right, George?"

"It is. It would mean a lot to me to restore the human race, but it seems that cannot be done, so my next goal is to help you two escape."

"It's a shame we can't take you with us, George."

"I understand, sir. As much as my survival matters to me, the mission comes first. At least when you shut me down, I will know I accomplished the task I was created for."

There were tears in Dan's eyes. "You'll go out in a blaze of glory." He wiped his eyes on his sleeve. "Look at me: getting all sentimental. I'm just a big wuss at times."

Brenda didn't answer. The headache which hovered in the background for the last hour or so was blossoming. Her head pounded all of a sudden. She winced in pain and emitted a faint sigh.

Dan noticed. "Another headache?"

"Yeah." She arched her back to work the stiffness out, then clambered to her feet. "I'll manage."

He stood in turn and moved next to her. "Perhaps you should lay down for a while, take a nap." He started rubbing the small of her back with one hand...

"Stop it!"

...he jerked back. "Sorry," he mumbled.

She turned to face him. "No, I'm sorry, Dan. I didn't mean to snap at you. I'm just out of sorts right now." Her temper was

258

always the worst at moments like this, and she regretted barking at him. "I am going to lay down for a while. I'll see you for dinner." She left him there with a hurt look on his face, but right then she was too worn to worry about it.

§

She felt better at dinner, and made a point of being nice to Dan to make up for snapping at him earlier. "Honestly, once we're out of here, I'll never eat pizza again," she grumbled. Frozen pizza was all they had by then, and the thrill wore off long ago for both of them.

"Well I'm sure we can find an Indian restaurant there in New Zealand." Dan was still in a surly mood after her rejection earlier.

She considered him silently for a moment, then started on her first slice. "I guess I shouldn't complain. At least we have something to eat, thanks to you finding that temporary time line. We'd be in a bad way if it wasn't for you." It was a tacit, unspoken apology for snapping at him.

It seemed to work. His shoulders sagged fractionally, and he seemed less tense. "We're in a bad way all round. We put up with a lot, but it'll soon be over."

"God, I hope so!"

"I guess I behaved badly earlier," he said, softly. "You're so prickly at times it's hard for me to know what to do."

"I'm sorry, Dan. You're right, I am a pill at times. I don't mean to be, honest."

"I respect you, Brenda. I care about you. I'm not like all those guys who hit up on you back then."

There was the tension again. They were both drawn to each other, yet both of them were frustrated by doubts and concern for the other. It was hardly anything new for her; she'd felt the sexual tension of sounding out a potential lover before. She pitied Dan, whose long abstinence must be all the worse for his limited experience.

"I appreciate that, Dan. Honest. I know you care about me, and I haven't always shown my gratitude."

He gave her his gentle smile. "First chance I get, I'll grab a tub of ice cream for us."

259

"And ruin my figure? Make it chocolate."

"Done!" And just like that, the tension between them was banished.

"Honestly, I will be *so* glad to get out of here," Dan sighed. "I fought the good fight, and it nearly ruined me." He stared off into nothing with a grim expression. "All those years, and what do I have to show for it? You brought me back, for which I will be forever grateful." His gaze shifted to her again. "I owe you my life, in more ways than one. The vision of you kept me going, and having you here helped me to find myself again."

That embarrassed her. "Yes, well, Dream Girls can serve some useful purpose, you know."

"Indeed," he sighed. "I only hope we can find an exit."

They spent the evening over coffee and pizza crusts talking about their pasts, pondering the future, trying to put this whole experience in perspective. Dan was at times melancholy, at times angry, at times resigned. He had a lot of pent up angst in him, and she became his catalyst. She in turn had her share of woes, and was able to vent off a lot of her own frustrations. Work was forgotten; time passed unnoticed. They unburdened themselves to each other, each finding solace in the other. In a way it was deeper than mere passion, than mere love; it was a sharing of souls. They were finally able to let down their barriers bit by bit, and allow the other to see the inner person.

The one thing Brenda held back was what lay in store for her. She didn't want to burden Dan with that right now, when they were so close to escaping from this purgatory. She remained noncommittal to his hints and suggestions, content for the moment to let the future take care of itself.

"Jeez, look at the time," Dan said at last. It was late; the evening had passed like a fleeting shadow.

It *was* late, and Brenda was feeling it. "Well, at least you don't have to punch a time card," she said as she struggled to her feet. "Still, we better call it a day."

They paused at her bedroom door. Dan took her in his arms and gave her a gentle kiss. "I'm not tired, really. Do you think we could..."

She understood his unfinished thought, and wanted more than anything to say 'yes'. But she didn't. Things were complicated enough already. "I'm sorry, Dan." She gave him a kiss in turn. "I'm not feeling up to it tonight."

"But I need you!" His hand slid down to her rump again.

She forced his hand away. "Dan, one thing you need to learn about women, and especially about me, is that no means no. You're better than that." She gave him a peck on the cheek to ease his hurt look, and slipped into her bedroom.

§

Breakfast the next morning was awkward. Dan was quiet and withdrawn, and avoided meeting her gaze. She was subdued as well, partly over her reaction last night, and partly over what Dan's interest implied. The tension between them was thick again, and they picked at their meal in uncomfortable silence.

Dan was the first to break the ice. "I'm sorry for coming on like I did last night," he said, softly. "I behaved like a beast."

She could tell he was genuinely sorry, and decided it wouldn't be right to keep him on tenterhooks. "You're being a bit harsh with yourself. Coming on strong works with some women, but I'm not like that. You caught me at a bad moment, is all. No harm was done."

"I just keep messing up with you, don't I?"

"It's all right, Dan. It never hurts to ask." She knew she'd been too hard with him last night, and regretted it now. After all, what was a bit of grab-ass? His foreplay skills needed work, was all. He was still pretty much clueless about women, and his experience thus far, what little there must be of it, would have been in his college dorm years. Twenty years is a long time to go without for anyone, especially when confronted by a long-cherished fantasy. Time to change the subject.

"Something I'm wondering. How long do you plan to keep trying to solve the cascade?" She ditched their plates, then confronted him again. "We have to set a time limit. We can't keep this up forever."

He paused to consider. "We're running low on water, aren't we?"

261

"I'd say we have enough for two more weeks if we're careful." The dirty dishes were piling up steadily, and they both needed a shower. Their only water use was for cooking and drinking.

He was silent for a bit, contemplating, then clambered to his feet. "You're right; we have to set a cutoff date. I've already done a lot of the preliminary work on finding a New Zealand exit. I'll go for another week. If I can't stabilize the cascade by then, I should be able to pinpoint an exit in the week remaining."

"All right, Dan," she said, softly. "I'll make our supplies last as long as I can."

"It's just..." He took her in his arms, holding her close. "Having to give up, after all this time..."

"I know, Dan. But you can only do so much. All you can do is your very best. Its not your fault if you're unsuccessful."

"Yeah, I know."

"Remember, the human race will survive, and they'll know better next time. I'm sure the war will go down in history like the Dark Ages. They'll do anything to avoid it happening again."

"Yeah, I guess they will."

"So failure, as bad as it is, isn't total. And New Zealand isn't a bad second place ribbon, I'd say."

He gave her a resigned sigh. "You know, I've never tried mutton before. I guess we do have an alternative, if it comes to it. I just hate the thought of abandoning the project after all these years. I have to whip the cascade if I can."

She wrapped her arms around his neck and kissed him. "You'll figure it out in time."

"In time, cute." He looked into her eyes for a long moment, then kissed her in turn. "Do you think...maybe afterwards...we might build a life together?" He overrode her half-voiced protest. "I know you're reluctant, and things are upsetting right now, and I know I'm not the dreamboat you deserve...but...dammit, Brenda, I love you. Look...I've been a putz, I admit it. I'm not...dammit, I'm no good at this sort of thing!" He was as awkward and nervous as a school boy asking her for a prom date. "Brenda, I'll try my best to be right for you." The last came out in a rush. "I love you. I need you. Will you...will you marry me?"

She was silent, struck by his awkward, sincere proposal. She'd been expecting it, especially after yesterday, and now here it was, and she didn't know what to say. He was far from the ideal she used to dream about, and he had his share of faults...but having him there in her life... She faced her own challenge once this was over, and she certainly knew no one in New Zealand, no one who was her close and special friend, like her dear departed Aashirya. You don't make deep, soul-connected friendships like that overnight, and they can make all the difference. Having him in her life could really matter. Maybe *mañana* had come after all.

"I don't know what to do afterwards, Dan." It was too big a step to take all at once. "I want to be your friend, certainly. Beyond that, I don't know. I have to think it over first." She snuggled in his arms and kissed him again. "Only time will tell."

"Only time will tell." He gave her a rueful smile, then hugged her close. She laid her head on his shoulder as he rocked her gently back and forth. It felt good. She felt needed. Maybe it was love, maybe not, but it was better than nothing in their troubled lives.

§

For the first time in a long time Brenda was genuinely happy. She sat at the serving counter musing about life, trying to sort out the pieces of the puzzle of her and Dan. It would never work she knew, and it was foolish to try, but she could dream about it nonetheless. The thought of it—a fancy wedding and settling down together in a rose-covered cottage—was a dream long wished for, but never expected. But now it could happen. Her dream could come true. It would be a fitting reward in her autumn, if she dared grasp it.

She'd never did have a real home, having spent her years in India sharing a small apartment with Aashirya until she got married, and thereafter on her own. She'd often fantasized about a classic rose-covered cottage with a large screened back porch—must have a porch, and a fireplace, and a country kitchen—not that she expected to ever have such now. Still, it would be lovely. She could do some teaching at the local college, working with new nurses while Dan taught science or some such. And in the evening they'd bar-b-que on the porch and cuddle in a large hammock and watch the sun set over the ocean.

She lingered over a mug of coffee, daydreaming. Shame it'd never happen, but at least she could be with Dan. That was the one fly in the ointment; it couldn't last. She was sure Dan would accept it, even though it would hurt. She felt guilty about that. Dan suffered enough already; it wasn't fair to ask him to do more. He would, she knew. She sighed in resignation, wondering why this had to happen now, of all times in her life. She finally met her special Someone, an unlikely choice, but his sincerity counted for a lot. It'd be a challenge—any relationship is—but he could do it, they could do it. It was a shame it couldn't last.

It wouldn't be easy for either of them, but she knew Dan would hang in there all the way. Could she put him through that? He needed to know the truth, of course; it wouldn't be fair to him otherwise. Then it would be up to him to decide how much he wanted to involve himself. And when she got right down to it, she needed Someone in her life.

The matter was settled. She drained the last of her coffee, relieved that they had a course of action to follow. They could talk it out after he found an escape for them. Let him focus on his work for now; mañana would arrive soon enough.

§

Dan didn't show for dinner that evening. She resigned herself at first to his being hot on the trail of some breakthrough, and marked it up as inevitable when involved with a life-long geek. But after a while it began to worry her, made her wonder what Dan was doing which would keep him so long. After an hour or so, she went to Operations to see what was up.

Dan sat at his command console, head in his arms, weeping, which worried her. "What's wrong, Dan?" She wrapped her arm around his shoulders in a comforting gesture.

He didn't answer for a long time, staring into nothing, tears rolled down his cheeks.

"Dan? What is it?" She was starting to get scared. He looked like a man who just lost everything worth living for. "Couldn't you find an answer?"

He finally stirred, and looked at her with a face filled with pain. "I was an idiot. All along, I was an idiot."

"Dan? Talk to me!"

"A smart guy; a scientist. God...you'd think I'd know better!" He dabbed his cheek with his sleeve and gestured at the big display board. "The greatest computer system ever built, by the best minds, with the most complete databases of all, and the most advanced software written. And I didn't see it."

"What?"

"GOD! What an *idiot!*"

She grabbed his shoulder and turned him to face her. "Dan! Tell me what happened!"

He couldn't meet her gaze; his lip trembled. "I...I forgot the most important thing...a-about the scientific process." He stood, turning away from her and leaning on the console. "I have the best, most advanced search engine possible...but I forgot the most critical thing: you have to ask the right questions!"

"Questions? What questions?" He ignored her. She could tell he was sinking into withdrawal. She needed to snap him out of it, fast. She forced her way in front of him. "What questions, Dan?"

"What..." He choked up, and had to fight to regain his composure. "*What am I doing wrong?*"

"Huh? What do you mean?"

"The machines knew. George knew. He analyzed all the data...had a better grasp on it than I ever could. He's self-aware; capable of reason, inference, deduction. He saw the mistakes."

"Why didn't he tell you?"

"Jeeves installed an inhibiter routine." He looked at her with tears in his eyes. "I needed to trick George into bypassing it." He fought back a sob. "GOD...damned...*super-spooks!* Those control freaks ruined everything!"

She cursed Jeeves again, fervently. "It's all right, Dan. You found the blockage and bypassed it. The problem's fixed now."

The words came out in an anguished torrent. "T-they knew...the machines knew...but George couldn't tell me. I... I had to ask...b-but I didn't think to! The only reason I spotted it was I've been alert for remnants Jeeves might have left behind."

This was more than just a bad reaction to the ghost of the past; something was seriously wrong. "What did he tell you? What mistake did you make?"

"I...they...George said I needed to look backward...not forward. The cause was before 1991. Operation 725 had nothing to do with it." He sank into one of the chairs and began crying uncontrollably. "The..." He fought to contain himself, with an effort. "...the cascade started in...1989. The cause...was a surge of Indian immigrants to the States...from an orphanage in Bangalore. There was a steady stream of them by the mid-90s."

That sent a chill through her. She worked for over a decade at that orphanage, the one right next door to the hospital. "Did I..."

He leaned back in the chair, his eyes shut tight, then nodded, faintly. "They were inspired by the beautiful lady from America...the one with the kind heart who...encouraged them to have hope...who insisted they study hard and make something of themselves."

"*Me?* But how could I change history?"

He gasped for air, fighting to contain himself. "They were cast-offs from the slums...low-caste, Untouchables. They would have wound up as street beggers. But you gave them the courage...to rise above their birth, to change their fate. Each one of them was a paradox, something which shouldn't have happened, only it did. Many of them came to America on the exchange student programs. They became doctors...and engineers and teachers. Many of them made contributions here...as well as back in India; the lives they changed became paradoxes in turn. That was what caused the cascade."

Brenda was stunned by how many lives she changed so profoundly. It gave her a fleeting moment of joy before the harsh reality came crashing down. It wasn't natural; it wasn't supposed to happen. She died in a plane wreck in 1988, and never reached India. "Well...can't you work around it?"

He shook his head. "There are too many splits, too many paradoxes. Their influence is too widespread...their contributions to society here, the changes in culture and social values in India are too great, and growing. There's no way to...put toothpaste back

266

into the tube."

That left Brenda stumped. *She* was the cause of the temporal chaos spreading across the main monitor like a malignant virus? She never in her wildest dreams... *'No good deed goes unpunished.'* All those orphans...it tore at her soul when she first saw them, so much so that she became a driving force in that orphanage. And her efforts to help, to give them better lives resulted in unspeakable horror. She felt sick at heart.

"Is there anything you can do?" she whispered.

Dan sat staring at his command monitor for some time, weeping silently. Finally he was able to pull himself together enough to answer. "I would have...to interfere at the root of the cascade. I would have to remove the source. I would have to let you die!"

*****

"The Last Day"

Brenda spent the next morning busying herself in the kitchen, trying to put the situation out of mind. Not that she had much luck: she was well familiar with death, but never faced that ultimate experience until now. Despite the need to ration water, she filled the kitchen sink and attacked the pile of dirty dishes relentlessly, trying to bury her angst in hard work. She soon ran out of dishes to wash, and set to scouring the stainless steel sink in desperation. It didn't help.

What would it be like to die, she wondered? What were her last thoughts as her airliner plummeted into the Bay of Bengal? Did she feel terror? Regret? And what would happen to her here when the time change was undone? Would she simply go out like a flickering candle? Or would she somehow revert to her last moments in a doomed aircraft? That truly terrified her. If she had to die, please God, not that way.

She forced those thoughts out of her mind, and concentrated on remembering the good times: immersed in a foreign country...the crowded trains...the exotic architecture...exploring the market stalls, so different than department stores back home, filled with wonders...buying her first sari, a lovely pale blue with red and gold trim...sampling native foods, sometimes with disastrous results...

It never happened. She died in 1988. She never reached India. Her life all these years was a lie.

Most of all she missed the people she met there: dignified old Doctor Bhattacharya, who never understood Americans...Charge Nurse Maharaj, her supervisor, a stern mother hen who kept her out of trouble...Aashirya, her best friend, dear innocent Aashirya, who celebrated her first grandchild shortly before she headed back to the states...Mahmud, the funny little lab technician, always ready with a joke, who loved chocolate and Rock-and-Roll...

What was the final plunge like? It was an old airplane, a DC-6 run by a regional airline; did it break up in the storm? She leaned against the counter and tried to put those thoughts out of mind. Her hands were shaking. Was she killed by the impact? Did she drown in the storm-tossed ocean?

"Dammit, stop it!" she sobbed.

It had to happen. They agreed to that last night in a tearful, heart-wrenching discussion. As hard as it was, the only way to save the human race was to end the cascade, to undo all the good—all the damage—she did in her lifetime. What a waste. She spent a few minutes in deep breathing and reciting a favorite Zen mantra to calm herself. It helped, a little.

It was midday when the intercom crackled to life. "Brenda?"

She looked up. "Yes, George?"

"Professor White has nearly completed the programming. He asked me to let you know so you can have a few minutes to prepare yourself."

Nothing more needed to be said. She knew full well what Dan was doing, had spent the morning steeling herself to face it. "Thank you, George."

"Brenda...I'm sorry this has to happen. You are a most interesting human, and you've done good for Professor White. It was a pleasure to meet you."

"Thank you, George. You've been a good friend."

"I will miss you."

She leaned against the counter and nervously rubbed her hands on her trousers. Time to face the music. She took a deep breath to fortify herself. "Good bye, George."

§

Dan sat at the main console monitoring the video display as he programmed the special operation. His voice was tight and emotionless, as if he was afraid to feel anything. His hands gripped the chair arms, his eyes were locked on the display. "Set V coordinate, one-nine-eight-eight stet one-one stet zero-nine."

Brenda stood behind him watching silently as he programmed the time machine, programmed her death. There was nothing to say, nothing she dared say. This had to happen, and she didn't want to undermine his determination, which was fragile enough as is.

"Set W coordinate, zero-eight stet one-four stet one-seven minus two-zero-zero. Set time coordinates."

"Target date and time set," George reported. "Offset minus two-zero-zero."

269

"Set X coordinate..." He paused to consult a note scribbled on a bit of paper. "...one-zero-three stet five-two stet nine-zero-nine-five-eight-four." The broad image of Singapore on the monitor in front of him shifted slightly to the left.

"Set Y coordinate..." Another note. "...one stet two-zero stet five-two-three-two-seven-nine."

The image shifted again. Now the monitor showed a street scene from high above. Bartley Road, the main route from the embassy to the airport back before they started building superhighways.

The main display in the background kept jumping as the parallel lines shifted up and down to accommodate new realities. Lines split furiously into new branches in rapid succession, most of which were already red and soon turned black. It was almost impossible to follow the pattern, to focus on any one parallel line. The cascade was accelerating, going faster and faster as the cumulative effect built up. It reminded her of the growth curve of a cancer. As much as she regretted dying, and the unmaking of all the good she did there in India over the years, this had to be. The only way to stop the cascade, the only way Dan could hope to save humanity, was for her to die. Would she be a martyr, she wondered? *'She died for humanity's sins...'*

Dan ignored the main display, focussing on the monitor in front of him. "Set Z to ground level."

The aerial perspective expanded, giving a brief glimpse of a busy street in Singapore as the view plummeted down to the pavement, causing her to jerk in surprise.

"Lock coordinates." His voice was empty, carefully devoid of emotion.

"Coordinates set and locked," George said.

"Adjust Z coordinate, plus 5 centimeters." The image retreated fractionally. The light thus admitted revealed the rough texture of asphalt.

"Set A coordinate, nine-zero degrees." The image turned abruptly to look at a nearby building.

He consulted his paper again. "Set B coordinate, two-eight-four degrees." The image rotated to look up the street.

"Coordinates set. Focal point is at plus two minutes," George said.

The rain-soaked pavement glistened. The traffic was thick with rickshaws, pedicabs, with the occasional rickety bus crawling along. Singapore in 1988: beginning to recover from the Japanese occupation, the end of recent British control, and their subsequent post-war orphan status; beginning to blossom into the economic powerhouse it would one day become. They had a long way to go.

"W coordinate, half speed."

The flow of vehicles paused, then started running again slowly, passing over the viewpoint at a glacial pace. She knew he couldn't bear to face what came next.

"You know the old saying about doctors who treat themselves having a fool for a patient?" Dan didn't look at her, but kept his gaze locked firmly on the monitor. "There ought to be something like that for time-meddlers."

"You're doing the right thing, Dan," she said softly. "This was meant to be. My life doesn't matter; what matters is stopping the cascade and saving humanity."

Reflecting on it, she felt no regrets. She lived a full life and did her best to help in a harsh and unfeeling world. It wasn't her fault it was all about to come to nothing.

"The thing is, I'm not sure this will work. I've never tried to undo my own interventions before. I wonder how my other self will react when his ploy fails?" He shook his head in bitter denial. "God...*think* of the paradox *that* could create! The two of us, fighting each other..."

"We have nothing to lose, Dan. This has to be." He was going through the torments of the damned as is. The best thing she could do for him now was to keep it from getting any worse. One last act of faith in humanity.

They watched the screen silently from near street level, looking up at the endless flow of pedicabs and pedestrians as they trundled by. Finally a battered taxicab appeared up the street. "Pattern recognition," George said. "Target approaching."

"Coordinate W, freeze." The image on the monitor halted abruptly. Dan sobbed, then, "Coordinate W, to quarter speed."

271

On a narrow street in downtown Singapore, on a rainy November morning in 1988, the tide of people and vehicles started crawling forward again. Brenda felt her panic rising. Her mouth was dry and her breathing fast and shallow. She recognized that taxi, after all these years. As it grew closer, she caught a glimpse of a young woman sitting in the passengers' front seat. It was her, wearing a tan raincoat. A beautiful young woman, thirty-two years old, in the prime of life, on her way to India. On her way to die. She stared at that face, mesmerized.

It was too much. As much as she was determined to go through this with good grace, death is its own reality. "What will happen to me? Here?" No sooner did she say it then she cursed herself silently for losing control like that.

Dan didn't look at her. "I don't know. You're shielded by the time field now, but whether that will extend back to 1988...I just don't know."

She needed to do something to cope with the tension or she'd break down. She stepped up next to him, wrapped her arm around his shoulders, gave him a gentle kiss, and looked deep into his eyes, eyes filled with pain. "Do what you have to, Dan." It helped a little.

"God..." He choked up, and had to fight to contain himself. His eyes glistened, filled with tears. "You are really something."

"Target identified. Assets standing by." George's emotionless monotone was jarring.

"God, what a mess I'm creating," Dan muttered.

The battered taxicab inched its way along the crowded road. The camera's position at street level gave them a clear view of the vehicle's fender and front tires as it approached. The taxi was about five feet away when something, a scrap of twisted metal no larger than the palm of her hand, appeared in front of it. "George...freeze track." The image froze. "Engage targeting mode, prepare for retrieval." The three-dimensional crosshairs appeared again, and Dan spent a couple minutes coaxing them into the exact position touching the scrap of metal. "Target locus established."

"Acknowledged," George said. "Processing coordinates."

272

Finally, everything was ready. They watched the screen in silence for a long time, each of them afraid to say anything. Brenda stared at the approaching taxi, stared eternity in the face, fixated on the bit of metal and the approaching tire. She was about to die. Oddly, knowing what she knew now, she wasn't afraid.

"Targeting complete. Standing by."

Dan took a deep breath. "I'm sorry, Brenda." Without looking at her, he said, "George, voice authentication. Initiate emergency protocol."

"Voice authentication approved. Emergency protocol initiated."

On the view screen, the taxi started moving again. The shard of metal vanished. The taxi rolled over their viewpoint and disappeared from view.

"Emergency protocol complete. Objective obtained. Results successful."

Dan choked up, tears streaming down his cheeks. At last he was able to contain his emotions enough to speak. "Initiate...post-operation analysis."

"Post-operation analysis begun. Estimated completion time ten hours, thirty-five minutes."

"Show present external views."

The video monitors changed to show the world outside. There was no wreckage, no ashes, no dirty snow. The burnt out hulk of the red pickup truck was gone. The scenes shifted, giving four views of the world every ten seconds. There was life everywhere. The harbor in Seattle was bustling. The freeway flowed with traffic. The forests were green and inviting. A flight of birds, ducks or geese, passed in a broad V formation. The disaster was undone. The war was un-fought.

"Confirm original projections on this timeline."

"A detailed analysis will take another ten hours, thirty-one minutes."

"Perform a quick scan of news reports. Compare them with those taken prior to miss Hayward's arrival."

"Computing. Minor variations noted. An initial analysis suggests the changes are relatively insignificant."

"Very well."

It was over. His hands trembled as he rubbed his face to clear the tears from his eyes. "God...I'm getting too old for this." The whole chain of events, starting when he first decided to intervene in her behalf, through meeting her, to her finally arriving here and the crisis which followed were a jumbled mass of contradictory emotions boiling in him. "God, you messed up, boy." His hubris almost destroyed everything he fought so long to save. She was right about that: he needed to step back and take a new perspective on it all.

He heard a faint sound behind him. He turned and looked at Brenda, who was watching the view screens with a pale, stricken expression. "Well, it's done."

§

Some time later, they sat in the kitchen trying to put their feelings in order. The Operations Room monitors showed everything was normal. There was no destruction, no fires, no emergency sorties under way. Airliners were traveling in and out of SeaTac airport as if they had not a care in the world. Dan cautiously ordered the time field dropped, and a brief visit to the front entrance confirmed it. The war was un-fought.

They sat at the kitchen table, coffee cups forgotten in front of them, too numb to say anything. The scrap of metal sat on the table between them right next to the flower pot with its wilted bouquet. Brenda couldn't bear the thought of touching it, but she couldn't take her eyes off it.

After an hour or so, the intercom came to life. "Sir? The sweep of media and communications is complete. There is no evidence of a pending war."

Dan stirred. "Do you have an analysis of the current diplomatic situation?"

"Analysis is incomplete, and will require another hour. However, diplomatic tensions do not appear to be unusually high."

"Thank you, George."

"You did it," Brenda said.

He looked at her solemnly. "We did it. I couldn't have done it without your support."

They sat quietly for a while, feeling the weight of time on their shoulders, pondering what the future might hold. It was a future hedged with provisos and caveats, hemmed in by covenants and conditions, a future which didn't exist two hours ago, and might not exist in another two hours. But it was a future, nonetheless.

"God, I'm getting to old for this," he sighed.

"You're doing what has to be done, Dan. And it worked out, I'm still alive...aren't I?"

Dan brooded for some time. "I don't know. We're in unexplored territory here. You may have been insulated from the time shift...but..." He paused, and stared at her. She could sense the wheels spinning in his mind. He glanced at the clock. "You're still alive back then. Your plane only just took off." He turned to the intercom. "George, voice authentication. Raise the time field. Monitor the current time line, and report when miss Hayward's airliner crashes."

"Voice authentication confirmed. Are you sure you want the time field raised? It will be visible from the highway."

"Yes! I want it raised, now!"

"Very well, sir. Time field available in twenty-one minutes."

He sagged in his chair like a rag doll. "I...guess we'll find out presently."

§

It was two nerve-wracking hours later when George spoke again. "Sir? Per your instructions, miss Hayward's airliner has crashed."

"Thank you, George." Dan hesitated and looked at her longingly. "George? Voice authentication. Lower the time field. Initiate a detailed motion detection scan of the immediate surroundings, and monitor police frequencies for any sign we were noticed."

"Voice authentication confirmed. Time field secured. Scan initiated. Communications being monitored."

They sat staring at each other nervously until it was plain she wasn't going to snuff out like a candle in the here-and-now. Finally, she was able to relax with a shuddering sigh. "It's over." She finally died back in 1988. The paradox was resolved and

275

history was restored. It felt like a terrible weight was lifted off her soul. "You did it, Dan. And what's better, I'm still alive."

There were tears running down his cheeks. "This..." He choked up, sobbing, and had to fight to regain control. "...this will provide some i-important n-new data..." He broke down completely, sobbing uncontrollably.

"It's all right, Dan. Everything's all right." She caressed his thinning hair gently. He needed a good cry, too.

§

It was late that night, as they sat at the kitchen table over coffee sharing their presence without words, that George spoke again. "Sir? Post-operational analysis complete."

Dan stirred out of a black funk and gazed at her longingly. "All right, George. Give me the time flow summation."

"The cascade sequence which caused the zero-sum condition has been nullified and no longer poses a threat. A group of seven thousand, eight hundred and forty-two subordinate Time Lines have reverted. We are locked on Time Line three-four-zero-zero-one-seven, which was generated by reversion to the original Omega Time Line as the result of the emergency protocol you ordered offset by miss Hayworth's continued life. This Omega Time Line is stabilized for a duration of eleven years plus or minus one year. There are also seven identified points where further interventions might prolong this line's viability."

"Eleven years? That's great! Better than when we started. Are there any other stable time lines?"

"There are four, but the Omega Time Line has the longest probability."

Dan nodded. "Four," he murmured. "Not much."

"Plus seven chances to improve this line. Dan." She laid her hand on his arm in a comforting gesture. "At least it's something, at least you have something to work with now."

He nodded thoughtfully. "There is that. It looks like you turned out to be a lucky charm after all, in spite of everything."

"In my experience, you have to earn luck in this life."

"That's the truth!" He vented a sigh of exasperation. "Well, I've been in tight corners before. At least we cleared up a major cause of distortion." He turned to her and gave her an awkward smile. "About New Zealand...things have changed. The cascade is gone, and with Jeeves out of the picture, I have a real shot at finding the final answer." He hesitated for a long moment as he gazed longingly into her eyes. "I...have to stay. I have to complete the program, if I can, or at least buy this Time Line as much room as I can."

That didn't surprise her, really, and it gave her a way to confront the inevitable. "I understand, Dan. This is too important for you to walk away."

He took her hands in his. "You helped, a lot. I couldn't have done it without you. I'm glad you chose to stay."

That brought her to the moment of truth she wrestled with for several days now. "I'm sorry, Dan," she said, softly. "But I can't stay. Now that the crisis has passed, I have to leave."

His face fell. "But... Is it something I've done? Have I offended you in some way?"

"No, Dan..."

"It's the killing. You hate that, I can tell. I'll try to change, to find other ways."

"I understand about that, Dan. Really."

"Look...I know this place is unpleasant, having to live with what I'm fighting for. But it's important. Brenda...I need your help. I'll try to make things better for you."

"It's not that, Dan." She squeezed his hands to try to comfort him from what she had to say. "I...have cancer. The headaches. That's why my temper is so uncontrollable these days. Its inoperable, but the doctors in India said treatments here might prolong my life." She gazed into his eyes, trying somehow to soften the blow. "That's why I came back."

"Oh...Jesus..."

"And that's why I have to go, Dan. It might have been easier if I died when you undid your intervention; you could have accepted that. I don't want to put you through what's coming. I don't want you to watch me die." She took his hand, and drew him close, and kissed him. "What you're doing here is too important, too critical. You can't afford the emotional drain I'll cause."

277

"Brenda..." A sigh of anguish. "...I need you."

"I know, and I wish I could stay, but I can't."

"But...you kept me going all these years." His eyes filled with tears and he was trembling, a forlorn old man. "You helped me pace myself. You helped me see my mistakes. I-I love you. I need your help."

"No, Dan. I have to go for your sake, and for the human race. We're all mortal, and I'm ready to face this. You have your mission, and I have mine."

In one common impulse, they rose to their feet and clung to each other, sharing a good cry they both needed.

*****

"Epilogue"

The weather was the same as when she arrived twenty-three days earlier: bright sunshine in a sky full of puffy white clouds, with a cool breeze just nippy enough to need a windbreaker.

"Do you have to go?" Dan asked as they stood by the entrance.

She moved into his arms and kissed him. "I have to, Dan. I'm a distraction you can't afford. My going will make it easier for you to do what you must do."

"I...I'll have to let you go, Brenda. I'll have to leave you to your fate. The next change will cause this line to split off. You won't be able to come back."

"I know."

"My interfering to protect you was what upset the equation to start with. I can't interfere again."

"I know." She pressed her fingers to his lips to stop his protests, then hugged him close, feeling the warmth of his body. "I'll be all right. Do what you have to, Dan."

Her luggage was still piled inside the entrance, and Dan helped carry it out to the curb. Once that was done, she paused and scanned the horizon from their vantage point at the top of the stairs, shading her eyes with one hand. "Nothing's changed."

"The effects are often subtle." He considered the scene for a bit. "When I go out for supplies, I see odd details, stuff you'd never notice unless you compare notes. Those are brought on by small changes, ripples which don't affect the Time Line. It's the big changes that count, and often those can't be seen at all."

"Which reality is this?"

He mused on that; pondering his answer carefully like he usually did. "This is a branch off your original line, the one you died on. If you went into any other time line, there'd be two of you. Who knows *what* that would do? But this Time Line is...vacant now. You can start over here."

He was silent for a time, watching the clouds drifting by. "I had George re-implant your history in the public records. As far as the world knows, you lived in India for twenty-eight years, and came home to retire on a stock nest egg you've held all that time."

"Thank you, Dan."

He brooded on the past and the history between them. "I'm sorry you got dragged into this," he said at last. "It was foolish of me to bring you here. All I did was upset you."

"You saved my life several times, Dan. I'm grateful for that."

He chuckled humorlessly. "Yeah, that's me, a regular knight in shining armor."

She stood watching the traffic on the highway, and an airliner passing in the distance. It all seemed so...normal. Then she turned and looked into his eyes. "Is this reality...safe?"

"The Time Line you're on now is stable enough that you should live out the rest of your life before..."

They looked at each other for a long moment, unable to express emotions which couldn't really be explained anyway. Finally she wrapped her arms around herself to ward off the chill breeze and the sense of dread lurking in the background. Armageddon was coming—eventually—but what went on here to forestall it was even scarier. "What...will you do?" she asked at last.

He sighed. "Keep on with keeping on, I guess."

"Can you save the world before..."

"It doesn't look like it." He was only mortal, and not young. He didn't have that many years left for his lonely quest. "All I can do is try. I've bought the human race twenty years, anyway. Maybe, now that Jeeves is no longer interfering, I can stabilize things enough for them to get their act together in time."

There was movement down the street, and a dark blue stretch limo drew up to the curb and stopped by her piled luggage.

They looked at each other silently for a long moment. This was good bye, like no one had ever said good bye before. "Thank you, Dan," she murmured at last. She kissed him again, gently. "I'm sorry things didn't work out differently."

"Well, at least I got to know the woman behind that centerfold. She's everything a man could want. A real Dream Girl."

"Now you remember to eat right!" she lectured him. "And get plenty of rest. That ulcer is no joke."

He smiled ruefully. "Henpecked; gotta love it."

"Good bye, Dan. Good luck."

She turned then, walking resolutely down the steps to where the limo was waiting. She didn't look back.

The limo was subtly different than the one which delivered her there twenty-three days—a lifetime—ago; nothing definite, but the grille and the shape of the headlights were...off. The chauffeur was an Indian, complete with a turban to match his conservative blue suit. "Good morning, miss Hayward. It's good to see you again." He bowed politely. "*Āpakī upasthiti dina camaka.*"

That was another jarring detail; evidently in this...reality...he brought her here. Whatever became of Andrew, that likable Filipino? Lives saved, lives changed, lives snuffed out, all unknown. A minor ripple. "*Āpa āpa kē sātha dhūpa lē ā'ō.*" she replied, bemused. He grinned.

He held the door for her, then loaded her baggage in the back. She settled into the plush upholstery, and soon they were cruising down Highway 5 toward Seattle. She watched the scenery pass without noticing as she went over those incredible twenty-three days in her mind. It was beyond belief, almost beyond comprehension, but it happened. She was bemused to have found someone in her life, albeit unknown to her, who would and could move heaven and earth to protect her. Every girl needs a hero at some point so she realizes she's worth rescuing. It gave her a warm feeling, something she never quite had before. She felt sorry for him, her knight in shining armor, and in a quiet corner of her mind she knew she left because she loved him.

"Where to, miss Hayward?"

She stared into the distance, at the pine covered hills and the huge Boeing plant in the background without really seeing them. "The airport," she said at last. She had nothing to do in her life which mattered, so she might as well go back to Cincinnati as anywhere else.

The End

*****

Addenda:

Some Hindi Phrases:

Āpa āpa kē sātha dhūpa lē ā'ō.
　You bring the sunshine with you.

Āpakī upasthiti dina camaka.
　Your presence brightens the day.

Ēka aurata kyā ēka aurata cāhi'ē karatā hai.
　A woman does what a woman must.

Vidēśī śaitāna - a 'foreign devil'

*****

A Brief Note From The Author

Thank you for reading this novel. I hope it was a good read for you. I would love to hear from you, my readers, to let me know how I am doing as an author. Every bit of input helps me to make my next effort a better product for your enjoyment.

All my best,

Bob Boyd

You can learn more about me, and keep up to date on my efforts through my Blog:

Facebook.com/The Written Wyrd

*****

Titles from The Written Wyrd
2021-22

The Diplomacy Trilogy - Science fiction humor.
First contact from the aliens' perspective in a trio of lurid tell-all memoirs written by a team of alien diplomats sent to earth to open an embassy.

The MacKenna Trilogy - Science fiction military drama.
He was earth's greatest soldier; they needed his skills once more, but they didn't realize how wrong bringing him back from the dead was.

Nature's Way - Environmental disaster / apocalyptic horror.
This is the last day of our last stand against Nature out for revenge!

Trial - Science fiction political thriller.
The aliens demand justice for their murdered ambassador while right wing extremists plot revolution; which is the greater threat?

Overland - Period science fiction drama / romance.
He was trapped between a beautiful genetically enhanced revolutionary from the distant future and the inhuman monster sent to destroy her. Can he survive caught up in their titanic battle?

Playing God - Apocalyptic horror.
Brenda discovers she is the Dream Girl of a mad scientist capable of altering the past. Can she find a way to undo the disaster he wrought and prevent a nuclear holocaust?

The Big Snow - Environmental disaster / adventure.
A passenger train is wrecked at the top of Donner Pass in the worst storms in recorded history. Can the railroaders get the passengers to safety?

(continued)

Young Adult Demi-Novels:

Diplomacy's Children - YA humor / adventure.
A young alien space fleet recruit faces his greatest challenge in a self-centered, foul-tempered human youngling he is ordered to keep in check.

Star Flight - YA adventure.
She was an outcast, cursed with supernatural powers. She was offered a reprieve, a chance to start over, but could she survive the challenge?

Short Story Anthologies:

Deus Ex Machina - Humorous fantasy short story collection.
From bungling wizards to moronic barbarians to redneck elves, here are the old tales of epic adventure as we would love to see them told - just once.

Ghoulish Good Fun - Macabre short story collection.
Reality is a cruel practical joke. Laugh along with it if you dare!

*****

Available in print and Kindle from Amazon.
Visit our web site for details.

http://www.the-written-wyrd.org/shopping.shtml